Infinite G

K.T. Morrissey

ISBN-13: 978-0-9853068-4-7
ISBN-10: 0-9853068-4-X

First Printing: June 2012

10 9 8 7 6 5 4 3 2 1

Printed in the United States of America

For Nan and Len, who love me regardless of all my faults

And…

For Tarod, who is my heart

Prologue

Baphomet leaned on one shoulder against the door frame, his long blond hair hanging in a loose, sleek curtain down his back. His broad chest and wiry, lithe figure housed a highly restrained energy, though no one but Suriyah knew the extent of his abilities. He had his arms folded in a deceptively calm manner across his chest and his feet crossed at the ankles as he studied Suriyah.

She sat in profile to him, painting her lips a dark shade of plum. She was the most beautiful creature on the planet… *Hell*, in the *universe*… as far as he was concerned. She always had been. Her long white hair was caught up in several twists and braids, with some parts hanging freely and other parts clasped and bound so tightly to her head it looked as if it might actually hurt. The effect, however, was pure perfection.

Her Jinn certainly know how to make their queen look regal, he thought. The Jinn regarded her as something next to divinity, he knew, and they always expected her to dress the part. Suriyah never disappointed, either. But Baphomet knew her better than that.

She would rather wear a pair of jeans and a t-shirt than to have to stand on ceremony all the time. She hated make-up and heels and all the other pomp and ceremony she had to endure day in and day out. She loved her people, though, so she did what they wanted her to do. He had to give her that.

Not like him.

A frown marred his perfect features and he pushed himself away from the door frame, turning his mind back to the reason for his visit instead.

"You will never guess who has moved into the Badlands," he said as he approached the vanity where she sat. He picked up a small bottle. Squeezing the little rubber bulb attached to the bottle produced a fine spray of the fragrance from within, and Baphomet wrinkled his nose at the strong smell.

Suriyah snatched the bottle from his hand and returned it to its place on the vanity. "Who?" she asked, annoyed. She had to finish dressing for yet another of the damned interminable ceremonies the high council of the Jinn Central Government was always having. She didn't have time to be wasting with Baphomet, even though she would much rather spend all of her time with him. He was fun. The JCG wasn't. Baphomet never had council functions to attend. She always had them. It wasn't fair. Then again, her people wouldn't punish her physically if she ever failed to do something they wanted her to do either, so she tended to forgive Baphomet for just dropping in unannounced this way.

Suriyah knew the Shaitans were wont to kill their own kind for even the simplest of infractions against the Shaitan laws they still held sacred. She did not envy Baphomet his position within Shaitan society at all. If anything, she wished he would just finally come live with her in her stronghold. He would be much safer with the Jinn and Suriyah wouldn't have to spend so much of her time worrying about him. She was so preoccupied with these thoughts that she missed his response to her question.

She sighed and shook her head, saying, "I am sorry, B. What did you say?"

"I said," her brother repeated as he watched her spray another perfume from the myriad bottles on the vanity onto her wrists, "*Mikhail* has moved into the Badlands."

Suriyah made only the slightest pause in her action, but Baphomet noticed it.

2

"Hmm," was her only response. She continued with her preparations.

Baphomet walked around her and picked up a brush from the other side of the vanity, pretending nonchalance. "Yes," he continued as he studied the brush, "he and some woman have taken up residence there it seems, along with a whole house full of followers." He concentrated on his sister from the corner of his eye. She had gone still… very still.

After a moment, she resumed spraying the perfume in fine mists here and there, stating, "No doubt there are hundreds of lower Angels in agony at the thought that he is no longer on the market. I wonder who the lucky Angel was."

Baphomet replaced the brush and turned fully toward her to stare for a moment before baldly stating, "He chose another Seraph."

Suriyah's eyes immediately shot toward him, her confused ice-blue gaze burning into him. "What the hell does that mean?" she demanded.

"Mikhail has found himself a female Seraph to mate with… and has, it seems, judging from what I saw."

Suriyah was stunned. She lowered her eyes to the mirror attached to the vanity. This was impossible. There were only six Seraphim and always had been only six. Where had this new Seraph come from? Without turning or taking her eyes from her own reflection in the mirror before her, she quietly asked, "Are you certain of this?"

Baphomet placed a hand on her shoulder. "I spoke with her, myself," he said, his deep voice deadly serious. "She is Seraph, all right. Or at least, she was at one time. But, there is… something different about her, some greater energy within her than I have ever experienced before."

Suriyah jerked her face around toward him. "Like with Enki and the others?" she asked urgently.

3

Shaking his head slowly, Baphomet simply said, "Greater."

Suriyah returned her gaze to the mirror before her. So many years had passed since she'd had the visions, but it seemed like only yesterday to her. Could it be?

She reached down to pull the tiny crystal on its chain from beneath the bodice of her dress and she could virtually taste Baphomet's anticipation rising. She never took off the crystal and now she needed to look into it to discover if perhaps it would aid her in finding an answer to this latest development. "You are sure he has mated with this creature?" she asked.

"She carries his offspring in her womb," Baphomet declared, earning himself a rare glimpse of Suriyah's shocked face. She'd been stunned earlier, he knew, but this announcement hit her much the same way the information had hit him.

For a Seraph to be able to reproduce was crazy to even think about. It was insane. They all knew Seraphim couldn't do it, yet Baphomet knew he wasn't wrong. He'd seen the glowing patch on the female's abdomen. He'd caught enough of Mikhail's thoughts through his own psychic shields to know Mikhail believed it. He'd heard the female's thoughts she'd intentionally projected to him. The two had mated and the child growing in the female's womb was the result.

Baphomet knew all too well the risks in Seraphim trying to conceive, but there was something about this new Seraph female that made him believe there just might be a chance the pregnancy would go to full term. A little chill stole down his spine at the mere thought of such a possibility and he watched Suriyah intently as she gazed into the small cut of crystal hanging from the necklace she held before her.

"Damn it!" Suriyah barked in exasperation a second later as she slammed her hands down onto the vanity top, the crystal

4

and chain falling back to rest against the skin of her chest. "I still get nothing."

"Well, try again," he urged heatedly. "Somehow he found another Seraph to mate with and I bloody well want to know how!"

"You know I cannot control it," she rasped, wishing she could just induce the state of mind she needed at will to be able to bring the visions on. "I want it just as badly as you, you know?" Her voice caught on her last words and Baphomet immediately knelt to console her, wrapping his strong arms protectively around her.

"I am sorry, Suri," he crooned, rubbing a hand along her back as he held her. He knew she couldn't control her visions. But this, this was something they'd dreamed of for so long, since even before they'd been banished. Her visions from that time had led them here, in a roundabout way, but here never-the-less. "It is not necessary for you to try just now, okay?" he soothed.

She pulled slightly away from him and studied his face, tears streaming freely down her cheeks, marring her perfect make-up, dark mascara tracks running heedlessly down her cheeks with the tears. "Do you really think it could be starting?" she asked quietly.

Baphomet looked away for a moment. He didn't want to jump the gun and get them both all excited over nothing, but he wanted this so much, as much as he knew she wanted it. After only a moment's hesitation, he looked back up at her, nodded and said, "I do."

A great sadness filled her eyes, and Baphomet felt just the tiniest prick of guilt at being happy at the thought of something so horrible about to happen to the world, but he immediately brushed it away. Suriyah's visions were never wrong – never. That meant the things she saw were inevitable, beyond anyone's control, so Baphomet wouldn't allow himself to feel guilt for something he had nothing to do with causing or controlling.

Also, according to what she'd told him of this particular vision, their lot would finally make out the way they should. Baphomet saw nothing wrong with justice finally being served, even though he thought it wouldn't be enough. He planned to see to it after everything was said and done that the one responsible for what Baphomet and those he held dear had suffered ended up paying for those crimes.

Suriyah suddenly stood and walked away from him. "You know he was only following his heart," she choked in a tear-clogged voice. "He loved us both and does still."

Baphomet stood, a deep vein of anger welling up within him. "Do you honestly still believe that, Suri?" he sneered.

Suriyah turned. One look at Baphomet's face told her exactly how much hatred he still carried for their brother, Mikhail. She returned to stand before him, reaching both hands up to smooth away the lines of pain marring his beautiful features. "He loves you and me to this day, I swear it." After a moment, she dropped her hands and turned away again. "As for the visions," she said, shrugging her shoulders and shaking her head, "I simply do not know. I guess we shall have to find out how he did it some other way."

Baphomet heaved a great sigh of frustration. "I guess I could return there, where they have built, and see if I can find out something, anything," he said. "The female seems willing enough to allow me access to her thoughts, but she is so *strong*." He paused a moment and then quietly continued, saying almost absently, "If she wanted to, I think she could crush me mentally."

Suriyah regarded him in silence, disbelief warring with awe within her. She believed him. Baphomet was far superior to her at reading other people and catching their energies, though her gifts were nothing to dismiss, to be certain. It was just shocking to think of anyone, Seraph or not, being strong enough to cause Baphomet to have a care. After all, he was the strongest psychic on the planet as far as she was concerned. She'd gotten the vision ability, but Baphomet, she knew, had developed so much more than that.

Suriyah agreed that Baphomet should return to the place where Mikhail and his supposed female Seraph had settled to see what more could be learned. In the meantime, Suriyah would continue working with the crystal to discover whatever it would show her, if anything.

She wished she could just take off with him, now. The two of them together would be a formidable team, she knew. The JCG waited though, and she knew she could not alert her people to anything before she knew for certain there was something to worry about. This would all just have to go in the journal she kept, for now. Tonight, after the celebrations, she'd write everything down in hope of creating the right atmosphere within her mind to bring on the visions. That seemed to have become the best way for her to induce them over the past few years and she would try again tonight when she was all alone again.

She took a deep, reinforcing breath and returned to her preparations for the evening's events. Baphomet's reflection in the mirror before her merely nodded once and then he left without further comment. However, each of them now carried within a sense of anticipation they hadn't felt before. Things were finally about to change and they each would do whatever they had to do to see to it they were ready.

Thirty minutes later, Suriyah sported a small, if inappropriate, smile as she finally made her way toward the council chamber for the rest of her evening. *Soon*, she thought, *soon.*

Chapter 1

Baphomet watched as Mikhail's mate moved slowly through the little garden at the back of the large structure he assumed was to be the main house on the estate. He'd glimpsed other, smaller structures around where other Angels worked and he could hear the sounds of hammering and building going on all around. He knew Mikhail was within this building, though. He could *feel* him in there.

He sent out a soft buffering signal, not overpowering, but enough to keep Mikhail from becoming aware of his presence near his mate. The woman interested him more than Mikhail for the moment. Certainly, he would seek his revenge against Mikhail later for his crimes. For the now, however, Baphomet was more interested in discovering more about this female.

How had she eluded the Seraphim for so long? If she had been on the planet as long as they all had been, why had she only just made herself known? She was so much stronger than any of the other Seraphim that Baphomet found it difficult to get a good read on her.

It just didn't make sense. Where had she been all this time? Who was she? *What* was she?

I was wondering if you'd come back. Baphomet suddenly heard her soft voice in his mind. He was yet again stunned. She'd blown past his considerable psychic defenses without any warning. Her mind was unbelievably strong and a tiny frisson of fear and awe lanced down his spine, even as he stepped forward onto the small garden path before her to reveal his presence.

Her brighter-than-bright eyes looked up at him. She was short, too short for his tastes, but pretty all the same.

A smile split the plane of her face and she chuckled aloud. *It's a good thing you've concealed yourself from everyone else or you'd be dealin' with a very angry Mikhail right now*, her voice floated through his mind on butterfly wings. She had an odd accent, he noticed.

"Humph!" was Baphomet's only response as he approached her, taking in the flowers she was tending to. They were beautiful, whatever type they were, and he wondered where he'd seen them before. They seemed familiar, but he knew they were not indigenous to this part of the Angelic realm.

The female shook her head, agreeing with him and saying aloud, "No. They're orchids – from the human realm."

Baphomet's eyes narrowed and he reached out to touch the tip of one of the tiny flowers' frail petals.

"These were my favorites when I was human," she said.

Baphomet was floored and he stared at her in shock. She'd been *human*? He didn't understand. "You mean you lived in the human realm?" he asked, his deep voice echoing slightly throughout the tiny garden. That would make sense. She could have remained quite well-hidden from all Seraphim there.

Again, she stunned him as she shook her head. "No, Baphomet," she explained. "I was human before comin' to the Angelic realm. Only after I came here and met Mikhail did I become Seraph… and then somethin' more."

He stared at her in confusion.

The creature moved toward her swing, the same one Baphomet had seen her on when he'd originally encountered her here. He followed her and joined her on the swing when she silently indicated he should sit beside her.

He kept looking down at her lower abdomen. He couldn't help it. He was fascinated by the little patch of lighted skin there showing through her clothing every now and then as she moved. He could hear some sort of prattle coming from the light and he wondered how the female and Mikhail could function with the little thing constantly chattering away.

The creature smiled up at him and chuckled once more. "She does get a little annoyin' every now and then," she said softly, "but she's our little Sheely, so how could we stay annoyed?"

Baphomet could feel tenderness coming from within the female and a part of himself railed at the injustice that Mikhail should be gifted with this when he had caused such strife within Suriyah's and Baphomet's lives.

A new anger built within him. It wasn't fair. Why should Mikhail get what Suriyah and Baphomet deserved more than any of the Seraphim? How had he found this creature, anyway?

"Your name is Sarah, yes?" he asked suddenly.

"That's right," she answered, studying her mate's brother. She'd thought about him a lot since she'd first encountered him in the garden. Mikhail had told her he hadn't been able to access any of her memories from her meeting with the beautiful Seraph, so Sarah had surmised the beautiful, deep-voiced man must have the ability to block her powerful mate somehow from sensing his presence.

When she'd first sensed him a few minutes ago, she'd felt his buffer go out, and recognized it for what it was immediately. Anyone with that much ability was definitely someone Sarah wanted to get to know.

Mikhail had told her a little about his brother, leader of a group of Angels called Shaitans. He'd told her the majority of humans thought Baphomet was the only Shaitan, like the devil, but that there were actually a whole host of Angels known as Shaitans who had followed Baphomet, and others known as Jinn who'd followed his sister, Suriyah, who was the queen of the Jinn, out into the Badlands of the Angelic realm.

All of them were reported to have the ability to access the human realm in areas other than the one natural rift at Mt. Hermon, just the same as Mikhail and Sarah had recently learned they were able to do. Mikhail had told her both the Shaitans and the Jinn went into the human realm regularly, even though crossing over without official sanction was forbidden by the Angelic governing body in Seraphim City. Those who lived out in the Badlands of the Angelic realm didn't exactly follow the rules of the land, though, since they'd been banished by Mikhail from Seraphim City so long ago.

Mikhail had warned Sarah not to associate with any of these Angels from the Badlands, as he'd said they had all been corrupted by living in this lawless region for so long. He'd said they had all changed into evil beings over the millennia.

He'd warned her to alert him immediately should she ever encounter his brother, Baphomet, again. He'd said it wasn't safe for her or Sheely to be around Baphomet. As Sarah studied the face of the beautiful Seraph sitting beside her, a blond brow rose sardonically above an ice-blue eye and a cruel, lop-sided grin flashed quickly across his face. She hadn't hidden her thoughts from the Seraph and he was showing her he knew exactly what she was thinking.

"You won't harm me," she said with confidence, returning his grin with her own confident one. "You need information from me."

Baphomet's grin faded. Sarah reached out a hand to touch his arm and he jerked quickly away from her touch, immediately going to stand on the opposite side of the path, as a jolt of electricity shot up his limb and into his chest. As soon as she'd touched him, a flash of images had flown through his mind at such a speed he'd been unable to catch anything of any

11

substance from her – just vague impressions. He turned to regard her, wondering if she'd intentionally transmitted the images to him through her touch, his face a mask of confusion.

Sarah's head tilted a bit to the side as she watched him in silence.

He swallowed a lump in his throat. He could still feel her energy racing through his body and he wondered what on earth a being as powerful as she was doing here. She belonged with the gods, not here with the puny beings of this planet.

Again, she smiled her pretty little smile and then chuckled aloud.

Baphomet frowned. She was making fun of him, laughing at him. No one but Suriyah did that.

"Come, my dear Baphomet," she suddenly said, patting the bench beside her on the swing. "I'll see what information I can give you."

Baphomet hesitated. What if he was wrong? What if she was the only one? What if there wasn't someone else out there, either in the Angelic realm or the human realm, who was to be *his* counterpart? What if Suriyah's visions had been wrong, just this once?

I will show you what I have seen, Sarah's voice said in his mind, *and then you will have faith once more. Come... come and find the answers you seek, dear Baphomet.*

Baphomet shivered. The allure this creature's energies sent out was very powerful. But, more than that, he felt compassion and even love coming from her. Suriyah had been the only one to think of him in such loving regard for so long he wasn't sure he knew how to deal with it from someone else. How could this stranger feel affection for him? She did not know him. She did not understand the darkness that enveloped the majority of his soul.

12

The brighter-than-bright eyes glowing up at him radiated something very closely resembling affection, however, and she reached out a hand to him as if she trusted him entirely and they'd known each other for an eternity. Baphomet shivered again, but, after only a moment's hesitation, he took her hand and resumed his seat next to her on the swing.

The energy from her touch immediately zinged up his arm again, but this time he was able to follow the flashes of visions whirling through his mind, though just barely, and the story shown him there was nothing short of life-altering...

Sarah's mind took him on a journey from the moment just before some giant explosion, where there was just one mass of energy comprised of all there was, to the next instant when that mass of energy was suddenly expelled outward in all imaginable directions in a burst so powerful that nearly every particle within the energy cloud was split apart on the most minute level.

He quickly grasped that what he was witnessing was what was commonly known in the human realm as the moment of the "Big Bang." He watched as energy particles were pushed out from the force of the explosion in every direction, some shooting out faster and farther than others to reaches unknown. Many bunched back together, causing even more and more explosions, like a chain reaction. Still others bunched together and traveled in groups as they whizzed through the darkness toward unknown destinations.

He eventually recognized the passage of time as other entities formed within the blackness through which the energy particles traveled and Baphomet came to know these as stars. More and more of these formed and, in so doing, planets were formed around some of them.

It seemed a very violent and turbulent time in the universe, as giant forms burst through clouds of star sediment and collided with other bodies, creating massive explosions and forming new floating entities, but Baphomet understood this was just one portion of the universe's formation he was witnessing and that there were probably many other regions where calmness reigned, or regions where perhaps even more explosions and collisions were occurring. He thought about the older regions they'd passed through first and he wondered if stars and planets had formed there as well after they'd gone.

When the first particles of energy traveling within their group broke away and pulled in a direction closer to one of the planets, Baphomet wondered how they'd managed to move themselves in a trajectory other than that to which they'd been assigned by the initial blast's force. He did not comprehend how the change was accomplished, but he marveled at the particles' individual abilities.

Soon others followed, but there was still a great deal of force pushing at their group of energy particles, so those who had pulled themselves off to the side were left and forgotten as the group moved ever onward and outward. Baphomet wondered if those they had left behind ever made it down to the surface of any of the planets they'd approached.

Time and again their group would come to new stars and, surrounding them, new planets. More and more of the energy particles within their group would divert their trajectories in order to head directly toward the planets and Baphomet finally realized it was a matter of concentration and consciousness. If one realized one was some*thing* and that an actual place was where one wanted to be, one would automatically find oneself at that place, or at least headed directly toward it.

Each thought, he knew, was energy, and thoughts had the ability to direct the flow of energy to such an extent that the latent energy the travelers within their group were made of was helpless in the face of such direction. All it required was one lucid thought and the energy particles would zing off into whatever area the thought directed them.

Eventually, their giant but dwindling group approached a star system with multiple planets and Baphomet recognized Earth. There, the energy particles closest to him all came to know one idea: *go there*. The group moved toward the planet and took up a stationary orbit around it while the larger group within which they had been traveling moved silently onward.

The group stayed that way for a very, very long time. Baphomet did not know how much time passed as they waited, but none seemed to know how to do anything more. There was some type of invisible barrier preventing movement closer to the surface of the planet, even though there was an imperative inherent within each of them pushing them to somehow find a way down to the surface. With no knowledge of how to do that, however, all the group could do was to wait.

While they waited, however, it appeared some of the energy particles chose to gather together with one or more of the other energy particles, at which point they would form into a single unit, or even a close-knit society. Baphomet realized each would emit different vibrations and tones and he found himself taking note of these unique emissions from the little energy units grouped around him. He became fascinated with the differences between each unit or group. That was when he realized he was searching for one he liked, one that had vibrations similar to his own.

He soon discovered one to his liking. It was smooth and soothing to his own energy patterns and he formed the thought to be next to that one. Almost immediately, he was with it and, as it seemed his energy patterns did not offend the other particle, it took no thought at all for the two to eventually meld into one single unit of energy.

Throughout all of this, there still had not been a single energy particle to make it down to the surface of the planet. All still remained in a holding pattern in orbit just on the outskirts of the planet's atmosphere, their mass of energies returning to a resting period similar to the stable state in which they'd been prior to the massive explosion that had started all this.

It might have been an eternity later, or just a short while later, Baphomet did not know, but he next observed what he, as a Seraph, knew as Designers approaching the planet's surface. The beings arrived in great hulking ships constructed of different types of materials from some other part of the universe. They would then use smaller vessels to propel themselves down to the surface of the planet. More and more of them came, each arriving in different types of ships. Baphomet could see what appeared to be writing on the sides of some of the ships, but he couldn't decipher any of it.

The next thing Baphomet realized was that single units of energy from within their group were suddenly making their way down to the surface of the planet by piggy-backing on the Designers' smaller shuttle ships. It also seemed, after a short time, that the Designers were somehow pulling the energy particles down onto the surface through the use of some device they had set up there.

Once pulled through to the surface, the bits of energy would be manually merged with other types of energy to take on entirely new physical forms. These forms did not last very long on the planet's surface and the individual energy units soon could be observed returning to the holding pattern back on the outskirts of the planet's atmosphere where all the other energy units waited.

When they returned, it seemed there was something wrong with them, as if they were unable to accomplish anything more than the slightest vibration. They seemed exceedingly depleted, as if the experience on the surface of the planet had been almost too much for them, and those still in a holding pattern would gather close to these energy units to comfort and aid them as best they could.

This practice went on for an indeterminate amount of time, during which the Designers' larger ships in orbit around the planet would leave and then return continually. Sometimes, all of the Designers would leave the surface of the planet and there would be no new energy formations happening down on the planet's surface. The planet, itself, would undergo massive geological changes during these times. Then, once the planet's atmosphere cleared again, the Designers would eventually return and start up their practice of taking energy bits and changing them into different forms of matter on the planet's surface.

Once, during a time when the Designers had left the planet's surface and the surrounding areas as far as could be observed, Baphomet noticed there were other, different energy forms moving among those with which he and his other half moved. These forms of energy looked similar to the way Mikhail and his new mate now looked, though their energy glow was not quite as bright as that of his brother and his mate.

These strange creatures moved within synthetic devices, similar to those the Designers used, but it was the "where" through which they traveled that so fascinated Baphomet. They did not exist on just one plane, these new forms of energy. They existed within space, for certain, but they also seemed to exist out*side* of space, as if they traveled *between dimensions.*

The new forms of energy came and captured the group's attention. That's when it was observed that *they* were taking individual units of energy from within the group too and splitting them apart right there where they surrounded the planet. As had the Designers, this new group used some sort of mechanical device to change one half of the energy unit into some other type, effectively splitting the energy unit in two, and the agony experienced by both halves of the split energy units had the majority of the remaining units within the group fleeing as far from the new energy forms as possible.

Baphomet, by contrast, moved closer with his other half. He saw and understood that one half of the now-split energy unit the creatures had just taken was being "processed" somehow and that it was then being forced down onto the surface of the planet below where it took on an entirely new form. As he drew closer to the strange energy forms and the odd device they used to accomplish this, Baphomet could see clearly the form now springing to life on the surface of the planet.

It was an infant Mikhail. Several of the strange creatures were there with the infant Seraph and they nurtured it and protected it from the elements until it was capable of caring for itself. Baphomet was so engrossed in watching what was going on down on the surface of the planet, that he failed to realize the strange beings were approaching his small energy unit. Too late, he felt the pull of the strange mechanical device they used, and then he experienced a gripping pain so powerful, he thought he would pass the brink of insanity.

His other half was ripped from his side and he felt as if he would bleed out. Then, all was confusion and more pain as his entire width and breadth was forced into the tiniest space imaginable and confined there with no discernible avenue of escape. The light there was blinding and it hurt to breathe, though his form then didn't even know what that meant. Every particle of his being throbbed with severe pain and the whole process seemed to be never ending.

Chapter 2

Upon his return to the Shaitan city of Knor, Baphomet had immediately ordered his travel luggage packed for a journey into the human realm. He still didn't know how he was going to find his other half, but after what he'd witnessed through Sarah's visions, he very much believed there was another half out there for him to find. He also knew he wasn't going to find her by simply waiting around for it to happen by chance, as Mikhail had done.

Unfortunately, Baphomet didn't believe in blind luck like that. He didn't know what forces of the strange creatures were at work here, but he wasn't about to wait another minute before going to find *his* other half. If she existed, he was bloody well going to find her himself now, and those other creatures be damned!

Sarah had shown him the visions of everything she'd been shown. Then, she'd shared all of her experiences since encountering Djibril, whom she called Gabriel, in the human realm and then on until she'd met up with Baphomet in the garden of the new home she shared with Mikhail in the Badlands. She'd held nothing back and Baphomet appreciated that.

He felt a cautious liking for this new creature and he hoped he'd have the opportunity to visit with her again. A part of him was vaguely thrilled as he wondered exactly how pleased Mikhail would be to know his mate had become such great pals with his sworn enemy, even though he was his brother.

Baphomet didn't really care, though. Mikhail could go take a flying leap, as far as Baphomet was concerned.

Five beautiful Shaitan females tended to his bathing and fed him by hand as he waited for his bags to finish being readied for his journey. Though his head was still throbbing from the vision-quest he and Sarah had taken earlier, Baphomet touched these Shaitans to ease the excited energy coursing through his body. He delighted in their smooth skin, as he wondered what his other half would look like.

He only knew her as an energy mass. He could recall the specific vibration of her energies and her tone from the part of the visions when he'd been connected with her in stasis around the planet, but he had no clue what her human form would look like. Would she be short like Mikhail's mate? Baphomet shuddered and shook his head. He hoped not. He couldn't stand bedding short women!

One of his servants fed him a grape and he reached up with half of it hanging out of his mouth, offering her the other half. She pounced at the invitation, moving down quickly to nip at the offering, pressing her lips upon her master's fevered mouth.

She and those like her lived for moments like this, when their master was feeling generous and giving. Most of the time, they had to keep well away from the Shaitan King as much as possible to avoid his black moods. For centuries now, he'd become quite an ogre, flying into rages over the tiniest things.

He was the most beautiful Seraph any Angel could ever dream of, yet he was the most feared for his sudden rages. If he'd been just an Angel, he would have been formidable enough. The fact that he was a Seraph, however, made him all the more dangerous, for *Seraphim* possessed abilities that would astound most.

There was a quick knock on the door to the bedchamber and then it opened to reveal one of the lower-classed Angels who, without waiting for an invitation, walked right into the room where Baphomet was being bathed. The Angel was tall, though not quite as tall as Baphomet, with jet black hair, which he wore cut short with just slightly long bangs that always seemed to hang down over his forehead in the most attractive, devil-may-care fashion. His skin was, by contrast, as smooth and white as pure porcelain.

Baphomet smiled. "Iblis, my friend," he said, pushing aside without a thought the Shaitan Angel he'd just been kissing. There would be time for fooling around with that one and maybe a couple of others as well, later. For the now, he wanted to do a little hanging out with his best friend, Iblis. He'd sent one of his Angels to summon Iblis just after his arrival home earlier. If anyone could help Baphomet find someone in the human realm, it would be Iblis.

Baphomet and Iblis had been hanging out for eons, even since before Baphomet and the human, Lilith, had had their time together. Iblis had helped Baphomet get through things after he and Lilith had split up. He wasn't always the nicest Shaitan, and Baphomet wasn't always so comfortable with some of the things he learned Iblis liked doing both to and with humans who were unfortunate enough to become associated with him, but Baphomet had learned over the millennia to forgive Iblis his little foibles.

After all, he was stuck on this chunk of rock for all eternity the same as all in the Angelic realm were, so why shouldn't he be allowed to pass his time here the way he wanted? Humans were not constant members of the planet, so why should Baphomet intercede on their behalf if a couple of them dying brought a bit of joy to his friend? Only now, however, did the thought that it was possible Baphomet's other half could someday fall subject to Iblis' ill treatments cross his mind and Baphomet wondered if he wasn't wrong in allowing such behavior to continue.

"You left too early the other night," Iblis said as he plopped down onto a nearby chair. "Satariel almost ended up losing his head to that Kaumatua. We had to raise all kinds of hell to get him out of the Wharenui!"

Baphomet frowned as he recalled the tribal elder Iblis was referring to. The most respected elder of the Maori tribe had been in the middle of a religious ceremony when Iblis and his gang of miscreant Shaitans had decided it would be fun to intercede. Baphomet had been their ride that night, though he didn't normally like to stick around once the Shaitans got riled up.

They'd caused all manner of havoc within the meeting house, which is what the Maori call a Wharenui. The Shaitans had made a mockery of the ceremony by "suggesting" a multitude of thoughts to multiple members of the tribe. Baphomet had very quickly become bored with the whole thing and had left, but apparently Iblis believed he should have stuck around.

"I mean it," Iblis continued, laughing as he recollected the evening's events. "We all thought Satariel was a goner when that old man started shouting spells and incantations designed to ward off all evil spirits. I even thought the creature was going to pull something out of the Book of Solomon, for a moment." He nearly doubled over with laughter as he said, "You should have seen the look on Satariel's face when the old man came at him with a crowd of his warriors backing him up. They were all making the most horrifying faces at him and he was just standing there, shocked by their wide eyes and their tongues poking out. I tell you, I have never seen a Shaitan move so fast in all my life!"

One of the five Shaitans who'd been bathing Baphomet offered food to Iblis as he sobered and he took his time choosing a nectarine, watching the backside of the Shaitan who'd served him when she walked away. When his gaze returned to his friend and leader, however, he stopped beating around the bush and asked, "So, what was so important it pulled you away from our sport and kept you away for several days?"

Baphomet stood to allow the Shaitans attending him to dry him before he slipped into his robe. He wished his head would stop hurting. After looping and tying off the belt, he took the seat opposite Iblis. "I am just not feeling right, lately," he said. He picked up the glass of wine one of his Shaitans had placed on the small table next to him and continued, "I needed a little time near my sister, I guess, so I went to see her." There was no way he was going to let on that he'd come up with a plan to find his one true mate, not to this one certainly.

"Hmm," Iblis murmured. He looked once again to the backside of the attending Shaitan who'd served him earlier. "So, am I to assume you have overcome your little issue with the help of your sister and your overly-beauteous staff?" he asked.

Baphomet followed his friend's gaze, but he shook his head, saying, "No. The type of sport I am interested in will not be found in the Angelic realm, I am afraid."

Iblis hiked an eyebrow over one of his light blue eyes. "Is that so?" he asked, a grin lifting the corners of his cruelly beautiful mouth. "Well," he continued, "I believe the boys and I can assist you with whatever... *quest* you have in mind."

Baphomet's eyes lit up. He knew he had him. He immediately dismissed his attendants, even though Iblis clearly wanted to have a go with at least one of them. But Baphomet had bigger fish to fry. "I am looking for something rather specific, I am afraid," he told the Shaitan. "However, I do not really have anything more to go on other than the fact that she will have a *lot* of soul-energy on her."

"Ha!" Iblis barked. "A human female... with above average soul-energy? Well, that ought to stand out like a Seraph in a stack of Angels! The boys and I should have no difficulty finding that for you." Iblis sat back for a moment, thinking about a particular human female he and his followers had recently discovered. They hadn't yet taken her and Iblis believed she might do for whatever Baphomet was looking for. Then, a disturbing thought occurred to him and he leaned forward to regard his leader, asking, "We are not looking to regurgitate the past here, are we?" The experience with Lilith had been the worst Iblis had ever witnessed, nearly driving Baphomet past the brink of insanity.

Baphomet shook his head vigorously. "No, no," he quickly denied. "I am just looking for this one particular human female I am told is out there somewhere." He leaned forward in his seat, propping his elbows on his knees as he warmed to his subject, the pain in his head momentarily forgotten. "I do not even know where she might be found," he explained, "but, I believe she is out there."

Iblis frowned. "That sister of yours been seeing things again?" he asked dubiously. Iblis knew of Suriyah's psychic abilities, as did everyone else in the Angelic realm.

Baphomet distractedly shook his head. "It is nothing from her I am working on," he said, his thoughts returning to the visions Mikhail's mate had shared with him. There'd been such a deep connection between Mikhail and Sarah, right from the very beginning. Baphomet had felt what Sarah had felt during the visions and he wanted to feel that with his own mate. It was crazy, he knew. Hell, there was no guarantee a human even existed out there for him. What if she had never been "processed" by the machine the strange creatures used or if she had never figured out how to possess a human body?

Why would Sarah have shared her experiences with Baphomet though, if she didn't believe there was a human counterpart out there for him? It didn't make sense, unless she believed there was someone for him to find. He knew he had to trust that this Sarah was correct.

Baphomet looked back at Iblis and said, "I assure you, this is not sheer lunacy I am working with here. This being exists. I just need to find her."

"Well," Iblis said as he stood and stretched, "I am going to go get cleaned up, myself. Then I shall come back to collect you and we shall start our search. Will that do?"

"That will be fine," Baphomet nodded. "I shall be ready as soon as you are."

∞

Lisa Murdoch stared out the window at the front of her empty shop. A few passersby on the street just outside stopped now and again to look at the window displays, but none ventured into the store. There was just no money left in Barrow Creek. Lisa sighed. There was no money left in Australia. Everywhere, everyone was strapped tight. No one had enough for food, even, let alone for extravagances like designer clothing.

Every now and then, someone would see Lisa out and about in one of her creations and she'd make a sale or two because women wanted to look like her, to be her, and husbands wanted their wives to look like her, but Lisa had never been enough of a socialite to be able to make her name known like that. Anyone who saw her, though, knew she had something. It wasn't that she was model material or anything, but she knew her craft and so she knew how to combine certain fabrics and pieces of clothing that worked well together to produce an overall spectacular effect.

A fat lot of good it did, however, when no one had any money to buy anything!

Lisa sighed again and opened up her laptop on the shop's glass countertop.

She checked her store's website for any new clothing orders; she then checked a couple of her favorite social media accounts. A friend of hers from school, Kiley Plimpton, had sent several links to a story about an American blogger she knew Lisa followed and so Lisa checked out the articles and an attached video. It was sad.

Apparently, there were a lot of people all upset about what the blogger had written and they had somehow managed to find out the woman's real name and physical address. Now, it seemed the blogger had gone missing and there was a big to-do over what had happened to the woman and her family.

The article said the blogger's real name was Sarah Baker and that her parents and dogs had last been seen entering the house one evening after having taken the animals for a walk, but that when police had entered the house a couple of days later after having received no response to repeated attempts at contact, there had been no one inside.

There had been one last entry made to the blog and its point of origin had been traced back to that very same house where Sarah Baker had lived with her family, but no one could discover any information as to where Sarah or her family had gone.

The video showed crowds of people still camped outside the house in a suburb of a city called Dallas. There were a lot of protesters shouting and vying for face-time on camera in the video, but there were also several groups of supporters of all ages for Sarah. She'd apparently gotten herself quite a following, judging by the number of people camped out on the large common area next to the house where she'd lived just North of Dallas.

"We're here to show our support for Sarah and her family," one of the supporters said. "She's done nothing wrong and we're gonna stay here 'til she comes home so we can tell her just how grateful we are for the things she wrote. So many people need answers right now and she provided a different way of looking at things. That's all."

Lisa clicked on the link to the woman's blog she'd saved on her favorites tab just after she'd started following her writings, but it didn't work. She tried typing in the blog's web address and then looking for any archives that might exist out there, but that didn't work, either. It was like it had never existed. She looked up the blog on her favorite search engine and discovered through linked news articles that the web host had been pressured into dropping service for the blog a week ago.

Figures, Lisa thought. It was amazing to her to see that, while all manner of ridiculous and insulting ideas were perfectly acceptable to the online community, whenever something of true insight and value came along, it was shut down so quickly your head would spin because it wasn't politically correct.

What had been so wrong about the woman's blog?

Lisa went back to her favorite social media site account and looked up what was being said about the blog there. Of course, there were plenty of the religious nuts ranting and raving, saying the blogger, Sarah Baker, was doomed for hell and that the devil had already come to take her and her family away with him. Then, there were the nut jobs who swore she was the prophet of doom and that her writings were a dire warning and any who didn't follow her words would be lost.

Lisa skipped over all of that, browsing through the posts until she skimmed a few lines of a thread that actually seemed to make sense.

"Her family was seen entering the house, but not leaving. Sarah posted her last blog entry that same night from that location. Once the cops went in, no one was found, not even the dogs. There was a report that the feds found some kind of evidence, but there's been nothing released to the media, yet. The kid hasn't been to school in weeks. The rest of the family has officially filed missing person reports on all four of them. And so far, nobody has a clue as to where any of them can be found? Come on!

"This has to be one of only four things: Either the whole bunch of them was abducted by aliens... not likely; or, they were transported through some trans-dimensional portal..., again, not likely; or, they were taken by the men in black to some secure locale where they'll be grilled and then debriefed and then set up somewhere else in the world under the witness protection program, which I guess is possible, but it still requires a lot of belief in something that really hasn't displayed anything that would require government involvement; or, and I believe *this* is the most likely scenario, this is all just the beginning of some elaborate hoax put on by some Hollywood film company in promotion of some new film or television series they've got coming out and we'll find out about it in a couple of months when the trailers are released. It's like Occam's Razor..., the simplest explanation is the most likely one, right? Other than that, you've got me.

"It's like that UFO sighting over the Temple Mount in Jerusalem in January of 2011... No one's been able to totally debunk that one, and yet, no one's talking about it still. Yet, there were more public vantage points filmed of that sighting than of practically any other in history and it's still not making headlines. Again, you've got me!" – blogcipher96

"If they left the house via inter-dimensional travel, wouldn't they have left behind some sort of residual energy field? Maybe that's what the feds found when they went in?" – idigufos4real

"It would have had to be traced within a short amount of time of their passing through the portal for it to have been detectable. Plus, there were feds all over that place within a week. Whatever they found when they went in, if anything, it was actual physical evidence, not anything so intangible as a residual energy field. If anything *had* been left behind there when they went in and they found it, you know they either took it or wiped it clean or, most likely, totally scrambled any trace of it." – cnspiracjnke193

Lisa typed in a question and posted it. "What do you think this Sarah meant when she said she hoped people would follow her?" – walkaboutwonderer42

Very quickly, there were multiple snide remarks posted by people she didn't know in response to her question. However, eventually there were a couple of serious responses from her usual online friends.

"Sarah most likely found a way to contact beings residing in another dimension and that's where she's gone. Her last blog was posted just before she and her family were taken by those beings to their dimension to live. They can't have humans knowing about them because they either use us as slaves or for experimentation. If humans found out about them and found a portal through to the other dimension, then there would be a war between the dimensions." – cnspiracjnke193

"Sarah wants people to follow her through the portal to the other dimension where she's gone. She left clues to the portal's whereabouts in her writings throughout her blog. All people have to do is to find the clues in her writings and figure them out. Then, they'll discover where the portal is and they'll be able to get through to the next dimension. There are hackers all over the world combing her blog entries for those clues for just that purpose as we write here." – truthckr179

Lisa typed furiously. "The blog's been banned. How can I access it?" – walkaboutwonderer42

Several links appeared on the page. Lisa checked each one, finding bits and pieces from the American's blog. She copied everything she found and put it all into one document, in as close to chronological order as possible. In the end, she didn't have it all, but she had managed to recapture most of it. She wrote a quick "thank you" to those who'd helped her, and then she signed off.

She didn't understand it. Why were people so obsessed with revenge against someone who was only trying to offer a little hope to the world? Wasn't there enough anger and madness out there already? Did they truly feel the need to create more strife for others simply because they didn't happen to believe the same way she did?

The world seemed to have gone crazy, as far as Lisa was concerned. Each day, she came to the shop and read stories online about how this country was falling apart under its corrupt government rule or how some kid had gone into a school in some other country and shot a bunch of the teachers and students. The world was definitely feeling the effects of having reached the shallow end of the gene pool and, quite frankly, Lisa had had enough.

She wanted out. She wanted to find a way to get out of this insane world and into the kind of place where she wouldn't always have to live in fear of everything, the way she did now. Sure, she was an independent woman who owned/rented her own shop and made a living for herself, meager as it was. But, each night, when she walked home from the shop, she felt to the depths of her soul how very alone she truly was in this world.

Of course, she had her mum. But, *she* was over a thousand miles away and wouldn't understand anything Lisa talked about with her anyway. She was a traditionalist and she didn't understand why Lisa didn't identify more with her native background, whereas Lisa was a more modern girl who wanted nothing more than to live the dream of being able to become independently wealthy. In Barrow Creek and in this economy with the world the way it was? Lisa knew she was dreaming. She knew she was completely alone and she hated it.

She'd recently read an article online that suggested this was the lost generation. Lisa understood about lost people. Her mum had been one of the "lost children" of Australia. All the kids these days growing up with laptops, hand-held computer pads, and smart phones as friends instead of actual people did seem to be lost, for they weren't learning social rules and they had no clue how to relate to other people on a face-to-face basis. Lisa didn't want to be like that, but neither did she wish to be a part of a continually maddening world.

She sighed as she realized it was almost closing time. Lisa closed up her laptop to perform her usual routine for closing up the shop. She would read through the bits of the blog she'd been able to recover once she got home. She just hoped there would be some sunlight left, even if it was just a little bit, for her short walk home tonight. It hadn't rained today, but it was being called for in the forecast.

Chapter 3

Baphomet carried Iblis and his followers in the direction Iblis had indicated, barely paying attention to their whereabouts. All he could think about was his human counterpart. What would she look like? How old would she be? Would she come with him willingly? Would she recognize him for what he was? All these questions plagued him, occupying his mind until he suddenly realized Iblis was telling him it was time to stop.

Baphomet settled their group down onto a nearly-deserted street, looking around as he dropped his shields to see why Iblis had chosen this place to stop. A second later, however, Baphomet could not think clearly at all.

There was something here he'd only ever felt once before... and yes, it was a *feeling* he was getting. Looking around the sleepy little town, he saw nothing out of the ordinary, but he could *feel* it, he could feel... *her*. All of a sudden, Baphomet knew what he was experiencing was the feeling of being in his human counterpart's presence for the first time in his long life! He looked around wildly, searching, desperate to catch sight of his supposed other half, though at the same time he wrapped one of his shields back around himself to keep out of sight.

Iblis and a few of his followers were across the street from where Baphomet stood by now, and he barely took notice of the clothing boutique outside which the group of Shaitans stood. Baphomet could feel her energies, could almost taste her essence sliding along his nerve endings, and he searched the

32

nearly-empty streets of the sleepy little town again with his heated gaze.

Suddenly, Iblis' group let go a great howl of excitement as the light outside the little boutique switched off and the door opened. The Shaitans all whooped and laughed gleefully as a tall female with dark skin and long, kinky black hair emerged from within the small store. Immediately, Baphomet was swamped by her energies.

It is her, he thought furiously.

He was across the street in a flash, knocking each Shaitan he encountered as far away from his counterpart as he could, even Iblis, who hoisted himself up on an elbow after landing painfully a few yards away and demanded angrily, "Hey! What was that for?"

Baphomet stared at his friend, rage still pouring through him that his underlings would dare try anything with their future queen. After only a moment's hesitation, however, he knew he must tread carefully.

He stepped back. "You were right, old friend," he said. "This was an excellent idea. But, you know I am not in the habit of sharing my toys."

Iblis immediately cast his eyes downward. "Of course," he replied abjectly. He was so filled with rage he wanted to burst! He and his minions had searched far and wide for one such as this human. So, when the Shaitan leader had come with his request of just such specifications as could be met only by her, Iblis had known his time had finally come. He would finally be welcomed as an equal to the Seraphim. He had even imagined a scenario in which he'd be invited back into Seraphim City to live. What a coup that would be!

Instead, however, the spoiled and petulant Seraph who was their leader, and whom Iblis secretly believed was solely responsible for all the Shaitans having been kicked out of

Seraphim City in the first place, now stood before him demanding full and sole ownership of this special human. Iblis wondered for a moment if perhaps his master's interest in the female human ran deeper than just as a means of escape from his day-to-day humdrum life, but he quickly discarded that notion. The tryst Baphomet had had with Lilith, another human female with whom he'd once dallied, had left him broken and near the brink of insanity. Iblis could not imagine anyone, even the Shaitan King with all his powers, ever risking something like that happening again.

No, this human female Baphomet wanted merely to use until she was broken and he grew bored with her. That's what the Shaitans did with humans. Why should their king be any different? Of course, the methods Baphomet would use on the girl would be far different from those Iblis and *his* followers used. Baphomet's mental abilities went far beyond even what Iblis could do, and Iblis licked his lips in hungry urgency as the thought of getting to watch as his master broke the human coursed through his mind.

What would that be like? he wondered. He might get to learn some of his master's secrets..., things he could use to his own advantage later on. He looked back at the human as she turned and made her way down the deserted and dark walkway from the little boutique. She was definitely worth the trouble he and his followers had gone through. He could feel something special about her, as if she was made of much more soul-energy than the other humans. He watched her moving through the late evening light and figured that must be it, for she almost seemed to him to glow with an inner radiance as she walked.

What the hell? he thought and he turned back to his master, hope springing to life in his eyes, as he said, "Of course this human was meant only for your pleasure, Master." He ignored the gasps of surprise and indignation coming from the

Shaitans flanking him. Instead, he focused on Baphomet as he asked, "Would you like us to collect her for you, Sir? We have just the right place back in Shaitan territory where you would be perfectly safe while taking your pleasures with her." If the Shaitan King agreed to that, Iblis and his followers would all be able to watch and learn from his masterful ways.

The King thwarted his plans, however, when he said, "No, no. Just leave this one to me. I shall deal with her myself, in my own time." Baphomet turned and walked in the opposite direction, heading away from where the human had gone.

Iblis, along with each and every one of his followers, was stunned as he watched his master walk away. He and his team had gone to all this trouble, had even traveled all this way, just so the human could walk away unscathed? If they didn't follow Baphomet now, it would take them at least two days to return home.

He had flown them all to the rift. He had made the crossing of the barrier so much easier for all of them. It would take hours without his assistance just to reach the rift alone and a whole day and night of walking over untamed lands after crossing the wicked and painful barrier to reach Shaitan territory, *if* they all didn't lose consciousness during the barrier crossing. That was a mighty big "if". Iblis shivered just at the thought of the crossing.

He wondered briefly why the Shaitan genetic make-up was such that the crossing of the dimensional barrier was an extremely painful thing to endure for them, while Seraphim, and even humans, seemed to suffer nothing more than a slight annoyance when they crossed over. It wasn't fair! Iblis believed there had to be some way to change things so that a Shaitan could cross over without such pain.

As he came out of his thoughts, he realized Baphomet was now some distance from him while the remaining Shaitans still stood nearby, waiting on some signal from Iblis as to what action to take. The human female was now almost out of sight as she continued on her way. Iblis knew he'd lost yet another round to those higher in rank to him and his blood boiled as he reluctantly turned to make his way toward Baphomet.

His underlings immediately turned to follow him, though Iblis heard plenty of grumbling coming from them. He ignored it all. He was too busy fuming silently and hatching plans to stage some sort of coup so that the Shaitans would one day be able to rise up and take over all of the Angelic realm, if not the human realm, as well.

∞

Baphomet resisted the urge to turn around and make sure his underlings were following him. It was the most difficult thing he'd ever done in his entire life, walking away from the female. He knew the majority of the members of the group of Shaitans wouldn't dream of defying his order, but Iblis was an altogether different story. Iblis had defied those whom the Seraphim in Seraphim City called the blessed Great Designers, even. Of course, that had been *after* Baphomet had defied them. But if Iblis didn't follow along with Baphomet's wishes, there could be trouble. Baphomet was not afraid of Iblis so much as he was of the influencing power Iblis had among the Shaitans.

In his own way, Baphomet had unwittingly nurtured that power by favoring Iblis all this time. He'd treated Iblis more as an equal over the years because of his innate courageous spirit. No other Shaitan had ever displayed even one tenth the... *gumption* Iblis regularly displayed, so they all naturally tended to follow his lead, just as Baphomet naturally tended to favor such spirit. The Shaitans knew this, too, and so they showed more respect and deference to Iblis than they did to any other Shaitan because of it. Now, however, it was becoming abundantly clear how dangerous the situation was because of Baphomet's favoritism toward Iblis.

Baphomet *could not* allow Iblis, or anyone else, to interfere with his plans of uniting with his human counterpart, not now that he was so close to succeeding. He'd been alone on this planet far too long to let that happen. As a steely resolve began forming within him, he both felt and heard Iblis and the others following along behind him. He breathed a sigh of relief as he continued on toward the rift they'd used to cross dimensions close to the human's location.

Once he reached the rift, Baphomet turned and waited for the others to catch up. They all eventually gathered together in a close crowd and Baphomet released his shields, surrounding all of them at once while simultaneously concentrating on a certain part of the brain of each Shaitan called the Reticular Formation, forcing each one into a peaceful slumber so that none would suffer any ill-effects during their travels across the barrier back into the Angelic realm. Once all were unconscious, Baphomet lifted off and crossed the barrier. He didn't awaken anyone until just before setting the entire group down near the heart of Shaitan territory.

As each one regained his footing and gathered himself together, Baphomet waited. He couldn't be seen rushing off to get back to the human. If anyone guessed how urgently he wanted to get back to her, she would be in grave danger. For anyone to suspect his interest in the female as anything more than a mere passing fancy would be an open invitation for blackmail, and in Shaitan territory, such a thing could be lethal.

Nearly all within the original group immediately dispersed in all directions. Once they were gone, Iblis approached Baphomet from behind, clapping a hand on his shoulder and saying jovially, "A few of us are heading over to Belial's place for a night of gaming. You in?"

Baphomet wasn't fooled by the Angel's tone. Iblis' eyes were as sharp as a hawk's and trained directly on Baphomet's face as he waited for an answer. Baphomet was no fool, however, and without hesitation, he cracked a wicked grin and whacked Iblis on his own shoulder, drawling sardonically, "Pass up an opportunity to take everything from such wicked and cunning Shaitans? Of course, I am in!"

He and the shorter Shaitan walked off toward the direction of Belial's abode, telling jokes to one another and recalling past escapades. Just one night. That was all Baphomet had to wait. If he remained within the Shaitan stronghold until dawn, everyone would retire to their own homes, their own beds, and Baphomet would finally be free to go to her and take her. She belonged to him already, she just didn't know it.

As they arrived at Belial's place, Baphomet put on his game face. If he could just keep his cool and resist using his abilities for the next few hours, he'd be home free. Just a few hours more. Even suffering through the rest of the night, during which Iblis drank excessively and even described several terror events he and his group of fiends were planning on causing within the human realm, Baphomet managed to keep his cool. He would have his mate safely back in the Angelic realm long before anything ever happened in the human realm, so he had no need to worry about her being caught up in Iblis' plans. Again, the main thing was to keep his cool.

If not, several among the assemblage would notice and the jig would be up.

∞

Lisa was creeped out! It had been two days since last she'd been at work. Sunday evening, as she'd been leaving the store, she'd gotten the queerest feeling as if there'd been at least

38

one male presence standing just behind her out on the walkway, just outside the boutique's front door as she'd locked it.

Oddest thing was that she'd even imagined there'd been *more* than one male presence out there with her. She'd even imagined she'd heard them laughing at her, though, when she'd looked, there'd been no one there. She sure had *felt* as if someone had been there. She'd spent her whole two days off trying to shake the feeling, though she now felt stupid since she hadn't actually seen anyone there at the time.

Now it was Wednesday. As she unlocked the door to the boutique, she quietly made her way through to the back rooms. Her office was all the way at the back of the darkened building and she became even more creeped out with each step she took. She still felt as if there was someone around watching her, waiting to jump out and get her just when she least expected it.

There was nothing out of place inside the office when she entered, however, and no one appeared around any doorway as she went about preparing the shop for another slow day in July. It was still a little chilly out and Lisa wished the summer season would hurry up and set in.

The hot Australian days did wonders for both her own personal and financial outlooks and Lisa yearned for the summer months with a passion. Local folks flocked to the city during the summer, and the tourists! Lisa could sell enough in one summer just to tourists alone to be able to make it for the remainder of her fiscal year. Today, unfortunately, wasn't going to be like that. It was overcast and very humid outside and the weather forecast was calling for rain again. There weren't likely to be many people out and about today.

She spent the next few hours standing behind the counter sketching outfit after outfit, all LM originals. By the time evening came, she'd almost filled her sketch pad, but she'd had not one single customer all day.

As the grandfather clock in the front corner of the boutique struck eight, she sighed and started her closing procedure. There wouldn't be much to do tonight since there'd been no transactions for the day and she was soon standing outside on the walkway at the door of the boutique making sure everything was locked up tight for the evening.

As she turned to walk away, out of the corner of her eye she thought she saw the reflection of two bright blue eyes staring out at her in the boutique's storefront window. She gasped as she whipped around, ready to take on whoever had snuck up on her.

There was no one there.

Lisa felt a distinct chill race down her spine that had absolutely nothing to do with the weather. She could *feel* that presence again right there next to her, as if she were to reach out with her hand, she'd be able to touch it... to touch *him*.

For a second, she was actually brave enough to do just that, though she felt foolish for having done so afterward. Whatever it was, it definitely felt masculine and menacing, and Lisa turned and broke into a run. She only lived a few blocks away, so she'd never bothered with a car. During the Wet, she normally wore a slicker and just rode her bike if it was raining. Now, she wished for the safety and speed of her bike, or even a car. She didn't own a car, but she wanted one tonight. It wasn't supposed to rain until later this evening, so she hadn't bothered with her bike this morning, either.

The streets were all empty and it seemed she would have to handle whatever might happen on her own. As she ran, she envisioned scenarios starring herself as the pathetic victim of whatever serial rapist/killer who'd recently moved to town. However, she reached the door to her flat without incident and, when she finally dared to peek behind herself as she fumbled frantically for the door key, there was still no one there.

There was no Johnny-come-lately serial rapist/killer lurking in any of the shadows, waiting to make her his first victim in his new hometown. The streets were still just as empty now that she was home as they'd been when she'd left the boutique.

Lisa quickly went inside, double-locking the door just to be safe. It was crazy, she knew, and she felt like she was becoming paranoid. Where did she think she lived? Sydney? Nothing ever happened in this one-wallaby town. But she couldn't help what she felt. Each time she tried to reason with herself, she just ended up in an argument about how it was better to be safe than sorry and she ought never to have moved to such a lonesome and derelict place anyway.

This last, of course, was always said in her mother's voice as it flitted through her mind. A thousand miles away from the woman, even enough space so the fool woman couldn't logically take out on foot to come see her "just 'cause she'd had the urge to talk to her little girl," (as if she'd never heard of a telephone), and yet Lisa still couldn't escape her nagging!

She decided what she needed was some hot tea and a quick shower. Then, she'd get to bed early, for a change. That was all she needed. She set the little two-cup electric kettle her mum had given her on her seventeenth birthday to brewing and then she went for her shower.

By the time she was done with her quick shower, the water for the tea was good and ready and Lisa poured a piping cup and settled into bed for the evening. Once the tea was all gone, she placed the cup in its saucer on her bedside table and switched off the light. Her head felt as if there was some sort of pressure building up within it and Lisa sighed in relief as she snuggled down under her covers. Her last conscious thought was that she hoped she wasn't coming down with something, and then she was out.

∞

She felt as if her head might explode from the pressure inside it and she wanted to grab it with her hands to keep it together. There was something binding her hands above her head, though, and she couldn't move them. She opened her eyes to see why and how her hands were bound, but found herself instead engrossed in trying to figure out why she no longer seemed to be in her bedroom in her flat. Her bedroom was tastefully decorated in muted hues of soft brown and green. Wherever she was now, it most definitely was not her bedroom!

There were garish nudes hung on the walls of the spacious room with a few miniature statuettes on white pillars placed sporadically throughout. Each one depicted a man and a woman in sexual pose, as if someone had sculpted the figures from the paintings and drawings of the Kama Sutra, itself.

Lisa discovered she was clothed in some sort of see-through red, gauzy material and sprawled out on a round bed with no headboard. Whatever the bindings on her wrists were attached to, she couldn't see. There were the requisite filmy nettings hanging down from the tacky ring suspended above the bed for a scene like this and Lisa felt the urge to roll her eyes at how cliché the whole scene seemed.

The thing was, she was still bound at the wrists and lying on the round bed inside the typical love nest à deux without any knowledge of how or why she was there. There didn't even appear to be anyone else in the room… and her head still felt like it was going to flippin' *explode*!

"Relax, my sweet," a deep voice suddenly said softly.

Lisa's eyes widened and she looked around, searching as much as she could see through the netting for signs of the voice's owner.

It was a deep, husky voice unlike any other Lisa had ever heard. In fact, if someone would have asked her to imagine a rugged, good-looking man, this was the voice she would've imagined for him – without the creepiness factor, of course! This voice, though it was deep, dark, and sexy, also held a bit of danger to it.

The voice suddenly laughed a bit maliciously and a shiver ran up Lisa's spine at the timbre of it.

"What?" the voice asked suddenly. "Is this not the perfect setting for our little tryst? Does it not excite you to have visual examples of all the ways in which I plan for us to be together?"

Lisa looked nervously around, ignoring the statuettes and paintings that displayed every sexual position possible and trying to find the voice's owner. All she saw were the four corners of the gaudy bordello-style room.

"Oh, come now," the voice came again. "You cannot tell me this does not please you. After all, I took it directly from your own mind, sweet."

Lisa began struggling against her bonds and the pain in her head intensified ten-fold.

"It will only abate if you cease your struggles and cooperate," the voice calmly said.

"Forget you!" she shouted and she struggled harder, pulling and twisting frantically against the bonds. As she struggled, the pain inside her head became too great and she eventually lost consciousness, her body slumping back onto the round mattress to lay still, her breathing leveling out and deepening.

Back in the small bedroom of Lisa's flat, Baphomet reached a hand out from where he sat next to her bed and gently wiped a few strands of her strange, thick dark hair from her forehead, careful not to touch her skin lest he should wake her. His face sported a frown of confusion as he whispered, "Why did you not like that, my sweet Lisa?"

He had finally gotten free of the seemingly interminable games at Belial's place and had returned to the human realm as quickly as possible to relocate his counterpart. He'd caught her coming back to the building she'd been leaving the last time he'd seen her and he'd watched her inside her little shop all day. No one had gone into or out of the shop the entire time she'd been there and Baphomet had taken his time learning things about his human counterpart.

After erecting a wall of buffering energy around himself so as not to disturb any of the electrical devices in her world, (which was something he'd long ago learned to do) he'd walked around inside the little shop with his shields keeping him concealed from her. He'd touched the clothes she'd designed and watched as she'd filled page after page of a sketch pad with drawings of new designs. He'd liked some of them. Some he could live without. She was talented, though, and he liked that about her.

He'd smelled her breath as she'd worked. It was fresh-smelling and he could tell from her bright teeth and her flawless skin that she took good care of herself. Her dark skin *was* flawless. Several times he'd had to resist the urge to reach out and touch her.

Now, as he sat beside her sleeping form in the tiny bedroom, he was truly confused. He'd gone home with her, had watched her fall asleep, and then he'd gone to work delving deep into her mind to find out what her idea of the perfect sex-filled evening would be. Then, he'd pushed into her dream, some silly one she'd been having about her mother, and he'd quickly taken over the show.

He'd become hard as a rock watching her take her shower earlier and he was ready to take her for more than one reason. Of course, they were meant to be together, but he *really* wanted her now. However, although he'd made everything according to the specifications he'd found in the hidden depths of her mind, she had rejected it all.

Why was that?

Baphomet leaned back in the rocking chair he'd taken from over by the wall, frowning even more. He was going to have to take things a bit more slowly, he realized. If everything was left up to him, they'd already be back in his giant bed in Shaitan territory in the Angelic realm. However, she was human and he acknowledged that he really needed to give this whole plan a bit more thought before he took her as his own. He frowned, more in frustration now than confusion.

He couldn't just go off and leave her now. She'd already been targeted by the most dangerous group of Shaitans out there. Without his supervision and protection, she'd end up the victim of one of the lethal games Iblis liked to play with humans. Baphomet had never actually seen in person any of Iblis' human victims, but he'd gleaned enough from the minds of some of Iblis' Shaitan companions to know the victims' endings weren't pleasant or pretty, ever.

He thought of the possibility of taking her to stay within Suriyah's people's land, but he immediately rejected that notion. The Jinn loved humans, but they were still Angels. The idea of having a human living within the Angelic realm would not be well-received, he imagined, even by such as they. He sighed in resignation as he realized he'd just have to stick around in the human realm guarding his Lisa until he could figure out what to do about this whole situation.

Chapter 4

Lisa woke with a start. After blinking a few times to clear her vision from such a deep sleep, she looked around. She was still in her bedroom in her flat and it was just the way it had been when she'd gone to bed last night. She frowned as her gaze strayed onto her old rocking chair over in its usual place along the wall in the far corner, but it, too, was where she'd left it. For some reason, when she'd first caught sight of it just now, it had seemed out of place, somehow, as if someone had moved it from there and then put it back, just not quite exactly in the same position it'd been in before. That was crazy, though.

"You're losin' it, girl," she said to herself as she sat up and swung her legs off the bed. She ran a hand through her nappy hair, scratching her scalp and yawning. First, she'd imagined she was being followed by some serial killer, and then she'd dreamed she was being held prisoner in some sado-masochistic bordello, and now she was imagining... what? Fairies or evil furniture gnomes were breaking in during the night to move her bedroom furniture around just to make her crazy?

She yawned again as she got to her feet. "Short trip," she said around the yawn. She then pulled sharply to a halt as she thought she heard again that deep, dark laughter she'd heard in the dream. It was gone before she'd even had a chance to catch hold of it, though, and she just shook her head and continued into the bathroom.

Pulling down her panties and squatting down onto the toilet, she thought about the dream of the bordello. It shouldn't

46

surprise her to have such a dream. This town wasn't exactly bustling with eligible bachelors, unless one wanted to include the uneducated homeless, jobless, shiftless, lazy, lay-about, no good, wandering, walkabout, follows-no-man's-rules drifters who passed through town almost on a weekly basis. She could have a date with at least one of them every weekend. Or, she could always go for one of the outback's overly-abundant toothless octogenarians. There were several of those that made their way into town each summer, so she knew there was an ample supply readily available.

She shook her head again as she finished up and flushed. Taking a step to one side, she looked at her reflection in the little mirror above the sink. "Leece, you're going troppo," she said. Again, she thought she heard the echo of that same deep, dark laughter and she asked her reflection, "See?"

Shaking her head, she reached for her toothbrush.

∞

Just as Baphomet had predicted, only two more days had passed in the human realm before the same Shaitan group reappeared for Lisa. She was in the process of closing up her little shop, again. Baphomet had been watching her for the past two days, listening to the wacky jokes she'd tell herself. The woman talked to herself all the time, it seemed. Of course, she'd only had two customers in the last two days and she didn't seem to have any kind of a social life, so he could understand her need to keep herself company.

It was fascinating watching her and learning her habits, but it wasn't enough. He knew she didn't enjoy talking with her mother whenever that one called on the telephone, but she did it anyway. He didn't get it, but that's what she did. He'd learned she was *very* heavy into aboriginal artwork, though he just didn't see the appeal. He thought all those paintings looked like the work of kindergartners.

The most fascinating thing he'd learned about her, however, had been that she knew of Mikhail's mate, Sarah. Last evening, he'd watched and read the posts Lisa made on her little laptop thing to this comment about something Sarah had written while she'd been in the human world or that comment made by someone else doing the same thing as she. It appeared that Lisa, along with countless other humans in their realm, was searching through Sarah's writings for clues as to Sarah's whereabouts.

Baphomet had nearly dropped his shields the first time he'd realized it to reveal himself to her when he'd discovered what she was up to. It seemed there was quite a "to do" over Sarah's disappearance and Lisa was hot on her trail. He'd decided to use information regarding Sarah's whereabouts as a way to introduce himself to his Lisa. He figured all he'd have to-do was to obtain one of those computer machines and learn how to use that internet thing. Then, with just a little patience, he'd have his Lisa safely in the Angelic realm in no time at all without too much damage to her mental state.

Of course, mother time, as everyone knows, is the biggest Be-*otch* in existence!

Time… he'd run out of it. As evening set in on this, what was called Friday in the human realm, Baphomet could sense that Iblis and his crew were here now, and he knew they wouldn't just be looking for a little fun. They didn't even *start* having fun until there was screaming and the first few drops of blood had been spilled. Then they really geared up for some fun… *all* of them. Some would just watch, but most wanted in on the action, all at the same time, if possible.

Not with his Lisa, though. He couldn't let that happen. Whatever he was going to do, he'd better get to it fast, he knew, for he could sense that Iblis and his group were practically on top of her!   The Shaitans' physical make-up, like all from the Angelic realm save for Seraphim, made it so they could not be heard or seen in this realm, not by most humans, at least. A *very few* humans could either sense them or see them, or both.

Although a Shaitan was limited in his ability to influence anything physically in the human realm, he was certainly able to influence the thinking and the actions of the creatures within their realm. They could by just their mental abilities alone cause humans to do terrible things, sometimes to others, and sometimes to themselves.   The more damage caused, the happier the Shaitans.

Baphomet narrowed his eyes and pricked up his ears as he suddenly noticed Iblis sidling right up next to Lisa as she turned to walk down the street toward her flat. Of course, Baphomet was much stronger, both physically and mentally, than any Shaitan. He was a Seraph, after all, even if he'd been expelled from Seraphim City by his most beloved brother.

However, some of the Shaitans had developed certain abilities over the millennia and Baphomet knew he would be detected by Iblis the very moment he dared use any of his vast store of mental abilities. He might not have much choice, but for the moment Baphomet was still hoping to find some way of getting his Lisa out of this situation without alerting Iblis to his presence. It would take a miracle, he knew, but hey, he was a Seraph.   Miracles were what the Seraphim were known for, right?

∞

Lisa turned from the now-locked boutique door and stepped out onto the deserted walkway. It didn't *feel* deserted. A few blocks down was O'Halloran's Pub. Fridays were ladies' nights and, as the only pub in town, it really drew in the crowds. Lisa shivered. She still felt like she was being followed or watched. She'd felt that way all week. Tonight, however, she felt almost as if she was *surrounded* by evil spirits, or by a ravenous pack of rabid dingoes. She could imagine them yapping and their jaws snapping at her ankles as she walked.

Something about the whole situation just didn't seem right and Lisa was really getting freaked out! A truck-load of migrant farm workers approached on the road from one of the local ranch stations, heading for O'Halloran's, and Lisa caught sight of a couple of the workers in particular standing up in the back of the truck and a plan suddenly formed in her mind. The two she'd spotted were members of the Aboriginal Ngarinyin people, judging by the tattoos they sported. If she could just get their attention, she might be able to get out of this mess.

As the truck passed, there were many male whistles and wolf-calls from the workers in the truck and, even though they sounded almost as bad as whatever or whoever was hounding her, Lisa ignored them because she knew *those* particular demons. Rude men she could handle. It was the demons she *didn't* know that concerned her.

The two men she needed finally looked from their places at the back of the truck to see what the other workers were so interested in and Lisa gave a sigh of relief as she signaled them in the special way her mum had taught her when she'd been just a young girl.

The two men did a double take and then looked at each other. After only a second later, they both jumped right over the high sides of the back of the moving farm truck and came running to her rescue. Lisa heard the chants they were already using to drive away evil spirits and she quickly moved behind the two men as they approached her.

The two bent and grabbed handsful of the thankfully dried dirt, grass, and rock from a nearby lawn. With those, they made a crude circle around where Lisa stood and adorned it with symbols they made from the blades of grass, chanting their powerful protection spells the whole time. The farm truck had moved on down to O'Halloran's and was parking. A couple of the other workers from the back of the truck called out to the two aboriginal workers, checking to see if everything was okay. Lisa and the two chanting men ignored them.

After another minute or so of chanting, Lisa suddenly felt as if a heavy weight had been lifted off her shoulders and she took a deep breath. She realized this was the first time she'd been able to really breathe deeply for days and she smiled up at the two young men who'd helped her. Their chanting was done and they watched her speculatively to make sure she was completely free of the annoying Murngin, or evil spirits.

"Here, what's this, now?" asked a voice from behind Lisa and she turned within the stone and dirt circle in which she stood to see the two men who'd called out to them earlier from the farm truck curiously regarding her. "You two doin' some sort o' aboriginal marriage ceremony, then?" the taller one asked, his accent the distinctive tones of someone from the Northern Territory.

One of Lisa's rescuers smiled, completely embarrassed, while the other said, "Nah, mate. We was just helpin' her along a bit. But she's fine, now."

The four men moved off back toward the parked truck and eventually went on into the pub to join the other workers they'd come into town with. Lisa stood staring down at the circle the two men had made around her. She took one more deep breath and then stepped outside it. She was once again alone on the walkway. But now she actually *felt* alone. She didn't feel as if she was being watched by anyone or anything. There was no mad serial rapist/killer about to jump out of nowhere to attack her. All she heard were the usual night sounds and the brawly noises from the men in the pub.

She sighed and slowly made her way down the street, a smile on her face and a feeling of complete security welling within her as she said to herself, "I'm gonna find a way to thank those two," thinking of the two tribal men who'd helped her. She didn't even know their names, but she'd find a way to thank them both, even if it meant she would have to contact her mum to do so.

$$\infty$$

Baphomet snarled aloud as he fought against the forces keeping him from his Lisa. He'd been exultant when he'd realized what she'd done in signaling the two men the way she had. He had been on the verge of revealing himself to the entire assemblage, both Shaitan and human alike, in order to save her, but the two dark-skinned human men had saved him from having to take such drastic measures.

The barriers they'd quickly erected around her had immediately put her out of even Iblis' reach and Baphomet had foolishly grinned as he'd watched the group of Shaitans eventually move reluctantly off in the direction of the nearby dimension barrier. With their sport spoiled for the evening, they'd either have to return back to the Angelic dimension, which meant they'd have to cross the barrier on their own, or they would have to find some other means of entertainment within this realm.

Iblis, he knew, would be very embarrassed and upset at having been bested by the two humans, so Baphomet believed the Shaitans would be returning to their dimension as quickly as Iblis could get there. Baphomet chuckled with delight at the thought of Iblis' defeat. He was soon to sing a different tune, however, as he felt his own psychic connection he'd established with Lisa days ago rip to shreds.

Suddenly, he was no longer connected to her and the loss of her constant flow of thoughts was deafeningly quiet. He pushed against the newly-erected barriers to no avail as the two humans continued chanting and moving around her. In the end, it appeared Lisa may as well have been on another planet, for all the access he had to her mind.

Baphomet pushed, shoved, pounded, and kicked against their barriers, mentally speaking. It was all for naught though, and Lisa just calmly walked away in the direction of her flat. He followed, of course, his conniving mind still poking at the men's barriers in search of any chink, no matter how small. But there just wasn't any way through, and Baphomet screamed in agonizing rage. How dare they block him from his counterpart! It took only a moment more of him fuming before he realized he had to get those men to reverse what they'd done, and he immediately left Lisa's side to go back in search of the pub.

The place was packed when he finally got there. Humans filled every inch of space inside the one-room establishment and Baphomet had to stay as far above the crowd as possible just so he could look for his quarry. Of course, that meant he got to travel at about the same level as the smoke cloud that filled the upper tier of the room.

It took him a few minutes, but he soon spotted the two dark-skinned men he was after and lowered himself toward them to see what he could discover. The taller one looked directly up at him upon his approach, with the shorter one taking only a second longer before looking him directly in the face. This was almost unheard of because Baphomet still sported at least one shield, which should have made him invisible to just about every human on the planet.

Baphomet cautiously stepped up to the pair. He was taller than both of them, but neither showed the slightest hint of fear or any sign they might back down. Of course, Baphomet couldn't tell if they were just putting up a brave front or not, because both of their minds were shut tight against his intrusion.

He knew *too* that if they could block him from being able to intrude on their minds that that meant they were probably in possession of some pretty powerful spells and incantations that might possibly be able to cause either psychic or physical harm to a Seraph, if not both. After all, there was always someone more powerful, no matter how much ability one had.

Baphomet knew that. He also knew there were still aborigines being raised in the old ways, with the old beliefs, and that somewhere back in the sands of time, the aborigines and Seraphim had been great friends. It was even rumored that the Jinn could still regularly be found guarding over this tribe or that, as they'd done for hundreds, if not thousands, of generations.

Finally, Baphomet nodded to them both. Neither man moved a muscle. This was going to be more difficult than he'd thought. He couldn't wait, though, so he swallowed the lump of consternation in his throat and plunged in headlong, saying, "I am sorry to disturb you, but when you helped out the young lady earlier out on the street, you incidentally managed to block *me* from her. She is very special to me and I can assure you I mean her no harm. If you would, I should like you to either reverse that part of the warding you erected around her or to explain to me how I might get around it so I shall once again have access to her." He took a breath while the two merely continued staring guardedly at him.

Baphomet stared back at them, perplexed. Had they heard him? Could they even understand him? The other humans and they had spoken English earlier, so he'd thought that would be the appropriate language to use. Each one merely continued staring at him, however, unmoving and silent.

"She and I are meant to be connected to each other, you see?" Baphomet asked as he frowned in concentration, trying to think of a different way to word his plea, when suddenly, he felt an incredible force of energy behind him. A shiver ran down his spine. The two in front of him shifted their gazes to someone, or something, behind Baphomet and he turned to face this new threat.

There, in the middle of the crowded pub, stood the oldest Koradji Baphomet had ever seen. A Koradji was the Aboriginal version of a medicine man or holy man. This one was a few feet shorter than Baphomet, dressed in full ceremonial garb, which basically meant he was wearing a colored cloth diaper and was covered in different colored mud decorations all over his face, arms, and torso. However, no one else in the pub paid any attention to the old man. It was almost as if... as if humans *couldn't* see the Koradji.

Baphomet's eyes widened at this thought, and then suddenly he was choking as the old man held a fist to his mouth and blew a fistful of red powder directly into Baphomet's face. He coughed and brushed at the red powder until very quickly, his muscles stopped working. Baphomet panicked as he realized the red powder had been some sort of neurotoxin that worked on Seraphim. Basically, this meant he was at the mercy of the three humans now surrounding him.

The old Koradji turned without a word and walked toward the exit. The two aborigines behind Baphomet grabbed him just as his leg muscles stopped working and they both half-carried/half-dragged him off in the same direction the Koradji had gone. Baphomet's eyes became dry and a flow of tears started out the corners of his eyes. The shorter of the two men carrying him noticed the tears and reached over to close Baphomet's lids.

Baphomet could only hear now, but for how long, he didn't care to take a guess. He began feeling a pressure in his chest and midriff. The muscles there that helped him breathe, such as his diaphragm, his intercostals, and his heart, were coming under the effects of the neurotoxin. Soon, Baphomet realized, he would be dead. He would exist no longer on this planet, in either dimension. He had lived for around a million years and now he was going to die.

Lisa's face popped into his mind from whatever part of his brain that was still functioning enough to allow it and Baphomet suddenly felt furious. He'd just found her! He hadn't even had time enough to talk with her or to truly get to know her! He couldn't let this happen! He just had to have more time with her, but how? Baphomet searched his sleepy mind for some way out of this situation.

He no longer felt a weight on his chest. He no longer felt the pain in his head he'd felt since the day Sarah had shown him the visions. In fact, he no longer felt anything, and Baphomet wondered if he was already too late. He could neither see, nor hear, nor feel anything. *Is this death?* he vaguely wondered with whatever part of his brain that still functioned. In the silent solitude of his eminent demise, Lisa's face crowded his inner eye once more and he thought *Lisa..., Lisa..., Leece...*

∞

Pain was searing throughout his entire chest. He couldn't breathe. He sucked as hard as he could for any available air, his throat making a rasping sound as a little air finally managed to get down it into his lungs. It hurt bad, and he coughed.

He felt something hit him hard on his back. He suffered another bout of hacking and coughing and something again hitting him on his back. His entire body felt as if pins and needles were being stuck into his skin all over, and every muscle he possessed seemed coiled up as tight as it could be. His head now felt like it was going to explode. Then, the pain slowly eased a little and Baphomet finally found the strength to open his eyes.

He found he was sitting on the ground, or really, being held up in a sitting position by the arms by the two young aborigines as he hacked and coughed, still trying to get air into his lungs. He managed to raise his head a bit and discovered the ancient-looking Koradji standing before him, watching as Baphomet struggled for air. Baphomet's gut instinct was to fight and he immediately released his shields.

Nothing happened.

He tried again, but still nothing happened.

The mud-covered Koradji standing before him spoke quickly in an ancient language Baphomet had long forgotten and one of the two young men holding his arms said, "My father wants to know who this Lisa is to you, Mate."

Baphomet blinked. Lisa's face swam before his mind's eye and he caught up a breath and said in a heavily slurred voice, "L-Lisa?" How could he explain to these humans what Lisa was to him? She was the other half of his very soul, supposedly, if one was to believe what Sarah had said and shown to him. Baphomet certainly already felt that way about her.

He was definitely interested in her. He didn't understand her, to be sure, but he wanted to. He wanted the opportunity to get to know her. He *needed* to be with her, as if there was some physical force compelling him to be near her. She was his perfect mate, even though she was human and he was Seraph.

If what Sarah's and Suriyah's visions had shown them was to be believed, then Baphomet believed Lisa and he needed each other in order to evolve into their next evolutionary stage. He hadn't shared this belief with anyone, but that was what he'd come to believe over the past couple of days.

The old Koradji spoke once again, rapping words out at break-neck pace to the two young tribesmen still squatting on either side of Baphomet. The one who'd spoken before said, "My father says you are fated to be with this woman, that the spirits have arranged for the two of you to meet. You may go to her now." Baphomet's bright gaze darted back to the old Koradji standing before him as he once again rapped out a rapid-fire litany to the other two. "He says the woman has been waiting for you and you must take her back with you to the dream world now so she no longer poses a threat to those in this world," said the young man.

The two young aborigines helped Baphomet to stand, not letting go of him until they were certain he could stand on his own. The mud-covered old man spoke once more, and then turned and walked off into the dark night without looking back. Baphomet looked over at the young man who'd spoken to him last and asked in a weak voice, "What did he say?"

The young man looked up at him and said, "My father says he's glad you finally came for her. He's been worried about her for a long time and it makes his heart feel glad to know you have finally come to take her back to your world. He also said he hopes you won't forget the children of this world once you return to the dream world." Without another word, or even a glance, the two dark young men walked off into the black night, the same as the old Koradji had done.

Baphomet watched them as they disappeared into the darkness. The ancient-looking Koradji had obviously been inside Baphomet's head. For a human to be able to do something like that, some pretty awesome power was required. When Suriyah and he used to visit these parts of the human realm, they'd always been impressed by the skills of the humans living here. Apparently, some of those skills and knowledge of ancient times truly had survived to be passed down through the generations.

When the two young men were no longer visible, Baphomet turned to regard his surroundings. They hadn't taken him far, he realized, as he saw the pub down at this end of the town and he wondered how much time had passed. Would Lisa have already reached her flat by now?

He attempted to release his shields once more and a feeling of pure bliss spread through him as he felt them sleekly unfurling and wrapping around his form. His head was still hurting, but that was just the pain he'd felt since sharing the visions with Sarah and he was quickly learning to ignore that. He flexed his shields and rose into the night sky, darting smoothly off in the direction of Lisa's flat. In mere minutes, he'd spotted her.

She wasn't quite to her street yet and Baphomet wondered for a moment why. Then, it occurred to him that perhaps the old Koradji had been influencing more than just Baphomet's mind. Maybe the old man had gotten inside Lisa's mind, as well? Had the old man even influenced time, itself? Baphomet would not put it past the old Koradji.

But he didn't care. All Baphomet truly cared about was the fact that he'd been granted a second chance with Lisa.

As he neared her location, he tried pushing into her mind, testing himself to see if what the old man had said was true. He smiled as he caught the sweet sounds of her mental voice in its constant flow of chatter. It felt so good being back inside her head, he fairly cackled with glee as he swooped down toward where she walked below.

He studied her. She moved seemingly without care. Before, when he'd been watching her for a few days, when she would walk down the street each step was a practice in putting off any approach. She'd so very obviously wanted to avoid attracting anyone's attention. Now, her step seemed to be light and comfortable. He wondered why she'd been like that before. After all, she wasn't unattractive.

In fact, with the right clothes and make-up, maybe a different hair style, she'd be quite comely, he imagined. She had nice legs, from what he'd seen over the past few days, along with curves in all the right places. Her breasts were of average size and she wasn't heavy. She might could stand to lose up to a stone, but that would come once she shared his bed on a regular basis.

Baphomet was never easy on those he took to his bed. He knew it and so did they. That's why each one of them lined up – they wanted the hurt he had to dish out to them. He made sure they got what they wanted too, even managing most of the time to give them a little more than that, just to ensure they'd never forget his presence inside their bodies.

Foolish females!

The Shaitan weren't exactly known for their intelligence, but they loved and craved every physical experience available, and they partook of them all, every chance they got. Baphomet knew of the exploits of his people, especially those like Iblis and his gang. He had those loyal to him willing to share information in hopes of gaining his favor. But very rarely did Baphomet intercede. Who was he to dissuade his people from taking whatever pleasures they could from this life? They were trapped here, the same as he. Why shouldn't they at least enjoy themselves as best they could?

And yet, as he watched his Lisa move through the mostly deserted streets on her way home, a tiny voice in his mind reminded him of the fact that she wasn't like the Shaitans. She was human... mortal. Hurt *her,* and she might not eventually bounce back as those in the Angelic realm did.

Humans were so fragile. For the millionth time, Baphomet wondered why on earth those strange, glowing creatures he'd seen in the visions Sarah had shared with him had created sentient life on this planet by such design so that some of those from one realm were meant to be with some of those from another. It didn't make sense!

Mikhail's woman had told him she'd been human before. He'd seen it in the visions she'd shown him. Whatever she and Mikhail had evolved into now, he wasn't sure, for although they resembled those strange, glowing creatures, they were somehow different from them. Baphomet had even imagined they were more powerful than those glowing creatures from parts unknown.

However, he knew this human female walking before him, this Lisa Murdoch, was intended for him and him alone. Once he'd caught wind of her energy tones that first night, had felt her frequencies sliding along his nerve endings, he'd known. This creature belonged to him, utterly and completely. She just didn't know it yet. And Baphomet had never liked sharing his toys with anyone, not even with Suriyah.

What had triggered the changes in Mikhail and his woman, Baphomet wondered as he followed along above his Lisa, simply enjoying watching her walk along the sidewalk for a moment. Suriyah had never mentioned anything about any physiological changes in her visions. Baphomet had never gleaned anything from her mind even remotely related to any type of transformations from Seraph to something else, so Baphomet found himself pretty much flying blind for the first time in his life, and he didn't like it!

Would *he* change, now that he'd felt his Lisa's energies? Could she feel his? Would that make her change as Mikhail's woman had? Baphomet wanted to know. He actually *needed* to know before he took her from her realm back to his own.

The Badlands was a lawless province, to be sure, but to bring a human there would only invite chaos. The Shaitans would take issue with having a human living among them in their capital city of Knor and Baphomet knew there would be trouble from others within the Angelic realm as well. But, the Koradji had instructed him to take her back to the Angelic realm, or dream world as the aborigines called it.

Lisa ducked into an alcove and Baphomet lost sight of her. He could still feel her, but he felt she must be moving upward in the three-storied building because her energy emission was becoming fainter and more difficult to detect and the building wasn't that big around. It was tall, though, so the idea that she was in an elevator or going up a flight of stairs was the logical conclusion.

He made a whistled sound of frustration and turned away. He would just have to wait for her to come out again because he was still feeling a bit jittery, and the idea of supporting a buffer around himself actually brought on a feeling of nausea. He let out a harsh sigh. He hated waiting.

He thought of the things he'd seen in the visions Sarah had shown him. She and Mikhail had started transforming almost immediately after they'd first come into contact with each other. It had seemed like it had only been hours after their first contact when their eyes had started flashing, if he recalled correctly. Would it be that way with Baphomet and Lisa? They hadn't actually touched physically yet, so did that mean they would *not* change anytime soon?

It was all too confusing and frustrating because Baphomet didn't know what to expect or even *when*. On top of that, there was the whole issue of where he was going to hide her in the Angelic realm until she had transformed from her human form into at least her Seraph form so she'd be safe. Baphomet threw his head back on a growl of frustration, closing his eyes and sighing deeply. He was just going to have to deal with things as they came at him. He had to make this work… he just had to.

Chapter 5

The moment Lisa exited the back of the library and then made her way around to the walkway out front, she froze. She could *feel* him. A chill stole down her spine and she dropped down into a crouch. It was stupid, since there was nothing she could hide behind, but it made her feel just a fraction safer.

Her eyes quickly scanned the area, darting first to the left, then the right. She slowly turned her head and looked behind her. About twenty feet away, she thought she caught sight of some sort of light. She couldn't be certain, but it looked almost like someone or some... *thing* was coming with a light just around the corner of the building to her left.

The light grew brighter and Lisa turned more fully toward its direction as quietly as she could, her tennis shoes making a slight scraping noise on some small pieces of broken glass that were strewn all over the dark street. The light got brighter. Lisa swallowed a lump in her throat and half-rose, her heart racing.

She'd been feeling so good after the two young men had performed their ritual earlier. But now she felt as if she was about to have a heart attack, she was so scared. This thing, or person, or whatever it was, she could *feel* it approaching her. Goosebumps ran all over her body and she jerked up and around just as a large hand landed on her shoulder from behind.

Lisa screamed and immediately took off running in the opposite direction from the light. Before she could take two steps, however, she suddenly found herself trapped inside a warm, leathery-feeling bubble that immediately surrounded her entire body and then conformed to her shape, like shrink wrap, pressing against her form until she was tightly cocooned within the leathery wrapping from head to toe. She couldn't move her head more than an inch or two and discovered it was pressed against a hot chest that seemed as hard as stone, though it was covered in some type of fabric. A silk shirt?

It didn't matter! What was she *thinking*?

She struggled to break free, pulling on this arm, pushing with that foot.

Rest easy, baby, a strong male voice said in her mind.

Lisa froze. Was she going insane? It was that same voice she'd heard the other day in her flat, all chocolaty and smooth.

Chocolaty? Seriously? the voice asked in her mind and she thought she heard a deep, rumbling laughter from inside the chest pressed against her head. Now he was making fun of her? Great! Lisa struggled against the leathery shrink wrap even harder, and again the voice came to her in her mind, saying, *Ow! Stop that!* Lisa stilled again, afraid she'd hurt him now. Again, she caught and felt the rumble of his laughter. *Go to sleep now, baby*, he seemed to whisper from some faraway place as Lisa suddenly felt more exhausted than she'd ever felt in her life. *Crossing the barrier is not something I want you to remember from our first moments together*, she thought she heard him say. Then there was complete silent darkness.

∞

Baphomet carried her through his own private entrance to the Shaitan stronghold from the dark forest. It would have to be a temporary arrangement, just until he could find a place where Lisa and he could be alone during their transformations. It wouldn't do to have any of the Shaitans discovering Lisa's presence within the stronghold before she had at least completed her transformation from human to Seraph. Before then, she'd be vulnerable to attack and Baphomet wasn't going to allow her to be put in harm's way ever again.

He made his way through the dark maze of tunnels only he and Suriyah knew about and finally emerged in his darkened bedroom. After placing Lisa gently upon his bed and covering her to keep her warm, he closed and locked the main doors to the room and then removed his shirt and crawled part way under the covers onto the bed beside his other half.

In the dim light of dawn, he allowed his fingers to gently touch her face, her neck, her arms, and her hands. It was safe to touch her now and he needed to. She was so soft. Baphomet had never been one to forego any pleasures available to him, but for the life of him, he could not recall ever having touched any female, Angel or human, who was as soft as she.

The thing that really thrilled him beyond measure, however, was how his own skin tingled with her energies each time he touched her. It was a delicious feeling and he wondered if sub-consciously she could feel his energies, too, whenever he touched her. He hoped so. He recalled the things Sarah had shown him from when Mikhail touched her and how it had felt to her. As he ran his hand along Lisa's collar bone, he resigned himself to having to wait until she woke to find out how his touch affected her.

He leaned in to take in her scent, nuzzling his nose against the softest part of her neck, inhaling the special fragrance that was her. His touch must have broken through to her on some level, for he caught the first stirrings of her thoughts emerging from what seemed to him to be some sort of nightmare with monsters chasing after her through a dark alley.

He pushed a little into her mind and softly said with his mental voice, *Wake up, my sweet. You are in your new home now.* He was anxious to see the color of her eyes and wished she'd hurry and wake up. It wasn't that he didn't like her beautiful brown eyes. It was just that he needed to know if they were both close to transforming or not. *Sweet Lisa*, he said, brushing his mental voice over the landscape of her mind. *Come on, Leece. Open those beautiful eyes for me, sweet.*

∞

It was that voice again! It had haunted her dreams forever, it seemed, and Lisa just wanted it to go away. Everywhere she turned in her dreams, it was there. It wasn't that she didn't like it, for she did, a lot. It was just that she couldn't find its owner and that both frightened and frustrated her. She was near to panicking, when suddenly those big strong arms and that rock wall of a chest surrounded her again.

She grabbed hold of the chest and held on for dear life. This was the one who'd saved her in the alley near her flat. She was sure of it. Somehow, she knew she was safe with whoever this was… her guardian Angel.

One of the Angel's big hands smoothed comfortingly down her back as the voice came again. *Yes, you are safe. I shall never allow anyone to harm you. Now, come, my lovely*, it persisted. *It is time for you to officially meet your new master.*

Lisa frowned, even in her semi-sleeping state, as her mind processed his words. She didn't *belong* to anyone! Who the hell did this disembodied voice think he was? Her ire instantly rising at such words, she pushed away from the safety and security of her guardian's arms and finally opened her eyes to confront her nemesis. Immediately, she wished she'd kept her eyes shut.

Everywhere she looked, stark images of lovers entwined in every sexual position possible, and several she had no doubt were quite *im*possible, were displayed in paintings, sculptures, and even woven into hanging tapestries. The colors in this room weren't quite as bawdy as they'd been in that other room, but they were still disturbing. She felt dirty just being there and she instinctively tucked her limbs in close to keep as much of herself as possible from touching anything.

Welcome, sweetness, to your new home, the voice came again and Lisa jerked around, suddenly realizing she was sitting on a giant bed, and that she wasn't alone! Her eyes widened in shocked amazement as she beheld the most beautiful creature she'd ever seen in her life lying right next to her on the bed! He had long, thick blond hair that hung in a straight sheen well past his shoulders as he lay on his side, his head propped up on his hand, his gleaming ice-blue eyes smiling mischievously up at her.

His entire upper torso was bare, revealing a broad, well-muscled chest and abdomen lightly dusted with dark blond hair that led down under the covers he'd pulled up over his waist. His arms were muscular, though not "beef-cake" muscular. As this thought slid through her mind, the beautiful man before her chuckled softly and she immediately realized it was he who belonged to the voice. "Finally, my sweet, we meet," he said as he reached to touch her cheek, his voice deep and delicious.

The moment his skin came into contact with hers, Lisa felt a jolt of electricity shoot through her, stemming from his heated touch, and she gasped and jerked off the bed to stand staring down at the beauteous vision the man made. *What is he?* she wondered. If there were male supermodels, Lisa knew this would be the king of them... and his touch... it had been so hot and electrifying. Was she still dreaming? She pinched herself, just for good measure, and winced.

The man looked at her for a moment like she was crazy, then chuckled softly again, saying, "I have waited so long for this day, sweet Lisa. I know you must have, as well." He patted the mattress between them. "Why not lie back down, now and we shall get started on seeing just how well-suited you and I are, pet?"

Lisa stood rooted to the spot, her mouth hanging open in astonished disbelief. How could anyone be so goddamned arrogant and presumptuous... and blunt? Who the hell did he think he was?

Apparently, the guy took no notice of her growing outrage because he then said, "Of course, I do hope you are not harboring hopes of conceiving too quickly, for I am a very sexual being with a large appetite, and I am going to want to do some... *exploring*, if you will, before I have to share my new toy with anyone, offspring or no." The truth was that Baphomet was secretly afraid. He still didn't believe it was actually possible for Seraphim to conceive. He wasn't about to admit to anything like that, though, and he looked expectantly up at his future bride.

Lisa had had enough! She leapt onto the bed and, reaching back, slapped him as hard as she could, stunning herself almost as much as it appeared she'd stunned him as the sound of her hand making contact with his face seemed to echo throughout the room. She was so filled with rage she didn't even recognize herself, mentally speaking. As horrifying realization gradually dawned, Lisa bolted off the bed again, this time not stopping at the side of it to look back at her tormentor.

Instead, she frantically ran away from him, looking for any available escape route. There were several doors to the room, but only one open one and, as it was nearest, she took it, plunging headlong into the black depths beyond it, uncaring that she didn't know where she was headed or that she could see nothing. What mattered was that she escaped *him*.

"Wait, Leece," Baphomet called out, as soon as he realized what she was doing. He'd been so stunned by her violent reaction to him that it had taken him a moment before he'd figured out she was trying to escape. He'd rolled and tried to stand, but found himself suddenly tangled in the covers and he fell, face-down onto the floor beside the bed.

"Lisa!" he shouted, as he frantically disentangled himself from the silky bed linens. If she was seen by any Shaitan, she'd be in grave danger. He had to get to her, and quick! "Lisa, wait!" he yelled. Finally, he broke free of the silken covers and gained his footing, already in a dead run for the open door to his secret passageway.

"Master?" came the voice of one of his harem suddenly, followed by a knock on the main bedroom door, and he stopped dead in his tracks. His heart sank as he realized all was lost. He'd carelessly left the passageway door open and then he'd thoughtlessly called out to his Lisa too loudly.

Of course his upper Shaitan servants had heard him. That was their function, to tend to his every whim at all times. He'd be expected to let them in, now that they'd discovered he was there. Why not? He'd never before *not* let them in. And, Lisa was gone.

He couldn't go after her, not immediately, anyway. Another knock and another of his hoard calling out to him proved that.

Baphomet wanted to scream as a rage so black and foul filled him at the circumstances. She was his and she was in mortal danger, literally! The minute she was spotted by a Shaitan, which he knew was inevitable, she would be lost. No self-respecting Shaitan, male or female, passed up an opportunity for pleasure. Humans represented the most delicious pleasure a Shaitan could experience, other than the pleasure of being favored by a Seraph, of course. But, with humans, a Shaitan got to be the master, and that held an appeal unrivaled in the Angelic realm. She'd be taken for certain.

Another knock, more urgent this time, followed by a panic-stricken, "Master?" and Baphomet hung his head in defeat.

A heartbeat later, he silently closed the door to the secret passageway, once again concealing it from any and all, and then he made his way over to unlock the door where his Shaitan harem waited, wrenching it open to glare at the women standing just outside his bedchamber. There were about fifteen of them standing there and they all stepped back in the face of his rage.

"What?" he demanded, petulantly taking his anger out on the innocent women. He knew it was wrong. He knew they were just doing as they'd been trained to do for millennia. But his loss was too new and his pain was too fresh and raw. He wanted to hurt someone. He wanted to squeeze the life out of them and laugh at their agony. He wanted to punish someone for putting him through this pain. To have found her, his other half, only to immediately lose her was more than he could stand.

As Baphomet's thoughts whirled, a black aura settled in around him. His vision clouded with the torturous images of the things he wanted to do to his imaginary foe and he didn't bother to notice the actions of his servants.

Near the front of the crowd of women was an older Shaitan who'd been with Baphomet since long before he and his sister had been banished from Seraphim City. Although she'd been his bed mate many a time, she'd actually come to regard him more as a son than as a lover. She cared very deeply for him and she'd become increasingly concerned for him over the past few centuries – most especially lately.

Baphomet advanced onto the crowd of females with a dangerously ravenous look in his eyes, seemingly unaware even of who they were, and the woman stepped forward suddenly and slapped him hard across the face. Fourteen simultaneous gasps sounded behind her as Baphomet stopped in his tracks, his hand covering his now twice-insulted cheek as he stared at his servant in astonishment.

The Shaitan female stood her ground even as realization dawned on her. Realization then dawned on him as well and Baphomet felt an almost overwhelming urge to flee. These women were not his enemies. They'd been his sounding boards, his confidants, his comforters throughout much of his life, and here he was contemplating punishing them in the most gruesome manner possible, and for what?

It wasn't their fault Lisa had escaped. He never should have brought her to Shaitan territory before they'd both evolved. It was his fault she was now out there somewhere, as vulnerable as an infant, in the wilds of the Badlands. She would die a mortal death, most likely in some excruciating manner, at the hands of one of his people, and Baphomet would have to wait however long it took her to be born again to the planet before he could once again track her down and try again.

He stepped back from his servants. "Forgive me, my dears," he softly said. "I have treated you unfairly." With that, he stepped around them and disappeared down the labyrinth of hallways within his mansion.

The fifteen women stood stock-still, staring after their master, at first in astonishment at his apology and then in devoted concern for him. One by one, fourteen pairs of eyes turned to regard the eldest of their group. After only a slight hesitation, the woman held out her hands on each side and solemnly said, "Come, my sisters. We must go pray for our beloved master."

∞

Baphomet squinted his eyes at the early-morning sunlight streaming through the solarium's Eastern-facing wall of glass. Somewhere out in the vast, dense forest stretched out before him, his Lisa wandered unknowingly toward her death, if she wasn't captive already. The forests in Shaitan territory were densely populated and one such as she would quickly be discovered. It would be useless for him to go after her now. That was assuming she'd made it through the labyrinth of tunnels leading from his bedchamber to the forests beyond.

If she still lived by the time he tracked her down, *if* he could, he knew she'd already be in the custody of one of the Shaitans living within the forest. Shaitan law declared one's property as sacred and possession *was* the law. Even he, with all his status as a Seraph, was not above Shaitan law. But, perhaps there was another way…

Baphomet took a seat at a nearby chair and concentrated. In seconds, he felt the welcome connection springing to life between Lisa and him and he heard her voice. A frown immediately marred his perfect features, however, as he realized she was talking with someone… someone he couldn't detect. He concentrated on her thoughts, trying to catch a glimpse through her eyes of her mystery partner, but he was being blocked somehow.

In an instant, he was filled with rage again.

How dare *he* interfere!

Baphomet's shields whipped out and he catapulted soundlessly through the glass ceiling of the solarium and then high into the morning sky, hell-bent suddenly on intercepting and reclaiming what was his, his bloody brother be damned!

∞

Lisa had run until her legs would function no more. She'd fallen a few times and her hands and knees, and even her chin, bore vicious scrapes from which blood still flowed freely. She was on the verge of tears from the ordeal of trying to find her way through the dark tunnel when she suddenly caught sight of a light coming from somewhere just a little way up ahead. A warm, calming feeling suddenly enveloped her and she heard a soft voice coming from parts unknown.

"Have no fear," the soft, feminine voice said. "You are safe now."

"Wh-Where are you?" Lisa asked aloud. She suddenly felt like a little girl, small and helpless, searching for her mother, needing her protective strength.

"Come toward my voice and you will be safe."

Lisa slowly stumbled forward toward the light, trying not to touch anything, but having to reach out to the walls to keep from falling every now and then as she kept her eyes focused on the light up ahead. She finally stumbled out into a brightly-lit clearing and was temporarily blinded.

As her vision cleared, she realized there were two huge men standing in the clearing watching her. For a moment, she felt a frisson of panic and fear skitter down her spine as she took in how much they resembled the beautiful man she'd just escaped from, but then the soft female voice said, "You are safe. These two will serve as your guardians and will guide you safely to me."

After only a slight hesitation, Lisa approached the two gentlemen and regarded them expectantly. Each man quickly bowed and then extended his hand in greeting.

"Welcome, Miss. I am Djibril," the first said as she shook his hand. She then turned toward the other.

"Welcome, Miss," he said, also shaking her hand. "I am Israfil. Please allow my brother and me to escort you to safety."

"Go with them," said the soft voice and Lisa didn't hesitate. She didn't see anyone else in the clearing, but she wasn't going to wait around for anyone else to find her. She felt only the slightest sense of uncertainty as she found herself suddenly being wrapped in the same type of invisible leathery-feeling cocoon the other man had used. She was amazed this time, however, as she watched the ground drop away beneath her feet when she and her two guardians rose up into the air and then again when they took off flying in a northwesterly direction. Lisa felt no fear at all as the cold winds whipped around their little group. Not once did it even twitch a hair on her head and she wondered what kind of cloak wrapped around them to protect them so.

In mere minutes, she noticed they were slowing and she looked around below them, eagerly searching for the female voice's owner. That voice had been so warm, so soothing. It had comforted her like nothing ever had before and Lisa *needed* to find its owner. She *needed* to feel protected from that man. It was crazy, but Lisa felt sure that, had she not escaped him when she did, her life would've been irrevocably changed for all time.

There was another clearing below them, and as their trio descended, Lisa noticed several people standing along the edge. Off to one side stood two men and a woman, each watching the group descend from above without much movement of their own.

Standing a short distance from those three was a pair of people so odd-looking Lisa's gaze became transfixed. They had long white hair that was constantly being caught by some breeze or other in their area. Lisa found it odd that the others standing below didn't seem to be affected by any breeze.

That wasn't the only peculiar thing about them, though.

As Lisa and her two guardians neared, she studied the couple.

The man was much taller than the woman as he stood behind her; one arm was banded across her chest with his hand resting on her shoulder while his other arm was banded across her waist. It struck Lisa that these two actually seemed to be *glowing*.

As she and her two guardians finally settled onto solid earth, Lisa gasped, for that was when she finally caught her first glimpse of the couple's eyes. She almost had to look away from their bright gazes, it was so intense, and a resurgence of fear and uncertainty crept back into her mind. *Have I just exchanged one dangerous situation for another?* she wondered.

"Rest assured, Lisa Murdoch," the glowing female said in her soft voice. "You are quite safe here."

Lisa returned her gaze to the two and stared at them, particularly the female. She seemed somehow familiar. That couldn't be, could it? As she continued staring at them, Lisa realized suddenly that there was no breeze making their white hair move. It just moved on its own! It was like it was alive, flicking up here or there and then softly floating back down to settle next to the other strands, only to flick up again a moment later. It was almost like watching a cat's tail twitching just at the end, but on the much broader scale of thousands of individual strands of hair all flitting about individually.

Lisa wondered if they got tangled up regularly and then shook her head at such a randomly insane thought. Judging from the slight lifting of the couple's lips at the corners, Lisa could almost believe the couple had heard her crazy thought, and that's when it hit her out of nowhere – the glowing female standing before her was Sarah Baker, the American blogger who'd caused all the hullabaloo world-wide with her Vision Blog. Lisa remembered her from the pictures she'd seen of Sarah on the internet.

As if acknowledging such, the glowing woman slightly tipped her head down in a half-nodding gesture.

Just then, again from out of nowhere, the man who'd kidnapped her dropped onto the scene with a frightening snarl and Lisa uttered a fearful cry at the sight of him. How had he found her? She broke free of her two guardians and quickly darted around the glowing couple, instinctively moving toward Sarah Baker for protection. The male standing with Sarah dropped his arms and moved to Sarah's side, effectively blocking Lisa from harm's way.

Lisa stood where she was as she realized the white strands of hair, which before had only flicked here or there, were all now whipping about, wrapping around to position themselves so they could seemingly "face" their owners' foe. If one were to look at the scene objectively, Lisa supposed, it would seem quite fascinating, she was sure.

"Give her *back*, Mikhail!" her bare-chested lunatic kidnapper snarled.

The glowing man beside Sarah calmly said, "Go home, Baphomet."

The man, Baphomet, snarled viciously once more and shouted, "You had no right to take her! She is my *mate*!"

Then, the strangest thing happened... Everyone became completely silent, except for the enraged Baphomet, who grunted and snarled on occasion. Other than that, there was silence. Lisa watched the scene in utter confusion. They all kept looking about at each other, the way people do when they're carrying on conversations, but not one word was being uttered.

Chapter 6

Baphomet stood rooted to the spot, unable to move his legs the slightest twitch. Sarah's voice wafted across his mind. *Baphomet, you will listen to me, my new-found brother… You are in no state to be with this woman at the moment*, her soft, yet firm, voice said.

Baphomet snarled aloud at Sarah, and Mikhail quickly piped in, warning, *Watch yourself, brother! This is* my *mate you are facing and I shall rip to shreds anyone who dares disrespect her!*

Baphomet growled aloud at Mikhail as his mental voice scathingly rebutted, *You can go to hell*, brother!

Mikhail sucked in a sharp breath and started toward his brother. A small, soft hand on his arm immediately had him stopping to look down at Sarah. Her beautiful glowing eyes looked pleadingly up at him as her soft voice lightly whispered in his mind, *My love, have mercy on him. We're keepin' him from his mate.*

That still does not mean he has any right to offend you, my love, Mikhail thought back to her.

Sarah's eyes softened. *Please, Mikhail*, she continued. *Imagine how you would behave if someone tried to take me from you.*

Mikhail stilled instantly. He knew he would kill anyone daring such a thing.

Sarah was right. He needed to help Baphomet, not fight him.

She is mine! Baphomet bellowed silently. *I'll kill you all if she is not returned to me immediately!*

Both Seraphim and Mikhail and Sarah winced from the volume echoing within their minds.

Mikhail turned to look at Israfil, his silent request immediately answered in the affirmative.

They both turned back toward Baphomet. *Brother,* Mikhail silently commanded, *you will return to Shaitan Territory until such time as this female is ready to accept you. Until then, you will refrain from coming near this complex.*

You cannot keep her from me! Baphomet barked silently. *I will kill you all!*

Mikhail looked toward Israfil as Baphomet struggled against the forces binding his legs. Though Mikhail didn't understand how she did it, he knew Sarah was the one holding Baphomet captive, so he knew his brother had no chance of breaking the bindings. Sarah had grown incredibly strong over the past few weeks.

Israfil stepped forward then and slowly raised his gaze to Baphomet's. Immediately, Baphomet ceased struggling as his gaze met Israfil's. Seconds later, Israfil turned back to Mikhail and Mikhail blinked in surprise, asking aloud, "Is it done, then?"

Israfil nodded once.

Mikhail glanced behind himself at the girl named Lisa. *I'll take care of her,* Sarah's voice softly assured him in his mind. *You should take him home before Israfil's magic wears off.* He looked down upon her radiant upturned face.

After only a moment, he quickly leaned forward and kissed Sarah on the lips before turning back to Baphomet. He released his shields, wrapped them quickly and securely around himself and the still-mesmerized Baphomet and promptly vanished into thin air.

"Um… What just happened?" Lisa timidly asked, her eyes rooted to the spot where the two large men had just disappeared into thin air.

Sarah turned to her and just the slightest twitch of her lips gave the impression of a smile. "Everything will be okay," Sarah said. She turned toward the others standing within the clearing. "Please, allow me to introduce my friends," Sarah said. She introduced each person in turn.

Of course, Hantsushept immediately requested that Lisa be taken to the clinic for tests. "The more information I have to work with," he explained, "the more complete our picture will be of how this evolutionary transformation takes place."

Lisa, of course, had no idea what the man was talking about, but Sarah seemed to think her going with him to submit to the tests was a good thing, so she agreed to go. She needed to get her scrapes and cuts tended to, anyway. The group silently moved off toward a small building to the left of the clearing.

∞

Thomas and Samuel stopped, pulling up behind a pair of thick-trunked trees so those on the other side of the clearing wouldn't see them. The two young men had been on their way to the clearing for their daily sparring match when they'd noticed the area was already occupied. Thomas' mom and dad stood with their backs to a woman Thomas did not know while Gabriel and Israfil both stood near some other really tall guy who looked like he wanted to kill everybody else around.

"Who is that with your mom and Mikhail?" Samuel asked quietly.

Thomas studied the woman for a moment. Even though her skin color was quite a bit darker than anyone else's in the clearing, she still kind of fit in. The waves of energy coming off her were patterned the same as Mikhail's and Thomas' mom's, though on a much less intense scale, and Thomas believed he knew, if not *who* she was, then at least *what* she was. That remained to be seen, however, so he merely shook his head and said, "I dunno." He turned his attention to the others. That's when he noticed Hantsushept and his aides standing nearby.

The old physician saw Thomas and Samuel, but made no move to alert the others to their presence. Instead, the old Angel merely turned to more fully concentrate on what was going on with the others in the clearing.

"Who's that with Gab... I mean, Djibril, and Israfil?" Thomas asked.

"I dunno," Samuel said. "I have never seen him before." After a moment of consideration, he continued, saying, "Maybe he is one of the outlanders everyone is always warning us about? I mean, look how mean and angry he looks."

Thomas nodded, but said nothing more on the subject.

The two boys watched and listened as best they could, though from this distance they couldn't hear much of any of what was being said. They were amazed when Mikhail suddenly stepped forward and took the angry man up into his shields and disappeared into thin air. Then, however, disappointment set in because the show was over and everyone except Thomas and Samuel left the clearing.

Though Thomas had an idea of what was going on, he didn't care to share his thoughts with Samuel just yet. Instead, now that the clearing was again available, he moved out into the center of it and took up a fighting stance, saying, "All right. Knock me down, if you dare."

Samuel's eyes lit with anticipation, his face taking on a sinister look as his upper lip curled into a wicked grin and he took up an offensive stance opposite his opponent, and the matter with the others was promptly forgotten amid the thrill of battle.

Without warning, he let go a volley of energy blasts directed straight toward Thomas. Just in time, Thomas twisted and bent his form to avoid the first few, allowing him enough time to erect a barrier for the remaining ones coming at him. They hit his invisible shield and he was pushed backward a bit from the force of the blasts. The patterns the energy blasts made as they skittered along his shield were like little starbursts of lightning all around him. Thomas paid them no attention, however, as he readied to fire his own round of blasts right back at his opponent.

Samuel was on the move, as he and Thomas had practiced time and time again. He kept his body moving while he erected his own energy shield. Whenever he felt his shield weakening, he would move his arms around in a round, circular movement, never breaking stride. He moved his arms in such a manner in order to draw more energy from within to add to the protective layer he already had in place. As soon as the protective outer layer was complete and stable, Samuel changed the movements of his arms, sometimes even involving his entire body in the movements as he pulled on the energies surrounding him to gather enough to make a proper strike.

Thomas watched as the energy mass Samuel was gathering grew and he knew he was in trouble. Samuel poised himself in a strike position and readied to release the energy mass. Without even knowing what he was doing, Thomas raised his hands and then waived them in a new pattern he'd never used before. It resembled the movements a massive tree would make as it waved in a violent wind.

"What the…?" Samuel muttered in wonder just before he was hit full on and went flying through the air.

Thomas watched in confused fascination as his friend hit the trunk of a nearby tree hard and then fell to the ground. He could still feel the effects of his unexpected connection with the molecules comprising the air around him and he looked with wonder down at his hands. Somehow, he'd known how to control the wind and he'd used it to defend himself.

Could he do it again?

Thomas lunged to the right, away from the area where Samuel was struggling to his feet, and moved his arms in much the same manner as he'd done before. The connection was still there and Thomas felt a sense of elation as he realized he was actually controlling the wind, its speed, its direction, its force, its content even… everything about it.

"How did you *do* that?" Samuel asked in awe from behind him.

Thomas dropped his arms and turned to face his friend. "I don't know," he said, grinning. "I just did it and you were down."

"But, your eyes," Samuel said.

Thomas frowned. "What about my eyes?" he asked.

Samuel shook his head and softly said, "They kind of glowed for a minute, like those of your parents."

Thomas raised a hand to his face, wondering if he could be experiencing the same kind of change his mom had gone through. "Are they still glowing?" he asked, a strange excitement building within him.

"Nah," Samuel said. "They just kind of flashed for a minute when you knocked me down."

Well, so much for that. Deflation was all-consuming and Thomas said, "Oh."

"So," Samuel said, cautiously approaching his friend. "You think you could show me how to do that?"

"I-I think so," Thomas said as he thought back over the steps he'd taken to perform the maneuver. It seemed simple enough and the two were soon embroiled in an intense training session on wind control maneuvers. The rest of the day whizzed by without either of them noticing the passage of time.

∞

The clinic was just a short walk from the clearing and Lisa soon found herself sitting on an exam table as two beautiful people, whom Lisa assumed were either nurses or interns, poked, prodded, and cleaned up her cuts and scrapes. They took various forms of samples from her person. After only a few minutes, the bright-eyed man Sarah had introduced as Hantsushept walked into the room to start his own examination.

"So, what's all this for, then?" Lisa asked him.

Without pausing in his examination of her, Hantsushept explained, "It is vital we get as complete a physiological and anatomical history on you as possible during each stage of your transformation. Stick out your tongue now and say, 'Ah.'" Lisa did as instructed and he poked a tongue suppressor into her mouth so he could check out the back of her oral cavity. With that done, he then grabbed his stethoscope and went to work listening to her heart and lungs as he instructed her on when to take deep breaths.

Lisa complied without hesitation, but in her mind she was puzzling over what he'd said. When he looped his stethoscope back around his neck like any regular doctor would do, she asked, "What did you mean about my 'transformation'?"

That halted him immediately in his tracks. He stared hard at her for a long moment in silence and then asked cautiously, "What exactly has the Seraph Baphomet told you so far?"

Lisa blew raspberries through pursed lips and said, "*That* nut case? As if I'd listen to anything *he* said! I hope that other guy drops him off a cliff somewhere, or locks him up tight in some far out-of-the-way asylum where he belongs."

Hantsushept frowned and murmured, "Hmm," but said nothing more.

Just then, the door to the small examination room opened and Sarah stepped inside.

Hantsushept stepped away from his new patient to give a half-bow to the creature he was very quickly coming to regard as being the closest thing to divinity he'd ever encountered. His eyes, of course, went immediately to check on the glowing patch on Sarah's abdomen.

Hantsushept, as always, was fascinated by the fact that Sarah and her mate, a former Seraph named Mikhail, had actually managed to conceive and he wished for the umpteenth time he still had access to all his equipment at the medical facility within Seraphim City. There were so many tests he'd be able to run on these creatures then.

However, he'd lost his access to that equipment when he'd fled the city with Sarah and Mikhail. So, he'd have to just make do with the simple tests he could run with the bits and pieces of equipment he'd managed to bring along. He and the two Seraphim who'd accompanied Sarah and Mikhail had returned to the city not long ago in secret and had managed to bring some supplies back, but it was nowhere near what Hantsushept would have liked.

Sarah politely cleared her throat to regain his attention and he quickly refocused. "How may I be of service, m'dear?" he graciously asked.

"I would like to show Miss Murdoch to her quarters now, if I may," she softly said aloud. Within Hantsushept's mind, however, she explained, *I believe it would be better for her if I explained things to her before she starts experiencin' the physical changes, don't you agree?*

Hantsushept nodded silently, but mentally he said, *You had better make it fast then, m'dear, for her eyes have already changed to a light blue color from the brown which I believe they used to be.* He knew Sarah had heard and understood him as he saw her own glowing eyes dart to see this evidence for herself.

Hantsushept had already read through Lisa's human medical history file, which he'd downloaded after hacking into the medical database on the human web, prior to commencing his physical examination of the young woman. Although he was a man of science, he'd recently learned he had a particular talent for the humans' computers and he made good use of his hacking skills.

Sarah smiled slightly at Lisa as she silently informed Hantsushept, *This changes matters, then. She'll have to be monitored since Baphomet's not here with her.*

She could remain in the clinic, Hantsushept offered hopefully. *She would have constant supervision that way and we would be able to document and observe each phase of her transformation.*

Sarah turned back toward him with a raised eyebrow of reproach. *Listen, you old Angel*, she silently chided. *I know you're just itchin' to discover everything you possibly can about us lab rats for your records and all, but I wish you'd remember that we're still living, breathing creatures who're tryin' to deal with somethin' no one else in Earth's history has ever had to deal with before. So, for the time being, you're just gonna to have to wait things out with everyone else, I'm afraid.*

Hantsushept bowed in apology to her. It was true he wanted to study these creatures, to find out how they were evolving at such an unprecedented rate. Evolution, if that was what this was, simply didn't happen this way! The rate of the changes these creatures were experiencing was more like that of genetic disorders, activated by this protein or that genetic coding error.

If only he could convince Sarah to allow him to track and observe the changes in this new subject, he might be able to discover why they were all transforming at such an unprecedented rate *and* what more they could expect. But the stern look of warning she threw him when he glanced hopefully in her direction had him backing off that train of thought immediately. "I shall step out while the patient gets dressed," he said aloud as he quickly made his escape.

As the door clicked closed, Lisa hopped down from the examination table and began dressing. "The two of you were communicating telepathically just now, weren't you?" she asked Sarah as she slipped on her jeans and buttoned up the fly beneath the exam gown. She'd sat riveted to the spot as she'd realized what Sarah Baker and the physician had been up to. Now she wanted answers.

Lisa had been an avid fan of Sarah's blog for the past couple of years and she was excited to be in her company. More than that, though, she felt a kind of connection with the woman, even though Lisa found her presence a bit daunting. Sarah's glowing eyes and white, moving hair were striking, for certain, but they did nothing to help someone feel at ease in her presence.

If Lisa hadn't learned all about Sarah's entire human history from all the recent news articles online and programs on the telly, then she never would've believed her to have ever been a human at all. She certainly didn't look human now!

Sarah handed Lisa her shirt, then turned away to offer her some privacy while she dressed and said, "Perhaps, we could talk about this, and a few other things, over lunch? I don't know about you, but I'm starvin'."

∞

Suriyah gasped as two figures suddenly appeared out of thin air in the middle of her bedroom. She'd been simultaneously writing in her journal and getting ready for yet another formal function of the JCG, so at least she was dressed, but the sight confronting her was quite astounding and she stared in shock at the two standing before her.

Baphomet looked as if he was in some sort of mind-numbing daze as he stood staring stupidly off into space. His companion, however, was the main attraction. Suriyah hadn't actually seen Mikhail in a few thousand years, but never would she have expected such physical changes within him.

His hair, his eyes, his radiance, his power... these were all so much... *more* than Suriyah could ever have imagined possible with him. Her visions definitely had not prepared her for the changes her beloved brother had suffered and she stood with jaw dropped and eyes wide as her confused mind tried to assimilate everything she saw.

Sister, Mikhail's mental voice said in her mind. Suriyah gasped again in surprise. Mikhail had never evidenced any type of psychic abilities. How could this be?

"You look... different," she said aloud after quickly clearing her throat.

Mikhail's glowing eyes blinked. "You look beautiful, as ever," he finally said.

Suriyah dragged her gaze away from his face. She closed her journal and placed it back in its place within the drawer of her vanity. She felt both confused and frightened and she wished all of a sudden that Baphomet was standing by *her* side, not by Mikhail's. She looked at her favorite brother, King of the Shaitans, and suddenly asked, "What is wrong with him?"

After a quick glance at his brother, Mikhail returned his gaze to his sister and explained, "He has merely been temporarily stunned. He should awaken within the next half-hour or so. We did not think it wise to leave him in Shaitan Territory in such a state."

"No," Suriyah agreed guardedly. "They would destroy him." She studied her most trusted brother. He was her best friend, her confidant, the only person who really knew her, and now, somehow, something within him had changed. Suriyah narrowed her eyes as she searched for some clue as to what was different about him, other than the obvious.

Baphomet stood perfectly still, his gaze never wavering, as if he was an empty shell with no one steering the ship, if you will. Suriyah stepped closer to him, reaching a hand up to touch his beautiful face. That's when she saw it.

Baphomet's eyes were different. Instead of his pupils bearing the light blue all members of the Angelic realm had been born with, it now appeared Baphomet's eyes were losing their blue pigmentation in the iris area. In fact, one had to look closely to detect even the slightest hint of blue within the dull eyes staring out at the world.

"What have you done to him?" Suriyah demanded as she threw an accusing glare at Mikhail. Without waiting for his reply, she slowly guided Baphomet's witless form over to a nearby chair and somehow managed to get him seated there.

"Rest assured, sister, what has happened to Baphomet is not our doing," Mikhail stated calmly as he took a seat in a chair to the left of where Baphomet sat.

Suriyah squatted down next to her seemingly catatonic brother. Baphomet was always so full of life, so full of energy. It almost hurt her physically to see him in such a still state.

After a moment more of studying his quiet form, she got up to take a seat on the other side of Baphomet, placing her opposite from where Mikhail sat. She studied his face, finally realizing Mikhail's eyes had probably gone through the same thing Baphomet's eyes were going through now. "So, he will be all right?" she finally asked.

Mikhail's glowing eyes stared steadily at her. "Baphomet has encountered his other half."

Suriyah stilled. "He actually found her?" she whispered.

"He did more than that," Mikhail explained. "He kidnapped her and brought her to the Angelic realm without so much as a by your leave."

Suriyah frowned. "I guess that did not go over well?" she asked. She couldn't imagine Baphomet's other half being a mousy-type person who'd allow something like that, human or no. Any female designed to be able to handle someone as strong-willed as Baphomet would have to be pretty formidable in her own right.

"She escaped almost immediately, of course."

Suriyah chuckled as she imagined a mental picture of this. After a moment's silence, she asked, "Where is the girl, now, in Seraphim City?" There'd been just the slightest hint of acidity laced within her tone on her last question.

Mikhail's glowing eyes never even wavered. "She is at our new complex in the Northwest," he simply said.

Suriyah nodded. This confirmed what Baphomet had told her earlier.

Silence took control of the room.

Suriyah studied Mikhail, not even bothering to hide her inspection of him. He merely sat staring back, placidly allowing her to look her fill. "What happened to you?" Suriyah finally asked in a choked whisper. She only had memories of her beloved betrayer brother. The thing sitting opposite her barely even resembled the Mikhail she'd known.

Mikhail slowly said, "We… wish there were words we could use that would give you some hint, even, of what we have been gifted with…" He looked briefly at Baphomet's still form before continuing. "There are no words, though. The only way to know is to experience it for yourself, as our brother is doing now." He returned his gaze to his beloved sister. "We can only hope your experience is not as difficult as Baphomet has chosen to make his," he said, just the slightest lifting of the corners of his lips softening his censorial words.

Just then, Baphomet heaved a deep, relaxing sigh and blinked on its release. It took only the space of a heartbeat before he jumped wildly to his feet, immediately attacking the still-seated Mikhail. "Where *is* she?" he growled in the most vicious and hate-filled tone Suriyah had ever heard from him. He was clutching the fabric of Mikhail's shirt with such a fierce grip Suriyah had no doubt the thing would rip momentarily. "*Where is she?*" he shouted when Mikhail didn't immediately answer.

After a moment of silence, the two men looked down at the grip Baphomet had on Mikhail's shirt and Suriyah was amazed to see Baphomet reluctantly release the shirt and stand. He turned and walked over to a nearby window, raking a hand through his long blond hair in frustration. "You did not even allow me to tell her good-bye," he softly said in a broken voice, his head and shoulders slumping in defeat.

Mikhail stood and said, "We have no wish to keep the two of you separated any longer than is absolutely necessary."

Baphomet whipped around, his eyes filled with an eager glow. "Fine," he said urgently. "Take me back to her now. I shall work things out with her and we shall be out of your hair before nightfall. You can do that for me. You *owe* me at least that, Mikhail!"

Mikhail's glowing eyes regarded him steadily. "We cannot allow you back at the complex until you and your mate are *both* ready to be together. What you did by kidnapping her and bringing her into our realm was not only wrong, but dangerous, as well. It will take some time for her to adjust to life in this dimension and we are going to make sure she gets that time. She deserves it, the same as anyone would."

"But she is my mate!" Baphomet screamed in his deep voice, the sound echoing off the walls of the room.

There was a discreet knock at the door of the room and Suriyah quickly stepped over to it to assure her personal Jinn Guard that everything was fine. Her assistant reminded her of the JCG meeting she was to attend in a matter of minutes and Suriyah stepped back into the room, closing the door behind her and wishing for the millionth time she didn't have to attend such functions.

Mikhail's calm voice brought her back to the situation at hand as he said, "You may visit her in one week's time at the complex to see how she feels about the situation. That should give you enough time to put your own affairs in Shaitan Territory in order and then the two of you can stay where you can be cared for by our physician. He has been caring for my mate and me throughout our transformations and so he and his staff will be able to handle any emergencies that might arise."

"You will *not* keep her from me for a week!" Baphomet shouted. "And, I shall be damned if I shall stay one single night in your complex! You will release her into my custody immediately, or I shall rip your bloody head off!" He moved toward Mikhail, his eyes insane with anger.

The moment he got within striking distance, the long white strands of hair, which up to this point had been hanging placidly from Mikhail's head, suddenly whipped up and out, slicing cruelly deep into the skin on Baphomet's face, arms, chest, neck, and back... anywhere it could reach. It sliced into the flesh, drawing blood and then freeing itself only to strike out again and again.

"Stop it!" Suriyah screamed in horror. She plunged in between Baphomet and Mikhail, uncaring of the danger, thinking only to save her beloved brother from the lethal hair strands. To her surprise, the blade-sharp white strands immediately dropped away, returning to lay in a shiny curtain around Mikhail's long frame, barely even twitching at the ends and perfectly clean, with no trace of blood. Baphomet, on the other hand, was covered in the free-flowing red liquid.

Suriyah helped him back over to the chair he'd been in before and then went to get some help from her staff. Once she'd returned with the bandages and antiseptic her staff had supplied, she suggested, "Maybe Baphomet and his mate could stay here while they get to know each other."

Baphomet looked up expectantly at Mikhail, a glimmer of hope shining in his bright eyes.

Mikhail merely said, "Until the girl either requires or requests his presence, we will not force Baphomet upon her. He will just have to wait until she is ready."

Baphomet threw back his head on a growl of angry frustration. He'd come so close, and now the one person in the world he despised the most was once again seemingly in control of his fate. In his mind, Mikhail's voice said, *You must consider Lisa, brother.*

Then Sarah's voice chimed in as well in his mind, saying, *Don't worry about Lisa, dear Baphomet. She'll be safe enough here with us, and we'll make sure to tell her only good things about you until you return.*

Baphomet stood and threw a glance in Mikhail's direction.

"Give us one week to repair the damage that has been done, brother, just one week. Then you may come to her," Mikhail said.

Baphomet looked down at Suriyah, who still sat beside him. She was scared for him. He could see it in her eyes. But she could have no idea of the depth of emotion coursing through his entire being at the mere thought of being kept from Lisa for an entire week. "I-I wish I could tell you how wonderful she is," he said to her, his hand caressing her just below her chin, "but there are no words." He shook his head in utter helplessness. His eyes squeezed tightly shut and he dropped his hand. Then, after one last look at Suriyah, he released his shields in a flash and disappeared from the room.

Suriyah blinked in surprise. He'd never disappeared on her like that. She'd seen the sheer agony in his eyes, had felt it coming off him in waves. After a moment of thinking on this, she jumped to her feet and went straight to the door to inform her aides she was canceling all appointments for the day *and* for the next week. The entire place was immediately in an uproar.

"Right," she said as she turned back into the room to face Mikhail. "You may as well have a seat, my dear brother, because it is going to take me a while to pack and you are not leaving this room or this house without me." With that, she turned to go about preparing for at least a week-long sojourn to the Northwest Territory of the Badlands. "By the way," she said as she worked with her assistants to pick out clothing for her journey. "I have been meaning to ask you something. Why did you choose to leave Seraphim City for the Badlands?"

All Mikhail said was, "It is a very long story," as he sat watching her preparations.

Suriyah decided to drop the issue for the moment. She felt an excitement she hadn't felt in eons. A part of her felt guilty because she knew Baphomet was suffering so. She'd even witnessed it first-hand. She also knew many bad things were about to happen to many others, if the prophecy she'd envisioned in her crystal was indeed beginning. However, there were so many wonderful things happening all at the same time that she just couldn't truly feel bad about being at least a little excited.

First of all, Mikhail was back in their lives, miraculously. Suriyah had always believed he'd come around, she just hadn't known when. Now, here he was – and out in the Badlands, no less! Who would've guessed?

Secondly, for some reason, Mikhail had actually *chosen* to move out to the Badlands and Suriyah was curious to know what had prompted the decision to move. Her own spy network within Seraphim City had informed her of none of this and Suriyah wanted to know what was going on.

Third, Suriyah wanted to know why Mikhail suddenly seemed possessed of multiple psychic abilities, not to mention his lethal hair and glowing eyes. How had that all come about?

And, lastly, Suriyah was curious about her brothers' mates. She wanted to meet these women, to get to know them so she could get a feel for them. After all, they were to become Suriyah's sisters, if the behaviors of her brothers were anything to go by. Suriyah just wanted to form her own opinions on the matter.

She and her assistants finished packing and, after checking with her aides that all official matters had been successfully postponed a week, she and Mikhail donned their shields and were off, gliding through the clear mid-afternoon sky toward the Northwest Territory. Suriyah's assistants, since they couldn't fly like Seraphim, were to follow along behind Suriyah with her luggage in vimanas to a location Mikhail had indicated on a map of the Badlands.

Chapter 7

Sarah and Lisa stood in the garden behind the main house of the complex. It was so green and beautiful, Lisa thought she'd died and gone to heaven. They had enjoyed a huge lunch and afterward, Sarah had shown her to a suite of rooms, yes, a suite, which Lisa had been informed was to be her place of residence for as long as she wished to stay. Lisa had been bowled over!

In the suite, there was the most exquisite bathtub Lisa had ever seen and she ached for the chance to have a long, gloriously hot bath. Where she lived, everyone had to conserve water, which meant only quick, lukewarm showers. The idea of having a really long, really hot bath in the giant tub filled to the neck with water like she'd seen in movies had Lisa's toes curling in anticipation. However, that bath would have to wait.

Sarah had informed Lisa they were expecting another guest at the complex and they were waiting in the garden for the guest's arrival. Lisa looked around, wondering which direction the person would be coming from, when suddenly, out of thin air, appeared the man who'd taken Lisa's kidnapper away earlier, except now he was in the company of the most beautiful woman Lisa had ever seen in her life.

The woman was almost as tall as the man, and where he had long white hair like Sarah's, the woman had even longer blond hair that was so artfully arranged on and around her head that Lisa felt sure the woman had just come from hours at a salon.

Sarah immediately moved into the man's waiting arms and Lisa suddenly felt, first of all, a twinge of jealousy at the idea of having someone who cared for her that much, and secondly, as if she ought not to be witnessing this moment. The two people standing before her holding each other seemed connected somehow, as if each wasn't quite complete without the other, and Lisa looked away, embarrassed for having stared at them so long. She noticed the beautiful woman was looking away, as well. They both stood silently studying each other while the glowing couple completed their greeting.

After a moment, the beautiful woman cleared her throat politely and the couple broke apart and returned their attention to the other two women in the garden. "Yes, Suriyah," the glowing man said. "This is my mate, Sarah Baker." The two women remained still, each staring intently at the other.

After a moment, Sarah stepped toward the beautiful woman, extending her hand, saying, "Suriyah, it is so nice to finally meet you." She shook Suriyah's hand and Lisa frowned as she noticed Suriyah's quick gasp at Sarah's touch. Next, Sarah turned to Lisa and said, "And this is Lisa Murdoch whom Baphomet brought to us just this morning." Lisa suddenly felt like she'd been put under a microscope as all three of the others turned to look at her. "Lisa," Sarah continued, "this is my mate, Mikhail, and his sister, Suriyah. They are brother and sister to Baphomet."

Lisa stopped herself from offering her sympathies to the two as she stepped forward to shake each one's hand in greeting. That guy was nuts and Lisa didn't think anyone could be happy to have him as their relative. Lisa experienced a slight tingling sensation going up her arm with each hand she shook, kind of like when she'd been touched by that Baphomet guy, though not as intense. When Suriyah shook her hand, however, Lisa was surprised to hear her say, "I am so pleased to meet you. My brother has had only wonderful things to say about you."

Lisa frowned. Baphomet hadn't spent enough time with Lisa to have been able to learn *anything* about her.

Sarah quickly stepped forward and took control of the situation. Apparently, this was the first time Suriyah and Mikhail had seen each other in a long time, judging from the conversation that followed, and Lisa walked silently along with the group. She wasn't the only one who seemed uncomfortable and Sarah ended up doing most of the talking. She seemed intent on doing her best to make everyone feel comfortable and welcome.

Mikhail never broke physical contact with Sarah, Lisa noticed, and it was interesting to see how the two of them seemed connected on some much deeper level with each other. The two even moved in tandem, it seemed, as if each could anticipate the other's movements. Again, Lisa found herself feeling almost jealous of the two, wishing she could meet someone she felt that comfortable with.

She suddenly recalled how good it had felt in that guy Baphomet's arms. He was a crazy, kidnapping, raving lunatic, and the world was better off without him, for sure. But it really had been one of the best feelings she'd ever experienced having his hard, hot chest pressed up against her cheek while his strong arms were wrapped around her like bands of warm steel. And his voice – Lisa shivered as she recalled how deliciously deep and sexy that voice had been.

The sound of the beautiful Suriyah clearing her throat suddenly brought Lisa out of her reverie and she was immediately mortified by the fact that she'd just been daydreaming, and perhaps even fantasizing a little, of the one person in the world she could never be with. He was nuts, after all, and he was gone now. Judging from the way everyone here kept bringing up Baphomet's name in their casual conversation, however, made Lisa wonder if perhaps he wouldn't be coming back at some point.

The rest of the afternoon and evening was very pleasant and Lisa was bone tired by the end of the evening. She truly just wanted to go to her suite of rooms, take a long, hot bath, and then go to sleep – for a week! Today had been a really, *really* long day. By the time supper was winding down, Lisa had yawned about twenty times and Sarah finally seemed to take notice.

Everyone was dismissed from the table and Lisa was finally allowed to go to her room. She didn't know if she had enough energy remaining for her bath, but she was bound and determined to have one.

To her surprise, when she returned to her suite the tub was already filled with piping hot water, including the bubbles resting atop the water like Lisa had always fantasized about when she'd dreamed of being able to take a long, hot bath. Lisa dipped a hand into the steaming hot water and her toes curled in anticipation. She'd been looking forward to this bath all day and she sighed with pleasure as she undressed.

The bathroom connected to this suite of rooms Sarah and Mikhail had given her was, in itself, almost larger than her entire flat back home. Lisa marveled at the fact that she was being allowed to stay in a place this opulent for free. Added to all that opulence was the fact that she got meals cooked for her as well as having someone waiting on her hand-and-foot, taking care of her every whim, to boot.

She'd felt very uncomfortable having people wait on her like that, but then Sarah had explained to her that those who served here did so by choice. She'd said they were loyal to Mikhail and that they had chosen to follow him out into the Badlands once Azra'il, another of his brothers, had banished him from a place called Seraphim City, which was where they'd all lived before this.

Lisa could only imagine what *that* place had looked like, since Sarah had told her the house here was much smaller than the one in Seraphim City had been. It didn't matter, though. As long as Lisa got her bath, she didn't care where the house was or how big it was.

According to what Sarah had told her earlier today, before Mikhail and Suriyah had arrived, Lisa was going to go through some physical change so that she would look similar to Mikhail and her, though Lisa couldn't imagine that. Sarah had told her it had already started and she'd pointed out that Lisa's eyes were no longer brown.

At this thought, Lisa stepped over to one of the mirrors above the double vanity and leaned in closer to look at her reflection. Her eyes seemed to be an even brighter shade of blue than they'd been this afternoon when Sarah had first told her about the change.

Lisa didn't care if she changed to look like Sarah and Mikhail. She thought they looked really cool, though she couldn't even imagine herself looking anything like that. She was just plain old Lisa, the half-breed aborigine. That's all she'd ever been. Why would nature have selected her for anything as special as what these people were? Lisa didn't want to think about it.

Instead, she finished undressing, used the toilet and then slowly dipped one foot and then another into the deep tub of piping hot water. Easing the rest of her body down into the water was sheer heaven and she sighed a little as she went ahead and slipped all the way under. All was suddenly quiet and Lisa closed her eyes, allowing a sweeping sensation of ecstasy to overcome her entire being.

∞

Baphomet let his shields drop silently as he finally landed in his bedchamber in his home in Shaitan Territory. He was out of his mind with the desire to return for Lisa. He'd agreed to one week, but he had no idea how he was going to be able to keep that promise. He'd flown over every known part of the Angelic realm, along with a few unexplored areas, all day and evening and yet, even now, Baphomet could still smell her on himself. He could almost recall how it had felt to have her soft skin beneath his touch for that brief period of time this morning.

The rest of his household seemed to be asleep already and he felt no need to disturb them. He ripped off his clothes and climbed into bed. He was determined to get through this week with as little thought as possible. The idea he had was to sleep his way through the week. It had come to him about an hour ago as he'd flown soundlessly, yet furiously, over the Western coast. That way, he wouldn't have to think about Mikhail having access to his own mate while Baphomet was made to wait for access to Lisa.

The only reason Baphomet had even considered this whole waiting a week idea was because of the images Sarah had shown him. She'd left nothing out of her visions when she'd shared them with him, so he knew there were about to be some serious changes going on and Lisa was going to need some help. She also was going to need him to help with all those changes and right now he knew Lisa didn't trust him at all. Baphomet would just have to trust that Sarah would do her best to talk him up to Lisa over this next week.

Baphomet had screwed up and he knew it. Lisa hated him already and rightly so. What had he been *thinking*? How could he have acted so carelessly with her? She deserved so much better than what he'd given her, but what could he do now?

He laid his head back on the pillow and closed his eyes, sighing in frustration and seeking the escape only sleep could offer. Immediately, however, an image of someplace else flashed before his mind's eye. He couldn't tell where he was or what had caused the image to appear, but he felt very warm, as if completely immersed in a hot tub of water. The image was fuzzy, but he could feel and smell with perfect clarity. It was Lisa's scent filling his nostrils and it was her skin he felt when he moved his hands. Everything was so soft and warm and Baphomet felt his eyes rolling back in his head on a wave of sheer ecstasy.

That's when the real sensations began.

Baphomet suddenly found himself being controlled by a very domineering Lisa. She was atop him, taking pleasure in touching him wherever and however she wanted. Baphomet moaned in agony. "Lisa…," he whispered, reaching out to touch her, but she pushed his hands away from her body. He wanted to argue, to take control of the situation, himself, but Lisa would have none of that. This game was hers to play and he was only allowed to sit back while everything played out.

Her mouth opened on his neck, her teeth nipping softly at the corded muscles there. Her hands lightly drifted over parts of him and then tugged not so nicely at other parts of him. One of her hands finally settled on the sensitive bud of his nipple, first barely flicking it, and then twisting and pinching it between her forefinger and thumb. The other hand came to rest along his hardened shaft, grasping at first lightly, and then getting rougher as she moved her hand up and down at an increasing rate. All the while, that glorious mouth of hers continued torturing him with its little nips and kisses all over his chest and neck.

Baphomet finally reached his limit, sitting up to push her off him as he ground out in a frustration-filled voice, "Enough!"

He opened his eyes…

The dark, still recesses of his bedroom were all that stared back at him. He was alone in the room. There was no Lisa here.

It had merely been a dream. It seemed he wouldn't even be able to count on sleep to help him forget about her for the next few days.

Jumping up from his bed in complete frustration, Baphomet reached for fresh clothing. He had to adjust himself within his underwear and pants several times, since he still sported a major hard-on from the dream he'd had. As he thought of the dream, he realized his head was hurting alongside his temples and he reached to massage them.

Suddenly, however, he fell to his knees, clutching his head on either side tightly, as a flood of voices crowded into his mind. Try as he might, he couldn't shut out the cacophony of voices and he squeezed his eyes shut as he yelled out in pain.

Almost immediately, there were Shaitans by his side, helping him to stand, all asking questions he couldn't hear, all looking at him as if he'd suddenly gone insane. Their voices added to the plethora of voices raging inside his mind and Baphomet knew he had to leave before his instincts took over and he ended up hurting someone.

"I am sorry," he whispered as he pushed through the crowd of servants who'd gathered around to try to help their master. Once outside the room, Baphomet let loose a couple of his shields and took to the skies, thinking only of escaping the deluge of voices inside his mind.

He headed south, away from his home and away from Lisa, and the voices seemed to weaken just a bit. The farther away from her he got, it seemed, the less he could hear of the voices. Perhaps Lisa was the cause of it? Perhaps not. All Baphomet knew was that he couldn't withstand another episode like that, so he decided the best thing for him to do for the next week was to go away.

He gathered his shields around himself more tightly and headed for a barrier rift he knew of that would deposit him out into the human world on the other side of the planet from where Lisa had resided. Crossing over, he felt the slight sting of the barrier. Usually, he crossed the barrier with all six shields up to keep from feeling it at all.

He was glad to feel it this time, however, because it distracted him from the pain still raging in his head and from the real reason for this trip. In fact, once he'd made it through to the other side, Baphomet found the voices in his mind had completely silenced themselves.

Well, if staying in the human realm was all he had to do until a week's time was up in the Angelic realm, then Baphomet was completely capable of that. It would mean being here for a little over half a month because of the time difference, but surely he could find some way of distracting himself. He thought over the matter as he came to rest on top of one of the towers of the Tower Bridge of London overlooking the Thames.

London had always been one of his favorite places to visit because it was so filled with life and culture. There were so many things to see and do in London that Baphomet felt certain he'd be able to lose himself there for the next three weeks. As he dropped his shields and made himself more comfortable upon the tower, he suddenly felt the presence of other Shaitans within the city. Curious, he pulled his shields back up around himself and went in search of whomever it was he was detecting.

∞

Lisa lay still on the big bed. She was doing whatever she could to forget about the past couple of hours. Her fantasy of having a blissful bathe had actually turned into a nightmare from which she'd thought she might never escape. If it hadn't been for Sarah and Suriyah, Lisa wasn't sure she would have emerged with her sanity intact. As it was, Lisa was certain she'd never take another bath in her life! It was only quick showers from now on, she decided.

She still couldn't figure out what had happened. One minute, she'd been stretched out in the giant bathtub, luxuriating in the feel of the piping hot water caressing her entire body. Then, in a flash, she'd found herself in the throes of the most erotic wet dream she'd ever had. What was so strange about the dream, other than the fact that she'd been the one instigating everything within it – controlling everything – was the fact that her partner in the dream had been that crazy guy, Baphomet.

Why on earth she would be having fantasies about a man who'd kidnapped her, she just didn't know. What she did know, however, was that what happened when she woke from that dream was something she never wanted to experience in this lifetime again!

Just as she'd come out of her dream about dominating her kidnapper, among other things, her head had begun a vicious pounding. Lisa had been drying off from her bath, about to go in search of some aspirin to help with the pain, when she'd suddenly been bowled over by so many voices she couldn't even hear herself think! She'd grabbed her head and started screaming, hoping someone would hear her cries above the wreck of a noise the voices were making.

Oddly enough, both Sarah and Suriyah had entered the bathroom almost immediately to help her, as if they'd been waiting just outside the door. They'd gotten her settled on her bed, all covered and cozy except for the voices, and then one of the brothers, the one who'd introduced himself to her as Israfil, had come in to sit by Lisa. He'd taken her hand and, immediately, the voices stopped.

Israfil had stared hard at her for several seconds before announcing that she'd be fine for now. Lisa hadn't asked what he'd meant by the "for now" bit, but she sure was interested in finding out exactly what had happened and why! She didn't think she'd survive another attack like that and she wanted to know how to avoid it.

However, as she'd lain there thinking about how awful the experience had been, her mind had drifted back to the erotic dream she'd had in the tub of her domination of Baphomet. She'd enjoyed touching him. She'd even found herself taking little nips now and then, wondering if he'd mind if she actually bit him. It was odd, but the thought of his lean, hot body pressed full-length up against hers made her want to do all manner of wild things to him and Lisa wondered if she wasn't going insane from lack of sex. After all, she was getting on up there, age-wise.

A masculine half-grin flashed across her mind's eye as her physical eyes slid closed. *I do not think you are old at all*, came the deep voice of her dream lover in her mind. Lisa's toes curled just at the sound of his voice. *Go to sleep, sweet*, the voice continued. *We shall be together soon, and then we can discuss your cannibalistic urges toward my body*. A full smile stretched across Lisa's lips as she sighed and fell asleep to the sound of her Baphomet's quiet, deep rumble of laughter, which no longer seemed very scary at all.

∞

Thomas finished up his fourth meal of the day and watched in dismay as Miriam cleared away his dirty dishes. He had no idea why he was suddenly so hungry all the time. It didn't matter how much he ate, either. It was always only a couple of hours before he'd be starving again. Miriam was always there with smile and a tray laden with food, though, as if she'd anticipated his hunger.

Thomas supposed he shouldn't worry about it, since he'd actually been *losing* weight instead of gaining it lately. That, he knew, was from all the training he and Samuel had been doing. That seemed to be all he and Samuel *did* lately. Even video games had taken a back seat to the training.

He wondered if there was something wrong with him. Weren't kids supposed to want to do things like playing video games?

Suddenly, Thomas found himself standing in the round room with Nera and several of the others like her. They were all busy at their monitoring stations and didn't even bother looking up to acknowledge his presence. Nera was the only one who even seemed to notice he was there at all, though even *she* took her time in greeting him.

What a pain she was!

Thomas waited patiently while she finished up whatever it was she was doing. When she finally logged off her station and approached him, she sported a cheerful grin and there was a twinkle in her eyes as she said, "Isn't it great? We never expected those two to get together so quickly. But, this helps with the timetable greatly, huh?"

Thomas merely looked at her in complete confusion.

Her grin slipped a little and she said, "I mean we were worried getting them together was going to be a monumental task, what with their personality difficulties. Now we don't have to worry about that. They seem to have taken care of matters for us just fine."

Thomas looked around the room, trying to find some clue as to what she was talking about.

"*What* is your problem?" she promptly demanded, immediately bringing his attention back to her.

"Who are you *talking* about?" he asked, shaking his head and frowning, looking at her as if she had lost her marbles.

Nera's own face screwed into a confused frown as she explained, "The next Seraphim couple, like Sarah and her

Seraph.   We saw they'd finally gotten together to start their transformations. That's why we were so excited. We'd thought the Seraph male was going to cause trouble, but we don't have to worry about that, now."   When Thomas merely frowned more deeply in response, Nera sighed and said, "Okay, out with it!"

"Well," Thomas replied, "I think maybe you missed a few scenes on your screens over there."   He indicated the monitoring station with a jerk of his head.

Nera's face paled, if that was even possible, and she asked in a quiet, cautious voice, "What do you mean?"

Thomas shrugged. "That Seraph, if that's what he was, left without the new girl. She's there at the complex with my mom and dad. I don't know where the guy went," he explained.

Blanching even more, Nera hysterically shouted, "But, they'd already touched! The proteins were already produced; the cascade of gene activations has already begun!" When he only continued to stare dumbly at her, she quickly approached him and grabbed both of his upper arms, shaking him as hard as her slight frame allowed, growling, "Do you not understand? Their bodies are going to change now whether they're together or not. The changes have already begun. If they're not together, though, there's no telling how everything will go. They could go mad, for all we know, and all will be lost!"

She broke away from him and paced a short distance away, her back to him. Thomas watched her hair rubbing her back and neck, as if trying to calm its owner by massaging her muscles. He wondered if his mom's hair ever did that to her and he decided that was something he could live without seeing.

As it was, he rarely visited his mom. It was just too weird looking at her glowing eyes and skin. When one threw in the whole living, moving white hair thing, it just kind of creeped him out, so he stayed away. Besides, she had Mikhail now. She didn't need Thomas.

Nera wheeled around all of a sudden and tromped back over to him. "You must find a way to get them back together," she announced. "I do not care how you do it – get Sarah and her mate involved, if you have to. Just do it!"

"I don't understand," he said.

"I know," Nera sighed heavily. "Things would be so much simpler if only y…"

"If only what?" he asked hesitantly.

She looked at him, and then shook her head. "Nothing," she said after a moment. "Look, it might not be too late. If you manage to get them back together somehow, we might still stand a chance at salvaging this batch. I mean, I know the odds are against us, but we got lucky once before with them, right? Maybe this time will work out as well, huh?" Thomas frowned again and Nera shook her head, saying, "Never mind. Just find a way to get those two back together. We have already started on the next one, so we need this end tied up quickly."

She reached out and turned him around, giving him a push from behind.

In the blink of an eye, Thomas found himself sitting once again in his room at the main house of the Badlands complex, exactly where he'd been before Nera had whisked him off to her place. He jumped up from the sofa he was sitting on. He had to get to his mom immediately. As he made his way through the house, he thought, *Mom?*

Immediately, her mental voice floated through his mind, asking, *Yes, sweetie?*

Thomas cringed at the endearment, but continued on his course. *I need to talk with you*, he silently informed her.

Chapter 8

Azra'il sat listening to each argument presented. One after another, members of the Great Sanhedrin took to the pulpit, each citing specific documented historical incidences as evidence, each determined to win over the vote of their new leader. The sole remaining Seraph in Seraphim City felt an odd sinking sensation as he watched and listened to each one of them.

It wasn't that he cared over-much for humans, or anything, it was just that he could see what was happening to their world and he felt at least a little sorry for them. His people, he knew, cared for humans, but things had changed over the last couple of thousand years and the Angelic society was becoming more aware of itself as an actual entity.

When the blessed Great Designers had last been on earth, all Angels had still thought of themselves strictly as human guides and protectors. Now, however, large numbers of them had had time to have offspring of their own, to live lives of their own, and they didn't want to give up that independence from the human world.

Of course, the Angels of Seraphim City still held to the directives given by their beloved Designers, but they also believed they would not have been given the ability to procreate as humans could without their beloved Designers having intended for them to do so. So, although the Angels had continued with their duties as guides and helpers of mankind, an entire Angelic societal structure had developed and they all liked it.

The difficulty with this, however, was that now there were humans in the Angelic realm, and *that* the Angels did not like one bit. They all feared more would come, and then more, and then more, until they took over the Angelic realm. Those few who were already in the Angelic realm had caused such chaos and disorder that Angels were now actually discussing the possibility of banning all contact between Angels and humans.

There were those who still took the job of human guardians to heart, believing it might be okay to allow certain humans into the Angelic realm. However, those in control of the governing body of the Angelic realm were unanimously opposed to actually allowing any other humans *into* the Angelic realm. Those who were already here they wanted gone, as well.

One council member stepped forward and waited for the room to settle. When it did, she said, "I have two small children of my own. We live simple, uncomplicated lives within these city walls. However, recently I was forced to discuss the subject of murder with my two young children. That came about because of two humans having been brought into our realm without this council's permission – just two.

"And, there have recently been reports from some of the guards who survived the skirmish with the recusants that there were two other humans seen among their numbers. If what they say is true, then that's already four humans in our realm. Imagine what will happen when more humans than our own numbers crowd this dimension!" There was a loud echo of agreement from the other members of the council, as tempers flared again, and the councilwoman held up her hand for peace.

When the crowd quieted, she continued, saying, "We are charged with guiding and helping humans *in their realm*. I do not recall any directives from our beloved Designers concerning bringing humans into our realm. Why, even our most gracious

Creators would not intrude upon the realm they created for us without our consent and escort.

"These humans, however, have proven time and again how destructive they are once they move into a new territory. Just look at what they have done to the lands in their own dimension. Look how over-populated much of their realm is, how bare the landscape is of forests and vegetation, how crowded the horizon has become wherever they have settled. Do not for a moment believe they would not over-breed in our realm, as well. And what has been done to the conquered races in the territories they've overtaken, well, I can tell you it is not a thing I wish for any Angel, let alone my own children to experience or even witness."

Another roar of agreement sounded from the crowd as the intense emotion within the chamber swelled to a great wave of fear and panic. Although he felt the pity he'd always felt for humans, Azra'il also felt his people's pain, for he knew the councilwoman was correct, and he wondered how his beloved brothers could ever have done what they'd done to cause this mess. As far as Azra'il was concerned, the blame for all of this lay at the hands of one person and one person only – Sarah Baker. She was the one who'd started this whole mess.

Before she'd come along, there'd been no trouble. Then, as soon as she'd been brought into the Angelic realm, both Mikhail and Djibril had been immediately drawn under her spell. They'd even fought and killed their own kind for this... demon, if that was what she was. Azra'il could certainly find no other term that fit. He *had* to reassure his people that the Angelic realm would return to being and then continue to be human-free while he ruled.

Azra'il stood and raised a hand for peace. Immediately, the entire chamber quieted. "My people," he said. "I have heard your cries and I have seen with my own eyes the destructive power of humans on our realm. As the last Seraph within the walls of Seraphim City, I have experienced loss due to this invasion, if you will, like no other. But, I assure you, from this day forward, I shall devote every waking moment of every day to warding off this evil.

"Until the day our blessed Great Designers fulfill their promise and return to us once more, my sole duty will be to ensure no more humans are allowed to cross the barrier into this dimension, and those who are already wreaking havoc within our realm will be hunted down and exterminated as punishment for their crimes against all Angel-kind."

A huge roar of agreement and acceptance resounded within the council chamber and Azra'il sighed heavily as he resumed his seat. He had just declared war on Sarah Baker and all those siding with her. He had no idea how ordinary Angels were to defeat two Seraphim and whatever Mikhail had transmutated into, but Azra'il knew his elite Guard and he had to trust in their ability to defeat them. After all, Mikhail had trained a good many of them. However they were to achieve it, Azra'il would *not* let down his people!

It was agreed upon that extra guards would be put on the barrier rift crossing at Mt. Hermon to ensure no one, human or otherwise, utilized it for any purpose other than official Sanhedrin business. It was also agreed upon that the elite Sanhedrin Guard were to be sent, this very day if possible, to do what they could against the humans and other militants currently residing in the Badlands.

The council was pushing for complete annihilation of *all* of the opposition, human and otherwise. Azra'il just couldn't do that, though. The only problem he had was with the human female and her ilk. Once they were eliminated, Azra'il was certain Djibril and Israfil would return to their old selves. As for Mikhail, Azra'il simply did not know what to think. Perhaps, he would return to his old self, perhaps not. Azra'il could only prepare for the worst and hope for the best.

Azra'il believed he could still sense all three of his brothers' energies, along with those of the humans, so he decided to track them and send the elite Guard in for an attack, but only after the humans were off on their own.

He retired from his already long day of sitting on hearing to his private chambers.

These had once been Mikhail's private chambers. After having been elected to lead the Great Sanhedrin, the main body of the council had insisted Azra'il move to these rooms. They'd handled everything, of course, without even considering that he might not wish to change chambers. Azra'il had been perfectly content to remain in his same chambers as before, since he had fully believed Mikhail would eventually return.

He sighed resignedly as he collapsed onto the chair behind his desk. He would have been happy to return to his home for the remainder of the day, but he still had another private meeting scheduled for this afternoon, about the same two issues: how to stop humans from encroaching on the Angelic realm and how to get rid of those already inside it.

The meeting was really designed to be more of a strategic planning meeting to map out exactly how and where the elite Sanhedrin Guard were to attack, but it basically boiled down to what the council had just been talking about. Authorization for an attack, which was what the earlier council meeting had morphed into, was merely the first step.

Now Azra'il had to use his special Seraph abilities to determine where and how the elite Sanhedrin Guard should best attack. Unfortunately, utilization of the particular tracking ability needed for this didn't come so easily for him. Djibril was much better at this particular skill than he and Azra'il fervently wished his brother was there to assist him.

Instead, Azra'il had to actually track Djibril and his other two brothers.

As for a new group of humans the council had recently learned about that was attempting to encroach on the Angelic realm on its own, Azra'il still wasn't sure what to do about that issue. This problem had been getting progressively worse over the past century or so after a group of humans called Nazis had first discovered it was possible to cross the barrier from dimension to dimension.

That group had forced breaches or rifts in the dimensional barrier which would remain open for mere fractions of a second. That had never allowed an entire human being enough time to be able to fully cross over into the Angelic realm, but *parts* of them had.

Azra'il shuddered as he recalled some of the pieces of human flesh Angels had found here or there throughout that time period. Once, an entire half of one human male had been found. The Great Sanhedrin had been on the verge of voting on some form of action against the humans at that time, when suddenly the breaches had stopped.

It was later discovered that the human society as a whole had moved against the leader of the so-called Nazis in what was called a "World War," the second one the humans had had they'd later learned, at which time the Nazi reign of terror was effectively quashed, allowing for the Great Sanhedrin to discard any notions of the preventative actions they'd previously planned to take against the humans.

Over the past few decades, however, there had apparently been renewed interest in the whole idea of human trans-dimensional travel and a fresh vein of fear had grown steadily within the Great Sanhedrin. It didn't appear humans were trying so much to force breaches in the dimensional barrier now as much as they were searching for, and were apparently on the verge of discovering, the naturally occurring rifts that already existed between their two realms. And, it appeared the female who'd ensnared Mikhail in her human web of energy may well have had something to do with guiding the humans directly to said rifts!

Azra'il didn't yet have all the details and he didn't know if the girl was actively working from this end to guide humans toward rifts leading into the Angelic dimension, but it appeared when she'd crossed over herself that she'd left behind some sort of manifesto containing clues as to the locations of these naturally occurring rifts. Angels within the boundaries of Seraphim City knew only of the one rift at Mt. Hermon, but Azra'il knew there were others in existence.

Ever since Mikhail had banished their brother and sister, Baphomet and Suriyah, to the Badlands, reports of interference by Jinn and Shaitans in the human realm had steadily streamed in. The barrier rift at Mt. Hermon was constantly guarded by elite Sanhedrin Guardsmen, as it had been for millennia, so the only way that could be possible was for them to be crossing the barrier somewhere else.

The barrier at Mt. Hermon had been guarded since the blessed Great Designers had first visited, so the council knew for certain that particular rift wasn't being used. Logically, that meant there was at least one other. The number of reports of interference, however, was from such a broad range within the human realm that Azra'il figured there had to be tens, if not hundreds, of naturally occurring rifts between the dimensions. He didn't know how they'd come about, but he believed they were there.

How he was supposed to protect against humans crossing at any of *those* rifts when he didn't even know where they were located himself, Azra'il did not know. If he could get his hands on either the human female or her supposed manifesto, however, he'd at least be able to find out where these things were. He'd already put his most trusted Angels on the case out in the human realm, but there'd been no word as yet from any of them.

Azra'il knew Mikhail would fight to the death before he'd allow anyone near his precious human, though.

What sway did she hold over him, he wondered, and how had she accomplished it? Was it her body? Was she controlling Mikhail strictly with sexual favors? Were human females that alluring? Azra'il had never bothered looking.

He mostly saw their glowing tether lines when he looked at humans, so he might just be missing something others saw, for he knew the blessed Great Designers had often taken human females to their beds, even reproducing with some of them. That was how humans had developed light-colored eyes, even. However, their beloved Designers had forbidden humans to Seraphim.

A frown crept over Azra'il's face as he thought on this. Was that all that had his three brothers defying the one rule – sex with humans? Azra'il certainly hoped not! Although, he'd read many a tale from human history of human males losing their heads over their female counterparts. Perhaps there was something to human females Azra'il just hadn't yet noticed.

A knock at the door broke into his reverie and he called for the visitor to enter. An old Angel named Gushmael walked in carrying a tray laden with hot tea and finger sandwiches. The Angel spoke not a word as he placed the tray before Azra'il on the desk and he left immediately afterward. It was always like that.

Ever since he'd been elected to his new position, hardly a soul other than council members and Azra'il's own servants loyal to his house had spoken directly to him. He supposed that was how Mikhail had existed for millennia, but Azra'il didn't like it. Now that his brothers were all gone, he found himself feeling completely alone in the world and, for some strange reason, he felt an interminable restlessness that plagued his nights and a good portion of his days.

Azra'il had never experienced anything like it and, without anyone he trusted around to talk about it with, he felt a growing sense of frustration building within his psyche. On top of that, he was expected to deal with everything else that was going on in the world and, to be honest, he really wasn't sure he was up to the task.

Mikhail had always had at least three of his siblings available as sounding boards whenever problems arose. Azra'il didn't, not a single Seraph. If only that human had never come into their realm, Azra'il was certain everything would be so much better.

An angry energy filled him and he moved over to a sofa along the far wall. Turning, he stretched out full-length along the well-cushioned piece of furniture and closed his eyes. If he could pinpoint the humans' exact location, he just might get lucky enough to catch them alone so that the elite Guardsmen would be able to take them out quickly and without interference from any Seraphim who might wish to protect the humans.

In seconds, he'd tapped into three separate energies within the Angelic realm with human tethers on them. The tether on one of them was very weak, the same as the female's had been the last time he'd encountered her, so he was willing to bet this one was hers. The other two were not with hers, but they were very strong and Azra'il didn't believe either of those could belong to the female. He wanted her gone.

He couldn't detect any other humans around her, but there *were* other energies there. He didn't recognize them as anything he'd ever dealt with before, nor as any kind of threat, though, so Azra'il took no notice of them.

It was like ignoring a flea on a large pet, like a Great Dane. They existed and he could feel the energies they emitted, but there was no danger associated with them, so he merely ignored them. He couldn't detect the fourth human and he wondered if perhaps his elite Guardsmen had miscounted. There was no time now for checking into the details of what they recalled, however. Instead, he got a fix on the location of the one he judged to belong to the female and then catapulted off the sofa, already in a dead run for the council chamber.

The Captain of the elite Sanhedrin Guard looked up from the maps he and several council members had been studying when Azra'il burst into the giant round chamber. Everyone in the room had been furiously poring over maps of the Badlands in attempts to discover likely areas the militants would have settled in.

The Guardsmen had been instructed by the highest-ranking council member in the room that their newly-elected leader was working to provide them this information, but that the Seraph had given no timeline as to how long it would take him to discover the militants' hideout, and as he'd not yet been tested in his new position with such a duty, they had all felt the need to make plans of their own – just to be on the safe side.

"I have found her," Azra'il said as he approached the heavy, map-laden table where they all stood. He immediately pointed out the region on one of the maps spread out before the group.

"Are you certain that is where she and the others are holed up?" the Captain asked.

"That is where she is right now," Azra'il confirmed. "Her tether has grown weaker, but it is still detectable enough." As the Captain and the council members began discussing strategies, Azra'il interrupted them, saying, "The human female is there now. I would not delay the attack. I did not detect my brothers' presences around her at the moment, but that does not mean they will not return to her soon."

The Captain looked to the highest-ranking council member in the room, and, as he received a confirming nod, he cautiously asked the Seraph, "The best way to kill a Seraph is by beheading, right?"

Azra'il was shocked! "What are you *talking* about?" he finally demanded, his face infinitely paler than usual. "You are only to engage the humans, not my brothers!"

"And if your brothers engage us?" the Captain whipped out, his tone lashing across Azra'il's psyche until he felt broken and bruised. The council member had warned the Captain of this possibility. Many within the walls of Seraphim City doubted the Seraph Azra'il's commitment to completely protecting the Angels of Seraphim City from the human blight and so this reaction was very much expected. It was not to be tolerated, however, so the Captain stood his ground.

After a moment, Azra'il realized that even this highly-trained elite Sanhedrin Guard Captain stood no chance against Mikhail, not as powerful as he'd been when last Azra'il had seen him. He looked the Captain up and down then and said honestly, "Then, may the blessed Great Designers keep your soul-energy." With that said, he turned and left the chamber, as a wave of fear passed over all those remaining within the room.

∞

By the time he reached the house's master suite, Thomas was as nervous as could be. He hadn't even *seen* his mom, except from a distance, since not long after they'd moved out to the Badlands. Of course, he'd caught glimpses of her out in her garden and he and Samuel would sometimes watch her and Mikhail, as they'd done earlier in the clearing, but always from afar and never did they actually converse with her or Mikhail.

Now, as he quietly knocked at the main door to their suite, he knew he couldn't avoid it any longer.

The door opened almost immediately and Thomas followed a beautiful Angel into a sitting room where his mom, Mikhail and another woman sat already. The Angel bowed and quietly left the room, closing the door behind him.

As Thomas faced the three beings before him, he felt like an animal in a zoo being stared at by creatures who'd come to see all the oddities. Strange that *he* should feel odd-looking when his mom and dad looked so weird. And, the new lady, she was undeniably beautiful, but she was very tall and her hair was so blond it was almost white, though it didn't appear to be the dangerous kind of white hair.

Smiles flashed across his mom's and dad's faces so fast Thomas wasn't sure he'd actually seen them, but he had a feeling they'd both been listening in on his thoughts, just now. The new woman merely watched him, her ice-blue eyes curious.

"Please, sit down," his mom said as she gestured toward a nearby chair.

Moving to take the seat, Thomas realized the new woman was like Gabriel and Israfil. That meant she was one of the ones Nera and her people would be working on to pair up with a human. Turning back to look at his mom and dad, Thomas again got the impression the two of them were listening in on his thoughts. They both regarded him with intense expressions.

Do not fear us, my son, Mikhail's voice said in his mind. Thomas softly gasped, blinking a few times in his confusion. He hadn't expected them to just come out and reveal such ability.

Sweetheart, his mom's voice suddenly said in his mind, *we can do a lot of things that will probably scare you a little, or at least make us seem really strange to you. But, like Mikhail said, you don't ever have to be afraid of us. We love you, honey.*

Thomas looked over to the female Seraph, who was still just sitting there silently watching. *Does she know?* he asked silently.

Mikhail and his mom turned back to look at the Seraph and Mikhail's voice said, *This is our sister, Suriyah. She does not know of all of our abilities, though she is quickly getting an idea about some of them.*

After a moment of curiously studying the silent Seraph female seated opposite him, Thomas sighed and silently said, *Okay.* He turned his attention back to the two beside him and continued, thinking to them, *I need you to do something.*

The two regarded him expectantly.

Earlier, Thomas continued, *you were in the clearing with two people...*

Both pairs of eyes narrowed as they regarded him and his mom's voice suddenly asked from out of nowhere in his mind, *Who is Nera?*

Then, without warning, Mikhail's presence filled Thomas' mind to such a degree he felt like he was being crowded out. He grabbed his head and his mom said aloud, "Mikhail!"

Immediately, the pressure eased and Mikhail cleared his throat and said aloud, "Sorry... I do not quite have complete control of things yet."

Blinking in an attempt to understand, Thomas looked at Suriyah, who continued watching, her eyes narrowed as she, herself, tried to figure out what was going on. Thomas stood suddenly and said, "Look, you just need to get the two of them back together because they've already touched, so they're gonna change like you two did."

Suriyah jumped up from her seat to demand, "Who is going to change like Mikhail and Sarah?" As three pairs of eyes turned toward her, she started shaking visibly. "Do you mean Baphomet and his mate?" she asked tremulously.

121

"Who told you about these things?" Sarah interrupted to ask Thomas.

Thomas looked away for a moment, the urge to flee swelling within him. Nera's words came back to him, *I do not care how you do it... get Sarah and her mate involved, if you have to. Just do it!* she'd said. He turned and said, "I can't explain things to you now, but you need to get them back together, like the two of you were while you transformed, or things might go bad for both of them – and for the rest of us."

Mikhail and Sarah stood. "We were hoping they had not actually had physical contact and that the changes we have witnessed within the girl were just because they had been in close proximity to each other," Mikhail said. "If they have actually had physical contact, however, there is no telling when their transformations will begin in earnest, or what type of transformations they will be."

He turned to Suriyah. "Suri, we need you to stay here to help with Baphomet's mate. If she starts any major transformations before we return, she might need others around to help get her through it. Sarah will know how to deal with whatever physical changes Lisa might experience, and Hantsushept, our physician, will be here to help as well. But, with your Jinn nurturing skills, you might be able to ease the process a bit."

"Where will you be?" Suriyah asked shrilly, a distinct sense of disquiet showing through her normally placid and unshakable demeanor.

"Djibril, Israfil, and I will go retrieve Baphomet from wherever he has gotten himself off to," he explained. Mikhail started toward the door, but then stopped to look back at Sarah in confusion.

A moment later, Sarah blinked and re-focused on Mikhail's face. "He's in the human realm, the Southwestern side of London, I believe. Hurry," she said. "You need to get to him quickly."

Mikhail nodded once and took off.

Sarah turned back to the other two, a deep frown covering her face, and quickly said, "Follow me."

Both Thomas and Suriyah followed her through the house to the suite Lisa had been given to stay in. Without even bothering to knock, Sarah walked right into the suite, straight on through to the bedroom. There, on the floor next to the bed, looking as if she was in a tremendous amount of pain, was Lisa, all curled up in a fetal position, shaking and clutching the sides of her head.

"What on earth?" Suriyah asked distractedly as she crouched down to tend to the woman, her natural nurturing Jinn tendencies immediately coming to the fore. "I thought Israfil said she would be all right."

Sarah looked as if she might fall over and Thomas quickly grabbed hold of her arm, shaking her and asking, "Mom? Are you okay?"

"Israfil was only able to stem the flow for a short while," Sarah said. Her eyes closed and she swayed a little on her feet again. After a moment, she opened her eyes, but stood still, staring off into some distant place only she could see.

"Mom?" Thomas quietly asked.

Suriyah cradled her brother's mate's head in her lap as her own gaze seemed to dull and she, too, became caught up in some far off vision.

Lisa fought for each breath as whatever pain she was experiencing continued.

"Is that..." Suriyah began.

Sarah sighed in frustration, angrily saying, "Great! Perfect timing, as usual!"

"Azra'il?" Suriyah finished.

"It's not him. Not in the flesh, at least," Sarah explained as she crouched down next to the two on the floor and sighed in frustration.

Thomas suddenly felt a shift in the energy in the room and he looked around for its source. Something was causing a rapid accumulation of energy in the whole place. It felt to him like something powerful was approaching.

"Here, you, boy," Suriyah said as she called for Thomas' attention. "Come sit with this human while we are gone."

Thomas looked hesitantly toward his mom as she and Suriyah both rose to their feet. "Wh-Where're you going?" he asked.

Don't worry, sweetie, his mom's mental voice intruded on his mind. *Suriyah and I will be back in a jiffy.*

"Just take care of the girl!" Suriyah said urgently. She and Thomas' mom raced from the room, leaving him standing there with the dark girl curled up on the floor. She was still in a lot of pain, from the looks of things. Thomas' face screwed up in discomfort as he looked around for some way to help the poor girl. He looked a little closer at her and realized she was much older than him. She had to be at least twenty, so him thinking she was a "girl" was probably inappropriate.

She is in pain, you know, Nera's voice suddenly said in his mind.

Thomas looked around the room and up at the ceiling, saying aloud to her wherever she was, "Well, duh! Why do you think I'm trying to find some way of helping her?"

It's her mind, Nera's voice explained. *She's using her new abilities unintentionally and she's lost control. You have to connect with her mind and help her control the flood of voices.*

"Flood of voices?" Thomas asked frantically.

Yes. One of her gifts is the ability to pick up on any thought wave in existence.

"In existence?" Thomas asked. "You mean like a really powerful cell phone? She can hear the thoughts of everybody in the whole world?"

No, Nera's voice quietly contradicted in his mind, a dark and sinister tone coloring it. *I mean she can hear every thought in existence, as in the whole of existence everywhere, in this universe and any other.*

Thomas blinked in appreciation of the enormity of such an ability. Cell phone companies would sell something like that by saying it was Infinite G, he supposed. A little sound from Nera brought his attention back to the situation and he quickly knelt down beside the dark woman.

Lisa! Nera yelled silently. *Her name is Lisa Murdoch and she is like Sarah Baker.*

Thomas frowned. So, this Lisa was like his mom? She didn't look much like his mom. Her skin was much darker and she had long black hair. He didn't know about her eyes, but now that he was paying attention to it, she did seem to have a bit of a glow about her.

She still looked like she was in a lot of pain, though, and Thomas wondered if his mom had gone through this much pain when she'd changed. He hoped not. He felt a quick pang of guilt for not having noticed things while his mom had been changing.

Reaching over, he touched a finger to her temple, thinking only that he hoped Mikhail had been there to help his mom through whatever she'd suffered. His thoughts were interrupted when he suddenly found himself pinned in by a tidal wave of voices. Thomas couldn't think and he couldn't make it stop! The voices were too loud and there were so many of them! He panicked.

Somehow, Nera's voice managed to be heard through the sextillions upon sextillions of voices inside his mind. *It is all right. Concentrate on my voice. Slow down your breathing and just concentrate on my voice.*

Thomas took a few deep breaths as he listened to Nera's soothing voice. Suddenly, he made out Lisa's voice from among the multitude. He could hear her sobbing somewhere in the background. She sounded so small and scared.

Link with her so she'll have somewhere else to focus her mind's attention, Nera's voice ordered. *You must pull her through this until her Seraph arrives.*

Without hesitation, Thomas linked with Lisa, forcing his presence into her mind, filling every available space until he found where she was hiding. Her energy was as scrunched up as could be into the tiniest little ball imaginable. Thomas surrounded her gently, he hoped, with his own energy, doing his best to protect her. He completely forgot about the voices. He focused on a soothing tone to his energy.

It took only a second or two before he felt Lisa's energy patterns change. Her wavelengths slowed in their frequencies, their amplitude increasing. The voices slowly subsided until there was just Lisa and Thomas left in her mind. Her energies still indicated she was scared, but she wasn't as freaked out as she'd been before, and Thomas loosened his hold on her mind a bit.

For a moment, the multitude of voices raged again, trying to force another coup, but then the little ball of energy that was Lisa expanded and asserted itself, fighting back against her attackers until Thomas felt confident enough to pull completely away from her mind.

Thomas slowly opened his eyes.

Lisa breathed in deeply as she opened her eyes.

The two silently stared at one another.

Chapter 9

Baphomet dropped down to the ground by an abandoned warehouse on the outskirts of town. He could feel more than one Shaitan's energies nearby, their patterns causing a distinct disturbance in the world's web work of energy. The patterns were much like those Iblis and his gang caused whenever they were around. Curious, Baphomet stepped closer to the warehouse. That's when he heard the pitiful cries coming from within the building. They were low, but definitely audible.

Stepping through the wall of the building, he caught his first sight of one of the scenes he'd only up to now gleaned from within the minds of others after the fact.

In the very center of the room, at the farthest point from any window or door, there was a human female lying on the dirty flooring of the building. She was nude and covered in blood and caked-on dirt. Over to one side, Baphomet could see what looked like black clothing – a dress of some type with something white tangled up in it. It was dark in the warehouse, but he thought he recognized the clothing as that kind worn by Christian nuns.

Whatever color the female's short hair had been was obscured by all the blood and dirt densely caked within the closely cropped sweaty tendrils. There was a small crucifix hanging around her neck on a thin chain of metal. Baphomet couldn't tell if the metal was gold or silver. It didn't matter.

In her right hand, she held a wicked-looking shard of broken glass and Iblis and several of his followers cackled and sneered in delight as they forced images into the female's mind, suggesting she do this or that with the shard of broken glass, and then writhing with delight whenever she followed through with their suggestions. Her piteous screams as she sliced the shard through her skin in shallow, painful cuts merely added to the Shaitans' enjoyment of this game and so it went on and on.

Baphomet frowned and shuddered at the sight.

Iblis moved and pointed to something lying on the dirty floor next to the female, making her believe she'd come up with some new thought. The girl looked to where he pointed and she reached to pick up a thick cylindrical tool there. Then, spreading her legs, she positioned the metal tool below her and then she lowered herself, pushing the short rod up and into herself, half-curling up in pain as she pushed it farther and farther into her orifice.

Whatever the thing was, a rusted pipe of some sort it appeared to Baphomet, it obviously hurt each time she moved it and he wanted suddenly to rush over to her to stop her from doing such a thing to herself.

She started pulling and pushing on the coarse metal pipe, eventually screaming with each move she made. The cackles of the Shaitans watching her became uproarious and Baphomet thought he was going to be sick. Iblis moved again and the girl had another "thought." She struggled to turn and crawl up onto her hands and knees with the metal rod still half protruding from between her legs. The smiling leader of the little band of Shaitans pointed to another object on the floor next to the female and she reached for it and then set to work inserting it up into her anus.

"Stand up on your knees and then position it and squat down onto it," Baphomet heard Iblis say, his voice dripping with delight as the female immediately complied, though again Baphomet knew she believed she'd come up with the idea of doing this horrible thing to herself. Her screams as the object ripped the sphincter open and then collided with the metal already lodged within her uterus were almost Baphomet's undoing.

Blood gushed from within the hollow metal pipe onto the floor and he knew it was already too late for the poor human. She grunted with each up and down movement she made, rocking back and forth, no longer capable of screaming. "Move them deeper," Iblis snarled, his upper lip curling as he rounded her side to take in the full effect of his influence on this pitiful human.

Baphomet wanted to vomit as the female rocked back and forth more forcefully, each time sinking lower onto the objects. It was almost a relief when something within her seemed to rip and she suddenly went very still and then curled over to the side. The sharp edge of the metal pipe inside her body tore through the skin of her side, just below her rib cage, as she hit the ground.

The group of Shaitans wailed with delight at the sight of the dead human lying in a pool of her own blood. After a moment of this, Iblis kicked the female's head and chuckled as it flopped to rest at an odd angle, and then he said, "Well, this one is done. We shall have to find ourselves another, boys!" There was a loud cheer and the group fairly danced its way out the side of the building and off into the dark night in search of its next victim.

Baphomet fell to his knees, staring at the mass of blood and dirt-covered flesh.

What had he done?

He had caused this by not teaching his people the way they ought to have been taught throughout the ages. Now, he could see they were a lawless, unruly, immoral lot well deserving of the things humans often believed of Shaitans. Baphomet had often rankled at the thought of being called a demon, and worse, but he saw now that his people's actions had caused humans to believe such things with good reason.

An image of Lisa's smiling face suddenly flashed across his mind's eye and he felt overwhelmed with a sense of dread. How could he be deserving of someone like her? He'd created this horrific band of demons and he'd set them loose on her world with no thought to the safety of those who lived here. He'd only thought of the pain his people suffered due to their immortality. Never once had he considered things from the human standpoint. By his omission to supervise and teach his people, he was responsible for each and every crime against humanity the Shaitans had ever committed.

How could he ever repent for such crimes? Even if he could find a way to repay both human and Angelic society for what he'd done, how could he ever force himself onto someone as sweet and innocent as Lisa? He was a monster. She deserved someone better, much better than he.

A dagger-like pain ripped through his heart at the thought of her with another, any other, but he knew he couldn't allow himself to go anywhere near her. He was evil, through and through, and she was lost to him forever. He choked on his breath as tears of guilt and shame spilled over onto his sunken cheeks.

Still staring at the mangled corpse of the dead human female, a vile and wretched anger built within him and he stood, his upper lip curling into a sneer as he thought of the first thing he would do to try to make this up to Lisa and all her kind. He would find Iblis and his band of miscreants and Baphomet would destroy them all, rip them to pieces, do to them what they had done to this poor girl and countless others like her. If Baphomet couldn't have Lisa, at least he could make her world a much safer place in which to live.

A steely resolve overcame him and he straightened on a deep breath. The flow of tears ceased and his face became a mask of determination. With his mind made up, he turned and made his way out the same wall of the building the Shaitans had used upon their exit earlier. He could still sense their energies, so he knew tracking them would be a breeze. It took mere minutes to catch up with them as they moved through the darkened streets of London's seedier side of town.

∞

Iblis' group of Shaitans walked unchecked through the nearly-deserted streets, laughing and joking about what they'd just finished doing. They weren't quiet about it, but then they had no reason to believe anyone in this realm would be bothered by their loudness, not that they would care one way or another. Baphomet swooped down out of the sky to land directly in front of the pack, immediately dropping his shields to reveal himself. He'd done it so quickly he'd startled each and every one of them.

Iblis, who was afraid of no one, Angel or otherwise, immediately overcame his surprise and stepped to the front of the group, saying, "Baphomet, old friend, what a surprise! Have you come to join in our sport?"

The look Baphomet threw him would have seared right through the very brains of any other. Iblis merely backed off a scant step or two. However, he wasn't about to bow before his master now, not after what Baphomet had caused to happen with the human they'd delivered to him in Australia. Iblis was still irked that he'd lost his opportunity with that one and he had no more desire to pander to his master's whims. That didn't mean he was above having Baphomet join him and his group in their next project, though.

Baphomet pointed a finger at the group, moving it back and forth, looking each member in the eyes. After a moment of this constant concentration on each one of them, nearly the entire assemblage fell to their knees, each clutching their heads and screaming in agony as the most horrific images flowed through their brains. He'd picked out each Shaitan's most desperate fear and had then exploited it to its fullest extent within the mind of each one of them. Each one believed himself to be involved with whatever nightmare vision Baphomet had created for him.

Iblis stood stock still, staring in stupefaction, wondering what on earth his master was doing. After a moment, he reached over and grabbed Baphomet's arm and, shaking him hard, demanded, "*What are you doing to them?*"

Baphomet broke his concentration only long enough to snarl, "I watched as you and this pitiful band of demons completely decimated that poor creature in that warehouse! For years, I have stood idly by while you and the idiots who have followed you have committed such horrible acts of terror upon the human population. I will no longer allow you to be a scourge on this or any other realm! The plans you told me of at Belial's will not be seen through to fruition. It is over."

He turned to look directly at Iblis and said, "I shall destroy your minions, yes, but then, then, I am going to completely annihilate *you!*" With that, he turned back to the group still kneeling and writhing on the pavement at his feet and he called once more on his energies as he concentrated on fulfilling their worst nightmares.

Suddenly, however, everything changed. There was a shift in the web of energies around Baphomet as he was once again completely overwhelmed by a flood of voices within his own mind. He clutched his temples on both sides of his head, screaming in agony as he fell to the street at his feet. Not now! This couldn't be happening to him at this very moment.

He couldn't think, couldn't move, he could only lie there helplessly, with pain completely ravaging his mind, as the others around him recovered. It didn't take long, either, before the entire group was surrounding him, standing above him with their anger building exponentially.

Iblis wasted no time as he watched his master writhing in pain. "You and your Seraph *superiority*," he snarled at Baphomet. "You have always thought you were *so* much better than the rest of us. Well, look at you now." Iblis laughed. "I am truly going to enjoy watching with Satariel as your precious humans blow themselves to smithereens, but I am afraid you will not be around to witness that." With that, he kicked Baphomet's head with one of his steel-toed boots.

That was all it took. Thirty-some-odd pairs of strong Shaitan feet immediately took up the action their leader had started and Baphomet was soon rendered nearly unconscious by the continuous blows to his body.

Without warning, however, several of the group involved in the frenzy of beating suddenly went flying through the air. The others barely registered this as they were all still so caught up in attacking the one they had served for so many thousands of years. Another bunch of them was suddenly brushed aside and the rest of the group finally turned to see what this new distraction was. That's when they stopped and stared in dumb fascination.

Two Seraphim stood on either side of the most powerful and fearful creature any of them had ever encountered. Its glow alone would have been enough to frighten even Iblis, let alone the energy vibrations coming off it, and the whole assemblage immediately turned tail and ran off, scattering into the darkness in terrified fear.

Djibril and Israfil immediately sheathed their shields. They'd been using them to beat off the Shaitans. Now, they both bowed beside Baphomet's badly beaten form. He was battered and bloodied, but his autonomic immune system had apparently already kicked into full gear with his advanced Seraph healing abilities, judging from how quickly some of the visible cuts on the surface of his skin were healing. However, many of the wounds ran very deep and there had been a great loss of blood.

"He is still breathing," Israfil announced, "but we need to get him to Hantsushept immediately."

Baphomet moaned and Djibril said, "Well, at least he is still alive."

"Lisa," Baphomet whispered and blood seeped from the corner of his mouth. He choked and coughed up more blood, and then he grabbed his head and let out a weak groan, "Ahh...!"

Israfil leaned in closer to where Baphomet lay curled up on his side. Placing a hand on his brother's forehead, Israfil immediately seized up, sucking in a shocked breath as his eyes bulged and his jaw dropped. He gasped again and then again and Mikhail stepped forward to kneel beside Israfil. "It is too much," Israfil said in a rush. "I do not know how he is taking it!"

"Easy, brother," Mikhail encouraged, placing a hand on Israfil's shoulder. He closed his eyes and concentrated as he linked his mind with Israfil's. Immediately, his mind was swamped with voices. There were so many of them! Mikhail sucked in a gasp of air and then called out to his mate, "Sarah, Sarah!"

Baphomet moaned again and whispered, "Leece..."

Mikhail pushed into Israfil's mind without asking permission and he was overwhelmed by the information suddenly bombarding his mind, so much so that it momentarily stunned him. He'd had no idea. When Mikhail saw that Israfil and Sarah had already discussed one particular issue, he became distracted. He felt a small sense of shame that he'd spent all this time with his brother and yet had never realized what had gone on with him.

"Mikhail!" Israfil screamed in terror.

Mikhail immediately pushed aside the issue distracting him and launched himself into a greater area of Israfil's mind, guiding and buffering the sea of voices. It took a massive amount of energy and control and Mikhail spared only one moment more in an attempt to contact Sarah again. When there was no response, he took a deep breath and then took on the entire force of the voices, essentially freeing Israfil's mind so that Israfil could work his magic on their injured brother.

Israfil didn't hesitate.

"Lisa," Baphomet said more clearly, his voice stronger now.

"Whatever you are going to do, Mikhail, I suggest you do it quickly," Israfil said in a gush as he struggled to maintain his grip on Baphomet's mind. "I cannot keep this up much longer!"

"Djibril," Mikhail gritted through tightly-clenched teeth, "get us out of here – now!"

Djibril had them all enclosed in his shields and airborne before the words were even completely out of Mikhail's mouth. He raced toward the barrier rift Mikhail had located for their journey to London and their entire group was soon speeding across the landscape of the Angelic realm.

Mikhail gritted, "Hold on, Iz, we shall be home soon." He gasped as another wave of voices bombarded his mind through the minds of his brothers.

"It is too much!" Israfil gasped again. "I am losing control of it – I am losing him!" After only a second, Israfil cried, "Ahh!" and then suddenly slumped against Mikhail and his other two brothers as unconsciousness claimed his mind.

Immediately, Baphomet and Mikhail screamed out in agony.

∞

135

Sarah and Suriyah stood side by side in the clearing as they waited for the attack. The air fairly crackled with the approaching energies of the elite Sanhedrin Guard and both of the women geared up for battle. Sarah trembled with the effort required to block out Mikhail. She'd heard his pleas a few moments ago, but there was no time to answer him. The best she could hope for was that Israfil and Djibril would assist him with whatever he needed. Sarah and Suriyah were needed here and they both had to concentrate to the best of their abilities on the task at hand, judging from the amount of energy they could feel approaching.

There was a hum in the air now and the two women took one last look at each other. Vimanas suddenly appeared over a nearby ridge and each of the females went into battle mode. Just as they moved into ready stances, an odd thing happened. The approaching vimanas went right around the clearing where the two women stood and on toward the main building of the complex.

After only a second of watching the little buzzing machines go by, Sarah gritted, "Crap!" as she took off running directly toward the structure. Suriyah immediately fell in behind her.

"What is happening?" Suriyah yelled.

"They're goin' after the girl!" Sarah yelled back at her without breaking her stride. Her shields whipped out and immediately lifted her into the air, as did Suriyah's, and the two were soon whirling through the building's walls only to stop in the bedroom where they had left Thomas and Lisa.

The sight that confronted them upon entry into the room was nothing short of astonishing.

Thomas and the young Angel Samuel stood in the very center of the room fighting Guardsman after Guardsman. Lisa was in the farthest corner of the room, huddled down and staring

136

in horror at the scene before her. The Guardsmen continued pouring into the room, each taking only a cursory glance to assess the situation and then joining in on the attack on the two in the middle of the room who were presenting the biggest threat at the moment.

The thing that astonished Sarah and Suriyah so much, however, was the way in which the two boys were defending against the attack. They moved in perfect unison, though the attacks came from all different directions. The Guardsmen used multiple weapons of various makes and models, some carrying knives, some swords, some whips that lit up with electrical charges and made a zinging noise whenever they lashed close to the boys.

Not once did Sarah observe anything or anyone touching either of the boys, though. Their movements were almost majestic as they moved in tandem, thrusting their hands out here, lunging into a stretch position there, their arms circling around the next moment and then thrusting out again. It looked like some type of martial arts movements, but more perfect than anything Sarah had ever seen and without any type of visible weaponry.

It only took a moment before the Guardsmen noticed Suriyah and Sarah standing off to the side, however, and they were both immediately forced into the fight as two Guardsmen rushed toward them with swords drawn.

Suriyah crouched down just in time to avoid being sliced in half by one of the swinging blades. She quickly sprang back up and, moving her arms in unison in a large circling motion, caused a battery of nearby loose objects to magically fly through the air to bombard her attacker. The Angel was dead after the first blow to his head and he dropped to lie motionless on the floor.

The second Guardsman spared only a glance toward his fallen comrade before he lunged at Sarah. Big mistake! Sarah's lethal white hair slid smoothly along the blade of the sword as Sarah merely turned to the side. Sparks flew as the strands of hair raced up the blade to make quick work of the Angel's fingers and hands and Sarah heard only the clank of the sword as it hit the wood flooring before the decapitated body of the Angel joined it. She didn't bother taking note of where the head ended up.

By now, the other Guardsmen recognized there were two new adversaries in the room and they split themselves evenly amongst the four fighters. There were still Guardsmen entering the room. But, for each one that entered, another two *at least* fell lifeless and bloody to the floor.

Sarah started as she caught a glimpse of one of the Guardsmen with an electric whip flinging the blue-lit weapon at Thomas, but she needn't have worried. The noisy instrument merely glanced off some sort of invisible energy shield Thomas had erected around himself and he quickly moved his arms in a beautiful series of movements that soon had the Guardsman screaming as he was thrust backward by some invisible force until he crashed forcefully against the far wall and fell unmoving to the ground.

At that moment, three Guardsmen chose to advance on Sarah simultaneously, two with swords drawn, one with some sort of wicked-looking spiked metal club. From the corner of her eye, Sarah caught Suriyah's movements and she knew what was coming. That would take care of the Guardsman on her left, but the other two, she'd have to deal with.

Without even thinking, her hair reached out and wrapped itself around one of the tall bed posts and Sarah's whole body went flying, flinging around the post and setting her up to take out the remaining two Guardsmen with swift kicks to each man's sternum. The second they were doubled over down on the ground, each straining to regain control of his stunned diaphragm, Sarah's hair finished off the job. Two lifeless, headless bodies collapsed onto the wood flooring.

The battle lasted only a few minutes more and ended with all of the Guardsmen lying lifeless at the feet of the four who'd fought so valiantly to protect Baphomet's human mate. Blood was everywhere and they were all exhausted, but the battle was done and none of the outlanders had been harmed.

Any victory celebration would have to wait, however, as Sarah suddenly stilled. There was a change in the energy frequencies she was receiving. She looked around quickly and said, "Thomas, you and Samuel make sure someone gets Lisa's things moved to another room. Then, I want you to make sure someone cleans up this mess."

"Where are you goin'?" Thomas immediately asked. He wasn't sure he wanted her around after what he knew she'd just witnessed him doing, but he didn't want to be without her, either, just in case more of those guards came back. His mom was a kick-ass fighter, judging from what he'd just seen, and he felt much safer just knowing she was near.

"Lisa, Suriyah, and I are needed back at the clearing. Mikhail and the others are almost home with Baphomet. I need you to take care of things while we're gone, okay?" she hurriedly asked as she turned to nod at Suriyah.

Thomas hesitated, and then reluctantly nodded. He wanted to be involved in everything and he didn't understand why he had to be excluded from the really important parts. But, he knew his mom and he knew she would make him do what she wanted him to do, whether he liked it or not.

Suriyah helped Lisa to stand from her still-huddled position in the corner and they both moved quietly toward the door, doing their best not to step on any faces or heads. The floor was knee deep with bodies, though, and it was impossible to avoid stepping on at least some of the bloody parts.

Sarah watched them for a moment, but then turned back toward Thomas and said, "We *will* talk about what happened in here later, I *assure* you." With that, she turned and made her way out of the room behind the other two women.

Thomas looked over at Samuel, who'd been quiet throughout the exchange. "Well," he said to the Angel, sighing, "I guess our practice sessions are pretty much over."

Samuel just nodded as he moved toward the doorway to go get some help with the clean-up.

Chapter 10

Djibril forced his mind to concentrate on moving as fast as he could. He soon felt another of his brothers become a dead weight in his grasp, though he wouldn't allow his attention to stray from the task at hand. He had to get his brothers to safety!

"Djibril," Mikhail whispered in a broken voice. His strength was almost gone.

Djibril grunted as he finally set down in the clearing just outside the Badlands complex where Hantsushept, Sarah, Suriyah, and Lisa waited. There were several of Hantsushept's assistants waiting alongside the clearing who immediately rushed forward to take charge of the two unconscious Seraphim. Djibril and Mikhail looped an arm each around the other's shoulders and helped each other to stand as they struggled for breath.

Suddenly, Lisa, who until now had been quietly standing at the far edge of the clearing with Sarah and Suriyah, screamed, "No!" and she ran forward to knock away one of Hantsushept's attendants from Baphomet's side.

Everyone in the clearing started in surprise as she immediately wrapped Baphomet's arm around her shoulders and growled viciously at the other attendant still partially supporting the unconscious Seraph. "Get off!" she screamed, her eyes lit with an insane light from within. The Angel didn't hesitate and Baphomet grunted, regaining consciousness a bit as the bulk of his weight landed heavily against Lisa's smaller frame with a thud.

141

"L-Lisa?" Baphomet stammered as he woke from the jolt and some semblance of awareness slipped in.

Sarah and Suriyah stepped forward, hands out-stretched, toward Lisa and her charge, but Lisa screamed, "Stay back, you! Y-You just stay away from him!" Her wild eyes darted from one face to another as she struggled to support Baphomet's weight while also trying to protect him from everyone in the clearing.

"Li-sa?" Baphomet repeated in a broken voice. "Leece?" He finally opened his eyes wide and focused on her face. Once he realized he was finally with her, he closed his eyes and bowed his forehead to her temple, repeating, "Lisa, Lisa, Lisa," over and over again.

"It's okay," Lisa said softly to him. "I'm here."

Sarah threw a quick look toward Mikhail. "Lisa," she then said, stepping forward once more. "You need to let Hantsushept examine Baphomet to make sure his wounds are healing properly."

"No!" Lisa screamed, immediately turning to position herself in front of Baphomet to protect him from those she deemed a threat to him. "Don't you touch him!"

"It is not safe," Mikhail said as he stepped forward to stand beside Sarah. "You need to let us take the necessary precautions, both for your sake and for Baphomet's."

Baphomet managed to fully embrace Lisa from behind and he whispered, "Let them do as they will, Leece, as long as we are left together."

Lisa half-turned to make sure she'd heard him correctly. He looked horrible, his beautiful features haggard and blood-covered. She reached up to touch his beautiful face, suddenly wondering how she could have survived this life without him.

He hugged her and nuzzled his nose into the hair at her temple. "We need rest, sweet Lisa," he finally said. His voice sounded horrible, even, and she knew she would do anything for him.

She turned back toward the others. "I stay with him – understood?"

Several heads nodded without hesitation. Hantsushept cautiously approached and started a cursory examination of the blood-stained Seraph. "And how exactly did this happen?" he asked as he lightly poked and prodded the cuts and bruises marring Baphomet's perfect features.

Baphomet winced and said through gritted teeth, "I kind of got caught off guard by some nasty blokes."

"Hmm," was all Hantsushept said. After a couple of more minutes, he stepped back and announced, "I believe the majority of your wounds have correctly righted themselves in the proper alignment, but we shall have to take some x-rays to see if your bones have properly knit together."

"I do not need any bloody x-rays!" Baphomet grumbled. "I just need some sleep… and Lisa."

Lisa immediately stepped closer to her Baphomet, tightening her hold on him only slightly for fear of hurting him. Baphomet gently hugged her closer, thrilling to the feel of her cool body pressed against his hot one. He knew he couldn't keep her forever, but at least she was his for the moment.

An Angel approached the circle carrying something that immediately had Baphomet's muscles tensing. "Seriously?" Baphomet asked as he looked from the Seraph energy binders to Mikhail.

"The last time you were here," Mikhail reminded him as he approached to take the bindings from the Angel and turned with them to Baphomet, "you threatened to kill us all."

Baphomet was too exhausted to argue and, after looking back over and cupping Lisa's cheeks for one long, deep gaze into her eyes, he sighed and turned and held out both hands to Mikhail.

Sarah conferred with Suriyah for a moment and then turned back toward Lisa and the beaten Seraph, saying, "Suriyah will lead you to your room," indicating that they should follow the tall woman. Hantsushept and his assistants disappeared in the direction of the clinic.

"Where is Israfil?" Mikhail asked Sarah as he situated himself behind her, his arms encircling her and his lower hand coming to rest on top of Sheely's spot.

"He and Gabriel are at the clinic. Hantsushept had Israfil taken there a little after you arrived and Gabriel went along to make sure he was okay," Sarah explained.

She leaned back into his embrace, turning her head to kiss him in a lingering open-mouthed kiss. Their tongues entwined and Sarah's breathing increased in tempo. She turned fully toward him and encircled his neck with her arms in a strong embrace.

Where did you go? Mikhail's mental voice suddenly asked in her mind.

She pulled back and looked up at him in confusion. Then, as the images of the moments he spoke of became clear to her mind, she frowned and said, "We were havin' our own issues here."

What do you mean? came his response floating across the landscape of her mind. He leaned down and latched his open mouth onto her neck, licking and nipping at her sensitive skin there.

Sarah moaned and ran her fingers deep into his hair, clutching great handfuls of the swirling white strands in her fists to pull him closer. *Later*, she thought to him.

Soon, neither of them was concerned with anything more than taking and giving pleasure. Of course, reality always has to rear its ugly head, however, and Sarah finally pulled back. "We have things to do," she said.

Mikhail moved to pull her back into his arms, needing her strength and comfort, wanting her close to him. "What things?" he softly asked as he nibbled gently at her neck.

"While you were gone," Sarah began, "we received another visit from the elite Guardsmen – around fifty of them, this time."

Immediately, Mikhail was on the defensive, looking her over to ensure she and Sheely were unharmed.

Sarah smiled at his concern, saying, "We're fine. They didn't come for us."

Mikhail's eyes narrowed, but then realization dawned and he said, "Let me guess, the girl?"

Sarah merely nodded.

After looking around the complex for a moment, Mikhail asked, "Where are they now?"

This was the tricky part and Sarah took a deep breath for courage before launching into the tale of what had happened. Mikhail listened without interrupting, but Sarah knew his heartbreak at the news that not one of the Angels had survived.

Afterward, Mikhail said, "They'll have to be taken back to the city."

Sarah nodded, softly saying, "I know."

"You had better take me to them, then," Mikhail said resignedly.

Sarah nodded again. She knew the only place the bodies could have been taken from the main house was over to Hantsushept's clinic, so she led Mikhail there. Neither of them spoke on the walk over. Once there, it was only a matter of moments before the assistants there tending to the burnt and mangled bodies allowed them entry to the cooled storage area.

Mikhail looked upon the faces of the dead Angels, some unfamiliar to him, some very dear to his heart. The bodies had been lined up in rows upon the ground. There were too many for the few autopsy and examination tables the room housed and so the staff tended to the majority of the bodies on the floor. Mikhail stopped to look down at a couple of Angels who looked very similar to each other in coloring and height. After a moment, he said, "I trained these two. I was there at their births. They were twins, sons of one of the council members."

A tear slowly slid down his cheek and Sarah gently took his hand in hers as she stood silently by his side.

"There will be retaliation for this, to be certain," he said. Sarah shook her head, sadly realizing that Azra'il would never let it go, would never end the battle to rid the Angelic realm of humans. Mikhail's voice came to her in her mind, saying, *He just does not understand, love. He has not seen and experienced the things we have. He still holds to the rules and laws laid down by the bless... by the false Designers*, he finished.

"So, how are we to end this," Sarah asked, "or, are we to merely continue living the life of refugees forever more?"

Mikhail turned to hug her, confessing, "I do not know." After a moment, he said, "I only know we have to return the bodies and then do what we can to get on with our lives."

"You don't think there's any way we can change Azra'il's mind?"

Mikhail thought for a moment and then said, "I am sure my brothers and I can come up with something. It is just going to take a little time."

Sarah studied him for a moment as she thought this over. "What about your siblings?" she finally asked.

"What do you mean?"

"They're havin' to deal with this, too," she clarified.

Mikhail nodded, saying, "I know." He moved out of the way of the workers and grabbed Sarah's hand to lead her back out into the reception area of the clinic. There were several chairs and settees there and Mikhail led her to an area farthest from the few Angels harboring about in that part of the building.

There, they sat and he continued, saying, "Djibr... I mean, Gabriel is doing his best to deal with things. He is more of what humans would call an anal personality. He likes rules and order and whenever anything is not in order, it bothers him. That was why he was fine living in Seraphim City. There were rules and laws there. There was order."

"And then Thomas and I came along and screwed up everything," Sarah said.

Mikhail took her hands in his, turning more fully toward her and shaking his head. "No, baby. You did not screw up anything," he said. "You and Thomas were a wake-up call. The only problem is that not everyone has gotten it, yet. Gabriel will come around. He cannot deny the logic of what he has seen since you came into our lives. After all, it was he who suggested you were something completely different than what we had seen before."

Sarah turned her gaze down to their clasped hands. "And Israfil?" she asked.

Mikhail was quiet for a moment. Then, he said, "You already know about Israfil, love."

Sarah looked up at him, eventually nodding because there was no denying it. "I promised him I wouldn't tell anyone, not even you," she whispered.

"I know," Mikhail said, reaching to tuck a few strands of her glorious white hair behind her ear. "I just wish, I just wish there was some way we could... *help* him, or *something*."

"I know." Sarah bent more toward him. The idea of having to endure what Israfil had endured made her instinctively want to be nearer to her mate.

Mikhail wrapped an arm around her and pulled her close. "Do not worry," he said on a sigh. "We shall work it all out, somehow." His words rang hollow, even to his own ears. He did not know how this would end. He could not see a clear path for any of them. All he did know was that Sarah and he and the two kids were now a family and he would do whatever it took to ensure they were all safe. A thought occurred to him then and he pulled slightly away from Sarah.

She immediately felt him throwing up a psychic buffer, shielding his thoughts from her as best he could. It didn't work, but since she had actually been practicing just such a maneuver herself since her last encounter with Baphomet in the garden, she went ahead and put up her own, which effectively blocked his thoughts from her momentarily. If he needed a bit of privacy, she would give it to him, though she worried about his reasons for needing such.

The two of them stood and, sparing a solemn glance toward the storage area where all the Angels' bodies were being kept, slowly made their way upstairs to the area where Gabriel waited with Israfil.

∞

Lisa never once lost physical contact with Baphomet as Suriyah and another Angel showed them to their new rooms. She wished they could return to the rooms she'd been given when she'd first arrived at the complex, but a quick memory of how the bedroom in that suite had looked the last time she'd been in it, with the bodies of all the dead Angels strewn willy-nilly all over the place, had her sighing with acceptance of these new smaller quarters they were given.

The Angel quietly informed her he would arrange for her things to be brought into her new quarters and then he left. Suriyah looked around quietly, as if trying to decide what she should do next. She didn't seem to want to leave her brother, but there really wasn't anything more she could do to help him.

Everything he and Lisa could possibly need seemed to have been provided and there was absolutely no way Lisa was letting anyone near Baphomet at this point. After a moment more of looking helplessly around the room, Suriyah sighed and informed them she was going to go check on her other brothers but that she'd return to them later.

As the door closed behind the tall blond, Lisa and Baphomet were finally alone for the first time since he'd kidnapped her and taken her to that awful sex room from which she'd initially escaped. Lisa didn't want to think about that. Instead, she helped Baphomet over to the only bed in the quarters and then helped him climb up under the covers.

Neither of them spoke, but the need for physical contact between them was overwhelming, so Lisa continued touching him, on his arm, his hand, anywhere she could to assist him in getting comfortable on the large bed. He was still bound at the wrists, so he couldn't do these things very well by himself.

Baphomet also still looked horrible and Lisa wasn't sure how much internal damage there might be. The physician, Hantsushept, had declared Baphomet needed x-rays, but Baphomet had, as was apparently his usual gruff manner, rudely declined.

What if he really did have internal damage that needed fixing? What if he was dying right now and Lisa was going to be left alone simply because she didn't have the balls to stand up to him to insist he get the medical attention he needed?

Baphomet's quiet deep rumble of laughter brought her out of her reverie and she looked questioningly at him. He reached his bound hands out to touch her cheek, swallowing hard and whispering, "Sweet Lisa. Do not worry so about your mate. I have survived far worse than this in my time." His hands fell with a thud to the soft bedspread covering the major part of him and Lisa finally broke physical contact with him and, turning her back on him, stepped away from the bed.

This was all so crazy. Who *was* he? *Why* did she feel so protective of him all of a sudden? Why did she also feel this undeniable pull toward him, physically? He was a complete stranger to her, and yet he kept calling her his mate and saying that he was hers. She went to stand by a window where the soft rays of the late afternoon sun gently shone through the glass.

Baphomet adjusted his position and cleared his throat. Already, he was missing her touch. He wanted her back over on the bed with him, but he didn't think it wise to demand such. After a moment, he quietly asked in a broken voice, "Tell me about yourself?"

Lisa distractedly turned back to look at him for a moment, asking, "Like what?"

Baphomet shrugged, saying, "Anything. Everything. I want to know everything about you."

Lisa turned back toward the window, gazing out on the beautiful gardens she'd sat in with Sarah earlier in the week. She laughed, shaking her head. "Why would you want to know about me?" she asked. "I'm nobody. Nothing."

"You are wrong," was Baphomet's quiet response.

She threw a side-ways glance over in his direction as if to sarcastically say, "Sure, I'm wrong."

After a moment's hesitation, Baphomet recalled how often she thought of her mother and he said, "Tell me about your parents."

Lisa quickly speared him with a look filled with accusation and, although he wasn't certain, he could have sworn he also saw sadness mixed in that look as well. A mere heartbeat passed and she was looking back out the window.

After a moment, she haltingly began telling him the story of her life. She told him of how her mother had been one of the "lost children" of Australia and of how the woman had been taken at the age of eleven from her tribe to live among the white Christian settlers because she'd been a half-breed.

There, the girl had been raped by the white ranch owner at the station where she'd worked. When it was discovered she was pregnant, the girl had been told she would have to get rid of the bastard baby. So, Lisa's mother had run away from the station and had found her way back to her tribe.

"That's where I came into the picture," Lisa said finally.

"So, you are an aborigine," Baphomet said.

"Part," she agreed. "Actually, I am Ngarinyin, a Djungun. If my mother had been allowed to stay to give birth to me, I would have grown up there with the people and would most likely be a Wodoi wife by now with several children of my own. She was banished, though. My father said there was no Wodoi for me and that I would not fit in the tribe."

After a moment's pause, she continued, "When I was fifteen, just before I went to study in Sydney, I returned North to ask my father why he had banished my mother and me from the Ngarinyin."

"Wait," Baphomet interrupted, confused. "Y-You said your father was a white farmer who raped your mother."

"No. That was the man who impregnated my mother with me. My father is the oldest of the tribal elders who decided my mother was to be banished from the Ngarinyin if she was to have me. He was the one responsible for her since she hadn't yet become a Wodoi wife at that time.

"And, so what was his response to your question?" asked Baphomet.

Lisa was silent for a short time. Then, she sighed and said, "He told me I wasn't meant to be there, that I had never been meant to be one of them." She fell silent. After a few minutes, she softly said, "I guess I should've expected something like that, you know? But, it still hurt for a fifteen year old to hear it. I mean, I know I'm different from just about *everyone* on the flippin' planet, but it really hurt hearing the tribe's patriarch tell me I was not welcome there with my own people."

Baphomet wanted to kill the tribal elder. How dare the man disrespect Baphomet's mate! He could feel the anger rising inside his body and mind and he suddenly wondered if he might someday get the opportunity to return to the human realm and hunt down this tribal elder to make him pay for what he'd done. Just then, however, Baphomet recalled the old koradji and how powerful that one old aborigine had been, and that was enough to quash that train of thought. But, for Lisa's sake, he would be willing to risk it.

"I shall kill your father for you, if you would like," he quietly told her.

Lisa looked at him, aghast. *"Kill* him?" she demanded. "Why on earth would you think I'd want something like that?"

Baphomet shrugged as best he could and answered, "Because he hurt you."

Lisa stared at him, astonished and repulsed at the same time. Even when she'd first encountered Sarah and her mate, Mikhail, she hadn't felt so out of her depth as she did at this very moment. The differences between Baphomet and her came crashing into her mind with a colossal thump.

What difference did it make? He'd kidnapped her. He was crazy. She'd seen it in everything he'd ever done. Why was she even thinking about this? But, the idea of not being with him made her heart sick. The moment she'd seen him in the clearing,

152

seen someone else touching him, she'd known he was hers and that she would do anything to protect him.

Who was he, though? She didn't know anything about him, not even really *what* he was. She decided the best way to find out was to just ask. So, she started with this latest issue of him offering to kill her father for her.

"Why are you like that?" Lisa asked brokenly as the realization that it was possible she shouldn't be trying to make things work with this being after all suddenly dawned on her.

Baphomet chuckled and said, "You cannot change fifteen thousand years' worth of anger in the blink of an eye, my heart."

She blushed a little at the endearment, an oddly warm feeling beginning to flow inside her despite her doubts, and then she blinked in awe as she realized what else he'd said. "You're *that* old... *really?*"

His beautiful smile faded and he looked away. After a moment, he looked back at her and grinned, saying, "What does it matter how old I am? I am still here, basically chained to a bed, and the only one who can save me thinks I am some sort of demon." His grin faded on his last words and he looked away again.

Lisa hesitated. Why did she feel sympathy for this creature? Why care at all? After all, he had kidnapped her and brought her to this odd place to be with these strange and dangerous people. And, then again, he, himself, seemed insanely dangerous. Yet, there was that feeling within her again. It just wouldn't let her go.

She recalled how wonderful it had felt being held by him when he'd first entered her life and she knew she wanted to feel that again. She'd never had that with anyone else, ever. Just watching Mikhail and Sarah together made her want that same kind of closeness with another. Could Baphomet be that one other in the world who could make her feel like that? Lisa blinked and then said shyly, "I-I don't think you're a demon. I just don't understand you."

Chapter 11

Djibril sat beside the bed, patiently waiting for Israfil to awaken. He, himself, was exhausted, but he wanted to ensure his brother was okay before he went to his own quarters within the main house for some rest.

Israfil finally showed signs he was regaining consciousness and Djibril leaned forward to him. "Iz?" he said softly, gently touching Israfil's arm.

Israfil's eyes blinked once, then opened wide and he shot up to a sitting position on a gasp. "Where is he?" he immediately demanded.

"It is all right," Djibril soothed urgently. "Baphomet is secure, and I am told Lisa is with him and that they are both fine."

Israfil hysterically shook his head. "No," he explained. "Where is Mikhail?"

Djibril frowned. "Mikhail?" he asked, confused.

"We are here," said Mikhail as he and Sarah entered the room.

Israfil turned toward Mikhail, saying, "Iblis and Satariel…"

Everyone looked at Mikhail as he stood there silently contemplating the implications of Israfil's statement. His eyes took on a somber glow as he rehashed everything he'd learned while he'd been inside Baphomet's and Israfil's minds. The name Iblis came up several times and it seemed primarily to be associated with a betrayal, and then with the beating Baphomet had endured.

Sarah stepped forward and entwined her fingers with his, allowing her mind and her vision to join with his again, the buffer between them dissolving instantly. Suddenly, a kaleidoscope of colors flashed before Mikhail's mind's eye before a scene from Baphomet's memory came onto him with perfect clarity. Sarah could detect so much visual information, and so much sensory data, that he could actually smell the stench from the Thames as he stood in the little room in the clinic.

He could feel the wind ruffling Baphomet's hair, could feel Baphomet breathing, could feel his sorrow and then his anger at what his friend, Iblis, was saying. Mikhail also felt the deep connection Baphomet had with Lisa, even stretched across dimensions as it had been then.

Sarah had gotten all of that, whereas Mikhail had mostly just picked up on their words. When he'd initially received the verbal exchanges from delving into Baphomet's mind, Mikhail had paid only cursory attention to it, concluding very quickly that this Iblis had somehow felt Baphomet had betrayed him and so he'd beaten him to within an inch of his life.

However, when he added the verbal context he had to all the sensory information Sarah'd been able to collect, he suddenly understood, as did Sarah, what had upset Israfil so much that he'd actually requested Mikhail's presence.

"We should go now," Sarah suddenly said, "if we're gonna have time to track 'em and stop 'em."

Suriyah entered the room at that moment and asked, "Who are we tracking and why?"

Mikhail turned to Sarah. "*You* are not going anywhere near Iblis *or* Satariel," he stated matter-of-factly.

"Oh," Suriyah said, rolling her eyes as she crossed her arms and leaned casually up against the frame of the door through which she'd just entered. *Shaitans causing trouble again... quelle surprise!* she thought.

Sarah stared at Mikhail as if he was insane. "So, we're gonna just sit back and allow this to happen?" she asked.

"Allow what to happen?" Djibril asked.

"Yes, please, what is going on?" asked Suriyah.

Mikhail ignored them, focusing instead on Sarah while he said, "I will not have you and Sheely put in harm's way again, either from Iblis or Satariel or from the simple act of crossing the rift."

"Yet, we live in danger here with Azra'il sendin' his elite Guard to attack at random moments. If you're not here with us, how can either of us be sure of the other's safety?" she finally asked. Mikhail stood silently looking down at her as he thought over her argument.

"Will you please tell the rest of us what is going on?" Djibril demanded in frustration.

Finally, Mikhail turned toward him and said, "Two Shaitans have influenced a group of humans to carry out a plot to commit a major act of terrorism somewhere within the human realm. Baphomet tried to kill them, but somehow they managed to beat him. Now, if someone does not find the Shaitans and the humans they are going to use and stop them from carrying out their plot, many innocent humans will most likely die."

Djibril looked at each person in the room in the ensuing silence, and then said, "Well, the obvious answer here is for me to go. I mean, unless Suriyah has suddenly developed extreme tracking abilities, I am kind of the only one here other than Mikhail and Sarah who will be able to find these people and the Shaitans quickly enough to be able to stop anything from happening, right?"

Mikhail and Sarah looked helplessly at him.

"Also, I know I cannot come anywhere close to defeating a whole platoon of elite Sanhedrin Guardsmen," he said. "If there is another attack like the one I learned of from one of Hantsushept's assistants, the two of you will be needed here to protect those within the complex, and you know it."

After a moment more of consideration, Mikhail and Sarah both nodded once, the lights from within their eyes swirling in tandem.

Suriyah stepped forward. "I shall go with you, Djibril," she announced. All eyes turned to regard her curiously. She looked at each of them, and then explained, "I am pretty good in a fight and my people would expect me to do something to save the humans. You know how much Jinn love them. As Queen of the Jinn, it is practically my duty to go."

Djibril nodded once and then turned toward Israfil. All others in the room followed suit.

Israfil shook his head and simply said, "I cannot." Confusion lit Djibril's and Suriyah's eyes, while understanding and gratitude shone in Mikhail's and Sarah's. "The transformations for Sarah and Mikhail proved to be very violent and painful for them sometimes. Lisa and Baphomet will need someone to help buffer some of that, if they are to get through this with as little pain as possible," he explained to the other two Seraphim.

Everyone nodded in understanding. There really didn't seem to be any alternative course.

∞

Mikhail and Sarah left the building slowly, each deep in thought. Sarah could sense he was trying to erect another buffer between them and, although the idea that he didn't trust her enough to talk with her occurred to her, she went ahead and reestablished the buffer between them again. She was unsure if

Mikhail understood she was the one maintaining the buffer, but it hardly seemed to matter. He needed some privacy and she was going to give it to him.

Clearing her throat, she said, "I'm gonna go check on my folks, if you don't mind?"

Mikhail was immediately filled with concern, asking, "Is something wrong?"

"No-no," she quickly told him, shaking her head. "I just haven't visited them in a few days and," she rolled her eyes, "you have no idea how paranoid my mom can get sometimes. She's probably drivin' my dad crazy by now."

Mikhail stopped and turned toward her, running his hands down her arms. He looked down at their feet for a moment in thought, and then looked her in the eyes, softly saying, "Do not visit overlong with them, hmmn?"

Sarah stared into his glowing eyes, wondering what demons were haunting his soul but knowing she would never ask. He had given her so much without question. The fact that he still wanted her to return to him was, to her, in itself a miracle. She would do whatever she could for him, even if it meant giving him time away from her.

Sheely chose that moment to launch into a tirade about something, though Sarah couldn't catch a word of what was being said, and Sarah chuckled.

"What?" Mikhail asked.

"Did you understand any of that?" Sarah asked around a smile.

Mikhail frowned. "Any of what?" he asked.

The smile slipped. "Sheely," she explained. "She was yappin' about somethin'."

Mikhail looked down at the glowing patch of skin on Sarah's abdomen and reached out to touch it gently. After a moment, he shook his head and whispered, "I didn't hear her at all."

Sarah blinked as understanding dawned. The buffer had kept him from hearing Sheely, as well.

Mikhail suddenly sighed and bent to place a swift kiss on Sarah's forehead, saying, "I shall meet you back at the house shortly." Then he turned and headed off in another direction, away from all the buildings in the area. Sarah stood staring after him for a moment, wondering what she could do.

He was obviously worried about something, but she didn't want to intrude without him wanting her to know about whatever it was. The last time she'd listened in on things he'd wanted kept from her, he'd gotten all upset and, although they'd ended up having great make-up sex afterward, Sarah didn't want there to be times like that between them. Again, if he wanted his privacy, she was going to give it to him.

She sighed and turned back toward the direction where her folks' new house was.

She hadn't fibbed in what she'd told Mikhail about her parents. Sarah figured her mom was probably going nuts by now since it had been almost a week since they'd seen each other. Back in the human dimension, it had been years since they'd gone a single day without at least talking with each other on the phone, let alone seeing each other. Lately, however, each time Sarah had gone to visit, she'd felt like her parents looked at her weird, or something, like they felt strange having her around because of the physical changes she'd gone through.

Sarah didn't like making them feel like that, but what could she do? She hadn't had anything to do with the physiological changes she'd endured. They'd just happened. Although, she guessed the changes had been brought about by the fact that she and Mikhail had experienced physical contact with each other, but Sarah would not apologize for that. Mikhail was the very best part of her life and she hoped never to be separated from him again. If she had to look like some kind of freak to everyone else in order to be with Mikhail, then so be it.

As she neared her parents' house, she heard someone manually sawing something from around the side of the house and she went to investigate. Her dad was just around the corner working on some kind of wood project. It looked like lawn furniture he was building.

"Hey, Dad," Sarah said as she approached.

He stopped sawing and turned to greet her. "Hi there," he said with a grin. He reached out an arm and Sarah easily slipped into his quick embrace. He was all sweaty and she wrinkled her nose as she stepped back from him. He chuckled and adjusted the safety glasses he wore over his regular glasses. "Your mom's in the house," he said. "You'd better get in there before she starts up again."

Sarah laughed as she headed for the back of the house. "I figured she'd be drivin' you nuts by now," she said.

Her dad shook his head as he repositioned his saw blade and said, "Been cryin' for the last 24 hours about how she's such a terrible mother and none of her kids love her anymore."

Sarah laughed and hurried along to the back door of the house. The sound of sawing started up again.

Once inside the back door, Sarah called out, "Mom?" Within seconds, the swinging door from the hallway opened and there stood Marian, all teary-eyed and red-faced. She looked a mess. "Aw, Mom," Sarah said as she made her way over to give her mom a hug. They stood there for a few minutes as Marian softly cried while holding her daughter as tightly as she could. Sarah's hair rubbed at her mom's back and arms, doing its best to soothe the older woman.

Eventually, Marian took notice of that fact and she quickly stepped back away from Sarah, eyeing the strange moving strands of hair fearfully, yet trying to make it look as if she was just giving them both the proper amount of space.

At least she's stopped cryin', thought Sarah. She followed her mom over to the kitchen table and they both had a seat. Sarah looked around the kitchen, noticing how well-decorated it had become. "This is really startin' to come together," she said, nodding as she continued looking around.

Marian looked quickly around, herself, preferring to concentrate on anything banal rather than having to look at her daughters strange glowing eyes or the moving, wickedly sharp white hair. She nodded and agreed, "Yep, we're gettin' there. I've had a bit of help from a couple of Angels Mikhail sent over to us, so I don't think it'll take too much longer to finish."

"I like it," Sarah said.

The silence stretched between them and Marian suddenly stood. "How 'bout a glass of iced tea?" she asked as she moved over to the cabinet for a couple of glasses. Soon, they were both seated at the table again sipping the traditional Southern drink, though they preferred theirs without sugar. "How're Thomas and Mikhail?" Marian asked.

Sarah quickly looked away. "They're both fine," she said. "I mean, things have been a bit hectic lately because Mikhail's other sister and brother have been visitin' and his brother's, um, fiancée is here, too, so the house is practically full. His sister, Suriyah, and his brother, Gabriel, just left, though and other than that, everything's goin' fine, I guess." She took another long sip of her tea and asked, "How've y'all been?"

Marian bent her head and scratched at an eyebrow for a moment before sighing and saying tearfully, "I just miss everybody, you know? I mean, since we came here, I hardly get to see you or Thomas. I don't have a phone, so I can't call your brothers or sisters. Tom's always out working on some project or other and the only people I have to talk to are a bunch of strange Angels." She got up and grabbed a dish cloth so she could start wiping down her already pristine countertops and sink. "I don't have any friends here and there's nothin' for me to do all day long," she finally said.

Sarah looked around, trying to think of something she could say to ease her mom's mind. "You know," she said, "you and dad are always welcome over at the main house. Y'all can come see us anytime you want, and Thomas, too. There's even enough room for you to stay the night, if you'd like."

Marian dropped the dish cloth back into the sink and turned, leaning a hip against the countertop and crossing her arms just below her chest. "I know that," she sighed. "I would just feel a whole lot better knowin' everybody's safe, not just us."

Sarah frowned in confusion.

"Your brothers and sisters should be here, too," Marian explained. "They're in just as much danger as we were when we were still there, don't you think? I mean, if the crazy people can find out your real name and home address, what's to stop'em from findin' out the names of your brothers and sisters?"

Sarah looked away. What could she say? Her mom was right. If people who had read her blog could track down *her* real name and address so that her parents weren't even safe, surely they'd be able to find anybody else connected with her. That would mean each and every one of her sisters and brothers would be in danger, just as Marian was suggesting. Sarah hadn't thought about any of this, though.

Mikhail's willingness to bring Marian and Tom, along with the two dogs, back with them to the Angelic realm had overwhelmed Sarah at the time. Sarah and Thomas had both experienced the racial tensions running throughout the Angelic dimension because they were the only two humans there. Marian and Tom had only been subjected to it once, when Narayana, one of Mikhail's servants, had tried to kill them all.

Her parents probably thought that had been just one nut case out of the whole dimension full of Angels. The Angels who'd come to live with them out in the Badlands all seemed extremely loyal to Mikhail and so they had only ever treated any of the humans here with the utmost respect and kindness, so Sarah doubted either of her parents even had a clue racism existed in this realm.

Sarah knew it, though, and she knew just how upsetting it would be for even more humans to be brought over into the Angelic dimension without the Great Sanhedrin's permission. There was no way she could ask Mikhail to allow her siblings to come live here with them. She'd have to think of some other way around this issue. How she could say that to her mother, though, was another issue entirely.

Chapter 12

Baphomet adjusted his hips, moving just a little closer toward Lisa. He was pleased to notice she didn't move away from him. Licking his lips, he asked, "Would you mind getting some water for me?"

Lisa immediately complied. She couldn't stand to see anyone, or anything, suffer. Someone had thought to place a couple of glasses and a pitcher of water on a side table, and she quickly filled a glass and, placing a hand behind his head for support, held the glass to his lips. The feel of her touch had tingles of electricity instantly shooting down his spine.

He'd never felt anything like this with any other, not even Lilith, who'd disappeared from his life so many tens of thousands of years ago. As Lisa moved in closer to him and he caught a whiff of her natural scent, his mouth suddenly *was* parched and he gulped thirstily.

He drank so fast that the water soon dribbled down the sides of his chin onto his chest. Lisa righted the glass and pulled it away from him, apologizing to him as she set the glass back onto the side table. She used the cuff of her sweater's sleeve to dry his chin, her touch slowing as she watched her wrist moving over his skin.

There was no stubble there, even though they'd been in this room for quite some time now. His chin and jaw still appeared as freshly-shaved as if he'd just finished the task. Her eyes narrowed as she marveled at this fact.

"You may touch me, if you want, my heart," Baphomet suddenly said, a lop-sided grin flashing across his handsome features.

Lisa quickly jerked her hand away from his chin and stood to go stare out the window again. She did want to touch him and that was the problem. Here she was, twenty-six years old, still a virgin, and alone in a bedroom with the most beautiful creature she'd ever encountered. Sure, he was crazy, but hey, who didn't have a flaw or two? Most of the girls her age she knew from her school days back in Sydney already had kids. Most of the girls her age from her tribe were already married with *several* kids. Lisa had never wanted that life. Not since she'd discovered everything that had happened to her mother.

She'd wanted adventure and romance and *money*... oh, how she'd wanted that. She'd spent a huge portion of her life just dreaming of the things she could do if she had money. But that kind of life wasn't easily come by for a half-breed aborigine. Half of Australia still regarded her people as being no better than stinking, ignorant slaves to be used either as migrant workers, hired help, or day-laborers. Lisa was pretty, so she'd had it a little easier than most like her, but she was still thought of as a lower-class person.

For the past few years, she'd received plenty of offers to become a kept woman. So far, she'd managed to keep focused on the goal of owning her own retail apparel shop in Sydney. The one she owned now was much smaller than the one she hoped to own one day in the big city. She'd decided long ago on this course so she'd be able to support her mom and herself. Since then, she'd remained focused. At least, she *had* been focused until Baphomet had come barreling into her life and screwed up everything!

She turned and glared at him. Baphomet returned her stare, completely unrepentant.

"Why?" she demanded simply.

A grin flashed across his face and he chuckled, asking, "What, am I not good enough for you, my sweet?"

She frowned. "I don't even know you," she said.

His grin vanished and he said acidly, "But, you belong to me, the same as I belong to you!"

Lisa reacted violently to his mercurial mood change, not to mention his words. "I belong to no man!" she declared vehemently through gritted teeth.

"You think I am thrilled to acknowledge the fact that a human holds sway over my entire being?" he threw back at her angrily. "I have been my own master for a million years, and now I am at the mercy and whims of a human whose years I bet do not even cover the fingers and toes on my person!" He struggled in frustration against the bindings at his wrists and then winced as they performed their function by causing pain to shoot up his arms in order to stop his struggling.

Lisa immediately returned to his side, concern etched on her young features. "I'm sorry," she said, placing a hand on his arm just above his bound wrist to soothe him. "Shh," she said finally.

He turned more fully toward her and sighed. His energy flow was calmer whenever she touched him. He'd noticed that before but had been too caught up in wanting her to concentrate on anything else. He moved his head to a more comfortable position on the pillow she'd put behind him and stared at her. She really was pretty, he realized. A lock of hair fell onto her forehead and he reached his bound hands up to push the lock back and behind her ear.

Lisa's eyes closed as a thrill raced across her skin and a rampant heat flashed into existence inside her core. Her nostrils flared and her whole world suddenly narrowed to the smell of him. Opening her eyes, she stared at him in wonder. It had only been a few hours since the others had locked Baphomet and her in this room, but Lisa could swear she felt as if she'd known him forever. His mood swings, his anger, and she could feel his loneliness inside. She could feel the hurt, the pain...

The moment their lips touched, Lisa realized she must have bent to kiss him. However, she didn't think after that. All she could do was feel. Lisa was on fire. Her skin burned from the inside out! She felt as if she would die if she didn't get closer to him, have more of him, just... more! His hands touched where they could, hampered as they were, but it wasn't enough for Lisa. With a moan, she climbed more fully up onto the bed to sit astride his form.

Baphomet's hands might be bound by those things the others had put onto his wrists, but she suffered no such encumberences and her hands explored his perfect form with relish. He was so hard in some places, and yet so soft in other places. And his heat...

Lisa wondered vaguely if he suffered from fever, but the allure of his neck and chest was too great for her to pay much attention to the stray thought as she slowly moved downward to lavish his heated form with her lips and tongue. Every now and then, she had to nip at his skin, just to make sure he was paying attention.

Baphomet reared up on a hiss when her teeth tugged on the soft skin at the juncture of his shoulder and neck. He reached to touch her and was immediately wracked with lightning bolts of pain spearheading up both arms. He hissed again and groaned in agony.

Oh, how he wanted to touch her! This was Hell, he decided. At least, he could smell her, and she was touching him... just not how and where he needed her to be touching him. It was almost as if she'd never done this before.

He moaned again at the thought of what *that* would be like. She was far too pretty for him to even conceive of such a notion, though, and he groaned half in frustration at not being able to lead in the dance and half in pleasure at the feel of her luscious mouth on his nipple.

She suckled his nipple, scraping her teeth lightly across the sensitive bud, and Baphomet moved to position her between his legs. It wasn't easy since her knees were on either side of him. But, he spread his own legs and pushed down on her shoulders with his arms.

Lisa instinctively followed his silent command and moved to settle her lower torso between his legs, delighting in the feel of his long legs wrapping around the backs of her thighs through the blanket covering him.

In mere seconds, she'd managed to unbutton the rest of his shirt and she laid bare his entire chest and abdomen. She leaned on an elbow and allowed her other hand to roam where it would, her eyes following voraciously over the heated flesh passing beneath her seeking fingers. Every now and then, she would bend over to lick where she touched, the need to taste his skin too tempting to resist.

When her wandering hand ventured onto the fastening of his twill slacks, she quickly glanced up at his face, as if seeking permission. His eyes were riveted to hers and he nodded in short, jerky movements, his teeth clenching and unclenching in tortured anticipation.

When she hesitated still, he pushed his pelvis upward and pleaded, "Touch me, Leece, please, just touch me!"

Lisa looked down at her hand and suddenly found herself unfastening his trousers and pulling down the waistband of the pristine boxer briefs he wore to expose the most wondrous thing she'd ever seen in her life.

It was enormous! He was longer than she'd thought he'd be, but that was no surprise. He was a tall man. She wasn't worried about that. She was an extremely tall woman, especially for her tribe, so his length shouldn't be a problem. His thickness, on the other hand, was what gave her cause for concern. She'd heard the girls in school talking about men's sizes before, so she knew a man of Baphomet's size could possibly cause a great amount of pain for her.

As her thoughts raced, she didn't realize what her hand was doing until she felt the steely-hard length of him heating her palm. Again, he hissed and pushed his pelvis upward. His head fell back onto the pillow behind him and she heard him release a tortured groan.

She felt something wet on her hand suddenly and looked back down to discover a bead of milky liquid pearling from the tiny opening at the center of the tip of him. Fascinated with the little drop of liquid, she found herself dipping her head and licking at it.

Baphomet jerked into a half-sitting position, his breath wrenching out on a grunt of disbelief.

Lisa heard his gasp, but she was too enthralled with the salty-tasting liquid emitting from within his heated length and she bent farther to take the top part of his flesh more fully into her mouth, hungrily licking and sucking at him for more.

He didn't disappoint as, with another groan, he lay back down and a small, short spurt of the salty nectar spilled forth onto her tongue. Lisa moaned in pleasure as she swallowed and licked around the shaft, adjusting her position so she could take him more completely into her mouth.

"Use your hands *and* your mouth, sweet Lisa," he ordered urgently, his breathing becoming labored. Without even thinking about it, Lisa placed a hand on the shaft and began moving both her hand and her mouth up and down the entire shaft, alternating them, sometimes fast, sometimes slowly, still licking and suckling him. She soon found a rhythm that seemed to work best for both of them.

Baphomet's breath was coming in gasps. Lisa was experiencing more and more pleasure, both from the tasty liquid and from his ever-increasing moans of pleasure. When he rasped out, "Take your clothes off, Leece, and climb on top of me," she didn't even hesitate.

In a trice, she had her clothing off, flinging the pieces of cloth wherever they would fall, and then she was climbing back onto the bed, flinging one leg over him and pausing just over his hardened flesh. She was breathing hard as she placed one hand on his chest and reached down with the other to guide his length into her sacred garden.

Baphomet lifted his head to watch as her cooler dark flesh eased down over his heated length. He'd been here before, but never like this. Lilith had been human, yes, and her flesh had been cool, but there the similarities ended. Lisa was fire and ice, the sun and the moon, everything light in the universe to soothe and excite the deepest black void that was his soul. As she moved on him, sinking down, adjusting to his girth and then sliding farther down, he suddenly felt a barrier of some kind blocking his entry.

His eyes shot to her face and he was stunned to find a look of utter ecstasy covering her face and he wanted time to stop. He wanted to be like this with her forever. His body wouldn't allow that, however, and Baphomet reached his bound hands up to place his hands on her neck, holding onto her as best he could with the bindings.

She opened her eyes and looked down at him. Then, as he gave just the slightest push with his hands, she used her own muscles to push down until he felt the thin barrier of skin give and suddenly, he was buried in the purest heaven he'd ever known.

"Ah!" he gasped, and then he hissed a breath inward. Lisa moved up, then down, then up and back down again… and again… and again… finding the rhythm they both needed until they were both so caught up in the pleasure that nothing else mattered.

Baphomet felt as if his entire insides were on fire and he felt a building sense of urgency within. He reached out once more for her, touching her as intimately as he could on her breast, her abdomen, and even lower.

Suddenly, both of them were riding on a wave of desire that was building and building. Neither knew how to stop it. They only knew they were each a slave to the other.

Baphomet couldn't hold back his voice, as with each push of his pelvis up into her, he said, "Ah…, ah…, ah…," with the volume increasing each time. His grip on her flesh tightened, pulling her harder down onto his body with each thrust.

Lisa felt the energy building within her body and unknowingly began holding her breath. Baphomet's thrusts forced out her air supply, but she would immediately take another breath and hold it again, only to have it pushed up and out of her upon his next thrust.

The energy inside both of them built to a crescendo all of a sudden and then it exploded on a crest of a wave that circled outward like a mega-tsunami across the entire ocean of the universe, its raging force barreling over any obstacle in its path before depositing their exhausted forms back onto the shore of the earth where they clung to each other, sweat-drenched and panting for oxygen, and each wondering if the world would ever be the same again.

Baphomet recovered first, as he felt her give a slight shiver. He moved his arms up and tugged at the covers with a foot. His slacks and underwear were still on and bunched around his ankles. "Leece," he said, raising his head and shoulders to look at her. "Sweetheart, you are going to have to help out here with the covers, if you will."

Lisa raised her head and looked down toward the covers that had become shoved in a bundle across the bottom of the bed. That's when she noticed the dark stains. They were all over everything, even his pants and her entire pelvic area. "I'm sorry," she quickly said, looking up at him with embarrassment and fear in her eyes.

Baphomet reached forward and ran the backs of his fingers of one bound hand down her cheek, assuring her, "No worries, sweet. We can clean up later. For now, though, we need sleep."

Lisa pulled up onto her knees and then off the bed, shaking her head. "No-no," she said. "We've got the water in the pitcher I can use to clean us up."

Baphomet watched silently as she poured the water into the glass he'd used earlier and then she found a wash cloth in the attached wash room and returned to the bedside.

She was lithe, he realized, as he watched her move. Her actions were graceful and beautiful to watch and he found himself hardening slightly again, just from watching her. She wet the cloth and then twisted it and crumpled it up between her hands to warm it before touching his skin with it. It was still a bit cool when she finally placed it against his heated flesh, but he managed not to flinch.

Lisa rubbed and scrubbed softly at his skin, delighting in touching him so intimately. She set the wet cloth aside for a moment to remove his remaining clothing so she could finish bathing him. She'd have to rinse out his pants as soon as possible before the stain set in, she determined as she dragged them off him.

He compliantly lifted his legs when she needed and was soon just as nude as she. Well, except for the shirt that still clung to his upper arms. She couldn't remove it without destroying the shirt because of the bindings, so she left it alone.

She returned to her task of cleaning and had him spotless, except for the few remaining dark bruises from his beating, in just a few minutes. Then, she pulled up onto her knees to wash herself.

Baphomet watched as her hands moved over her body and he felt himself hardening even more. His mouth was suddenly very dry and he ached to touch her, but he knew where that would lead. The fact that she'd come to him as a virgin meant he would have to give her body time to recover before he took her again. And, take her he would, again and again.

His appetite for her had not decreased in the least from their experience together. Instead, he found he was now starved for her touch and only by taking her time and again would he slake his need of her, if then.

Lisa finished cleaning herself, got rid of the glass of water and washcloth in the wash room, where she also managed to quickly rinse out his clothes, and returned to the bed. After pulling the covers up to cover him securely, she climbed beneath them herself to lie down next to him. He raised his arms to encircle her upper torso and she turned to rest her cheek against his chest, drawing a leg up and across his thighs. He adjusted his body to a more comfortable position and she asked, "You okay?"

Baphomet sighed and nuzzled the top of her head. "I have you in my arms, sweet Lisa. All is perfect," he said simply.

However, he wasn't comfortable, he discovered a few minutes later. He moved, trying to get comfortable. He wanted to hold her, *really* hold her, but the bindings kept him from doing so. He understood his brothers' thinking. He just wished it wasn't necessary.

Lisa grunted as he moved yet again and lifted her head to look at him. "Couldn't they take those damned things off now?" she asked angrily. "I mean, I think we can rule out you harming me now, right?"

He cradled the back of her head with one big hand and stared her directly in the eyes as he solemnly said, "It is not safe, not for you or for them." After a moment's hesitation, he said, "My brothers are very intelligent men, sweet Lisa. They wish to protect you, even if you do not understand the danger you are in."

She stared down at him, eye to eye, taking measure of what he'd said. Then, she shook her head and said confidently, "You would never hurt me."

Baphomet pulled her closer to kiss her forehead, closing his eyes and wishing what she said could somehow be true. After a moment, he whispered, "You do not know that for certain, my heart. I could do so many things to harm you."

Lisa settled in against him again and softly said, "No, you won't... ever. I can feel it."

Baphomet cradled her in his arms as best he could, rubbing his chin across the crown of her head so slowly she was soon breathing evenly in a deep sleep. All was quiet in his mind and he marveled at the effect of her energies on him. He'd never experienced such calming quiet and his usually-tense muscles relaxed for the first time in eons. His head wasn't even hurting very much anymore. Soon, his own breathing evened out and a blessedly quiet sleep overcame him.

∞

It was several hours later when Baphomet awakened, judging by the weak rays of morning sunlight filtering in through the only window in the room. Lisa's still-sleeping form remained snuggled up against him and Baphomet blinked in confusion as he wondered what had wakened him. He felt something wet drip onto his upper arm and he carefully moved without waking Lisa to see what it was.

Immediately, his heart began racing as he caught sight of a thick river of blood cascading forth from Lisa's back. "Uhn!" he grunted in shock. Then, he started screaming, "Help! Help me! Help!" He screamed, until he finally heard footsteps in the hallway outside the room.

Mere seconds had passed before the door was ripped open and Israfil and Mikhail rushed inside, followed closely by Sarah and the damned Angelic physician Baphomet had met previously.

As the four people stood staring in stupefaction at all the blood on the girl and the bed before them, Baphomet bellowed, "Help her, damn you! Can you not see she needs help?"

He raised his arms as best he could without disturbing her, tears streaming down his face, and as soon as she was free of his arms he got as far away from her still-bleeding form as he could, wondering what on earth he could've done to her to cause her to bleed so. Was she dead? He finally managed to get up off the bed, uncaring of being nude in front of everyone.

Baphomet walked over to stand in the farthest corner of the room from the bed and leaned his head into it, wondering what kind of monster he'd become. If he'd killed her, what was to become of him? She had become his very essence and he'd killed her, or at least mortally wounded her!

His brothers should have taken more precautions against this kind of eventuality! They knew what a monster he was! They knew, yet they'd allowed her to remain with him! Rage toward them suddenly filled his mind and he trembled with it. If she died, he would kill them all!

As this thought solidified in his mind, a cold, soft hand fell on his shoulder and he jerked around to see two brightly-glowing eyes staring up at him. *She's fine*, Sarah's voice said in his mind.

Baphomet directed an incredulous gaze toward the bloody scene on the bed where Israfil and the Angelic physician were attending to Lisa's still form and he frowned in confusion. She was still not moving and it appeared blood still seeped from the upper portion of her back, just between her shoulder blades.

Her body is evolving into that of a Seraph, Sarah's voice continued in his mind. Baphomet's eyes darted back to Sarah's face as he recalled the vision of her memories of the issues she'd endured after coming to live in the Angelic realm. Her body had changed, bleeding from between her shoulder blades as her spinal nodule and cutapi formed on the outside. Her six shields had formed inside just as quickly.

Baphomet recalled also the memory of Mikhail being knocked across the room immediately after Sarah's shields had formed and a lop-sided grin flashed across his face, even as Mikhail stepped between Sarah and him, clearing his throat and wrapping a blanket around his brother's nude form.

Baphomet chuckled and turned back toward the bed, completely ignoring Mikhail. The bindings on his wrists suddenly fell silently to the floor and he quickly turned back to Sarah. Mikhail stood behind her, his right arm wrapped around her chest, his left around her waist. Baphomet ignored him still, but as realization dawned, he bowed slightly to Sarah in thanks, and then turned back to see to Lisa.

Israfil looked up at his approach, his eyes narrowing as he noticed Baphomet was no longer bound, but he didn't remark on the observation. Baphomet ignored him, too, as he pushed past his brother to take a seat on the bloodied mattress next to Lisa's unconscious form.

The Angelic physician on the other side of the bed was cleaning the area around the open wound on Lisa's back and

Baphomet realized the bleeding seemed to be coming to an end as the skin there sealed itself up and her newly-formed cutapi came to rest peacefully over her fully-formed spinal nodule.

"She should rest now," the Angel stated as he finished up.

"Not here," Baphomet said. "I shall take her back to Shaitan territory, now that she is Seraph."

"She is in no state to travel," the physician asserted matter-of-factly. "You may move her to another room here, certainly, but that is the most I will allow."

Baphomet immediately reacted, ready for a fight, but once again Sarah's voice sounded in his mind, saying, *You must think of her safety, Baphomet. There's plenty of room here for you both and you're welcome to stay as long as you like.* He shot a glance back to where Mikhail still stood holding his woman. He hated the thought of accepting anything from Mikhail, but Sarah's voice persisted in his mind. *I welcome you here, my new brother,* me. *Nobody here's gonna oppose your presence in this complex as long as I endorse it.*

Baphomet wasn't sure how much, if any, of that Mikhail had been privy to, but he nodded once curtly and turned back to the physician, saying, "Fine. We shall move to another room here, but I am staying with her, myself – no one else!"

The physician nodded, his head bobbing up and down as he gathered his things together to leave. "I shall arrange everything with my assistants. Of course, it would be most ideal to have her stay at the infirmary where I could keep a close eye on her, but…"

Baphomet merely shook his head and the physician said, "I thought as much. I shall arrange for her to be moved to…" Again, Baphomet shook his head and the physician pursed his lips and then nodded, saying, "Very well. You move her to whatever room my assistants arrange for you. But, be careful with her!"

178

Baphomet glared at the Angel.

The physician merely shook his head and moved off to confer with his assistants awaiting him just outside the room.

Baphomet reached out to softly run his fingers over the newly-formed skin covering Lisa's spinal nodule. The cutapi looked as if it had been there all along, since her birth. He recalled the searing pain he'd learned Sarah had experienced during the formation of her own spinal nodule and cutapi. He wondered if Lisa had suffered while he'd slept soundly beside her. The thought had him cursing himself nine times a fiend.

He closed his eyes and wished he had the decency to leave her so she'd be safe, but he knew he never would. Never! She belonged to him, almost as much as he felt he belonged to her.

The sound of someone clearing his throat nearby brought Baphomet out of his reverie and he looked around to see Israfil standing a few feet away, watching him. Baphomet's first instinct was to express his anger at Israfil's recent behavior and actions that had led to Baphomet's capture in the first place.

However, as he studied his brother, he heard Sarah's voice once again in his mind and she informed him it had been Israfil who'd called the Angelic physician to come to the room earlier and that it was Israfil who was keeping Lisa asleep during all the painful changes that were going on within her body. The information coming from Sarah soon had Baphomet understanding that Israfil had actually been waiting just outside the room, monitoring Lisa's and Baphomet's energies for hours, in anticipation of this very thing happening.

Baphomet didn't know what to say. He hadn't expected... he had thought his brothers hated him. Suriyah's words about Mikhail came back to him and he wondered, *What if...?*

He swallowed a lump in his throat and said, "Th-Thank you for bringing the physician... and for helping her."

"Hantsushept," Israfil stated, completely ignoring the second part of his brother's thanks. "His name is Hantsushept, and he is a colossal pain in the ass, but a damned good physician. And, you are welcome... brother." After a moment of staring at him in an odd manner, Israfil turned and left the room without another word.

Baphomet blinked, frowning as he thought of his brother's words. He looked around and found Mikhail and Sarah still standing where they'd been before in the same position, and he wondered how anyone with so much energy coursing through their bodies could stay so still for so long. He could almost hear the energy vibrations from them all the way across the room.

Watching the two of them there, their glowing eyes seemingly staring blindly outward, was almost eerie and Baphomet wondered if that was where Lisa and he were headed, evolutionarily speaking. The two across the room had such power!

Baphomet looked back to Lisa's still-sleeping form. He didn't want to think about what might happen between her and him. He just wanted to know she was safe and to be with her.

Another Angel approached the bed and smiled nervously at Baphomet. He merely glared at the man. After taking a cautious step back, the Angel said, "If you will just bring the patient, sir, I shall show you to her quarters."

Baphomet nodded once to him and carefully gathered Lisa into his arms, surrounding her with the blanket he wore as gently as he could without waking her. She stirred once, but soon settled in next to his warm chest.

He followed the silent Angel down a couple of corridors to a set of rooms triple the size of the room in which he'd been confined earlier. There was a lounge area complete with two sofas, two comfortable-looking wing-backed chairs, a fireplace, an entertainment center and a wet bar. Off to the right was a door leading to what looked to be a large washroom. In the corner was another door, along the back wall, that led to a room where a huge four-poster king-sized bed could be seen.

Baphomet immediately went and laid Lisa down, covering her with the soft covers on the new bed, tucking them gently up under her chin. He was glad she slept on. After all their physical activity of earlier and the physical changes she'd just been through, he knew her body needed the rest.

The Angel waiting just inside the door of the first room softly cleared his throat to get Baphomet's attention. Once the Seraph returned to him, he said, "I will show you to your rooms, now, if you would like to follow me?"

Baphomet shook his head. "You may inform your master," he said quietly as he moved toward the man, "that, like I said, I shall be residing here with my mate." As Baphomet had advanced toward him, the Angel had backed up, so much so that by the time the Seraph was finished speaking, the Angel was already standing in the corridor outside the rooms. Baphomet gave him one nod and a plastic smile and then quietly closed and locked the door.

He then dropped the blanket he'd been wearing and went and crawled into bed beside his Lisa, covering them both up securely. Though she slept still, she snuggled up against his warm length, her arms wrapping around him, even as his wrapped around her.

Baphomet relaxed for the first time in hours and he lay there listening...

Chapter 13

Do we really seem so strange to everyone? It was Sarah's voice. Baphomet recognized it immediately.

Why would you think that? came Mikhail's response.

It's just that my parents and Thomas, and really all the others, look at us like we're some kind of freaks or something, every time they're around us. I mean, didn't you notice the way Baphomet was looking at us earlier?

Do not worry about what other people think, love. I think you are the most beautiful creature I have ever encountered, Mikhail responded sincerely.

Sarah was smiling at Mikhail. Baphomet could hear and feel it as she thought back to Mikhail in her mind's voice, *I am only considering how uncomfortable we seem to make other people. I, for one, could not wish for a sexier mate and wouldn't want him if he existed... especially when you do that one thing with your tongue.*

Baphomet received a mental image of what Sarah was talking about, complete with her recall of physical sensation and he wondered why his brother and Sarah were allowing him to listen in on such a private conversation.

At the experience of Sarah suddenly reaching climax, Baphomet jerked awake, half-sitting up on the bed as he came out of the dream. Lisa fell to his side and grunted as her head plopped onto the mattress. Baphomet instantly turned to comfort her. He was unbelievably embarrassed by what he'd just witnessed. Surely, they knew?

Lisa stirred, opening her eyes and stretching full-length before him. After a moment of just comfortably lying next to him, some instinct within her picked up on his discomfort and she reached up to cup his cheek as she asked, "Where are you?"

After a moment's hesitation, he smiled down at her, reaching to cover her hand with his, and saying, "I am right here with you, my heart."

She looked around and frowned, asking, "Where are *we*?"

Baphomet snuggled down next to her and nuzzled her neck. "That other room was not fit for my queen," he said, "so I had us moved here." He reached up to run a hand through her long hair up along the back of her head. It was surprisingly tangle-free and smooth and very easy for his fingers to comb through.

"Hey!" she said, as she finally noticed he was unbound. "How did you get loose?"

He kissed the tip of her nose and smiled gently. "Do not worry, sweet. I did not escape. My brother's mate freed me from the binders," he explained.

Lisa frowned again and pulled away from him, sitting up to turn and look down at him, asking, "How long was I asleep?"

He reached up to tuck a few strands of her dark hair behind her ear. "A while," he simply said, not ready yet to explain everything to her.

They stared at each other.

So beautiful...

"What was that?" Lisa demanded, frowning.

"What?" Baphomet asked, completely at a loss as to what she meant.

How could I ever become worthy of her?

"That!" Lisa growled in exasperation. "How are you talking in my head?"

Baphomet stilled. *You can hear me?* He silently asked.

Lisa's eyes widened as she stared at him. She nodded, even as she thought, *Yes.*

After a moment, his face slowly curled into a grinning mask of pleasure and he reached up to pull her down to him for a hungry kiss. The moment their lips met, he was on fire. He coaxed her mouth open and his tongue plunged inside, taking and returning all the emotion he felt for her. It wasn't enough. He grabbed her and rolled her onto her back, under him.

More, sweet Lisa…, more! he silently screamed.

Yes! came her husky voice in his mind and her hands seemed to be everywhere at once.

I cannot get enough of you, Leece! he thought. *Gods! I'm sorry. I need to be inside you, now!* He positioned himself above her and smoothly entered, plunging deeply into her waiting depths, growling aloud at the feel of sliding past her tight inner structures. As her muscles contracted around him, he looked into her eyes, marveling at the glimpse of heaven he caught within their depths. The swirling black pools of her pupils suddenly seemed to take on an iridescence deep within and his own eyes widened in wonder.

Lisa's eyes widened as she looked back directly into his eyes and he heard her in his mind. *How did you make your eyes do that?* her voice asked.

Baphomet didn't want to talk with her about their physiological changes yet, and so he bent and kissed her deeply. *No talking now,* he silently told her as he picked up the pace of his movements inside her.

Lisa wrapped her legs and arms around him, pulling him deeper inside her cool well of sensation and soon the only thing either of them heard was the other's grunts as they each got caught up in the rhythm.

Lisa tightened, sensation becoming all, her vision eclipsed by a thick gray fog over a backdrop of space until suddenly there was a cacophony of voices coming from everywhere. She heard everything like before, but on a much broader scale and she screamed aloud at the pressure generated inside her mind.

Her scream was in tandem with Baphomet's as the voices of every being in existence crowded into his mind as well. The two of them rushed in a fever to escape the wave of sound and then, as a supernova blasted across the entire known universe, both of them screamed in a gut-wrenching release and there was a sudden, all-encompassing silence as Baphomet collapsed upon her.

Each lay still, breathing as deeply as they could, shaken and afraid to move for fear of the wall of voices returning.

Baphomet didn't understand what was happening to him. He moved, pulling out of her liquid coolness and turning onto his back, hugging her tightly, protectively to his side as she settled in comfortably next to him.

He trembled as he wondered how he could be feeling so much for this person. They'd spent so little time together, yet he felt as if she had been with him for an eternity. She was part of him, as if his very soul had never before been complete until he'd first touched her.

From somewhere in the depths of his mind came the images he'd gleaned from within Sarah's mind of her visions of what had once been and, as he lay cradling his Lisa closely within his strong arms, he took himself even farther into the visions until he found a unit of energy more familiar to his soul than anything else ever could be.

He watched as strange beings forced the energy unit apart and changed one half of it into his now-familiar form on the surface of the planet. The other half remained floating near his form for a very long time… an eternity, it seemed, until it was then taken by the same beings, manipulated, and forced into an alternate form in a separate dimension on the planet.

Then, more memories of his own transformation came crowding into his mind. That's when Baphomet realized he was observing himself being "born" into the world. He remembered that he could see with his eyes and he looked around only to observe the planet from its surface for the first time. Mikhail was there, though he was larger than Baphomet, and he took Baphomet up into his arms and nurtured him and protected him, just as the strange beings had done to *him*.

All was very confusing for the longest time and there was still an all-encompassing pain that was felt for a very long time. As Baphomet aged, he realized these were growing pains and that his physical body was evolving into its adult form. His bones and muscles were lengthening and new proteins were forming and circulating throughout his body, causing change after change.

In time, Baphomet stopped struggling to get out of the body he inhabited, for it had become his soul's home, like a shell that grew with him. The half of the energy unit that he was became comfortable residing within its new shell and Baphomet took it upon himself to explore and to do and to experience as much as his physical body possibly could on the planet.

He came to know other Seraphim, those he claimed as his siblings. They did everything together and they watched over each other, protecting each other and nurturing each new one that came along. As time passed, he realized the vision of himself he was watching had forgotten the other half of the energy unit to which he used to be connected.

One day, the Seraphim found a new thing on the planet's surface, something they'd never seen before. It was different from them, but similar in a way. Then, just after they'd discovered this new thing, one of the strange creatures that had taken each one of the Seraphim from their stationary orbit around the planet appeared beside the new thing. The creature made it known to the Seraphim that this new thing was an Angel and that it would require the Seraphim to watch over it and to protect and nurture it as they had each other.

These new beings, these Angels, the creature explained, were to act as guides and helpers for the Seraphim for when their other halves finally made it through the processor. Then the Angels would lead each Seraph to his or her one true mate and they would be united. The Angels were to help the united couple through the changes they would then experience until complete evolution had been achieved.

Baphomet did not think to ask questions at this point because he was so very fascinated with the tiny Angel the creature had delivered to them. It was only after the strange creature had vanished again that Baphomet realized it had left a lot of unanswered questions among the Seraphim. Not one of them had any idea what a true mate was or even what that meant. All they knew was that there was now a being on this planet they all needed to look after.

The strange creatures came again and again, delivering more and more of the little Angel beings, until one day, they just stopped showing up. The little Angel beings grew into adulthood and then a very strange thing happened to one of them.

It was a female Angel named Epinoia, the first female Angel to have been delivered upon the planet by the strange creatures, who came forward to the Seraphim with what looked to them to be a physical ailment. Her midsection had swelled to such a degree that it appeared she might burst open and there was liquid spewing forth from between her legs.

This was the first birth of an Angel any of them had ever witnessed on the planet. It was the first time any of the Seraphim realized such a thing was possible. It was also the beginning of the end of hope for the Seraphim.

Baphomet was the first to try mating with an Angel. He tried and tried with Angel after Angel, but none conceived from unions with him. Soon, it was discovered all the Seraphim were mating with Angels. That was when it was discovered no Seraphim could conceive with one.

At that time, and only once, the idea that one Seraph might be able to mate with another Seraph to produce was brought up. No one wanted to be the one to do it, however, as they all worshipped the ground upon which Suriyah walked and the idea was very quickly thrown out.

It was hundreds of eons later that Mikhail, Suriyah, and Baphomet discovered a rift between dimensions leading to the human realm. It was quite by accident and they were not sure what they'd discovered until they actually encountered a human being.

The thing reminded them of young Angels, but it was very weak. The three of them thought it *was* an Angel and that there was something wrong with it. They followed it, wondering if there was something they could do to help it. However, when the creature finally reached its destination, the Seraphim discovered it was one of many of the same type of creature it was.

Some of the creatures lived in crude shelters, barely sturdy enough to keep the elements at bay. Some, the Seraphim were to learn later, lived in magnificent large cities built of stone and wood in many new and interesting styles. Their cultures were wildly varied and the Seraphim fell in love with the creatures immediately.

Again, Baphomet was the first to try mating with one of these new creatures. It worked, but the resulting offspring was stillborn. He tried again and again, but each time resulted in the same outcome. By that time, however, Baphomet had found himself enthralled by the tiny creature with which he'd been mating.

He took her into his confidences and told her all about the Angelic dimension, though he could not be certain she understood any of what she was told. His relationship with Lilith had soured after the fifth pregnancy attempt and she'd left him.

∞

Baphomet's breathing became labored as he realized what he'd just remembered. He didn't want to remember his time with Lilith. She had not been his true mate. His thoughts returned to the memories of being "processed" and he realized that was the last time he had been with his true mate.

Baphomet railed inwardly at those strange, glowing beings for having split him and his Lisa apart for so long. A hatred for them so strong and pure filled his very soul and he nearly cringed at the intensity of it, fearing that it would take over every part of his being, until suddenly, all the intense emotion that had been building within him just seemed to disappear.

He realized he was somehow connected to Lisa all of a sudden on such a basic level that he couldn't tell where he stopped and she began. A calmness the likes of which he'd never before experienced overcame him as he realized there was no him or her, there was only them.

They were once again one unit, but infinitely stronger than before. There was far more knowledge and insight than there'd been before and the bonding securing the unit was stronger than any force in existence.

She was there with him. He could feel her mind joining with his and he relaxed. His mind continued on its quest through the past, allowing Lisa access to the same memories he was seeing. Baphomet and all the other Seraphim spent millennia searching for meaning in their lives. They needed to know why they had been put upon this planet to live forever. They seemed to be the strongest and most superior creatures to inhabit the planet, but there was a great dark emptiness in their lives.

Mikhail, Suriyah, and Baphomet were again out one day when they came upon a different type of creature. It was a scouting envoy of the blessed Great Designers. Mikhail saw the creature's strength and immediately wanted to have contact with it, to communicate with it, to find out if it was as strong as it appeared, and to learn what he could from it.

Suriyah was immediately suspicious of the creature. Baphomet caught the tone of her suspicions within the thoughts he could hear from her. The more suspicious she became, the more Baphomet felt obligated to delve into this new creature's thoughts to learn for himself exactly what they were dealing with. Baphomet had always been very talented at accessing others' thoughts and he held nothing back as he pushed into the creature's mind that day. He couldn't understand the exact words it used, but Baphomet caught the general tone of everything the creature was thinking, and it was not anything good.

When Suriyah and Baphomet confronted Mikhail with their suspicions, he merely assured them they felt that way simply because this creature was so new and unknown to them. He explained to them that it was normal to fear the unknown and to wish to exercise caution where the creature was concerned. As time passed, however, and more and more of the creatures arrived on the planet, Suriyah and Baphomet's suspicions only increased. By then, however, it was too late to convince the others that the creatures were not what they seemed.

The very first task the creatures had set about accomplishing had been to convince Baphomet's brothers that all

Seraphim had been created by them. Baphomet recalled that none of the creatures was ever able to offer a believable explanation as to why all Seraphim and Angels had been created within the one dimension, while all humans had been created within an all together different dimension, nor why the humans were not immortal as were the Seraphim and Angels. The idea that the Seraphim had somehow found an opening into the other dimension and each and every one of them, along with all the Angels, had chosen to go live in that other dimension because they couldn't stand living within the human dimension with humans never sat well with either Suriyah or Baphomet.

Then, one day when Mikhail, Suriyah, and Baphomet had been at a place called Lemuria in the human realm, one of Enki's squadron of lackeys had arrived on the scene and, without a word of notice or concern for anyone, they'd begun collecting "specimens" to be taken to one of the mines the Designers used to obtain precious minerals from deep within the earth. Suriyah had long suspected the Designers were using humans for just such purposes, but she'd never been around to actually witness them in the act. Now, however, she was there, as were Mikhail and Baphomet, and they all witnessed the Designers' brutality.

Somehow, they managed to save a small portion of the humans who'd lived in the town. However, a good many of the villagers had perished in the flood resulting from the Designers' arrival on the scene. The rest who either did not die or could not make it to the hiding places with the three Seraphim were taken by the Designers to become slaves in the mines. Baphomet was sure of it.

Suriyah and he had used every argument they could think of to convince their siblings that the brutal act of the Designers proved they were not the benevolent beings they claimed to be. All, however, was to no avail and Suriyah and Baphomet were soon ordered to be banished for all time from Seraphim City.

What did you do then? asked Lisa's voice within Baphomet's mind.

He squeezed her close within his arms, thinking back to those dreadful first days of their banishment. He didn't want her to know of the anger, the jealousy, the hatred that had developed within him and his kind during that period.

Lisa rubbed a hand gently across his right breast and thought, *I don't blame you for those thoughts and feelings, Baphomet. I imagine I would have had similar thoughts and feelings, myself. In fact, I did, if you'll recall. When my father told me there was no Wodoi for me and that I was not to be allowed to live within the tribe? It was the same for me. I was very angry and jealous of all those who got to stay while I was forced to leave.*

I suppose, Baphomet silently told her. He lay there holding her, seeing the memories she was replaying in her mind of that time in her life. He wished he could have been there for her to help ease the pain he now felt she'd experienced during that time. Then, somehow, their two minds meshed so well together that they were soon tumbling back through memories of each and every one of her lifetimes on the planet. Sometimes she was male, sometimes female. Sometimes her life span was very short, sometimes it had been very, very long.

At the end of each lifetime she'd experienced, there would always be a bright light seen as her soul energy left the human body it had occupied. This was similar to what many humans who had reported near death experiences had described and which scientists had yet been able to fully explain. Lisa and Baphomet came to understand that this was an amalgamation of all the soul energies of all the others of her kind crowded together around the outside of the planet, waiting to have their chance down on the planet's surface.

192

Lisa could recall faces and specific bodies of those whom she'd known down on the surface of the planet. When first she would return from a lifetime on the planet, she would see these familiar faces and bodies. Eventually, however, as she recovered from the time she'd spent on the surface of the planet, those familiar faces and bodies would revert back to just a collection of glowing energy.

Lisa came to understand that what was happening was her mind could not change the way it thought of things and people it had known down on the planet's surface so quickly. It took time before her consciousness would return to thinking and comprehending things the way it had before she'd gone down onto the planet and spent time there as a human being. Eventually, her mind would forget how things had been there and the way she understood things would change back to how the basic energy forms surrounding her understood them.

In the end, both Baphomet and Lisa experienced her energy's first time through the strange creatures' "processor" when she was first sent down to the surface of the planet. Lisa and Baphomet both felt an incredible rage building within themselves toward the strange creatures who'd split up their single energy unit. They were angry for the fact that the creatures had put them into two separate dimensions when they'd forced them down onto the planet's surface. How irresponsible could one race of beings be?

As one, they tightened their grips on each other to ease the other one's suffering. It was over now. They were together and nothing and no one would be able to separate them ever again. They each sighed as this knowledge coursed through their joined minds. They were together. They would never part.

Baphomet's physical form opened its eyes at the same time Lisa's did and they gasped in unison as each took in the sight of a brilliant glow from within the other's eyes. Their eyes widened as long, white strands of hair seemed to come to life around each of them.

Where there had been long-ish blond hair before hanging from Baphomet's head, there were now much longer pure white strands. Lisa's hair was the most striking, however. The even longer white strands standing out against her dark skin color made a visually stunning picture. The individual strands from each person touched the strands of the other person, sometimes intertwining, sometimes merely touching, as if making love with each other on some hair-level.

There'd been no building up to this, no transitional period. The two of them had simply gone into this as separate entities and come out as one whole.

Only a second passed before both looked down at Lisa's abdomen simultaneously, as the memory of what had happened to Sarah flashed suddenly through their combined consciousness, and they found themselves fascinated by the tiny pinprick of light showing through Lisa's dark skin from within her form's core.

Baphomet reached to run his fingers over the skin covering the light, swallowing a huge lump in his throat. It was warmer than he, even, and the idea of it hurting his other half flashed through his mind. However, almost before the idea could even finish forming, he knew Lisa felt no pain. He could sense her elation, knew it as his own, and he closed his eyes as a peacefulness stole over them both.

Chapter 14

Sarah sighed. From behind her, Mikhail reached up to lightly rub her neck. His other arm was under her head acting as her pillow, as it usually did when they were in bed. It was strange, Mikhail reflected, thinking how different their lives had become since they'd found each other.

Before, he'd had so much undirected energy, just wasting away. He'd sent it wherever and however he could to fill his days and nights, sometimes with others, but most of the time alone.

I don't need to know everything, you know, he suddenly heard her voice in his mind and he smiled. It pleased him to know she was jealous with him. But he wouldn't dwell on thoughts of the Angels who'd helped him get through his eternity of loneliness before Sarah had come along.

Thank you, her voice said sarcastically in his mind. He relaxed a little more behind her, his lips barely curving upward at the corners in a smile, his thoughts turning back to his brother, Baphomet. He and his mate were going to be fine, though Mikhail worried that Baphomet might still have a few lingering anger issues due to their history.

We'll work through it together, he heard Sarah's soft thoughts saying in his mind, as she squeezed the arm covering her front. He closed his eyes as he leaned in to brush a kiss across the nape of her neck. How soft and sweet-smelling her skin was! He rubbed his lips over her skin, wondering how he could still feel this much for her on the physical level.

Her very essence was already so much an integral part of his being that he didn't understand his physical need for more of her, yet it was there, and it seemed to be increasing with each minute he spent in her company. She was the air for him inside the vacuum that was the universe. That was how vital she had become to his life.

As have you to my life, my love, her voice silently rippled across the surface of his mind's well. Opening his eyes and looking his other half over, he realized everything would be fine. They would work with Baphomet and Lisa in whatever way they could to assist with their transformations.

Just then, an image of Azra'il flashed through Mikhail's mind and the mood soured. He immediately erected what he thought was a powerful buffer between Sarah and him to keep it from affecting her the same as it had him.

As soon as Sarah felt him withdrawing from her, of course, she erected an impenetrable buffer to allow him his privacy. It irked her, though, that he still didn't feel as if he could trust her enough to share everything with her.

Hypocrite, an inner voice whispered. She was not telling Mikhail about her fears for the rest of her family members still living in the human realm, so she was just as guilty of not trusting him as he was of not trusting her.

Mikhail's voice suddenly brought her back to the here and now, as he said in a low voice, "I want you to promise me something."

Sarah rubbed the arm she held and waited for him to continue.

"If anything should ever happen to me, I want you to promise that you will go on and…"

"And, what?" she asked, turning a little to look him in the eyes, her body tensing up just at the thought of anything ever happening to him.

"I want you to mate with Israfil," he quietly finished.

Sarah was stunned! *"What*?" she shrieked.

Mikhail squeezed her tightly and explained, "The council will not stand for what has happened without demanding that Azra'il take action against us. We are all good fighters, yes, but I do not think even *we* could combat an entire army of Angels. And, even if we were to somehow, miraculously, be able to fend them off the first time they attacked, they would eventually return, and they would have better weapons when they did." He pulled her around to face him as he pushed up onto his elbow. "Look," he continued, "I just want to make sure that you and Sheely and Thomas will be well taken care of if anything should ever happen to me."

Sarah looked off away from him, wondering what on earth could have brought on this conversation. She didn't even want to *think* about not having him with her. She didn't want to think about the possibility of him ever dying and her remaining alive. He was her life. He was the very air itself to her. The idea even of any other man touching her made her skin crawl. How could she agree to mate with Israfil?

She shook her head and asked, "Wh-Why would you ask me to mate with Israfil? I mean, I can understand you asking me to continue on for the kids' sakes, but... mating with Israfil? Why?"

Mikhail sighed and said, "Because of *his* suffering." When Sarah merely frowned at him, he continued, explaining, "I consider myself one of the luckiest beings in existence because I have found my one true mate. My brother, Baphomet, seems to have found his, as well. I do not know if this has been by design or mere chance, but you know Israfil's history. He is not to be as lucky as his siblings. If something should happen to me, I would like to know that the one person I trust above all others to look after my mate and children would also then have a chance at experiencing at least some of the happiness I have been allowed to experience with you. I love my brother and I love you and, if that is the only way in which I can help to ease both people's pains, then I am willing to do so – if you are."

Sarah stared at him as she contemplated what he'd said.

"Sarah, my heart," he continued. "You and I both know if something ever happens to one of us, it will be very difficult for the one who survives. You will need someone if I am the one who goes first and Israfil is one of the kindest and most protective souls I know on this planet. He loves children and I know he would be good for you *and* for the children."

Sarah closed her eyes and, shaking her head a little, said, "I don't want to talk about this anymore. I'll-I'll think about what you said, but I just don't want to talk about it anymore." She turned back over onto her side, putting her back to his front again, and tried to clear her mind of everything in order to go back to sleep.

Mikhail pushed his arm back up under her head and lay back down on his side, pulling her closer again so that there was no space between their bodies on the bed. He wished he could let down the buffer between them so he would be able to hear her thoughts. He disliked having any barriers between them, but he was too afraid she would discover the other thing he was trying to keep from her if he took down the buffer right now. Sarah, he had learned, became far more powerful when she was upset about things than when she was calm. It was just one of her quirks, he guessed, because he knew most people worked the opposite way.

Just then, there was some sort of flash or image on the edges of his mind and Mikhail paused, searching for some clue as to what it could have been. "Too fast, I couldn't catch it," Sarah's soft voice echoed from in front of him.

It had been like this since their consciousnesses had joined. Sarah was used to receiving flashes and visions, but Mikhail just couldn't seem to get used to getting a quick glimpse of something and then having to figure out an entire story from the tiny bit of information he'd been shown. He thought it odd that he would still be receiving the flashes even though he'd erected a buffer between their minds, but he didn't dwell on that fact.

He bent in to softly kiss the back of her neck again, allowing his nose to rub gently across her delicate white skin. It didn't matter what the flash had been about. Perhaps they'd be shown the images again, perhaps not. This was the way of things. As long as Sarah and Sheely were all right and they were all together, Mikhail knew all would resolve itself eventually.

∞

"What do you think it will be?" Lisa asked absently as she rubbed Baphomet's new white hair. They were lazily lying in bed with him on top of her. Well, his head was lying to one side on her lower abdomen while the rest of him was situated between her legs. He'd been like that for the past hour and a half, just listening, trying to hear anything from the little dot of light there. So far, there'd been nothing.

"Hey," she prompted when there was no answer.

"Hmmm?" he asked absently.

"What do you think it will be? A boy or a girl?" she asked.

"Yes," he said.

Lisa chuckled, making his head bounce up and down a little with the movement of her lower abdomen. After a moment, she said, "Well, I want a boy. I want him to be tall and handsome, just like his dad."

Baphomet's head came up and he stared at her in silence for a moment. "A son," he finally said with a soft catch in his voice.

Lisa caught the drift of his thoughts and she reached for him immediately, pulling him up and half climbing onto him as she embraced him in a tight hug. "You'll be an amazing father, Baphomet," she whispered. "I know you will." She could feel him trembling and she squeezed harder, trying to pour assurance into the man she loved.

Baphomet instantly jerked back from her. They both lay there, each staring intently at the other. Baphomet swallowed a giant lump in his throat and silently asked, *You love me?*

Slowly, Lisa nodded as a shy smile tugged at the corners of her lips. *I didn't even know it until now*, she silently informed him. It took a moment, but finally Baphomet managed a soft smile for her, reaching to gently touch her beautiful face. It was odd seeing her glowing eyes staring out at him with her white hair against the contrast of her dark skin. But it was exciting, too.

Just touching her had him instantly ravenous for her, though, and he quickly rolled her back over onto her back so that he could settle in on top of her to give her a long, deep, slow kiss. He just as quickly jumped off of her, however, when he thought about the baby.

"What if it hurts it?" he asked.

Lisa looked down at the little dot of light weakly peeking through her skin. She didn't know anything about babies. She'd never been around any that she could remember. Had she been allowed to be raised within the tribe, she would have known all there was to know about kids, but she'd been raised outside the tribe, in the city.

She shook her head and asked, "Did Sarah tell you anything about her kid?"

Baphomet thought for a moment. "I have her thoughts, her memories, her emotions from the time she spent with Mikhail before," he told her. He sifted through the information Sarah had once shown him.

His eyes brightened as he finally came to the bit about humans being okay to make love up until the third trimester. It was only a momentary elation, however, as another thought suddenly occurred to him, and he asked, "Have you heard the baby, yet?"

Lisa slowly shook her head as her mind-link with him gave her access to the same thoughts and memories Baphomet had been sifting through. Realization dawned and they both looked back down at the tiny glowing dot with concern.

"Do you think there's something wrong?" Lisa asked in a tiny, frightened voice.

Baphomet immediately reached for her, pulling her into his arms and kissing her temple as he assured her, whispering, "Shh. I am sure everything is just fine, love." Doubts of his own crashed through his mind as he rubbed Lisa's back to comfort her. Their hair entwined together and all the strands seemed to sense Lisa's unease as they moved to rub at her temples and shoulders and back.

Lisa absently pushed them aside as she caught the drift of Baphomet's thoughts and she pulled back to stare in mortified horror at him, tearfully demanding, "What's wrong with our baby?"

Baphomet quickly pulled her close again, pressing her cheek against his chest as he soothed her, "Nothing. There is absolutely nothing wrong with our baby." When she merely continued crying, he pushed her gently away from him, grabbing both of her upper arms and giving her a slight shake, saying, "Listen. I am going to go get that Hantsushept guy and... and that kid, Sarah's kid, the boy. He can talk with Sarah and

Mikhail's baby, right? Maybe he would be able to talk with ours."

Lisa caught the memory of when the boy, Thomas, had informed the others he could communicate with Sarah's baby, Sheely, and a small sense of hope suddenly sprang to life within her. "You think he would do that for us?" she asked.

Baphomet hesitantly nodded. "I think so," he said. Then, a thought occurred to him and his voice strengthened as he said, "I shall go get my brother, Israfil, first and he will help convince the boy to come."

Lisa knew through Baphomet's memories and thoughts that this brother, Israfil, was one he trusted, and so she swallowed her fears and nodded, a small smile breaking across her tear-stained features. "Okay," she said.

Baphomet nodded and smiled reassuringly at her as he maneuvered himself up and off the bed. Donning some clothes someone had thought to place in the room before the two of them had arrived, it was only a moment before he was fully dressed and on his way out of the room.

Just before exiting, he looked back over his shoulder at Lisa as she lay alone in the big bed with the covers pulled tightly up under her arms. "Stay there and relax, sweet Lisa," he said. "I shall be back before you know it with the boy."

Lisa nodded and he left.

To Baphomet's surprise, he found Israfil lying on a cot in the hallway just outside the suite of rooms Baphomet and Lisa were sharing. Israfil immediately sat up and asked through a sleepy yawn if everything was all right.

"Why are you sleeping in the hallway?" Baphomet asked, and then the obvious answer came to him. He remembered that Sarah had said Israfil had been keeping tabs on Baphomet and Lisa since his return in case anything happened and they should suddenly need him. Baphomet felt terribly humbled before such graciousness from one he'd believed had hated him for millennia.

The fact that Israfil was still willing to play nursemaid to Baphomet and his mate after the last incident that had led them to this part of the house was overwhelming and he clapped his brother on the shoulder in thanks, giving a good hard squeeze to ensure his brother understood just how deeply appreciated the gesture was.

Israfil smiled a lop-sided smile up at him and said, "You would have done the same for me."

Baphomet's smile of appreciation faded a little. He wasn't so sure he would have done.

"You would have," Israfil assured him as he stood. "So," he continued, "what is going on?"

Baphomet quickly dismissed the useless thoughts of his former self and informed his brother of the reason he'd left his mate. As it turned out, Israfil knew exactly where to find both Hantsushept and the boy, Thomas, and the two brothers were soon rushing through the maze of hallways of the main house on their now-combined mission.

Hantsushept was the first to be found. If there was something physically wrong with the baby, Baphomet wanted the physician to be there. Baphomet didn't even want to *think* about the possibility of something being wrong with Lisa.

He knew all life on this planet was a miracle. He'd had enough lectures and stories from Suriyah and her Jinn to know that. She was always telling him how she was amazed any female survived pregnancy, let alone the actual birthing process itself. So much could go wrong.

Baphomet shuddered at the mere thought of it and he picked up his pace. Just as the two were almost to the physician's quarters, Baphomet felt the first stirring of the voices within his mind. That's also when he heard the first tiny whimper from Lisa within his mind. Not only was the wall of voices coming after him, it was coming after her, too. The only thing he could think was that he needed to get back to her to protect her in whatever way he could.

Baphomet stopped dead in his tracks. "I am sorry, Iz," he said. "I must ask another favor of you."

Israfil had, by this time, stopped and returned to stand by his brother's side, concern etched clearly across his features. "Of course," he immediately agreed. "Anything you need."

∞

Baphomet raced as fast as his legs would carry him through the maze of hallways. He wished for the millionth time he and Lisa were back in his mansion in Knor where he knew each and every square inch of the building by heart, but he then conceded that there they wouldn't have the luxury of having an Angelic physician who knew of their condition or the boy, Thomas, available to help in this situation.

The voices were now raging within his mind and he could barely even see to make his way down the hallway. He made two wrong turns and only found their suite of rooms by sheer accident, finally wrenching open the door and rushing inside.

Lisa was curled up into a fetal position, her arms clutching her head, covering her ears, as she softly cried. Baphomet fell onto the bed and grabbed her, turning her into his embrace and squeezing her as tightly as he could. Mere seconds had passed before the voices miraculously just faded into obscurity. "How did you do that?" Lisa softly asked after a minute of silence had passed.

Baphomet merely shook his head and brushed several errant strands of her glorious white hair from her forehead. It didn't make any difference. The strands returned immediately after he'd brushed them away. "I do not think I did anything," he whispered, caressing her cheek and neck. "I think just by being here with you, the voices could not get to us."

Lisa quickly grabbed a tight hold on him with both arms and urged, "Don't leave us again."

"Never!" Baphomet solemnly vowed.

∞

Thomas sighed in frustration. He'd been waiting for the past two hours for Nera to contact him. Where was she? He reached for a game controller lying on the table in front of the couch where he was sitting and, of course, that's when she finally chose to snatch his mind away from this dimension to wherever it was she existed.

She wasn't in the round room this time. It was the little garden area again with the bench and the cobbled stream running lazily nearby. Thomas liked this place. For some reason, he found it very familiar and peaceful, as if he'd spent many hours here with her.

Nera turned to regard him speculatively. After only a moment, she simply said, "You did."

After a moment's thought, Thomas nodded once and then looked around. Nera sat down on the bench, inviting him to come take a seat next to her, but Thomas felt an uneasy restlessness darting around inside him and he chose to keep on his feet. He walked around the little clearing for a short while, examining the flowers and trees, looking up at the sky.

"You were able to get the two together again, I saw," Nera softly said to break the silence.

Thomas nodded again, saying, "I had to get my parents to help. I don't know if it did any good, though, since I didn't get to go with them to see what happened when the guy was brought back."

"They are both doing quite well, actually," she supplied. "They are back on track to evolving into that which they need to be."

"You mean, they're becoming like my mom and dad."

Nera merely shrugged at this.

"So, their eyes are going to glow and their hair is going to turn completely white and long and be just as dangerous and freaky-looking as my parents' hair, huh?" Thomas asked.

Nera nodded, explaining, "They will transform, yes. Of course, no one can say how long this couple's transformation will take. Each coupling is different. It depends on how quickly their soul energies mesh back together to determine how long their physical bodies will take to transform. Some we have seen have transformed practically overnight, whereas others have taken weeks, if not months, to completely transform. One coupling I can think of even took as long as a full year."

"How come we've never heard of these couplings here before?" Thomas asked.

"On Earth?" Nera shook her head and said, "Because they were on other planets. There have never been any couplings here before, unless you want to count the..." She suddenly became oddly silent and looked away.

Thomas narrowed his eyes and studied her profile. Had his mom and Mikhail been together before? How could that be? Wouldn't they have already transformed to at least *some* degree, if they'd been together before, that is? Thomas shook his head.

That couldn't be right. There was no way he would have missed the changes in his mom all these years if she'd already transformed in some way. Then a thought occurred to him. What if the changes had been more on the inside than on the outside? If there had been things that had happened to her mind, instead of to her physical body, then would that not be something that could easily be kept from anyone else's eyes?

206

Just thinking the word "eyes" brought his thoughts around to those of his parents and Thomas suddenly asked Nera, "What's wrong with them? My parents, I mean." At her uncomprehending stare, Thomas approached the bench and took a seat next to her. Leaning forward, he continued, "I know we've talked about this before, but you never actually explained things to me. If I understand things correctly, here, all the Seraphim on this planet are meant to pair up with their individual human counterparts, right?" At Nera's cautious nod, he continued, saying, "And, if you and I knew each other before, then we used to be the same as them, right?"

Nera looked away. After a short silence, her voice came to him softly, as she explained, "No. You and I were never quite like them."

"What do you mean?" Thomas asked. When only silence confronted him, he reached over to grab her hand and softly demanded, "Nera, I need to know. If we weren't like them, then what – we came from some other place?"

Nera turned to look at him, nodding.

Thomas accepted this at face value and then continued, "Then we were once a Seraph and… whatever other species on another planet that eventually found our way together to transform into what you look like now?"

Nera nodded again, remaining silent, offering no more of an explanation to any of his suggestions.

"So, then I looked like you, at one point?" he asked.

Again, she merely nodded.

Thomas raked a hand through his thick brown hair and stood. Frustrated energy now raced through his body and he began pacing back and forth before Nera, barely even acknowledging her presence as he tried to figure things out in his mind. How could he have looked like her if he now looked like a human?

In the visions he'd had before, she'd told him that he had taught her how to fight with energy. It seemed he had also instructed her about things she should tell him now and things she shouldn't.

An idea suddenly had him standing directly in front of her demanding, "I order you to tell me everything you know about me!"

Nera threw a plastic smile up at him and said acidly, "Do you not think I would have already suggested that if it were a possibility? I cannot tell you anything more than I have already told you." At his look of utter frustration, she continued, explaining, "You were very specific about what could and could not be discussed. We do not know what kind of damage could be caused by exposing your mind to certain things before it is ready to deal with them."

"So, I'll be brain damaged!" he barked as he turned to pace a short distance away from her.

Nera stood and approached him. Laying a hand on his shoulder, she said softly, "I know you want to know more, but honestly, we just cannot risk losing this opportunity. Time is running out and you are our last hope."

Thomas turned to look at her. His eyes were on an even keel with hers, now. He'd grown so much over the past few weeks. In fact, it seemed almost as if she might be little shorter than he already. The absurdity of this thought had him shaking his head and he returned to the bench to sit, his elbows resting on his knees and his head cradled between both hands.

"You keep saying time is running out, that I need to remember things before it's too late," Thomas said without raising his head to look at her. "What does that mean? That there's some catastrophe coming and we're all gonna die if I can't remember everything you can't tell me?"

Nera sighed and came to sit by him again. "I can tell you this," she said. "We have to get all the Seraphim and their counterparts together before what is going to happen actually happens. If we do not, then all is lost and everything we have done will have been for nothing."

After a short pause, she finished, saying, "That is all I can tell you. The rest you must remember on your own and the only way to do that is for you to continue with your training. Once your mind and body are strong enough and have developed enough, you should remember everything, like you started to last time."

Thomas finally straightened and looked at her. "You've said that before, too," he said. "If I've been here before and have done this before, then how come there have never been any Seraphim on this planet matched with their humans before?"

Nera was silent for a long time.

Thomas watched her as he waited for her to answer. Her skin was almost translucent, but he found he liked it. It was pretty. *She* was pretty. At this thought, a strange sensation started deep down in Thomas' core and he swallowed a huge lump that suddenly formed in his throat.

Nera looked over at him at the sound of his gulp and seemed a bit embarrassed, as if she'd caught the drift of his thoughts. Finally, she said, "We could not have anticipated what happened. I mean, we did not even know there was a problem until then."

Thomas' eyes narrowed in confusion and Nera sighed in frustration.

"You might not understand what I am about to tell you, but it is the most I can tell you without breaking the rules. We did not know the Seraphim had formed in a separate dimension from the humans. They were supposed to have formed within the same dimension. It has always been that way. I mean, things are kind of made a lot easier for the couplings when each member of the couple is in the same dimension as the other," she explained.

Thomas chewed on this information for a few minutes in silence. When he finally spoke, he asked, "When you say 'we' – you mean me, too?"

"Yes," she said.

"How did the couples form in separate dimensions?" he asked next.

Nera bit down on one side of her bottom lip, holding it between her teeth for a moment before saying, "We did not notice while it was happening that there were two dimensions available for use."

Thomas didn't understand.

Nera could tell and she gave a frustrated sigh. "Look," she said, "I know this makes no sense to you, but it really was not anything we could have prevented, well, except for the interruption that pulled us away. But that was unavoidable and could not be helped, either."

At his continued look of complete lack of understanding, she continued, saying, "We have got one more chance now to save this batch, though, before it is too late and the whole thing has to be counted as a complete loss. If we can just get all the Seraphim and *their* counterparts together, and if you can just remember, then we might be able to salvage most of the rest of them."

Thomas sighed. He still didn't understand much, if any, of what she was talking about, but at least she was still around and talking with him. Surely, if there was no hope, she would already have gone? A moment later, he made up his mind. A steely resolve crept into his changing voice and he said determinedly, "Okay. If the only way for me to recall everything I need to remember is to practice, then I'll practice." He stood and turned to look down at her. "I'll call you if I need you, okay?"

Nera nodded, saying, "That is all you have ever needed to do."

After a slight hesitation, Thomas reached for her. Nera stood and slipped into his arms, pressing herself as close to him as she possibly could, her face tucked down along the side of his neck. Thomas was reluctant at first to squeeze her too tightly between his arms. This was all new and a bit uncomfortable for him. But then, he felt a great warmth spreading up within his body as she pressed against him and he went ahead and pulled her as close and tight as he could. He squeezed his eyes shut and reveled in the feeling of holding another being so close.

When he'd been younger, his mom and grandparents had hugged him all the time. His grandparents had hugged him whenever they saw him and his mom, well, she'd hugged him before bedtime each and every night, and she'd even asked for hugs randomly throughout each day, whenever they'd been together. She'd shown her love for him freely.

Since they'd come to the Angelic realm, however, Thomas hadn't experienced too much physical contact with her or anyone else. He could barely stand to be in the same room as his mom and Mikhail, so he avoided them, choosing to spend most of his time with either Samuel or Miriam. It wouldn't seem right asking Miriam for hugs, though, and Samuel – that just wasn't gonna happen!

Now, with Nera's form pressed so close to him Thomas experienced something he'd never before felt while hugging anyone else. There was that strange sensation deep down inside and it was growing, big time. Nera pulled back to look at him and, without even realizing what he was doing, Thomas bent his head just the slightest bit and touched his lips to hers.

Nera's hands gripped his shoulders and she pulled him gently closer, rubbing her soft lips against his. Thomas took her cue and moved his own lips a little, just a little, back and forth. His eyes slid closed and he was suddenly swamped by so many sensations at once that his head was swimming.

His breathing was labored, but he didn't care. Thomas merely wanted to continue kissing this magical creature, to continue feeling this... whatever it was. He tightened his grip on her and angled his head for better access to her mouth.

Nera was the one who finally pulled away from him. That's when he noticed the two tears gently tracking down her cheeks. He reached to wipe one of them away with a thumb and she smiled tremulously at him. "You should get going, now," she whispered. "They are looking for you."

Almost before he'd broken physical contact with her, he found himself suddenly back in his room at the complex, standing alone in the room with his hand still raised to where she'd been in front of him. His arm dropped and he turned on his heel. Someone was knocking at his door.

Chapter 15

Thirty minutes after the voices had dispelled, Baphomet and Lisa were still tightly wrapped in each other's arms when suddenly Baphomet *felt* something coming toward them. He pulled back from Lisa and searched the room with his eyes, his heart rate increasing in tempo as he frantically searched for whatever was causing such a tremendous amount of nervousness within his mate and himself. They could feel it, whatever it was, and it was getting closer, no doubt!

Baphomet jumped up off the bed and lunged for the door to the room, just as a knock sounded on it from the other side. Rearing his fist back in preparation to strike, his lethal white hair poised to strike, as well, Baphomet jerked open the door and then stopped in shocked surprise. Israfil stood on the other side with Hantsushept. Both men took a quick step back across the hallway as they took in the sight confronting them.

Baphomet's fist and hair immediately dropped as he stood staring at them in complete confusion. The next moment, however, had both his fist and his hair jerking back up into position as the boy, Thomas, rounded the nearest turn in the hallway and came into view.

The energies coming off the boy were unbelievable and Baphomet had felt them before. His mouth twisted into a vicious snarl and he all but lunged at the boy, only stopping at Israfil's shriek of outrage. *"Brother!"* Israfil yelled, somehow managing to avoid the wildly swinging lethal white hair while getting through to Baphomet on some basic level, enough, he hoped, to stop him from inflicting actual physical harm on the boy.

Thomas had immediately withdrawn to the safety of the corner he'd just turned and was cautiously peeking around it to see what was going on. The glowing eyes of the Seraph confronting him were enough to be frightening all on their own, but when one combined the lethal white strands of hair with them, the effect was downright horrifying. There also seemed to be a black aura surrounding this Seraph and Thomas knew he would never have the courage to face something this frightening.

After wrapping the lethal strands of hair around a hand to secure it back behind Baphomet, Israfil stepped closer to his brother and grabbed the closest arm at the bicep. Baphomet finally pulled his attention away from the creature huddling behind the wall at the turn in the hallway, his breath coming in short, angry bursts as the need to kill the creature burned within him. "What?" he barked, throwing a look of frustration at Israfil.

Israfil tilted his head slightly, his eyes narrowed, his face a mask of confusion.

That's when Baphomet realized Israfil didn't know. He jerked his gaze back toward the boy, wondering if even Sarah and Mikhail had been fooled by the creature. He narrowed his gaze upon the thing, wondering why it had come here, what its purpose in this dimension was.

The creature merely blinked back at him as it stared at the trio within the hallway. But Baphomet got no reading other than an energy signature from the creature, and that, in itself, was enough to give him pause as far as allowing the creature access to his mate.

"Brother," Israfil softly said again.

Baphomet looked back at his brother, wondering in amazed disgust why he couldn't sense the creature. It didn't matter. "That *thing*," he snarled, "does not come near my mate!"

214

Both Israfil's and Hantsushept's eyes narrowed in complete confusion this time, as the two turned to look at the subject of Baphomet's venomous command. It was Israfil who answered, saying, "But, you asked for him."

Baphomet turned a murderous look on his brother and shouted, "I will kill it if it comes anywhere near her! I *ought* to kill it now!"

"You ought to kill *what* now?" a deep voice demanded in whiplash fashion as Mikhail and Sarah suddenly appeared around the very corner where the creature hid. The two took up a defensive stance directly in front of Thomas, effectively blocking him from Baphomet's view.

One corner of Baphomet's upper lip curled up in crazed anticipation. He wasn't afraid of these two, not now, and he almost smiled as he said sibilantly, "That thing needs to be destroyed. I was merely offering my services to the house."

Sarah was quick to lunge forward, her voice sounding shrilly both aloud and within Baphomet's mind as she screamed, "You will not *touch* my son!" Her double voice playing tricks on his mind made Baphomet shake his head in an attempt to clear it all of a sudden.

Mikhail's hand on her arm interrupted Sarah's flight toward her new brother and she immediately turned a demanding look upon her mate, the fury in her eyes almost sparking out at him as she silently questioned his motives in stopping her from defending Thomas. *Calm yourself, my love*, his voice silently instructed her.

Sarah looked at him like he was crazy, but Mikhail merely stepped around her to confront Baphomet, himself, asking his brother, "Why use your venom on Thomas? He is just a boy."

A sharp bark escaped Baphomet and he viciously asked, "Is that what the thing has led you to believe?" At everyone's look of confusion, he continued, explaining, "That is no boy cowering behind that wall. I do not know what it is, but it needs to be destroyed and I shall happily do it, if no one else here is up to the task."

"No!" Sarah wailed as she once again made to jump Thomas' foe. Mikhail held her back once more, this time silently instructing her to listen to Baphomet from the inside.

Although her eyes were filled with rage when she initially turned to look at him, his silent words finally broke through to her and she turned cautious and wary eyes on her new brother. She allowed her mind to accept the thoughts Baphomet was gushing out for all and sundry to catch and that's when she finally understood that he'd seen something she'd missed. Somehow, there'd been some clue within her visions, something she hadn't figured out on her own.

Her eyes narrowed and Sarah took a step back toward Thomas, reaching back behind herself to grab onto one of Thomas' hands. He didn't disappoint, as his now large hand immediately encapsulated hers, their fingers weaving together in a tight grip. Sarah didn't turn toward him, as her mind was still picking apart the thoughts coming off Baphomet, her eyes darting this way and that as she processed the information.

Baphomet merely stared at Sarah, willing her to understand, showing her again and again the images he'd gleaned from within her own mind. He knew that if anyone within the complex could understand, it would be Sarah. This creature might have been able to fool the rest of them, but it couldn't hide from ones such as his new sister and him.

Sarah finally looked up at him, though she made no move toward him, nor did she turn to face the creature still cowering behind her. "I repeat," she firmly said with a steely resolve in her voice, "You will not touch my son."

Baphomet's mouth dropped open in obvious disbelief.

He made a move toward her, but was immediately halted by both Mikhail and Israfil. "Brother," Israfil said. "Have you forgotten about Lisa?"

Realization quickly dawned and Baphomet darted back into the room, all other considerations immediately forgotten. By the time all but Thomas and Sarah entered the room, Baphomet was already lying on the bed holding a crying Lisa who looked as if she was in a tremendous amount of pain.

Baphomet softly whispered, "Shh, sweet Lisa. Shh. I am here." He rubbed the back of her head, her white hair springing back up each time to gently smooth itself down her cheeks in comforting caresses as she softly whimpered. He wished he knew some secret word to utter to take away her pain. Her tears and pitiful sobs tore at his heart so much he would happily kill someone in order to ease her pain.

After a moment, Lisa's face cleared of all traces of pain and she was finally able to cautiously open her eyes and lift her head a little. She looked around piteously at the crowd of people standing around the bed, the tears finally ceasing their course down her cheeks.

"You okay now, sweet Lisa?" Baphomet asked as he helped her to sit up on the bed beside him. He adjusted his position so he could sit next to her while facing the others.

Lisa nodded, but kept a weak, but firm hold on his hand as she adjusted her position. "What happened?" she asked.

Baphomet thought for a moment, and then, shaking his head, he shrugged and said, "I do not know. I was standing out in the hallway, just outside the door, and then Iz reminded me about the reason I had sent him to get the others and then I came in to find you being attacked again."

"But, why weren't you affected?" she asked quietly. It wasn't that she was jealous or anything, she just didn't understand why she had been targeted and not he.

Baphomet's eyes narrowed in thought as he came to understand what she was really asking. He suddenly shot a glance at Israfil, demanding, "Did you do it? Did you keep them from affecting me?"

Understanding immediately dawned on Israfil and he said, "The voices. Yes. I remember feeling their energy coming on you while I was holding onto you out in the hallway. I guess I just automatically threw out a buffer for you without even realizing I had done it."

Baphomet looked back over at Lisa, then down to the covers on the bed. At least they now knew Israfil could help if Lisa and Baphomet were ever separated, but that still left the issue of the baby to be dealt with. Baphomet didn't think Israfil would be able to help with that one, unfortunately.

He quickly stood, though he didn't dare let go of Lisa's hand for fear the voices would return to plague her. Turning toward the physician, he asked, "Would you examine my mate to make sure there is nothing wrong with her or the baby? We have not heard it yet and we are getting... concerned there may be something wrong."

At the mention of a baby, everyone but Israfil immediately trained their gazes on Lisa's lower abdomen, searching for a bright spot of light like the one Sheely made on Sarah.

There was barely any light showing through there at all and everyone was soon filled with concern for their brother's child. Hantsushept lumbered forward and made quick work of examining Lisa, but he informed her and Baphomet there wasn't much he could do examination-wise for the baby without at least having access to the small amount of equipment he had back in his lab on the other side of the complex.

Baphomet stood there, his hand still holding Lisa's, his adam's apple bobbing up and down every few seconds as he swallowed lumps of fear forming in his throat. He looked over at Lisa several times, passing questions and information to her and then getting answers back. They weren't the answers he wanted, but what else could he do? He looked around the room, desperately trying to find some other way, *any* other way, but neither he nor Lisa could think of anything.

He looked back toward her as she reached up with her other hand to grasp his hand with both of hers. "Please?" she begged, her voice so small and pitiful it was almost his undoing. "I just need to make sure it's okay."

A fist of fear and anguish tightened the muscles within Baphomet's chest to such a degree he was certain he was experiencing what humans called a heart attack. After a moment's hesitation, he slowly nodded and sighed. "Iz," he asked, "Will you stay here with her while I leave the room?"

"No!" Lisa shouted. "Please don't leave me!"

Baphomet looked back down at her, shaking his head as he said, "Leece, I-I do not think I could stand here to watch that... *thing* touching you."

"Please!" she begged, tears starting to trace down her cheeks once more as she clutched his hand more tightly within her own two smaller ones.

To Baphomet's surprise, it was Mikhail who came to their rescue. "Use me," he said. When Baphomet and Lisa turned confused glances his way, Mikhail clarified, saying, "I will link with Thomas and he can link with the baby through me. We have done it before with Sheely. All I have to do is to place my hand on Lisa just above where the baby is and Thomas should be able to communicate with the child."

Everyone stared in shocked disbelief. To wield such a power was unheard of, though among their lot they should have expected it by now. Plus, it was better than having Baphomet go crazy while someone he considered to be some kind of monster touched his mate, *that* was for certain. There was no telling what he'd be driven to do if he had to endure that.

At Lisa's hopeful expression, Baphomet reluctantly agreed, saying, "Fine. If – If you can do that – that would be fine." He returned to sit at Lisa's side as Mikhail mentally contacted Sarah to make sure she'd understood what Thomas needed to do. She didn't like it, but she said Thomas was willing enough to try.

Mikhail rounded the bed and took a seat next to Lisa opposite Baphomet. Lisa was propped up on some pillows and so Mikhail had no difficulty placing his hand upon her lower abdomen. Immediately, he felt Thomas' mind link with his and, through him, Thomas' energies were soon linking with the life form housed within Lisa's lithe frame.

Unfortunately, Baphomet also felt Thomas' energies coursing through his mate and he nearly shot up off the bed in an attempt to knock Mikhail's hand off her. Instead, Israfil, who had silently moved to stand next to Baphomet, grabbed hold of Baphomet's arm before he could reach Mikhail.

Baphomet suddenly felt a dulling sensation within his mind. Somehow, he found the strength to silently say to Israfil, *I simply cannot stand having it touch her, Iz.*

Israfil responded in kind in Baphomet's mind, saying, *I know, Brother. I know.* Israfil concentrated and Baphomet's muscles were soon relaxed again.

To everyone else in the room, it appeared Baphomet was the perfect mate, sitting quietly by his mate's side, holding her hand while she endured this process. Inside, however, only those two who were linked with him knew of his suffering. Even under Israfil's mind-numbing ministrations, Baphomet still raged within as he felt the creature's energies coursing through his mate's body. He felt like he needed to go throw her in the shower just to wash the filth off of her.

This was Hell, he decided, and he wished he were anywhere but here as Mikhail began to tell them what was going on.

Mikhail repeated, word-for-word, everything Thomas was telling him. "It's a boy," he said. "He's very afraid. The voices… they come from everywhere, they're everywhere. Cabal cannot handle them. They overwhelm him and hurt him."

"Cabal?" Lisa asked.

"Yes," Mikhail said as Thomas said it. "That's the child's name."

Lisa looked down to where Mikhail's hand rested on her body. "Cabal," she whispered.

"He's hiding," Mikhail continued. "The pain is too much when the voices come. H-He doesn't want to talk anymore." And, that was it. Thomas pulled away from Mikhail's mind and Mikhail rose from the bed.

Israfil dropped his hold on Baphomet and moved to stand at the bottom of the bed. Baphomet had heard and understood everything being said throughout the entire process, but only now was he able to force his brain to function properly enough to make his body move and speak, though he felt like throwing up from the experience.

When Lisa looked at him, however, and whispered softly around a teary-eyed and watery smile, "Our son's name is Cabal," Baphomet knew it had been worth enduring. He didn't want to ever have to do it again, but he conceded that he was glad the creature had been willing to perform this small task for his mate and him.

Baphomet looked up at Mikhail and reluctantly said, "Tell them I said '*thank you*'." Mikhail knew he meant Sarah and Thomas and he quickly passed on Baphomet's words telepathically to his mate and son.

∞

Azra'il watched as the tally was finalized. All who'd been sent were accounted for... and all were dead. The council was in an uproar. Azra'il had been able to keep things on a civil level after the last show of force from his brothers, but only just, and there had only been a small number of dead then. Now, however, it was as if Mikhail and his little band had declared war outright on the governing body of the entire Angelic realm!

The Great Sanhedrin would *not* let this pass. Azra'il knew the council's response would be swift and, he believed, annihilating. His skin crawled at the thought of having his entire family wiped out by the very body he headed, but what could he do?

He straightened from his position against the wall of the main medical facility's makeshift morgue as one of his higher ranking council members approached.

"My lord," the Angel said as tears streamed freely down his face. "They are both there. Both of them, they are both dead. Why?" The Angel turned away as a fresh wave of pain wracked his body.

Azra'il leaned forward to place a hand on the Angel's shoulder. What could he say?

It had been three days since the Captain of the elite Sanhedrin Guard had led his men into battle, thinking only to take down one human, three, at most. Sometime during the night last evening, the bodies of each and every one of the Guardsmen had been returned to the city, perfectly pristine, well, except for those who'd been burned to the point of being unrecognizable or those who'd been decapitated or who'd had certain other parts of their bodies detached.

Azra'il shivered. The whole scene was gruesome, to say the least. How distasteful this whole business had become! There'd been a time when he and his brothers would have gone themselves to annihilate anyone who committed such a crime as this. Now, it seemed his brothers had taken it upon themselves to switch sides all together.

Not only were they harboring humans within the Angelic realm, but they were now actively engaging in murderous acts against their own kind – all in the name of humans! The very idea was unconscionable!

The council member suddenly recovered himself enough to turn back to Azra'il to declare, "I have called a special session of the council to discuss retaliatory action to be taken against these murderers." He paused for a moment as he realized what he'd just done.

However, as he took one last look over at the area where his two young sons lay upon autopsy tables, a steely resolve hardened within him and he looked again at Azra'il, saying, "I know they are your brothers, my Lord, but they must be held accountable for this massacre."

Azra'il looked away from the man. He wanted to scream, to rail, to hit something or some*one*. He wanted to believe his brothers could not have been capable of committing such a heinous act against mere Angels. But the proof was incontrovertible. No one else would have been able to defeat the elite Sanhedrin Guard so quickly or in such a crushing way. For each and every one of the Guard to have been killed was... *unthinkable*.

Azra'il looked to the skies, wishing for the trillionth time the blessed Great Designers would return. Their world was falling apart and there was no one to help them take control of the rapidly deteriorating social order, and that was just in the Angelic realm. There was no telling how bad things had become in the human realm.

Azra'il hadn't had any time to sit and monitor any of the goings on within the human realm since he'd banished his brothers from within Seraphim City's walls. He acknowledged the very real possibility that things there might well be even worse than things were in the Angelic realm. He also acknowledged that if the blessed Designers didn't arrive soon, there might not be a civilization left.

Azra'il sighed and turned back to the man, nodding. The two turned silently and headed side-by-side out the door of the Medical Facility. Today would mark the beginning of what might prove to be the dirtiest and most destructive war the inhabitants of this planet had ever endured. Azra'il, for one, said a quick prayer for the Designers to have mercy on the souls of those who'd transgressed against the law. He only wished his brothers weren't to be included within that group.

Chapter 16

Baphomet once again lay atop Lisa with his head positioned directly over the spot where Cabal hid within her womb. He softly crooned an old Angelic lullaby to his son. He'd been talking and singing to Cabal for the past few hours, hoping against hope that there would be some kind of response forthcoming. So far, all had been to no effect.

Baphomet's head jerked up as yet another sound from outside in the hallway intruded on the moment. Each time anyone out there passed by on his or her way to some other part of the house, both Baphomet and Lisa would catch their thoughts, as if the person had been in the very room speaking aloud for everyone to hear.

He frowned and sighed and returned his head to Lisa's belly, his ear pressed firmly up against Cabal's little lighted form showing through the dark skin there.

"Come on, sweet Cabal. Please, will you not talk to Mommy and Daddy?" he softly asked, his deep voice vibrating through Lisa's body to their son.

Lisa pushed her fingers through the silky white strands of hair at Baphomet's temple, gently caressing her mate's skin and reveling in the feel of his hair caressing her forearm. Her own hair reached down of its own accord to gently massage Baphomet's shoulders along his back. Baphomet began singing another lullaby, his hand gently squeezing Lisa's other hand, their fingers entwining and caressing each other with their thumbs.

Lisa heard another voice as someone else passed through the hallway and a part of her wished she and Baphomet could take Cabal far away from everyone. *They* were the reason Cabal wouldn't talk with anyone. *They* were the reason he was hiding from his own parents, even.

If only he would talk with them.

Lisa closed her eyes and silently called to her son, softly imploring him to come out of hiding. She believed everything would be okay, if only he would allow them to help him.

Suddenly, she heard what seemed at first like a very small child's whisper. Lisa stilled immediately, her action bringing Baphomet to the alert and he stopped singing. They each held their breath as they waited and listened.

Then, they heard it...

It was a very distant high-pitched whisper. Baphomet quickly peeked up at Lisa and grinned. Just as quickly, he returned his ear to its position and listened intently. There was more whispering, just a little louder this time.

Lisa couldn't understand the words, but she believed she caught the meaning. He was hungry! Cabal was hungry!

Before she could even form the words to speak, Baphomet was up and running for the door. He wouldn't get the chance, however.

The door was suddenly flung open and a very disheveled-looking Israfil stood there blinking and frantically looking for any signs of distress on the faces of his family members. Instead, he found only grins as Baphomet grabbed hold of him and gave him a great bear hug, saying softly but joyously, "Cabal is hungry! My son is hungry!"

For a moment, Israfil didn't know what to make of what his brother had said. Then, realization dawned and he quickly returned the hug his brother was still giving him and he softly said, "That is great, Brother. That is terrific."

Baphomet released his hold on his brother and asked, suddenly sobering, "Would you stay here with them while I arrange for food to be brought in?"

"No need," Israfil softly said. "It has already been arranged. You stay here and I shall go let them know you are ready now."

Baphomet clapped his brother on the shoulder, the sheen of tears in his eyes as, yet again, he was overwhelmed by everything Israfil had done for Lisa and him. "Again, thank you, Iz,," he whispered, swallowing yet another lump in his throat. What a baby he'd become lately!

"Thank you, Israfil," Lisa whispered as loud as she dared.

Israfil softly chuckled and nodded once before heading out the door.

Baphomet quietly closed the door, turning the knob to make sure as little noise as possible was made. Then, he returned to the bed and climbed back into his former position, laying his head back down on Lisa's tummy. A huge grin spread across his face again as he heard his son's high-pitched whisper sounding stronger and stronger.

"He likes the orange juice, I think is what he said," Lisa whispered. "We'll have to make sure to get some of that."

Baphomet looked up at her smiling face and, for a moment, he thought, *This is the happiest day of my life.* Then, as Lisa looked back at him and smiled just for him, his smile faded and he pulled himself up toward her. Moving to one side of her, he took her mouth in the most tender, heart-rending kiss he could give his mate.

Lisa responded immediately, reaching up to caress his cheek and neck and chest. She loved touching him and she didn't ever want to stop. Then, she heard Cabal's sweet voice again and she chuckled softly as she realized she *had* to stop, for

Cabal was swimming down there and she needed to go to the toilet!

She pulled away from Baphomet, but immediately halted as her fingers tightened on Baphomet's within their clasped hands. She looked back at Baphomet. They both knew what the question was. Should they risk it? They'd only just gotten him to start talking.

"I would rather not chance it, sweet, if *you* do not mind," Baphomet whispered. "Unless you would be too embarrassed to have me accompany you there?" he quietly asked.

After only a slight hesitation, Lisa shook her head, agreeing, "No. I'd rather be safe than sorry. We'll go together."

Baphomet helped her up. He sat on the floor, his fingers still entwined with hers, as she took her time in the opulent wash room. Afterward, they switched places, with Baphomet sitting on the toilet and Lisa sitting on the tile floor, both still holding hands.

Lisa found it wasn't nearly as embarrassing as she'd thought it would be. Of course, all she'd had to do was pee. She didn't want to think about when it was time to do more than that, yet.

Right now, she just wanted to make everything as comfortable as possible for Cabal so he'd keep talking to them. He seemed to be feeling much safer now, as his chatter picked up, both in volume, as in sound, and in volume, as in amount of chatter!

Baphomet chuckled softly as he helped Lisa back up onto the big bed and made her as comfortable as possible before crawling atop the covers to sit next to her. Sitting there beside her, he threw an arm around her and Lisa reached up on the side where his hand hung over her shoulder to grab it and entwine her fingers with his once more.

That was how they were seated when they caught the first strains of thoughts from Israfil and what seemed like a whole team of Angels bringing food down the hallway for them. Baphomet frowned a bit at all the noise the newcomers' thoughts were making and he quickly extricated himself from his position on the bed to try to head them off at the door.

"I shall only be a second, sweet Lisa," he assured her in a whisper as he crossed the room.

In the end, only one Angel was allowed entry into the room and the rest of the assembled crowd out in the hallway were quickly, if not politely, asked to put down their trays and leave.

Israfil was a little confused by Baphomet's request, but he held his tongue. As soon as the Angel serving the couple had gotten all the trays inside the room and situated where it would be accessible, she quietly excused herself and left. Israfil spared only one last glance around to ensure all was well within the room and then he too left, softly shutting the door behind himself.

Lisa pounced. She hadn't realized just how hungry she was until the smell of the delicious-looking foods reached her. She was starving! Baphomet apparently was, as well, for he sat with her and ate plate after plate after plate of the delicious meal.

There were several different kinds of meat, including chicken, beef, lamb, and one Lisa didn't recognize. Baphomet told her it was from an animal called a Dalbit that looked kind of like a lion and an eagle mix.

"Oh, you mean like a Griffin?" Lisa asked.

Baphomet nodded, explaining, "Yes, I believe that is what humans call them. They are from this dimension, but there have been a few throughout history that have managed to make it over into the human dimension."

"How is that possible?" Lisa asked as she tried some of the bright pink meat. It was delicious and she quickly gobbled up every bit of it on her plate.

"Most likely," Baphomet said around a mouthful of the delicious meat, "one of my people helped them to cross the barrier."

Lisa suddenly realized she was stuffed. She set aside her plate and leaned back in her seat to watch Baphomet as he ate. "This barrier thing," she said, "I don't understand how that works."

Baphomet finished off his drink and the rest of the food on his own plate. He then helped her back over from the table they'd sat at for their meal to the bed. Once they were both comfortable and could once again hear their son happily chattering away, he quietly explained, "Angels and some other animals were formed and exist solely in this dimension, as we saw in the visions supplied to us by Sarah. Humans and many other animals were formed and exist solely in what we call the human realm. There are no humans born in this realm and there are no Angels born in the human realm, at least not to my knowledge."

"But you said the animals had been taken across the barrier into the human realm from this one," she said.

"That was a long time ago, back when we had first been banished to the Badlands," he said cryptically. At her look of confusion, he said, "Many of my people were not happy with what Mikhail had done. Even I was not happy with his edict, and so we Shaitans sometimes got a little rowdy, doing things we knew would upset those in charge in Seraphim City."

He looked away from her, remembering some of the things he'd done and wishing beyond all that was holy that he could go back in time and erase those deeds. Lisa's hand reached over to turn him back to face her and she whispered,

"That's all in the past, now. I don't blame you for things you did years and years ago."

Baphomet reached over and kissed her softly, lingering over her lips as he whispered, "I love you, sweet Lisa, more than you will ever know."

Lisa smiled and moved to kiss him back. She never made it, however, as she suddenly exclaimed in a loud whisper, "Oh, my gosh! I wonder if that's how the Yeti and the North American Sasquatch legends were started?"

Baphomet chuckled quietly and reached up to pull her toward him, saying, "Sometimes, I think you are a little bit crazy, you know?"

With that, he fastened his mouth onto hers and didn't let go of her for a long, long time.

∞

Nikolai Shvedov adjusted his grip on his bag as he dug his vibrating cell phone from within his pants pocket. This was no simple task as he made his way as quickly as possible without running down the moving sidewalk within the skywalk between buildings. He finally managed to pull the flat chunk of metal out of his pocket and then nearly tripped over someone's bag as he searched for the talk button.

"Damn it!" he barked into the phone as he righted himself.

"Well, it's great to hear from you, too," his boss' heavily New England-accented voice growled from the other end.

"Sorry, Frank," Nick quickly apologized.

"Humph," was all Frank said.

"What can I do for you?" Nick asked, picking up his pace once again along the moving sidewalk.

"Your story's late," Frank said. Frank always said that. It was always late. Nick Shvedov was perhaps the best reporter he had on staff and Frank knew it. So did Nick. That was why Nick never bothered with things like deadlines.

Well, that and the fact that his parents had left him a boat-load of money when they'd passed away a few years ago. Nick didn't have to work, but he loved it and he was great at it. Frank also knew that and that was why he kept Nick on his staff at the paper.

"I know, I know," Nick said as he finally disembarked from the moving sidewalk only to turn a corner to discover yet another one he'd have to take. "Look, Frank," he said, exasperated. "The story's gonna be a bit later than usual, but I'll get it to you just as soon as possible. I've got another lead that just came in and I really need to check it out before I finish this thing. Could blow the whole thing wide open, if what I just found out is true."

Nick had more contacts worldwide than most people had as friends on those idiotic social networking sites everyone was so addicted to these days. Frank knew if Nick said he had a good lead, then he'd best give him some time and space to check it out. "Where are you?" he asked.

"I'm at the airport," Nick said. He heard the last call for his flight and he broke into a run. This damned lead had only just come in two hours ago and, as luck would have it, it was rush hour... in New York City. Nick had been all the way on the other side of Manhattan when he'd gotten the call. He'd taken one taxi and a helicopter to get to the airport on time and, now that he was this close, he was *not* going to miss his plane.

"Listen, Frank," he said. "I've gotta go."

"Where?" Frank asked immediately.

"Australia," Nick said as he handed his ticket and passport to the agent at the International Departures gate.

"Australia?" Frank demanded. "I thought you said this thing was happening down in Dallas?"

"It was," Nick explained, "but there's been a new development and I have to go to Australia to check it out." The agent handed his items back, all checked and approved, and he sprinted for the gate. "There's been another disappearance, this time down under, and it looks like the same M.O. as the Dallas incident. I'm gonna check it out and see where that can take us."

The airline employees were just closing the gate doors as he rushed up to them waving his ticket, wildly motioning for them to hold up. The closest one to him checked out his credentials, ticket, and boarding pass and waved him on through. "Look, Frank, I'll call you as soon as I know anything," he said, rushing down the gateway to the plane.

He pushed the END button without waiting for an answer and smiled politely at the flight attendant who'd been closing the plane's door before she'd spotted him. She pushed it back open and said, "I'm afraid there's not much left at this point, sir. You'll have to sit wherever a seat's available."

Nick nodded and passed on through to the main aisle of the airplane. He'd barely had time to pack for this trip, so he had only the one bag. He wasn't concerned overmuch with that, though. Whatever he'd need in Australia, he would just buy once he got there.

He found an empty seat between a blond woman who looked to be about eighteen, barely legal, and a businessman who looked as if he was *not* looking forward to the long flight. Nick usually flew first class, so this was not his ideal, either. But if he had to sit scrunched up next to someone, he would prefer it to be someone of about the teenager's height and build.

He gave her a crooked smile as he stowed his bag above the seats and then carefully made his way into the middle seat between the two.

"Hi, I'm Nick," he said to the blond, completely ignoring the businessman in the aisle seat.

"Hi," she said with a high-pitched cheerleader voice, "I'm Buffy."

"Of course you are," Nick said with a smile.

∞

Mikhail listened as Thomas, Samuel, and Sarah explained what had happened during the attack of the elite Guardsmen. He was amazed at the images Sarah showed him of Thomas' and Samuel's fighting styles. Even his most highly trained Guardsmen from when *he* had been the one in charge would not have been able to stand a chance against such formidable ability.

He was also amazed at how much Thomas had grown since coming to the Angelic realm. When he'd first arrived, Mikhail had been able to carry him like the child he was. Now, the boy was almost taller than Sarah and he looked more like a young man than a child. His voice was even changing… at age eleven! Mikhail had never heard of such a thing. *Perhaps that is how early human males go through puberty now.* Mikhail thought.

When the trio finished, Mikhail could tell they were all proud. Sarah was proud of Thomas, he knew, and Thomas and Samuel were proud because they'd defeated a dangerous enemy. "The thing to do now," Mikhail told the two boys, "is to learn to control the energies enough so that you can inflict just the right amount of damage necessary to thwart your enemy without killing them."

He hadn't meant the words as an admonishment, but he quickly realized that was how the two boys had taken them. The mood in the room changed and the two boys quickly made their excuses and left.

"I-I did not mean to…," he began.

"I know," Sarah said, interrupting him. "Don't worry about it. I'll talk with 'em." After a moment, she reached over

234

and took his hand in hers. "You've gotta understand, Mikhail. We were all fightin' for our lives when they attacked. We did what we could to save Lisa *and* ourselves because they weren't holdin' back at all, even though Thomas and Samuel are just kids."

Mikhail squeezed her hand and nodded, saying, "I believe you. I am just not looking forward to whatever retaliatory action the Great Sanhedrin will mandate because of what happened. I would much rather none of us have to enter into battle against anyone, let alone against our own kind, ever again."

Sarah once again felt the sting of his words as she thought how none of this would ever even have started had Thomas and she never come to the Angelic realm in the first place. Then, she thought of the request Mikhail had made of her should anything happen to him and her worry and sense of guilt increased a thousand-fold.

Do not do this, love, Mikhail's voice came floating across her mind. *You know exactly who is to blame for each and every death recorded here.*

Sarah looked over at him with surprised interest.

They deceived us all, my heart, and I, for one, will not stand upon this earth for one second more singing their praises.

Sarah blinked in understanding. The false Designers were certainly in for an eye-opener upon their return, what with Mikhail, their favorite Seraph, no longer clinging to his former fealty for them.

He gave her hand a quick kiss and said, "Do not worry. I will work with the boys to make sure they gain some control. That way, when the time comes, they will be good and ready for the fight, Designers or no." He stood and Sarah let go of his hand. She could feel him attempting to re-erect a buffer between them. Without even thinking about it, she threw her buffer back into place, effectively shutting off all psychic communication between the two of them.

Sarah remained silent as she watched him leave the room to go in search of the two boys. She still hadn't shared her fears regarding the safety of her siblings back in the human realm and she wasn't sure about a few other things she felt were going on here in the Angelic realm, but she was formulating a plan for the former and she had a whole lot of suspicions buzzing around in her head regarding the latter. She just wasn't quite ready to share them with anyone just yet. To that end, it was a good thing Mikhail wanted the buffer up.

Yesterday, when everything had been happening with Baphomet and Thomas, Sarah had realized the suspicions Baphomet had about Thomas were most likely true. She could tell the difference between Thomas' energies and those of humans, and he was definitely no human, at least, not anymore. She didn't know now if he ever truly had been.

His energy signature read more like that of one of the true Designers she'd seen in her visions before. But, Baphomet was livid with Thomas for the fact that he was not human and Sarah wanted to understand why. Was it merely because of the fact that the true Designers had separated each of their pairings and placed them into separate dimensions for all eternity?

Hell, she thought, *that would do it for me.*

Somehow, though, Sarah knew there *had* to be more to this story than they'd thus far been shown. She wanted to keep an open mind about everything, but Thomas wasn't exactly being forthcoming about his reason for being here.

The other day, he'd even completely *evaded* her question about who this Nera person is. Sarah believed that might be the best place for her to start digging for some answers, though, and she made up her mind. One way or another, she was going to meet this Nera. After all, Thomas was her son and she would do whatever it took to keep him safe.

Chapter 17

Sarah waited patiently while Samuel gathered his things and politely excused himself. Thomas and Mikhail were good-naturedly ribbing each other and cracking jokes as Thomas removed the protective tapes and pads he wore during practice. It was good to see them cutting up this way. Sarah had waited a long time for this.

Actually, she'd been afraid she'd never find anyone who would be able to form a semi-father-son bond with Thomas. But Mikhail seemed to be doing just fine, and Sarah was loathe to interrupt them. As they approached, however, Thomas looked as if he was readying to go off in the same direction as Samuel, intent on grabbing a snack and then spending the majority of the evening playing video games, which was how the two had spent the last few days after practicing with Mikhail.

Sarah couldn't allow that to happen today.

"My two men," she said. "You've both worked so hard. I've had a wonderful dinner prepared for us back at the master suite, so if you'll both go shower and change, we can all sit down to a nice meal together."

Thomas looked as if he might argue until Mikhail said, "That sounds great!"

After only the slightest hesitation, Thomas finally nodded his head and excused himself to go have a shower and change, *very* unlike an eleven year old. Well, he was getting close to turning twelve. He promised to meet them at the master suite for the planned dinner and took off.

After he was gone, Mikhail slid an arm around her and turned to walk with her back toward the complex. "You were not as subtle as you think, you know?" he asked quietly.

Sarah swallowed a lump in her throat. It was getting more and more difficult to hide things from him, not the other way around, even with a psychic buffer up between them. This had to be done, though, and she wouldn't let it go.

Mikhail sighed and gave her a quick squeeze. "I know you are concerned, but he seems to be doing okay to me. He is certainly stronger than he was when you first came here and he seems happy," he said earnestly.

"I know," she agreed. "It's just, I don't know anything about this Nera and she seems to be havin' a huge effect on Thomas lately. I want to know more about her, especially if she's the one who's been teachin' him things like these fightin' moves. I mean, don't *you* want to know more about someone who knows how to do these things?"

Mikhail sighed, nodding his head and saying, "Yes, but… I just would not wish to push the boy, you know? I do not want to interrupt the progress he has made here. I mean, if you think about it, Thomas is handling everything here pretty well, do you not agree? He was ripped out of his own dimension and forced to live in a new culture with a new people and everything, with only his mother and grandparents as those familiar to him. He did not get a choice, but he seems to be getting along with Samuel as if they were old friends and Miriam says he is the soul of kindness to her and has been since he came here."

Sarah's ears pricked up at that and she said, "That's another thing. This Miriam, I'd like to talk with her, myself."

Mikhail stopped and turned her toward him. "Sweetheart," he said softly, but firmly, "I have known Miriam since the day she was born. She has worked in my household for many thousands of years. Trust me when I tell you, of all the Angels within the Angelic realm, *she* is of no concern, here."

Sarah nodded, explaining, "I understand. But, Narayana worked in your house, too, and look what happened with her."

Mikhail sighed. "Narayana was prejudiced against humans," he explained. "And, I believe someone from outside my household got to her and convinced her to do as she did. We had suspected even before you and Thomas came to the Angelic realm that there was a traitor among us somewhere within the Sanhedrin houses. We were not sure who it was, but the suspicions were already there. Narayana's act of vengeance merely confirmed those suspicions."

"But how do you know there's no traitor here?" Sarah asked. "Thomas is my son and I'm just... He's goin' through changes that will affect the rest of his life and I don't know what's happenin' to him 'cause he's not talkin' to me about anything."

She sighed and looked off toward the main complex. "I just want to make sure everything's okay with him and I don't like not knowin' these people he's associatin' with, especially if they're more knowledgeable about war tactics than *you* are. Do you understand?"

Mikhail nodded and, after throwing a quick smile of thanks up at him, Sarah grabbed his hand and the two resumed their short walk back toward the main complex building. After a moment, however, Mikhail asked, "Was there something else you wanted to discuss with me, my heart?" He could feel the tension in her and he could find no reason for it in his recollection of thoughts she'd shared with him the last time they'd been connected psychically.

Sarah hesitated, coming to a halt on the little pathway they were walking along. There were bees buzzing around some flowers nearby and Sarah concentrated on those as she thought of how she could possibly ask more of him than he'd already given.

"Sarah?" he asked as he turned to take both of her hands in his. His heart rate was beating triple time by now with concern and he decided it was probably wise to drop the buffer so that she wouldn't feel so alone with whatever issue was eating at her brain.

Sarah felt his energies dropping and she knew he had decided this was too important of an issue to deal with while a buffer was up around them. She just didn't know if she had the courage to drop her own and face the truth with him knowing everything instantly.

As the seconds ticked by and the buffer Sarah had erected around herself remained in place, Mikhail frowned in confusion at the fact that he still was cut off from her thoughts. "Are-Are you blocking me?" he cautiously asked her.

She looked pleadingly up into his glowing eyes, her chin trembling and tears pooling along the bottom lids of her own glowing eyes. He looked so concerned for her and so eager, Sarah knew she couldn't deny him. She dropped the buffer and allowed him entry into her mind.

Immediately, Mikhail understood every second of every thought and every question and every worry she'd experienced regarding everything that had been going on for the past few days. He experienced her talk with her mother regarding her siblings back in the human realm. He experienced her doubts and concerns about Thomas not being a human being and the issue of Baphomet's hatred of the boy. He experienced the extreme sadness and fear she'd felt when Mikhail had brought up the whole issue of what he wished her to do should anything ever happen to him. Then, there were other, less urgent matters crowding her mind for attention.

241

Without hesitation, Mikhail bent and caught her up in a fierce hug, pulling her up and into his embrace right there in the open for all to see. He didn't care. Let the world, even the universe, see that he loved her and would do anything to continue to be with her for all time. Her small body shook as she silently cried. He knew she had only been helping him by erecting the buffer she'd carried between them and he loved her all the more for it. He had been trying to hide things from her without even thinking she might have things she felt she needed to hide from him.

As he thought this, she pulled back a little and looked up at him in surprise, a little smile of surprise and joy tugging at her lips as she caught a vision of the item he'd been working on so diligently over the past few days. Mikhail dipped his hand into his pocket to retrieve the trinket and she gushed, "Oh, Mikhail! It's so beautiful."

He laughed as he finally managed to dig its container out of his pants pocket and then handed it to her. "How do you know?" he asked teasingly. "You haven't even opened it yet."

Sarah took the tiny box and opened it to reveal the ring she'd seen him creating in the visions he'd just shared with her. It was small and very delicate, with a thin band of gold molded into what looked like mesh. Each link within the mesh even moved, until she put it on, that is. On top was an intricate pattern created entirely from tiny blood-red rubies along with tiny white diamonds surrounding a larger oval cut ruby. As she looked at it, the center ruby seemed to come to life and a bright light shone from within its center.

Sarah gasped at the beauty of it and then reached to hug him again. "Thank you so much for this," she whispered as more tears pooled in her eyes and eventually spilled over.

Mikhail pulled her closer and squeezed tighter. "You never have to thank me for things I give to you, my heart," he said. "You have given me so much more than I could ever repay."

He sought her mouth then and lost himself in a deep, promise-filled kiss.

Minutes later, when they broke apart merely because their brains were almost completely deprived of oxygen and Sheely was practically snarling at them, Sarah blushed a little and smiled up at him, saying, "We'd better hurry or Thomas will wonder what on earth has happened to us."

She turned to continue on up to the main house, but Mikhail's grip on her hand halted her. When she turned back to him in question, he said, "We shall find a way to contact your siblings. If they want to come live here, we shall make it work."

Again, the tears came. But they were humble tears this time, for she could not believe how much he loved her. "Thank you," she whispered again.

The two of them resumed their stroll toward the main house as he put an arm around her shoulders and whispered back, "You are welcome."

∞

Thomas approached the door. He'd showered and changed into his nicest outfit, a new pair of jeans, a new pair of tennis shoes, and a tight-fitting, short-sleeved American Joe polo his mom had brought back with her when she'd brought Thomas' grandparents over from the human realm. It was actually too small for him now, though he remembered this particular shirt as having been too big for him just before he'd left.

It seemed odd to him to think of things back in the human realm. He was glad he didn't live there anymore and he really wished he could just forget about that time in his life. He'd had friends, sure, and relatives, but they hadn't been anything like the people he'd gotten to know in this dimension. And, there he hadn't known Nera.

Thomas knew that was the reason his mom wanted him to have dinner with her and Mikhail tonight. He wasn't sure if he was ready to talk about Nera with anyone, especially his mom, but no one else knew. Mikhail had been helping Samuel and him practice over the past few days and the Seraph really seemed interested in what was going on with Thomas. In a way, over the past few days, Thomas had almost felt like he really *was* Mikhail's son – and it had felt good.

Now, his mom wanted to know about Nera. He was sure of it. Mikhail would be there listening. Maybe, if Thomas just told the two of them, they'd be able to help him figure out some things. Thomas still had plenty of questions and Nera wasn't talking, that was for certain.

As he raised his hand to knock at the door to the Master suite, Thomas sighed and thought, *Here's hoping they understand.*

∞

Surprisingly, the dinner talk was all innocuous, with very little of any true substance being discussed. Everything was kept on a light note and Thomas enjoyed himself tremendously. He and Mikhail talked at length about computers and video games and it was nice. Mikhail truly seemed to know what he was talking about, although Thomas did have to explain some of the older human game references he made during the conversation.

That was to be expected, though, since Thomas was certain Mikhail wouldn't have had any reason to bother with video games until after he and his mom had come to the Angelic realm to live. He hadn't even owned a gaming console until after they'd come to live with him.

All in all, Thomas spent a very enjoyable evening with his mom and Mikhail and he was quite relaxed as they all sat around the table finishing off the marvelous dessert the chef had made. It was some kind of chocolaty-gooey thing that had cream on top and fudge brownie underneath and Thomas thought he'd died and gone to heaven, it was so delicious.

That's when his mother chose to strike, of course.

"So, Thomas," she said. "I'd like to know more about this Nera person."

One thing about his mom, Thomas acknowledged, she didn't pull any punches. She just came right out and got to the bare bones of a matter. He supposed he liked that about her, technically speaking. It could be annoying, however, when one wasn't exactly ready to talk about certain things.

Thomas finished chewing the bite of dessert he had in his mouth and swallowed. He wiped his mouth on his napkin and placed it on the table beside his plate. After a moment, he raised his eyes to her and simply asked, "What do you want to know about her?"

"Well," Sarah asked, "how about who she is, where she's from, how you met her, how old is she, where does she live, that kind of thing?"

Thomas ran a hand through his lengthening brown hair and sighed. Again, appreciation for his mom's outright style of getting to the heart of a matter slapped him in the face. An image of Nera's face suddenly floated across his mental vision, though, and Thomas felt the strangest sense of responsibility toward her, as if it was his duty to protect her, even from his mother.

He looked over at the woman he trusted with his life and asked evasively, "Wh-Why do you need to know these things?"

"Thomas," Mikhail suddenly said, finally joining the conversation. "Son, your mother and I are just concerned, as we should be, about someone we do not know who has been communicating with you without your parents' permission."

Thomas looked down and thought for a moment, then said, "You don't have to worry about Nera."

Sarah and Mikhail exchanged a quick glance. "Sweetheart," Sarah said finally, "We *do* have to worry about her if we don't know anything about her."

Thomas ran a hand through his hair again and finally said, "I can't tell you everything about her because I don't know everything about her."

Mikhail came to sit beside Thomas at the table, turning his chair so that he was side-by-side with Thomas and he bent down to rest his elbows on his knees. He turned to look Thomas in the eyes. "Son," he said, "How about if we start with something simple, then? Tell us how you met Nera."

Thomas hesitated for only a short time before he told them.

He told them of the visions or dreams or whatever they'd been back at the other house in Seraphim City. He told them most of what Nera had said to him in those visions. He described the places where they'd met and some of the things Nera had taught him, though he didn't mention that all those things were things Thomas, himself, had taught to Nera. He described her looks and mentioned that there were others there within the round room that looked similar to her.

"So you're still communicating with this girl?" Sarah asked.

"Yes, though not so often," Thomas answered.

"And, you say she's got white hair that moves, like ours, and her eyes glow, like ours?" Sarah asked.

Thomas merely nodded. But then a thought struck him and he frowned. "Wait," he said. "There's something different."

Sarah and Mikhail waited patiently while Thomas arranged his thoughts.

"She's not *exactly* like the two of you," he finally said. "There's something about her energies that's different from yours. She doesn't glow as brightly as the two of you."

Mikhail and Sarah quickly shared a glance. "You can see our glow?" Mikhail asked.

Thomas nodded, looking at the two as if they were insane. "Can't everyone?" he asked derisively.

"What about Baphomet and Lisa's glow?" Mikhail asked.

Thomas thought about this for a moment, then nodded and said, "Baphomet's glow is even brighter than y'all's. I haven't seen Lisa since she's changed, but I could sense her energies the other day when I mind-linked with you and Cabal and they were pretty strong, like Baphomet's."

"So, was Nera a Seraph?" Sarah suddenly asked from out of nowhere.

Thomas hesitated. The need to protect Nera was riding him hard. His mother's questions, again, got straight to the heart of the matter and Thomas didn't know if he wanted to go that far with them, or not. He decided to take a chance. "I think she might have been a Seraph, but not from here," he said.

"Why did she pick you to contact?" Sarah asked. "Why not contact Mikhail or me?"

That was too close for Thomas' comfort and he stood, shaking his head and saying, "Look, you don't have to worry about Nera. Trust me, she's on our side."

Mikhail stood and said, "Son, we are just trying to make sure this person is…"

"I know what you're trying to do," Thomas interrupted. "But, I've told you, you don't have to worry about Nera. She's on our side, trust me."

"Thomas," Sarah said as she stood to round the table toward him, "I would like to meet this person to form my own opinion, if you don't mind."

"Well, that's not going to happen right now," Thomas stated matter-of-factly. "I'm not going to let anyone hurt her, even if that means I have to protect her from *you*."

"Sweetie, I'm not going to hurt her," Sarah said quickly. "I just want to make sure she's who and what she says she is and I think Mikhail and I would both feel better if we were to meet her, ourselves."

Thomas backed off, shaking his head again, and softly said, "I won't let anyone hurt her, Mom." With that, he turned and walked right out of the room. Sarah and Mikhail stood staring after him, thoughts and concerns whirling inside each one's mind.

Chapter 18

Nick Shvedov disembarked from the plane and moved on through customs with the rest of the passengers. He was never so glad to get off a flight in his entire life as he was to exit this one. The young Buffy had talked his ear off the entire way from New York to Sydney and Nick had had enough! If he never met another blond bimbo cheerleader type, it would be too soon.

Fortunately for Nick, the ditzy young woman had brought along a veritable shop-worth of luggage and he last spotted her with several of the bags lying open inside one of the inspection rooms in the customs area. He didn't think she'd be getting released anytime soon, so there was no danger he'd have to spend any more time with her before his next flight was due to leave.

The customs agent handed him back his passport and Nick grabbed his single bag and headed off in the direction of the gate indicated on his connecting flight ticket voucher. He still had another hour to wait before that flight was due to leave, but that didn't mean he couldn't get any work done during that time. His contact in Australia had instructed Nick to call the moment he landed in Sydney and that was just what Nick planned to do.

This case seemed kind of strange to Nick. Normally, serial killers tended to stick to one particular area, someplace close to home where they felt comfortable. This globetrotting theory bothered Nick in the extreme, even though he had at first scoffed at the idea that this disappearance in Australia could have anything to do with the Baker case in Texas. But after hearing what his source in Australia had had to say about what she'd heard had been found at the scene of the crime, Nick had quickly decided this new case was worth checking into and he'd booked his flight to Australia while he'd packed.

Now, as he sidled up to the counter at a pub near the waiting area at the gate where his next flight was to board, he dug out his satellite phone and, after ordering a pint of their darkest lager, made the call to his source. He sipped the lukewarm lager as he waited for an answer. Beer didn't taste good with ice cubes in it, but he sure wished he had some at the moment.

The airport was hot and muggy. It might be winter in the outback, but they still needed air conditioning in their buildings. Unfortunately, the Aussies didn't consider that a necessity. Nick knew it would be cooler outside, especially at night, so he guessed he should be relieved he was visiting during the winter instead of during the summer months. The outback got so hot during the summer it was almost unbearable to the non-native tourists. Nick had visited Australia many times as a child, but he'd long ago decided he would never visit again during the summer months because he'd recalled being stuck there during such hot times that he'd thought he would die.

"Yeah?" a sharp female voice asked in answer to the ring, bringing Nick out of his reverie.

"Kiley?" Nick asked. "It's Nick."

Immediately, the voice on the other end of the line turned smooth as silk and dripping with feline flirtation, as she said, "Nicky, darling, I was hoping it was you. Where are you? I'll come right over and pick you up."

"Ah, that's not necessary," he said. "I've just landed at Sydney Airport, but I'll be heading out for Alice Springs in less than an hour. I just needed to go over some of the fine points of the information you'd given me earlier so that I can contact the inspector on the case once I arrive there."

"You mean, you're not going to stop by and see me before?" she pouted over the phone line. Nick could just imagine her botox-filled lips doing their best to frown and he almost smiled. Kiley Plimpton and he went back a long way, even before his parents had died, and Nick knew if he gave her a minute, she'd take a week. She was just that good at time-suckage.

"I'm afraid I don't have time for socializing on this trip, love," he informed her smoothly. "This is strictly a working trip."

"Oh, pooh," she complained. "And I got all excited about your coming to Australia to see me. Surely there's some way you could manage to fit me in?"

"Not this trip, sweetheart," he explained. "It's strictly a fact-finding mission. My editor's already chompin' at the bit for this story and if I don't get it to him soon, he's gonna have my head."

"Ah, the plight of the working man," she sighed. "Well, I guess if you can't do it, then you just can't."

"Right," he agreed, relieved that she'd relented so quickly. "Now, tell me again about this friend of yours. Her name was Lisa…?"

"Murdoch," she finished for him. "Lisa Murdoch. She and I went to school here in Sydney together. She's a half-breed, but her mum always wanted the very best for her, so she made sure her daughter was accepted at the finest schools available. We took our A-levels together. She was very intelligent. Went on into Fashion and Merchandising. She always said her dream was to own her own shop here in Sydney. She's good at what she does, too."

"Uh-huh, and how old is she?" Nick asked as he wrote in the little notepad he always carried around with him.

"Twenty-six, same as me," she answered. "Oh, Nicky, you just *have* to help them find her. Where will I get my clothes if anything happens to her?"

"Uh, I'll do my best," he said, wondering how anyone could be so self-centered that she would think only of clothing at a time like this. This was supposed to be her good friend, right? Yet all she seemed upset about was the fact that the person who designed all the great outfits she wore was not available to do it anymore, not that the girl might be hurt, or worse. Nick just didn't get it.

"Hold on a sec, Nicky. There's someone at the door."

Nick held the line as he went back over everything she'd told him, both now and before he'd left New York. The whole bit about the evidence the locals had supposedly found was what disturbed him. From what Kiley had said, it seemed to match perfectly with what Nick's contact with the FBI in Dallas had told him had been found at the Baker household and that's what linked these two cases together, if what Kiley had said was true. Her description had been so close to what the FBI had found in Dallas, though, that Nick could see no way she could have faked it or gotten anything just right by accident.

"Okay," she said as she came back on the line. "It was just my lunch being delivered. Now, where were we?"

"You had said she was interested in the Sarah Baker case back in the states?" he asked, hoping to connect the dots even farther.

"Oh, yes," she agreed. "I remember her telling me all about that woman's blog, or something or other that she had been following on the internet. A few weeks ago, I just happened to catch a headline out on the internet while I was shopping for some new shoes. It was about this Sarah Baker woman and her blog and I immediately forwarded the link to the story to Lisa because I knew she would be very interested in it. I know she got the link because she emailed me back telling me thank you for having sent it to her.

"She'd said the woman's writings were causing quite a stir and that people all over the world were trying to track her down, but that's the last I heard from Lisa. Then, at the beginning of this week, I realized I had nothing to wear to this party I'm attending next weekend and I thought I would call Lisa to see if she might have any ideas. However, when I called, the inspector picked up and informed me she had gone missing. I did a little finessing and found out what little information I could, and that's when I called you."

Nick's flight was suddenly called. "Can you send me that link you sent to her about the American's blog?" he asked as he finished writing and then folded up his notepad and gathered his things.

"Of course," she said. "You want me to send it to your work email address or your personal one?"

She was fishing for his personal email address and Nick never gave that one out. "The work one would be great," he said. "Listen, my plane is boarding now, so I'm gonna have to get going. Thank you so much for the information, though. I definitely owe you one, sweetheart."

"I'll hold you to that, Nicky, darling," she said.

Nick pushed the End button on his cell and quickly gulped down the remaining half-glass of tepid lager. Damned Australians! Why couldn't they drink cold beer like Americans did?

He made his way over to his gate and boarded the smaller airbus along with his fellow passengers. There were several businessmen, but mostly families with two or three kids each who boarded with him. *Great*, he thought. *Just what I need, a bunch of screaming brats all the way to Alice Springs!*

Finding his seat, he stuffed his bag into the overhead bin and plopped down into the uncomfortable chair next to the window. The flight wasn't scheduled to be that long, but Nick wasn't overly fond of kids, and *any* time spent with more than one of them was way too much time in Nick's opinion. It turned out that the flight out to Alice Springs wasn't that bad, though. The kids that were on the plane were all well-behaved and Nick never once heard a single one of them whine or complain.

Before long, they were making their descent into the little airport there and Nick was soon standing outside it, waiting for a car at the rental desk. He still wasn't finished with his journey, as the woman, Lisa Murdoch, had lived in a small town called Barrow Creek, which was several hundred kilometres away from Alice Springs. Nick would have to drive the rest of the way on his own, unless he wanted to take one of the tour buses up that way. He'd seen several of the families with kids boarding one of the tour buses parked just outside the airport and he'd decided a rental car was definitely a better choice.

Nick didn't hold out much belief in the parenting skills of many in this day and age and he figured his luck with how well-behaved those kids were on the plane would run out very quickly if he boarded a tour bus with them. Nope, a rental car would be just fine by him. He had no idea how to drive on the wrong side of the car, or the road for that matter, since he'd always had a hired driver whenever he'd been in Australia before, but he was damned sure he would be able to figure it out!

All the car rental company had was some sort of SUV. The make was one he'd never heard of before and it looked like it was from World War I. Other than that, there was just a one-seater, and that was being generous. It was actually a European model, but it looked as if it would fall apart if anyone over 50 lbs. sat in it. Nick asked which had air conditioning and decided that way. The old one-seater European model it was.

He stowed his single bag in the spider-web laden trunk of the vehicle and then carefully folded himself down into the deep bucket seat. He spent nearly a half hour adjusting everything that could possibly be adjusted just so he would be able to see above the steering wheel enough to drive the rickety old jalopy. By the time he actually pulled out of the parking lot, the sun was heading down toward the horizon. Nick didn't want to be stuck out in the middle of nowhere in the Outback. That, he knew, was dangerous for a foreigner. After all, Australia not only housed the most venomous and deadly wild animals on the planet, but some of the deadliest humans as well.

$$\infty$$

Baphomet leaned back against the headboard and frowned. The things he'd just learned from listening in on Sarah's and Mikhail's conversation with Thomas merely served to confirm the suspicions he'd developed regarding the boy. Although, it did appear the boy truly did not remember why or even how he'd come to be on this planet.

"So we're not upset with him anymore?" Lisa asked quietly.

Baphomet hugged her closer with the arm he had around her shoulders. "I do not believe I am ready to send out the welcome wagon just yet, but at least I think we can relax our guard a little where he is concerned," he said.

"What I would really like to do," he continued as he moved to lay between her legs again so he could listen to Cabal's chatter, "is to leave the complex in favor of a less densely-populated area."

Lisa sighed and tilted her head, frowning as she, too, caught the thoughts from others within the complex. She knew if she and Baphomet could catch these thoughts, then Cabal probably could as well. He still wasn't talking, per se, but he had managed to keep up a steady stream of loud whispering, thus far.

Both Lisa and Baphomet had noticed Cabal tended to quiet down each time others' thoughts intruded on their little trio, and they both knew something would have to be done if they wanted to make Cabal feel completely safe.

Sure enough, just as this thought passed through her mind, Cabal's soft chatter stopped because someone else was passing by outside and their thoughts were coming through as if they were standing in the room with them yelling. Baphomet sighed in frustration. They were both frustrated, but what could they do? It was too dangerous for Lisa in Shaitan territory and they needed to remain somewhere close to the Angelic physician, Hantsushept, just in case anything happened with the pregnancy.

"M-Maybe, Israfil could help?" Lisa asked.

"No, sweet," Baphomet said, shaking his head. "He has done far too much already. We cannot ask him to…" A soft knocking on the door interrupted him and Baphomet said, "Come."

Israfil slowly poked his head around the door and asked in a whisper, "Is everything okay?"

Baphomet nodded once and held out a hand toward Israfil. "Please, come inside," he said to his brother.

Israfil entered and quietly closed the door behind himself. Then, he made his way over to stand at the foot of the bed near Baphomet's side, where he wrapped an arm around the high post there. He studied his brother's face and then whispered, "You seem… upset about something."

Baphomet narrowed his eyes as he looked at Israfil, suddenly realizing he couldn't read his brother. Ever since Baphomet had realized he had the ability to read the thoughts of others, he'd been able to read all of his siblings' thoughts, including Israfil's.

Now, however, as Baphomet thought back over each of the times he'd been around Israfil since coming to stay at the complex, he realized he had only been able to catch the thoughts Israfil probably wanted him to hear and nothing more.

Baphomet then realized he couldn't read the boy, Thomas, either, and that there was somehow a connection between Thomas and Israfil that aided them both from being open to Baphomet's mind. A jab in his ribs from Lisa's elbow suddenly brought his mind back to the present and he looked over at her to make sure she was okay.

I'm okay, but you're being incredibly rude to your brother, she silently told him.

Baphomet quickly returned his attention to Israfil and said, "We are not upset, it is just... we are having a bit of difficulty with something."

"Anything I can help with?" Israfil immediately asked.

"No," Baphomet answered on a sigh. "Leece and I will figure it out."

Israfil moved to sit on the bed beside Baphomet's legs. "Please," he said. "Whatever it is, I am sure I can help. At least, I can help figure out how to solve the problem"

Baphomet hesitated. He still wasn't used to having another Seraph, other than Suriyah, offering to help him with anything, and the old suspicions came crashing through his mind.

Baph, Lisa's voice silently implored inside his head, *maybe he really can help. Why don't we just tell him?*

Baphomet looked over at her. He could feel her hope and her need for it. Looking back toward Israfil, he decided he had no choice but to trust his brother. After all, Israfil had proven himself with all the things he'd already done for Lisa and him.

"We are trying to figure out a way to isolate ourselves away from everyone else without going too far away from Hantsushept, just in case we need him for something," he explained. "The complex is just too crowded and we think that is why Cabal is having such a difficult time coming out of hiding. We figure he will be more likely to feel safe and comfortable if there is no one else around. Unfortunately, Leece and I catch the thoughts of just about everybody here in the house whenever they are anywhere near this room, and sometimes when they are not even nearby."

Israfil nodded, thinking for a moment, and then said in a low voice, "Take my place."

Both Lisa and Baphomet narrowed their eyes in confusion and he explained, saying, "My people, those from my former household who chose to follow me out here, have been building a new house for us to live in. It is just about finished, but no one has moved in yet. It is about a thousand meters from Mikhail's house, so it is still well within the grounds of the complex, which would allow for Hantsushept to get to you should there be any kind of emergency or anything, and the staff here could still bring food to the two of you each day. Either that, or you could arrange for your own staff to come stay."

"Iz," Baphomet said. "We cannot take your home from you."

"Please," Israfil suddenly said urgently. "Please allow me to help."

Again, Baphomet felt a strange sensation of unease and he pulled back a bit, narrowing his eyes as he gazed at his brother. "Why is this so important to you?" he finally asked.

Israfil lowered his gaze and the couple sitting at the other end of the bed were suddenly horrified to realize this person they'd come to trust and care for was almost on the verge of tears as they noticed his chin wobbling and the dampness at the corner of his eye.

"Iz?" Baphomet asked.

Israfil took a deep breath and then turned to face the two. "Please take my home. Take anything. Take everything I have to offer and...," he shook his head. "Take it all."

"Iz," Baphomet began, "what are you...?"

Israfil interrupted him, explaining, "I owe you. I *owe* you – this, and so much more. You have no idea." The tears breached his lids and slowly slid down his cheeks as he shook his head. "You never knew and none of us ever got the chance to tell you. But it is time now and I shall do whatever it takes to make things up to you."

"Please," Baphomet said. "I do not understand what you are talking about."

Israfil nodded. "It was my fault Mikhail banished Suriyah and you from Seraphim City," he said.

Baphomet sat back, stunned. "What?" he asked in disbelief.

"It was my fault," Israfil said again. "I take full responsibility." When Baphomet merely continued staring at him, he continued, saying, "When Enki made his demands about Suriyah and you, I was the one who finally convinced Mikhail to do it."

Baphomet shook his head. He couldn't believe what he was hearing.

"Yes," Israfil continued. "At first, Enki wanted the two of you to be executed along with the humans who had rebelled. None of us wanted that. But then, he ordered the two of you to be expelled from Seraphim City. I think he believed you would both be forced out into the human realm and that there he would have the opportunity to have his human cattle kill you. He did not realize the two of you were more capable than that or that you would be able to live quite well in the Badlands on your own."

Israfil stood and paced over to the window near the far corner of the room. He stood staring out the glass, though the scenes flashing before his eyes were from long ago.

"Djibril would not agree to any form of punishment for you," he continued. "He did not care that Suriyah and you were speaking out against the Designers. He merely thought of you as young and naïve. Azra'il, of course, was completely taken in by them. He had no problem with the two of you being banished, though now I think he wished there was some other way."

Israfil looked over at Baphomet and smiled a sad little smile, saying, "I do not think he ever meant for either of you to be harmed in any way. He loved you both, but he was completely devoted to the Designers, just as he is to this very day."

He turned to look out the window once more, his mind replaying that dreadful day in Seraphim City. "Mikhail did not know what to do," he continued. "He was torn between his love for his siblings and his devotion to the Designers. In the end, I knew he was going to defy Enki's edict, so I convinced him otherwise."

At Baphomet's look of disbelief, Israfil said, "He even told me he was considering doing just that. That was when I did everything I could to stop him."

Israfil returned to the bed, sitting again at the bottom beside Baphomet's feet. "You see," he continued, "I believed them. At that time, I was as devoted to the Designers as Azra'il was. I had swallowed every line they had fed us and I could not *stand* the fact that someone would say anything bad about our creators. Hell, I wanted to banish you, myself. But Mikhail was the one in charge, so I did whatever I could to convince him to banish Suriyah and you from our city. It was not until a couple of millennia ago that I finally realized what a fool I had been."

"What happened then?" Baphomet asked, his voice stony and devoid of emotion. His heart was broken from watching this beloved brother's suffering, but he needed to know the entire story and he could get no reading off Israfil, no matter how hard he tried.

Another sad smile played about the corners of Israfil's lips as his eyes took on a faraway look. "That was when I first encountered Thomas," he softly said.

Baphomet and Lisa both narrowed their eyes in masks of complete surprise and confusion and asked simultaneously, "The boy?"

Israfil suddenly seemed to remember the couple's presence and he pulled himself together, stating, "Yes. But that was also when I realized the Designers had lied to us. I knew then what a mistake I had made and what I had done to Suriyah and you. I desperately wanted to find you both and do something, but what could I do? Both of you were lost to us by then and... so many other things were happening."

He looked pleadingly into his brother's eyes. "Please, brother," he requested. "Please allow me to help your mate and you, however I can, as much as I can? If for nothing more than so that I may repay you for all the happiness I caused to be stolen from your life." He looked down at his empty hands lying turned upward on his lap and his chin wobbled again in his grief. "Please..., forgive me?"

Baphomet hesitated for only a moment before suddenly leaning forward and clasping his brother's arm in a firm grip. "Brother," he said, "there is nothing to forgive. I have since discovered much about the false creators we called Designers and I have seen the effects of their duplicity. I cannot blame you or my other siblings for any crimes committed in the Designers' name."

Israfil looked up, disbelief clearly written all over his face.

Baphomet shook his head and said, "I will no longer carry hatred in my heart for my brothers for things they had no true

261

hand in causing." He paused and cast a loving glance at Lisa. When he returned his gaze to his brother, he said, "I am now complete. All I wish is for my mate and my child to be safe. So, I will accept your offer, my brother, and we shall forget the past and be done with it."

Another tear slipped over the edge of Israfil's eye and slowly tracked its way down his face as he nodded once more and simply said, "Thank you."

Baphomet nodded, a half-grin lighting his face. "No thanks are necessary, but I expect full consideration when it comes time for you to be naming your own son, assuming he does not already have a name," he said. "Baphomet is a fine name, after all."

A strange look crossed Israfil's face for just a split second before he smiled and nodded, saying, "Indeed, it is."

Baphomet had caught the look, but again found that his brother's mind was completely shielded from any outside prying.

Israfil stood suddenly and headed toward the door. "Well, I shall go and start making arrangements," he said. "Just, um, call out if you need anything." And then, he was gone.

Baphomet sat staring at the closed door. How had Israfil developed such extraordinary telepathic skills? For that matter, what had he meant when he'd said he'd encountered Thomas a couple of millennia ago? And what had he meant when he'd said *'so many other things were happening'*?

The only thing Baphomet recalled that had been going on during that time frame had been the Christian uprising with Jesus Christ in the Middle Eastern portion of the human realm. Baphomet had not interfered in that particular part of human history, so he didn't really know much more than what he'd later read about what had happened. Had Israfil been party to the uprising? Was *that* what he'd been referring to? And where did the boy, Thomas, figure into all of it?

Lisa suddenly squeezed his hand and he gave her a quick hug. "Do not worry, sweet Lisa," he whispered, as the soft tones of his son's whispers once more drifted into his mind. "There will be plenty of time for us to figure out the answers to these questions later. For the now, let us concentrate on making Cabal as comfortable as possible, hmm?"

She smiled and lifted her face to give him a quick peck on the cheek, whispering, "Thank you." After rubbing Cabal's lighted spot on her abdomen, she looked back up at him and said, "I would like to speak with Sarah and Mikhail before we leave, though. They've been extraordinarily kind to me, to us, and I'd like to thank them for all they've done."

Baphomet nodded and they both got up to make their preparations.

Chapter 19

The car rental attendant had informed him the road to Barrow Creek was a good one, but Nick knew one had to take words like "good" with a grain of salt in the outback. So, nearly an hour after he'd arrived in Alice Springs, he finally set off. The car jerked violently in the beginning until Nick realized it was necessary to shift into reverse first each time he needed to change gears. Other than that, Nick encountered no further difficulties with the vehicle. He had to strop three times to refill the gas tank, but he had plenty of fuel in plastic containers and he finally coasted into town around nine o'clock at night local time.

"Where the hell am I?" he asked of no one in particular as he drove through the small town.

The place was very tight-knit, with most of the buildings grouped as close to each other as possible. It reminded Nick of an old West town from those spaghetti westerns he'd grown up watching. It appeared not too many people actually lived in town, but that it was more just a meeting place where all of them could come together.

There was one pub and one motel, one bank, one grocer, and one petrol station. It seemed Barrow Creek was more of a place on the way *to* someplace else rather than one's final destination and Nick wondered if he, himself, wouldn't have done whatever he could to escape such a lonesome town. It would explain a lot in this case. The missing girl may well have just run off in order to find a better life for herself instead of having been kidnapped.

264

Nick mentally checked himself as he approached the address Kiley had given him for the kidnap victim, Miss Murdoch.

Don't go jumping the gun, Nick, he said silently to himself.

He'd come here to review as much of the evidence as possible. If she did leave without foul play, then he'd go home and turn in the piece he'd already written on the Sarah Baker case in Dallas. However, if there did turn out to be a connection between this case and the Baker case back in Dallas, he would be damned sure to follow through with the evidence until he had the whole story before he'd submit one word to Frank.

As he walked up to the front door of the little ground-level flat, his camera bag in hand, he noticed there were lights on inside the joint. Several loud, deep voices could be heard from inside and Nick wondered if he might need to return some other time. Just then, the front door opened and a whip-thin uniformed officer of the law stepped out.

He paused when he caught sight of Nick standing outside the flat. After a quick examination of the newcomer, the officer turned back to poke his head just inside the door of the flat and barked, "Inspector, I believe your American journalist is here." With that, the man rushed away from the building and walked quickly on past Nick without another word.

Nick raised his brows and said under his breath, "O-kay."

"Shed-off?" A booming voice called from somewhere deep within the little flat.

"Hello?" Nick called as he made his way back through to the small bedroom of the single flat.

There, a very tall, very large, and very hairy man stood in the middle of the room. "Shed-off? Am I sayin' that right?" the man asked.

Nick stretched out a hand and said, "It's Shvedov. It's Russian, but you can call me Nick."

"Right," the man said as he shook Nick's hand. "Gorman's the name. I'm the lead inspector assigned to this case." He turned and picked up a packet of photos from an open desk drawer. "I've been instructed to cooperate with you however you need."

Nick allowed his bag to drop to the floor as he took in everything in the room. "I appreciate that, sir," he said.

Gorman turned from the desk to regard Nick with interest. "You must have some pull with someone pretty high up to get that kind of clearance on a case like this," he said. When Nick merely shrugged, he asked, "So, what's so important about a half-breed Aboriginal girl goin' missin' that's got a New York City journalist flyin' all the way to the outback in such a hurry?"

Nick ignored the question, still looking around the room. Everything seemed to be in its place. "No signs of a break-in or a struggle?" he asked instead.

"Nah," Gorman replied, looking around the immaculate room himself. "The place is clean. Everything's in order. The girl's prints are everywhere, but no one else's."

"Nothing's been found?" Nick asked.

"Well, nothin' really conclusive," the inspector said evasively.

"Nothing at all?" Nick pointedly asked. "No DNA? No... hair strands?"

Gorman instantly stilled, going completely white with shock. "How did you...?"

Nick nodded and said, "There's the answer to why I'm here."

Gorman shook his head, explaining, "It's the damnedest thing I ever saw. You said it's hair?" When Nick nodded, he shook his head again and said, "I never saw any kind of hair like that. We thought it was some kind of snake or worm or something."

"You got your people working on it?" Nick asked.

Gorman nodded. "Sent it off to Sydney this afternoon," he said as a shiver raced down his spine. "I couldn't wait to get that thing out of the office. Didn't much feel like returning to this place, either, after we found that thing, I tell you. Had to threaten my officers just to get them back here."

Nick pulled out his camera and note pad from his bag and started filling a role while stopping every now and then to jot down a few observations. "Any idea who saw her last?" he asked as he worked.

"We got a couple of station hands who say there were two tribesmen who performed some type of ritual ceremony with the girl the last night she was seen," Gorman said.

"I'd like to talk with them, please," Nick requested.

"With all of'em?" Gorman asked.

"If that's possible," Nick affirmed.

Gorman scratched his great hairy head, his bushy eyebrows raised nearly all the way up to his hairline. "I can get you the two station hands easily enough," he said. "The two tribesmen though, they'll be a bit more difficult to track down, I'd imagine."

Nick stood up straight, reaching his full height of 6'6" and looking expectantly at the other man.

Gorman stared right back, considering his own height was still a couple inches higher than that, but then he sighed and shook his head again, rubbing the back of his neck in frustration. "I'll-I'll see what I can arrange," he said. "It's gonna take some doin', though. Word's got out that she's missin' and since then, we haven't had too many natives around town."

Nick nodded. "Whatever you can do, I'll appreciate it," he said.

Gorman sighed as if the weight of the world was suddenly resting atop his shoulders. "One of my officers is native to this region. I'll see what he can do as far as diggin' up the two boys."

Nick nodded again. "I'll be at the motel when you've got something," he informed the inspector as he packed away his gear back in his bag.

"Right," Gorman said, back to his gruff composure again. "I'd avoid the steak, if I were you. And, check the towels and the bed clothes for spiders before using them. Had a ton of bites there this past winter."

"Thanks," Nick said.

∞

Azra'il sat at his spot along the row of council members, wondering how things had gotten to such a state of utter chaos within these walls. The council chamber was as a sea of voices, with each member trying to be heard above the others. There were no coherent actions being discussed, merely accusations and reactions, and Azra'il knew no good would come from such discussions.

Every few minutes, he would attempt to interject a thought or suggestion to those within earshot, but the majority of the Sanhedrin members were completely ignoring him. Their sons and mates had been killed like no other time in history and they wanted blood.

For millennia, Angels had watched as those of the human race had warred amongst themselves, destroying entire civilizations, entire peoples, all for a piece of land or for a religious belief. Sometimes those wars had even begun because of suggestions the Seraphim had made to certain human individuals. However, such things had always been done with only the well-being of the overall human populace in mind.

Occasionally, the few had been sacrificed for the good of the many, but what else could the Seraphim do? They'd been charged with the maintenance and well-being of human society. The natural tendency of humans toward self-destruction was a constant threat to the balance the Seraphim were charged with keeping and they sometimes had to resort to extreme measures in order to maintain that balance.

Angels were not violent by nature, however, and each and every council member found the idea of having to engage in the type of civil unrest displayed by the human race over the millennia as repulsive as the idea of having humans living within the Angelic realm. No one wanted *that*!

"My lord, we must find a way to punish those responsible for the murders of our dear ones," a council member sitting near Azra'il said. The woman was so distraught that there was spittle clinging to the corners of her mouth, on the verge of becoming a glob of drool that would then run down the side of her chin.

She didn't seem to notice, however, and continued with her pleas, saying, "I understand your brothers are involved and that you have your loyalties to them to consider, but these were our sons and our mates! You must understand that this act of savagery cannot go unanswered, even if it was committed by individuals who have been completely duped by humans."

"My dear councilwoman," Azra'il said, holding up a hand in an attempt to gain some silence within the immediate area. A few of the council members standing and yapping nearby finally noticed his gesture and quieted themselves to hear his response.

At his continued silence, more and more of the council members around the room began to take notice of his raised hand and they, too, became quiet, with many returning to their seats around the room.

When at last there was complete silence within the large, round room, Azra'il continued. "I have been sitting here for the past few hours listening to this council's concerns," he said. "All of them, thus far, have been valid and unarguable. We have more than enough evidence for a jury to find those banished from Seraphim City guilty of each and every crime of which they are being accused, and to convict.

"However, at this time I would issue a word of caution to all of you." He rose from his seat and descended to the small stage area in the center of the room. As he looked around at the faces of the council members, many whose births he'd even witnessed, he wondered if there was any way they could possibly ever understand what he was about to tell them.

"Emotions are high within this chamber and such a state often leads to impetuous thoughts and actions. And, there is another matter that bears thinking about. The manner in which your sons and mates were killed in this recent battle should be concerning you more than anything else," he said. "I have been given the chief medical officer's report concerning the deaths and it is very disturbing in that the wounds and manner of the deaths are not typical to Seraphim.

"Seraphim are merely more advanced versions of yourselves, believe it or not. We do not have the ability to go around burning people with electricity from out of nowhere. We are not known for easily beheading others or for chopping off others' body parts on a whim.

"Yes, my siblings have been duped by this small group of humans they have allowed into our realm. But, I assure you, there is no doubt in my mind that it could not have been Seraphim who did this to your sons and mates." He paused to collect his thoughts, but already the smirks and rolling eyes could be seen on the faces of those all around him.

Azra'il spoke at once to dispel any notion of nepotism. "I understand there are those among us who will take my words of caution as a way to buy time for my siblings, as if I would allow this grave injustice to go unpunished simply because of my relationship with those whom you believe to be responsible for these deaths," he said.

"Murders," someone from the crowd yelled out.

Azra'il nodded his head in acknowledgement of the correction. "It is true," he continued, "I love my siblings. I love them as you love your own. I cannot think of any instance when I would not do for them to the best of my ability, as you would for your own. But, when I look out upon this collection of citizens of this great city and of this great race, I see the pain and anguish and confusion that has been brought on by these grave misdeeds, and my heart aches.

"It is true, I have no child. I have no mate. No Seraph is allowed such, by order of the one law set upon us by the blessed Great Designers 'lo these many thousands of years ago," he continued. "But, in living and loving with my Angelic friends and neighbors, I have come to regard the majority of the residents of Seraphim City as my own relatives. When one of you suffers, I suffer. When one of you fears, I share your fear. When one of you needs, I do whatever is in my power to see that your need is eliminated, either by providing for you or by helping you to provide for yourself.

"My Seraphim siblings have always believed the same way I believe. They are not parents. They do not have mates. They cannot, by order of the same law that compels me. I do not believe for one moment, therefore, that they have been so brainwashed by this puny collection of humans that they would be willing to commit such a heinous act against the very beings they have up to this point considered family members, themselves.

"Such a thing would be unconscionable, unthinkable. It cannot be true, I tell you!" As council members half-rose from their seats in an attempt to interrupt him, Azra'il held up his hand once more for silence, saying, "I cannot, in all honesty, promise you that this grievous savagery against your loved ones was not committed by my siblings' hands, for I was not witness to the act, itself.   But, that is why what I am about to suggest is so important."

He clasped his hands together behind his back and stared down at the floor as he paced around in a slow circle along the outside of the small stage area, nearly touching the legs of the council members seated along the lowest row of seats. After a moment, he sighed and stopped, looking up into the faces of those seated nearest him and saying, "I, myself, will go out in secret to the very spot where this massacre occurred. I shall go to the area where my siblings have settled in the Badlands and there, after I observe the situation with my own eyes, I shall determine for myself what punishment should be meted out to those responsible for your loved ones' deaths and I shall exact the vengeance you all seek. That way, the blood will be on my hands and none of the lay citizens within the walls of Seraphim City will have to know anything other than that their realm is once more human free and safe.

"Do not think, however, just because my siblings may be found to be involved in the massacre, that I will not assign a fitting punishment or that I will not carry it out with a swiftness and finality befitting the situation. *You* are my people. My siblings abandoned *all* of us when they chose the human way, not just me. They abandoned *all* of us, and they shall be made to pay the price. Of that, you may be certain."

Although it was not the war cry the council members had wished to hear from him, a few sitting around the chamber began to clap in a halting manner. Then, more hands joined in, then more and more, until the entire council was clapping for his words and his plan.

Azra'il's shoulders slumped in temporary relief. He had thwarted an outright war. *Only for the moment,* a little voice inside his head cautioned.

∞

Suriyah touched down in the empty clearing just outside the complex grounds, her shields finally unwrapping from around her form and slipping back down along the sides of her spinal column into their holding place. She'd been gone for only a short amount of time, but she was exhausted.

She and Djibril had discovered not one, but seven separate terror plots, all contrived and on the verge of being enacted by the groups of humans compelled by the Shaitans Iblis and Satariel. All but one of the plots had been thwarted at the last minute and Djibril was presently working on doing the same to the last cell of terrorists they'd found.

But things in the human realm were getting bad. Suriyah had not known it was so bad and she felt a tremendous desire to return to her people so she could inform them of the humans' current need. The Jinn had historically done whatever they could to assist the humans, though none would ever admit to it.

Hers was a meek people, not given to desires for praise or recognition. They merely wanted to help and that's what they did. They might not help in the way one wanted, but the Jinn always chose the path that would help the most. Humans didn't always appreciate that and so stories of the Jinn's duplicity and trickery had developed.

Suriyah also believed such stories had been assisted by her brother's people, the Shaitans, but she'd never said anything to him about it. She loved Baphomet and she would never hurt him by saying anything bad about his people. She didn't understand them, but neither did she begrudge them their way of life. At least, not until they started interfering with innocent humans.

As Suriyah entered the door to the main building of the complex, she came face to face with her brother... at least she thought she recognized Baphomet in the face staring back at her. The rest of him was completely changed! Suriyah turned to the person standing next to him and realized it was the human girl, Lisa, though she, too, looked completely different.

Suriyah stood with her mouth hanging open, not saying a word. Her brother's hair and eyes had been normal when she'd left. Now, the individual strands lifted of their own accord, as if on a mysterious breeze that only affected them, and then settled back down behind her brother's form. Suriyah shivered as she recalled just how lethal those innocuous-looking strands could be.

Baphomet's eyes glowed a bright white from within the pupil. There was no color remaining in his irises and one glance at Lisa confirmed hers had changed completely, as well. They each glowed with an innate light, though Lisa seemed to have a little brighter patch showing through on her lower abdomen. Suriyah wondered if that meant her new sister was with child and a swift pang of what could only be described as jealousy suddenly coursed through her.

Suriyah quickly looked away from the woman. How could she be jealous? The fact that Baphomet had found his true mate could only mean she should have more hope of finding her own, right? Hadn't the visions she'd seen showed her that much, at least? The prophecy had been pretty accurate thus far and Suriyah knew she should have faith that the rest of it would come to pass, but all in due time.

"Suri," Baphomet said softly. "I am so glad you made it back in time. Lisa and I are on our way to visit with Mikhail and Sarah to tell them good-bye."

Suriyah was floored! She burst out, "You are leaving?"

Baphomet immediately shushed her and reached over to place a hand over the little glowing patch on Lisa's lower abdomen. He then turned back to face Suriyah and said quietly, "Yes, we are leaving to go stay in Israfil's place until Cabal, our son, is born. There are too many people in this household and it frightens him whenever anyone even passes outside the door to our suite, so Israfil offered us the use of his new home on the outskirts of the complex."

Suriyah's eyebrows rose as understanding seeped in. "Well," she said in a loud whisper, turning to face her new sister, "I am sorry you and I have not had time to get to know each other better. I, myself, was on my way to see Mikhail and Sarah to tell them I would be returning to Jinn territory this very evening after I have gotten just a bit of rest."

She turned back to Baphomet and continued, "I cannot believe how bad things have become in the human realm, but I know my people would want to know, so I am headed home."

Baphomet's eyebrows narrowed and he softly asked, "Were Djibril and you able to find Iblis and Satariel in time?"

Suriyah shook her head as the trio turned toward the main suite of rooms within the house, explaining, "We could not find them, but we discovered several terror cells they had compelled and stopped them from wreaking havoc. Djibril is just finishing up with the last one and then he should be returning to the Angelic realm."

Baphomet reached the door to the Master suite and knocked on it as he absorbed this bit of news. An Angel answered the door and quickly allowed the trio entry into the suite, informing them they would have to wait in the parlor until Mikhail and Sarah could be notified of their visit. Baphomet and Lisa quickly took a seat on a comfortable sofa near the center of the room.

Suriyah stayed a couple of yards away from the two of them, choosing instead to sit on a nearby window seat facing the couple. As the Angel left the room, she studied her brother and new sister. The glow coming off the two of them was phenomenal. It was far greater than that which Mikhail and Sarah had emitted the last time Suriyah had been in their presence. She wondered how anyone could contain so much soul energy and not be continuously moving or nervous.

"Suri," Baphomet said in a low voice, "I would appreciate it if you would in future try to remember that my son can hear most thoughts emitted by those near him, as can his mother and I," he added as an afterthought.

Suriyah blanched and looked away, directing her attention instead outside to the gardens facing this wing of the house. There was a swing there she hadn't noticed before and a pretty little stone pathway through a maze of flowerbeds.

The door suddenly opened to admit Mikhail and Sarah, both of whom appeared flushed and out of breath, as if they'd both run to the room or been engaged in some form of physical activity just prior to coming to the room. The tender look they exchanged just after entering made it abundantly clear to everyone in the room exactly which it had been *and* what type of physical activity they'd been involved in, and Suriyah rolled her eyes. If that was all a Seraph could think about after finding his or her mate, then Suriyah wanted nothing to do with the whole business!

In truth, a small part of her heart wept at the fearful thought that she might never find her one true soul mate who could make her feel that way. But Suriyah was a survivor. She always had been. She sucked in a breath for strength and lifted her head, determined not to allow herself to get sucked down by her fears of such a fate. The prophecy was true. It had to be.

Suriyah would not allow the false Designers to conquer her mind as they had her siblings' minds for so very long.

Sarah was the first to break the uncomfortable silence, turning to Suriyah and saying, "Suriyah. You've returned with good news?"

"Yes," Mikhail chimed in quietly. "Welcome back." He looked around quickly and then asked, "Where is Djibril?"

"He will be back soon," Suriyah told the two. "He is following up on one last lead and then he should return."

Mikhail smiled at her, his bright white eyes shining softly out at her. "We are pleased you have returned to us safe and successful," he said. "We were beginning to worry about the two of you."

Suriyah gave a quick nod and a shrug, explaining, "Things are not exactly going well out there in the human realm. In fact, I cannot recall ever having seen it this bad before." At their looks of concern, she continued, "Actually, that is the reason I have come here. I shall be returning to Jinn territory this very evening to inform and mobilize my people. We must protect our charges as best we can from the evils currently plaguing mankind and I would be remiss in my duties as the Queen of the Jinn if I did not return as soon as possible."

"Things have gotten that bad?" Mikhail asked with concern.

"It is worse than I have ever seen," Suriyah reiterated. She looked at Sarah for just a moment before saying, "From what I gathered from the news reports, there is still a huge uproar over the things Sarah had published before coming to our realm. There are riots being held in the streets of several cities all over the world regarding her writings and… it seems there is a price on her head. It was announced on some Middle Eastern television station and then the information leaked to the rest of the world."

Mikhail's arm tightened its grip on Sarah's shoulders.

Suriyah merely shook her head and said, "I know everyone here is safe, but I do not think it would be wise for Sarah or any of her relatives here to go back to the human realm anytime soon." She sighed and shook her head again. "I know my people will want to do whatever they can as quickly as possible. I just hope we are not already too late to salvage things out there, at this point."

Mikhail stepped forward and placed a hand on her shoulder, saying, "Then you should go. And Suriyah, please know that you are welcome at this complex whenever you desire."

Suriyah still felt nervous around Mikhail and Sarah, but she'd done her duty and delivered the information she'd needed to deliver in order to make sure Mikhail and Sarah understood the dangers awaiting them should Sarah or any of her human relatives here try to travel back over into the human realm.

Suriyah's nervousness now extended to Baphomet and Lisa as well, now that they had changed, but there was not time now for dissecting her feelings on that issue. She would have to work that one out once she got back to her own stronghold on her own. She nodded to everyone in turn and then left without uttering another word.

When the door to the room was closed once more and the two couples were alone, Baphomet turned to face his brother and his new sister. He had a feeling Sarah had already been digging into his mind, even while she'd been conversing with Suriyah, but he went ahead and stated the reason for Lisa's and his visit this afternoon, saying, "We have come to offer our thanks to you both and to tell you we shall be leaving, ourselves, this evening."

Lisa stood and stepped forward, grasping Sarah's hand in both of hers and softly explaining, "Israfil has been kind enough to offer us the use of his house here at the complex until Cabal is born. We've been having such a difficult time with him so far and we all thought this might help him to feel safer."

Sarah rushed to ask, "Is there anything we can do?"

Smiling, Lisa shook her head and said, "No, no. And we're so grateful for everything you and Mikhail have done for us. I don't think we'll ever be able to repay you." She looked back over her shoulder at Baphomet, who had risen from his seat on the sofa and was now speaking very quietly with Mikhail. Perhaps now was the time for her to speak with Sarah about something she'd been wondering about since coming to the Angelic realm.

She turned back to Sarah and said, "I wanted to ask you something, if you don't mind?"

"Please," was Sarah's immediate response. The information Suriyah had just delivered to them still weighed heavily on her mind, but Sarah was determined to make Lisa feel as welcome as possible.

"Well," Lisa hesitantly began. "Before coming to the Angelic realm, I already knew about you." At Sarah's look of cautious confusion, she explained, "I used to follow your Vision Blog. Then, when you disappeared, I joined a group of online followers who were looking through the archives of your blog for clues as to where you might have gone and how you got there. You see, there was a theory out there, because of your last blog entry, that you had intentionally hidden clues within your blog so that others would be able to follow you to this dimension."

"But, I didn't," Sarah denied, shaking her head, wondering if this was the root of the cause of the riots Suriyah had spoken of going on in the human realm.

Lisa merely smiled and shrugged. "I just thought I would let you know there are people out there who believe in you," she said. "They're looking for you still, I'd wager." With that, she leaned in and kissed Sarah's cheek, and then returned to Baphomet's side to take his hand in hers.

He immediately asked, "Are you ready, sweet Lisa?" At her nod, he said, "Very well." He turned back to face Mikhail. "I am afraid it is time for us to be going," he stated.

As she approached Mikhail's side, Sarah noticed the sheen of tears in his eyes as he said, "You are both welcome in our household whenever you wish. I hope you know that." He held out his free hand.

Baphomet took his hand and shook it, chokingly saying, "Thank you..., Brother."

Mikhail and Sarah each slid an arm around the other's back as they watched the couple leave the room. It was sad to think two such social people would have to completely isolate themselves away from everyone at least until their baby was born.

I wonder if that will be the end of it? Mikhail's voice asked Sarah as it floated across her mind.

I don't know, she silently replied. *I just don't know.* She turned to look up into his glowing eyes, loving him with all her heart and wondering how she'd gotten so lucky.

No, my heart, he silently told her, *I am the lucky one.*

Sarah merely said aloud, "Hmm." Then, she narrowed her eyes and asked, "So, Baphomet has forgiven you, has he?" referring to the quiet conversation Baphomet had had with Mikhail while Lisa and Sarah had been talking about her Vision Blog.

"It seems so," Mikhail confirmed. "It appears Israfil told him I never wanted to banish Suriyah and him from Seraphim City, but that Israfil, himself, had convinced me to adhere to Enki's demands, which, if I am honest, is what actually happened at the time."

Sarah reached up and cupped his cheek, asking, "And so, have you forgiven yourself?"

Mikhail closed his eyes and raised a hand to cover hers, whispering, "I am trying, Sarah. I am trying. But, it was a long time to carry such guilt." He opened his eyes and looked directly into hers, swallowing a lump in his throat. "I know now at least *he* does not blame me for what happened anymore. There is still Suriyah left to deal with, though."

Sarah sighed and smiled and stood upon her tip-toes to kiss him tenderly on the lips. "She'll forgive you," she said with confidence.

I hope so, he silently whispered to her as he bent his head and kissed her long and full on the mouth.

Sarah had not once thought of putting the buffer back up once she'd dropped it earlier in the day when she and Mikhail had found themselves alone for a little while in the garden. She was getting very good at recognizing when he wanted a buffer between them, however, and when he wanted to share with her. She wasn't perfect at it yet, but she was getting there.

She was also getting very good at just blocking her own thoughts from him while still being able to pick up on his thoughts, as she was currently doing regarding the information Suriyah had given them. She would take those thoughts out and examine them later when she was alone.

Mikhail still didn't know how to do that very well on his own, but she was certain he would learn. Erecting a powerful-enough buffer on his own so that she would not be able to catch any of his thoughts would take time and she would give it to him. He was a male, after all, and Sarah knew just how prideful those suffering from the y-chromosome syndrome were, so there was no doubt in her mind he would continue practicing until he got it down pat.

Now, however, he didn't seem to want a buffer between them as he nibbled at her neck. Sarah happily tilted her head to the side to allow him greater access to her sensitive skin. She didn't care if he decided he wanted a permanent buffer between them and kept everything in the world from her, she decided, as long as he just kept touching her.

Chapter 20

Nick was truly thankful for the inspector's earlier words of advice regarding the towels and bedclothes as he stomped on two of the ugliest spiders he'd ever seen in the tiny bathroom at the end of the hallway in the little motel. They'd fallen from the towel that had been hanging on a peg on the wall next to the shower. Nick had remembered the inspector's warning just before he'd undressed and shook out the towel and there they'd been.

"Great," he said to himself after the two were finally mere pools of goo on the stained white tile floor. "I think I'll skip the shower tonight."

He made his way back down the hallway to his room and spent the remainder of the night in bed with the bedside light on, itching and checking to make sure he didn't have a spider on him with each new itch. By the time the sun rose the next morning, Nick was ready to jump out of his skin, he was so tired.

He jumped off the bed when someone knocked on the door and he practically raced to answer it.

"Good morning!" Gorman boomed with a huge smile on his face. He carried a brown paper bag and a tall steaming cup of what Nick hoped was very strong coffee.

Nick said nothing, but he quickly grabbed the steaming cup and sipped. It was coffee and it was *very* strong. After a couple of mouthfuls of the precious liquid, he bent around Gorman to peek inside the brown bag. Four muffins, giant and each one steaming and smelling better than muffins had a right to seemed to beam right back out at him and Nick quickly snatched a couple of them out of the bag, giving Gorman a quick wink and a nod, grunting, "Thanks."

Gorman chuckled. "You look like hell," he said. "Didn't get much sleep, eh?"

"Are you kidding?" Nick asked incredulously. "I probably would've been wrapped in webbing and sucked dry by now if I had slept."

Gorman guffawed. "Caught sight of'em for yourself, did you?"

"Too right, I did!" Nick shivered visibly as he caught the heebie-jeebies at the mere thought of the spiders he'd killed in the bathroom crawling all over his body.

"Well," Gorman said, sobering suddenly, "we got some information back on that, er, hair strand we found in the girl's flat."

Nick didn't even look over at the man as he replied, saying, "Yeah? Let me guess, it's nothing they've ever seen before."

"Not only that," Gorman confirmed, "it's not human or any other species known to man. They can't figure out even how the damned thing's still movin' about." He paused to stare intently at Nick for a second before quietly asking, "What the hell are we dealing with here, Nick?"

Nick paused in his feast and regarded the giant man seriously, then said, "I wish I knew, my friend. I wish I knew."

Gorman nodded, accepting the man's answer. "Well," he said, moving on, "I've got an appointment set for you to meet with the two station hands this afternoon out on the property where they work. I've come to take you out there since it's a ways off."

"What about the two Aborigines?" Nick asked.

"I've got my man working on it," Gorman stated. "I told you there's been very few natives in town since news of the girl's disappearance got out. But, if they can be found, my man will find'em. He's a top notch tracker, that one, and his kind still trust him, even though he associates with the whites so much."

"Good," Nick said, finishing off a third muffin. He peeked into the brown bag at the lone remaining muffin.

"Go on," Gorman said. "I've already eaten this mornin'."

Nick wasn't about to argue and he quickly wolfed down the giant muffin from the bag.

As soon as he was done, Gorman said, "Good. Let's get goin', then."

Nick nodded and grabbed his camera bag.

It took a couple of hours' driving deep into the desert to get to the station where the two men worked. *This must be the part of the map the Aussies list as "Nothing" on their tourism website*, Nick thought.

Gorman quickly introduced him to Erskine Banks and Nate Thompson when they arrived. They were the two men who'd witnessed the two Aborigines performing some sort of ritual with the girl the night she supposedly disappeared.

"I'd like to hear any information you can recall about that night, if I could," Nick said after the introductions and pleasantries were over.

Nate was the one who answered. "Me an' Erskine here were on the truck with them two tribal boys that night, when they just up an' suddenly jumped off an' went runnin' after this beaut we'd all been lookin' at on the side o'the road. It was like they knew her, or somethin'."

"And so what did the girl do?" Nick asked as he wrote in his little note pad.

"Nothin'," Nate said. "She just stood there while the two o'them set to work performin' some kind o'ceremony. When we got off the truck, Erskine an' me went over to see what was goin' on, but the two natives said all they were doin' was helpin' the girl out wi'somethin'. I didn't ask with what an' the girl looked fine, so we all just went on back to the pub. The two natives, too."

"Where did the girl go?" Nick asked.

"Dunno," Nate shrugged. "Didn't pay any attention once the two natives came with us back to the pub. They both proved themselves out here to everyone on the station. They're hard workers an' they've done a good job all season long. It's been sheer hell without'em since they disappeared. That's why we're hopin' you can get this all settled quickly so the two o'them can get back to work, soon. It's hard to find such good laborers these days an' we need'em back."

"Right," Nick said. "Anything else you can recall?"

"Nah," Nate replied. "Erskine?"

Erskine thought for a moment before shaking his head and saying, "I think Nate's covered everything. I just remember the two native boys leavin' the pub a little later that night. They looked kind of strange, the way they were walkin', but I figured they were just pissed, that's all."

"You mean, you thought they were drunk?" Nick asked.

Erskine nodded.

"Right," Nick said again, nodding to the two of them. "Well, if you think of anything else, you make sure to give me a call, will you?" He handed both of them his business card and turned to leave.

"Sir," Nate said, stopping Nick and Gorman in their tracks. "I wasn't kiddin' when I said those two were good men. I mean, I know they might've been the last two to be seen with the girl, but I have a hard time believin' they had anythin' to do with her disappearance."

Nick nodded once more.

"We'll do what we can to help them when they're found," Gorman assured the man.

∞

Thomas flinched as the pain in his side caught him up again and he straightened from his crouched position where he was tying his shoes. He and Samuel had just come from a grueling morning training session with Mikhail. Unfortunately, both Samuel and Thomas had *seriously* underestimated Mikhail's abilities and they were now paying the price for their overinflated opinions of their own skills as soldiers against someone as old and seasoned as Mikhail.

Old? Heck, thought Thomas, *Mikhail is friggin' ancient!* He suddenly paused as he realized Nera and he were probably much older than anyone on this planet and he just shook his head at the absurdity of his thoughts.

Thomas didn't want to think about things like that, though. In fact, he didn't want to think about Nera. It seemed he'd thought of little else lately and the stress of not being able to see her each day was starting to wear on him. It was weird, but she'd somehow gotten under his skin since they'd started communicating. Now he felt this strange need to be with her, to protect her, at all times.

But it didn't matter, because he was stuck here in the Angelic realm, practicing moves he didn't realize he knew until the moment he actually performed them, trying to remember a past that may or may not still be accessible to his mind.

If he didn't remember soon, some calamity was going to happen and Nera and her people wouldn't be able to prevent it. *So*, Thomas thought, *I don't know what I'm doing, I don't know what I'm supposed to do, and I have no clue why any of this is happening. That's just great.*

He sighed again and the sharp pain in his side made him wince. He quickly gathered up his things and headed for his room back at the big house. After a quick shower and change of clothing, he would be free to go play some online video games in Sam's room. It wasn't the greatest way to spend a day, but there wasn't much else to do here at the complex.

As he approached the door to his suite of rooms, a strange sensation came over him and he cautiously opened the door. The sun had not completely risen yet in the East and the room was still a bit dark, but Thomas could just make out a slightly glowing figure standing a bit farther back in the room just to his left. Stepping through the doorway, he suddenly realized it was Nera!

Thomas quickly closed the door and rushed to her side. She'd never come to his dimension before. She'd never appeared to him here. What kind of emergency could have prompted such a visit? *Maybe I've completed my training?* he wondered as an excited energy suddenly rushed through his bloodstream. One look at her tear-stained face, however, and he knew that was not the case. Something terrible had happened.

He gently took her in his arms and rested his chin on her shoulder as she quietly whimpered into his neck. He could feel her tears dropping onto his chest, but he didn't care. Nera was shaking and he suddenly wanted to kill whoever had done this to her.

Nera immediately stepped back a pace and gave him a watery smile. "It is not anything like that," she said through her tears. "Though, that would be so much better." She broke into quiet little sobs again and he embraced her once more, running his hand up and down her back to soothe her.

"Shh," he whispered. "It's okay."

She backed up again and wildly shook her head. "No," she said. "It is not okay. Something terrible is about to happen and we do not know what to do to stop it." A fresh spate of tears started down her cheeks and she whimpered, "We are about to lose *everything*."

Thomas tilted his head as he waited for her to explain.

"What can I tell you?" she asked finally. "We were watching them, the next ones we need to get together, and suddenly everything we could see was gone. It was like they were no longer there, or something."

"What do you mean?" Thomas asked.

Nera shrugged, explaining, "We have seen this before. If the mortal one among a coupling dies, then the immortal one has to wait for the one to cycle back around before they can be reunited. The difficulty here is that we do not have the *time* to wait even for one more cycle, if the odds were even kind enough to allow it within just one more cycle. If only one of them is not in place when the time comes, we cannot do this and the entire batch will be lost."

"So, everything was in place before you, I mean, *we* started all of this?" Thomas asked.

Nera merely nodded, tears welling up in her eyes again.

Thomas approached her again and cupped her shoulders. "Don't worry," he soothed. "We'll figure something out."

"How?" she demanded, looking up at him. "I told you, everything went completely black. There was nothing. We could see nothing. Whenever that has happened in the past, it has meant the mortal has ceased functioning on this plane."

He slipped his arms around her and hugged her close. "I don't know, but we'll think of something," he whispered.

Suddenly, the door to his room was flung open and Sarah and Mikhail walked in unannounced. Thomas turned and moved so that Nera was behind him, protected, shielded by his body from his parents.

Sarah narrowed her eyes as she took in the tear-stained face of the creature before her. She and Mikhail had been sitting in their suite monitoring Thomas when they'd suddenly felt a disturbance in his normal frequencies. He'd become agitated over something and Sarah, for one, had been waiting for just such an opportunity.

She knew her son. He might be harboring some deep, dark secret from everyone, but she knew the human part of him like no other. She could feel when he was upset about something and she'd felt it in a big way just a few minutes ago. That's when she and Mikhail had rushed to his suite of rooms to see what the matter was.

"Nera, I presume?" Sarah asked, hiking a brow.

Thomas held out a hand, saying, "Mom, wait… Please, just give us a minute, okay?"

Nera stared over Thomas' shoulder at the two newcomers, her glowing eyes not quite as brightly lit as the two pairs staring back at her. Her hair automatically wrapped around Thomas in order to protect him from any harm, though he was clearly trying to block her from their view in order to protect her from them.

Thomas kept brushing the strands of white hair away from his arms and chest, but they returned almost immediately of their own accord each time. Sarah's eyes narrowed at the action, but she didn't comment on it. After a couple of minutes of the four of them just standing there sizing up each other, Sarah finally raised her head and said, "I am Sarah, Thomas' mother. This is my mate, Mikhail."

Nera swallowed hard, but slowly made her way around to Thomas' side. She looked Sarah up and down, with Sarah doing the same to her. Then, Nera's eyes widened and she turned to look up at Thomas. He frowned, not understanding what was going on with her. Nera returned her gaze to the other two glowing beings in the room and made a decision. "We need your help," she suddenly said.

Mikhail and Sarah remained silent, watching the creature.

Nera suddenly turned to position herself in front of Thomas. "I do not know what Thomas has told you, but there is no time now. We are desperate. Will you help us?" she asked.

"I have a few thousand flippin' questions to ask you first," Sarah answered, her ire rising with each moment.

"There's no time, Mom," Thomas said, suddenly seeing the sense in Nera's request.

Nera stepped even closer to the other couple and took one of Sarah's hands in hers, saying, "I shall answer all of your questions, Sarah, but after everything is in place." She raised the hand she held in front of her and squeezed it tightly between both of her own, asking, "We need to know, will you help us?"

Looking at Thomas' face, all concerned and hopeful, was all it took for Sarah to say, "Of course."

∞

Baphomet and Lisa sat side by side, barely breathing, as they listened to the creature talking. They still couldn't breach the boy's thoughts, or even Sarah's for that matter unless she wanted her thoughts known, but since moving into the new house Israfil's people had built, they had discovered that, through Mikhail, they could catch just about everything Sarah and Thomas had to say. Now, this creature, Nera, had shown up, and Baphomet especially was very interested to know what *she* wanted.

His pulse jumped a bit when he discovered Nera wanted Sarah and Mikhail to monitor one of the Seraphim for her and her brood, but Lisa calmed him by laying a hand on his arm. Why would she need them to monitor anyone? What was going on?

The only thing Baphomet could think of to do was to continue monitoring Mikhail and, through him, the others. Then, if anything happened, he'd be able to decide if it was time for Lisa and him to become involved.

291

Baphomet didn't relish the idea of allowing others to lead, but he had little choice in the matter at the moment. Cabal was still shying away back into hiding each time any Angel even came *near* the house and Baphomet was not yet sure of Lisa's abilities.

At this thought, Lisa turned to give him an annoyed look, whispering, "Um, kind of right here! If I didn't give a damn about your son, I'd be practicing and gaining abilities. Somehow, however, I think you'd rather I take care of Cabal?"

Baphomet threw a sheepish lop-sided grin her way and whispered, "I know, sweet Lisa. I just do not want you put in harm's way until you are fully capable of protecting yourself." He eased back into the comfortable chair situated beside hers. "Besides," he said in a low voice, "I am sure this is nothing Mikhail and Sarah cannot handle without us."

Lisa recalled the way Sarah had moved during the battle with the soldiers who'd come after her before Baphomet had returned this last time and she had no doubt whatsoever that Sarah could handle any situation without any assistance from *anyone*. Just thinking about the way Sarah's hair had lashed against the soldiers and sliced off body parts made Lisa shiver and she noticed her own hair strands becoming more agitated around the ends.

I wonder if they do that automatically, she thought.

I would not be willing to bet on that, sweet, Baphomet's voice floated across her mind. *Not with Cabal so vulnerable and everything.*

I would never allow anything to happen to Cabal! she thought in a very loud manner.

I know, Leece, he thought back to her, raising her hand in his and kissing it along the backs of her fingers. *I simply will not risk either of you becoming involved in any type of dangerous situation until I am sure you are able to protect both Cabal and yourself. Please understand this and accept it.*

Lisa rubbed Cabal's spot on her lower abdomen. The little patch of glowing skin was quite a bit brighter and larger now, since they'd moved out away from the main populated center of the complex and Lisa knew she would do anything to protect Cabal.

She sighed and squeezed Baphomet's fingers and gave him a sweet smile. He loved her and his protectiveness of her was just another one of the ways he was showing her that. And, she loved him all the more for it.

There was a quiet knock at the door to the sitting room, startling the two of them, and Israfil's head peeked around the corner after a second. "Everything okay in here?" he asked quietly.

"We are all well," Baphomet softly answered. He made a motion inviting his brother to join them in the room and Israfil quietly closed the door and crossed to a nearby chair situated across a low glass-topped coffee table from where they sat.

"I thought I sensed something amiss," Israfil whispered.

"No-no," Baphomet assured him. "All is well. We were just discussing training options for Lisa after Cabal is born."

"Combat training?" Israfil softly asked.

"Yes," Lisa chimed in. "I've got the hair, may as well learn how to use it."

The two brothers chuckled, doing their best to keep the noise level down. Lisa always made them laugh whenever Israfil came to sit with them. Since they'd moved into his new home, he'd made his bed just down the hallway from the suite of rooms they'd chosen, instead of sleeping in the master suite on the other side of the enormous house.

Apparently, every single one of the Angels loyal to Israfil had chosen to accompany him out to the Badlands when Azra'il had banished him from Seraphim City and the house they'd built was large enough to accommodate all of them and then some.

Baphomet liked the quiet of the place, though, and the fact that Cabal felt safe enough here. He wondered if perhaps he and Lisa might not someday be able to build their own home nearby. But a quick look from Israfil put those thoughts to rest immediately. Baphomet might not be able to read Israfil's thoughts without his permission, but he was almost certain Israfil could read his with no difficulty. Baphomet did not like it one bit, either.

It was one thing for him and Lisa to be able to do it to others; however, when it came to others being able to do it to them, Baphomet wanted no part in that scenario. He preferred to keep his and Lisa's thoughts to just the two of them alone. It was no one else's business what they were thinking.

Israfil suddenly whispered an excuse to leave and Baphomet realized what had happened, as he turned to his brother and pleaded, "Iz, I did not mean for you to leave."

Israfil immediately shook his head, pointing to Lisa and saying, "It is all right. She looks as if she might fall over soon, she is so tired."

Concern for Lisa suddenly became Baphomet's only thought and he barely heard Israfil's whispered, "Call if you need me."

"What is wrong?" Baphomet asked as he moved to help her stand.

"Nothing," she said.

"How can I help?"

"I'm fine," she whispered, a little frustrated now. "I just need a nap. Somebody keeps me up half the night each night, you know, and an expectant mum needs a bit more sleep than just the two or three hours we've been getting."

"Oh, gods, Leece," Baphomet immediately rushed to apologize. "I-I did not realize. I-I promise, it will not happen again."

Lisa stopped in her tracks and stared up at him, asking, "Are you insane?" At his look of utter confusion, she smiled and whispered, "Don't you dare stop it. I enjoy the little games we play. I just need a nap during the daytime to make up for the sleep I miss. Plus, my mum told me once that, should I ever get pregnant, I should get as much sleep as possible while I'm pregnant because I won't ever get another full night's sleep after the baby's born."

Baphomet hiked an eyebrow and shook his head, saying, "Well, I guess I understand now from which side of the family your crazy genes come."

Lisa punched him in his upper arm as they made their way back to the bedroom where she intended to show him just how crazy she could be... in bed, at least.

Chapter 21

Azra'il packed his own bag, preferring to keep the number of those who knew he was leaving town for a few days to the barest minimum. The members of the Great Sanhedrin knew, of course, but no others had been alerted. There was so much upheaval within the walls of Seraphim City at the moment that he truly did not know what kind of effect the news that he was no longer within the city walls would have on its populace.

Azra'il had heard of riots in the streets having taken place, of violent outbreaks among the Angels who still believed in the old ways and those who now believed those of the Angelic realm no longer held any responsibility toward those in the human realm. There was great debate among the two groups and the majority of both Sanhedrin houses' time was being spent daily dealing with just this issue.

Something had to be done before the whole of Angelic society fell into complete and utter chaos. What could they do, though? To reveal themselves to the humans would be to invite chaos in both realms, not the mention the fact that it would confirm the very existence of an alternate dimension into which humans would then wish to intrude.

The only solution Azra'il could think of was to go, himself, out into the wilds of the Badlands to see for himself what was going on with his brothers. Only then would he be able to make a decision based on facts as to what was an appropriate course of action to be taken in this matter.

If he could figure out what the draw was, what appeal his brothers found for these humans, then perhaps he might be able to discover a way to bring his brothers back from the wrong side of the law. Azra'il knew it was too late where Mikhail was concerned, but he might still have a fighting chance as far as Djibril and Israfil went.

He had to try.

They were so close... so close to the time when the blessed Great Designers had been scheduled to return. Once they finally did return, the Designers would once again establish a rule of order within the human realm and those living within the Angelic realm would no longer have to worry about the wretched lives of those puny beings.

Azra'il was so sick and tired of having to deal with humans that he almost wished the Designers would just come back and wipe them all out, as they'd wished to do long ago. He remembered the time that Enki's father had declared all humans were to be abolished. Enki had pleaded for the lives of the beings he loved, however, and they'd been spared.

Now, Azra'il found himself wondering what things would have been like if Enki had not been successful in changing his father's mind. After a moment, though, he sighed in disgust with himself. Such thoughts were useless and he quickly returned his attention to packing.

This trip was to serve as a way to keep the two brothers he still had confidence in within the good graces of the Designers when they returned. There was nothing Azra'il would be able to do about Mikhail. And, certainly there was nothing to be done about Suriyah and Baphomet. Those two had been lost even before the Designers' last departure from the planet. But, Azra'il could still save Djibril and Israfil from whatever punishment the Designers would be sure to dole out upon their return to those who had strayed from the true path.

If only Azra'il could be certain when the Designers *were* to return. Israfil was the only one who was to be notified by the Designers when the time came. It was he who had been designated as the Seraph who was to alert all others of the eminent return of the Designers after he'd received their sign.

Azra'il stilled as he wondered if, perhaps, Israfil had already received a sign. Would his brother alert him or anyone else within the Angelic realm? Or, would the Angels of Seraphim City be lost to the Designers because they knew nothing of their beloved Designers' return?

None of the Angels of Seraphim City ventured into the human realm without having a powerful reason for doing so. But Azra'il would not have a way of knowing if the Designers had returned to the planet or not without Israfil.

Again, Azra'il shook his head and resumed his packing. These thoughts were enough to drive a Seraph crazy. He decided he would assign a team to monitor the human realm through their digital transmissions on the things humans called televisions and computers. Surely, the humans would immediately report through these media any sign of the Designers' return to their world. Then, Azra'il and the Great Sanhedrin would not need Israfil to notify them of any return. Of course, it would mean a delay in their notification, but it would be better than not knowing at all.

Azra'il, in the meantime, would go out and see what could be done to save Djibril and Israfil from these evil humans. Then he, Azra'il, would ensure his brothers' safe return to the city and all would be right again until the day of the Designers' return.

Only, it was not all right.

Mikhail would not be among their number.

Azra'il plopped down onto the mattress beside his one bag and hung his head. He missed his brothers, but he missed Mikhail most of all. How could Mikhail have done this to them?

How could Mikhail have done this to Azra'il? What kind of magic sway did this human have over Mikhail that could cause him to completely turn his back on his family, not to mention his fealty to his gods?

Azra'il just did not understand it. Of all the six Seraphim on this planet, he would never have figured Mikhail to be one who could easily be swayed by a female of another species. It had happened, though, and there seemed nothing anyone could do to undo the spell the vile creature had put on Mikhail.

Azra'il sighed and stood again, resuming his packing with a renewed sense of purpose. Mikhail may be lost to them, but there was still a chance for Djibril and Israfil. Azra'il would not fail them. Once they'd returned to Seraphim City, the three of them would work with the Great Sanhedrin to put everything to rights again so that, when the blessed Great Designers did finally return, things would be just as they'd instructed.

With his packing finally done and his mind resolute, Azra'il picked up his bag and headed for the door.

∞

Djibril sat in the vacant flat he'd occupied for the past three nights as he prepared for tomorrow's events. The light bulbs had all shattered the first night he'd entered the place, but it didn't matter. Djibril was just waiting, biding his time before everything was to begin.

He would be happy when tomorrow morning was over and done with. No, he would be happy when he was finally back home in the Angelic realm at the Badlands complex. It had become home for him and he already missed his brothers. He wondered how Baphomet and his new mate were getting on. When he'd left, they had just been left alone with each other and Djibril wondered if the human had killed his brother, yet. He chuckled to himself at this thought. She was a spirited one, he had to give her that.

The sounds from the city outside the open window on the far wall drifted over to him, disrupting his train of thought, and he shook his head in disgust. He'd been in the human realm far too long. Time moved faster in the human dimension than it did in the Angelic dimension, as did everything, it seemed, and Djibril felt it.

Suriyah had left nearly two weeks ago, human time, and Djibril was on the verge of insanity from having to deal with all things human since her departure. These creatures had absolutely no sense of *anything* and Djibril was nearly at his breaking point. If things didn't pan out tomorrow morning as he'd calculated they should, Djibril had decided he would simply have to return to the Angelic realm and have someone else come looking for Iblis and Satariel. He just couldn't take anymore.

He and Suriyah had followed up on every lead they could find and they'd come close a few times to actually nabbing the two Shaitans who were causing so much unrest within this realm. They'd thwarted several terrorist attacks and had even managed to see to it that several political assassination attempts had been averted without incident.

It didn't seem to matter, though. There was so much civil unrest throughout the entirety of the human realm that each little victory Suriyah and Djibril celebrated was merely a drop in an ocean of conflicts occurring throughout all of human civilization.

Gone was the world the Seraphim had once protected. Gone were the great cultures. Gone were the knowledge seekers, the great architects, the great philosophers. Now it seemed the entire human race was ruled by one thing and one thing alone: money.

There were a small percentage of humans that had the majority of the available wealth. However, the majority of *those* were politicians who took their wealth from the working masses through something called "taxes". These they justified by creating funds for those who were sick or unable to work, or for the under-privileged.

Of course, they collected far more revenue in taxes than that which was doled out. The extras were then supposedly divvied out to all manner of groups and causes designed to help the society. Instead, much of the time a good majority of it ended up being divided up among the lawmakers themselves. This was never enough, however, and so they continued increasing the amount of taxes the shrinking number of workers had to pay. After all, the sick and those who could not work were always in need.

Then again, there were far more of the under-privileged who seemed to need assistance than there were sick or those unable to work. So the working class ended up working to support the masses, along with the corrupt governments. But that would only last so long before the workers figured out what was going on and rebelled. Djibril had seen it time and time again.

There had been a time, about two and a half centuries ago in human time measurement, when the Seraphim had thought the human race might be turning itself around, learning to govern themselves, to grow, to become the race they were meant to be. That was at the birth of a grand new country, with its own very special government.

However, now it appeared *that* government had deteriorated to the same type seen throughout human history. The potential that had once thrived and heated the blood of the people of that country now trickled dully through the small capillaries in the eyes of its eldest citizens alone, withered and dying along with its hosts.

There was hatred in the young men's hearts one passed on the streets. Children were killing their parents and friends because they wanted to know what it felt like to take a life. Adults were raping infants and then burning their bodies for fun. Mothers were slicing open the throats of their babies in order to get demons out of them. More and more children were being born with genetic defects and there seemed to be a drug for everything.

Corrupt governments ruled and the masses were completely dependent upon them for everything. No one was allowed to speak his or her mind and everything had to be aesthetically pleasing to everyone or it couldn't be allowed to exist. No one was allowed a true voice.

Djibril had learned this was called "political correctness" and he hated it. He believed most of the older humans despised it as well, but they were powerless to do anything about it. The younger generations were all being indoctrinated starting at an early age to abide by this political correctness. Djibril listened each day as he passed young ones on the streets and he knew the things they talked about and how they took care when they talked, as if it was no big deal. But the younger generations did not seem to understand how dangerous such censorship of their thoughts and speech could be.

The governments encouraged it because it gave them control over everyone without anyone within the government having to do anything but punish those who disobeyed. As per the history of human governments, those in power came to crave more and more power, in conjunction with their concurrent rising fear of the loss of said power. The prevailing standard became a policy of not interfering except to make sure those who rocked the proverbial boat, so to speak, were punished.

Djibril had seen this societal state of being just before each and every single war in which he'd been involved in the human realm. He knew what was coming. The difficulty with this time, however, was that the weapons the human race had acquired over the last couple of centuries were powerful enough to wipe out every living thing within the human world, rendering it uninhabitable to all but the tiniest of creatures.

He started suddenly at the sound of gunfire from somewhere on the streets below. Shortly thereafter, sirens approached and there was more commotion to be heard. Djibril wished he was back at the complex, lying on his big, warm bed, where it was quiet and peaceful. He eased back into the rusty old chair he'd found in the vacant flat and thought of home. He wondered how Mikhail and Sarah were doing. He thought about their child, Sheely, and he wondered if he'd ever be able to conceive someday. If Mikhail and Sarah were able to, then why should Djibril not be able to?

This thought led his mind back to Baphomet and his new mate. He wondered if either of them had started changing yet. The changes Mikhail and Sarah had endured had not taken very long after Sarah had come to the Angelic realm, so it would make sense that Baphomet and Lisa would have already started transforming, too.

It was odd thinking of Baphomet after all this time, but the last time Djibril had been around him, he'd seemed as if he genuinely cared for the human girl named Lisa. He'd seemed more focused on her than anything else, as she had on him, and Djibril wondered again if there could possibly be someone out there in the human realm for him, someone who was just living her life, waiting for him to come along and complicate the hell out of it.

He smiled at the thought, though he couldn't really imagine it.

Djibril and his siblings had been on this planet for a million years, give or take, without ever having the option of mating with anyone other than the lower Angels. *How would it be*, he wondered, *to hold my own child in my arms?* The thought boggled his mind.

Again, however, Mikhail and Sarah had mated and conceived. It was not unthinkable, as it once had been. Djibril had seen it with his own eyes. He'd heard the Angelic physician, Hantsushept, speak of the baby they'd created within Sarah's womb. Djibril hadn't imagined that. He'd seen the evidence in the glowing patch of skin on Sarah's lower abdomen. He'd felt the thing's energy patterns, he believed, when he'd linked with Sarah through Mikhail and Thomas. There was no doubt in his mind that Mikhail had actually done it.

That meant it was actually possible. And now, Baphomet had found this Lisa whom he believed to be his one true mate. Would they conceive? If so, what did that mean?

Djibril leaned his head back, closing his eyes and rubbing his hands along the tops of his thighs. This was too much to think about. He ought to be concentrating on his plans for the next morning. As far as he could tell, there were nine men involved in the plot, but there might be more.

Since coming back to the human realm, Djibril had utilized his tracking abilities to trace the energy patterns of Iblis and Satariel as best he could. He'd soon picked up their frequencies and he and Suriyah had quickly discovered the first terror plot in Sydney, Australia. The Australian government had taken pleasure in stopping that one, after having received an anonymous tip from Djibril.

The second terror plot Suriyah had discovered through a vision she'd had regarding a world-wide games competition. The timing on that one had been too close to get anyone else involved, so Djibril and Suriyah had handled it themselves, ending up with six dead individuals from the Middle Eastern portion of the human realm instead of hundreds, if not thousands, of dead athletes and spectators from all over the planet.

Iblis and Satariel were slippery, though. With each botched plot, they'd secretly moved on through the crowds of humans to the next group gullible enough to listen to and believe the Shaitans' tripe. They always stuck to those of Middle Eastern descent, for some reason. They'd also become more cunning as the days and weeks had passed without some fiery explosions to entertain them, and soon Djibril and Suriyah had been forced to separate, dashing off to different parts of the globe in order to stop plots designed to work in tandem so that, even if one failed, the Shaitans would still have the other for their sport.

For the past few weeks, however, Djibril had been unable to detect any signal from either of the Shaitans, and Suriyah and he had concluded that the two evil Angels must have returned to the Angelic dimension.

Suriyah had been away from her people for too long and Djibril had told her to go. It wasn't as if there was anything more she could do, especially if there was nothing going on. Djibril also knew Suriyah had become as repulsed by the turmoil filling the human realm as he had, so he'd urged her to return home.

Djibril, himself, had considered returning, until he'd caught just the slightest hint of a strange energy frequency. It had caught his attention while he'd been enjoying a late afternoon tea near the small, but exclusive hotel near downtown London, England where he and Suriyah had been staying for the last few weeks of their time there.

Suriyah had just finished up her last assignment and she and Djibril had decided it was time for both of them to return home. On the day of their scheduled departure, Djibril had, on a whim, thought he would take tea once more in a wonderful little shop he'd found before departing for the Angelic realm. He so enjoyed some of the little pleasures humans had created.

The odd frequency that had caught his attention while he was there, however, had disturbed him on a much deeper level than any of those he'd detected with the previous terror plots. This one had seemed to hold a much more sinister vibration to it. Its tone had been vile and repulsive, causing chills to race up and down his spine when he'd caught bits and pieces of it through the bioplasmic universe.

There were still no signs of Iblis or Satariel, but this group, yet another collection of Middle Easterners, had a plan and they were close to executing it. Djibril was certain of it. He could feel their excitement and their hatred. They wanted all others to pay and they wanted everyone to know who they were once the deed was done.

There were a lot of pieces involved in this one. The group's vile frequencies were vibrating all over town, easily detectable by Djibril once he'd realized what he needed to look for. There was another essence near this one that he recognized from several of the other plots he and Suriyah had thwarted, so he believed Iblis and Satariel had to have had a hand in this one, as well, although he did not detect their specific energies attached to anything having to do with it.

Djibril had quickly informed Suriyah of the fact that he'd detected warning signs and, although she'd offered to stay to help him with the issue, he'd instructed her to go on without him. He had then gathered all the intel he could from the various sources he'd managed to find. Computers had become a hobby of his in the Angelic realm since he'd come to know Sarah and he now knew quite a bit about the internet and its uses as far as tracking source codes and hacking into the necessary databases without being detected.

Now he had a date, a time, and a location where everything was set to go down. He just had to wait for the appropriate moment and then he'd be able to make his move to stop this heinous deed from happening.

How anyone could even conceive of such a plan, let alone enact it, was so far beyond his ken that Djibril almost wished the blessed Great Designers would return and abolish the entire human population, just so the very possibility that this could ever happen again would be deleted.

There was suddenly more commotion from down on the street and Djibril sighed. This might well be the longest night of his very long life.

Chapter 22

On the drive back to town from the station where the two work hands had been, Gorman got a call from his native officer. He'd found the two tribesmen and had arranged a meeting with them for Nick for later in the evening. Apparently, there had been a week-long ceremony going on and the tribal elders had forbidden their sons to return to the city until it was over. Now that it had ended, however, the two young men were to be allowed to return.

Again, Nick was glad Gorman had volunteered to drive him around, as they proceeded out into an area even more remote than the station had been. When they finally rolled to a stop, Nick looked around. There was nothing around, just brush. No one was there and there were no landmarks outstanding that Nick could detect, either. He was about to ask Gorman why they'd stopped when he suddenly caught sight of some movement off to the far right of the road.

"Ah," Gorman said. "Here they are."

Two very dark-skinned slender black men with crazy, short-cropped hair atop their heads approached the vehicle. They were both shirtless and barefoot, wearing tight-fitting jeans held together at the top with wide leather belts. The thing that made them so very striking, however, was the light blue color of their eyes. Both of them had light blue eyes and it made a striking contrast against their dark skin color.

Nick opened his door and stepped out of the utility vehicle to greet the two. They both merely nodded upon being introduced to him.

"Nick, here, needs to know exactly what happened the night you two were seen with the missing girl, ah, Lisa Murdoch. You know the one I mean?"

Both young men nodded, but remained silent.

"We've come to believe that was the night she disappeared," Gorman continued, "and we just need all the information we can get so we can locate her."

The two young men stared at Nick for a moment, then said something to each other in a language Nick didn't recognize.

"What was that?" Gorman asked.

The shorter of the two responded, explaining, "The girl was bein' bothered by some Murngin. We just helped to block'em from her. It was our father who allowed the powerful one to take her over to the dream world."

Nick had no clue what the heck a Murngin might be.

"Are you sayin' you know who took the girl?" Gorman asked, interrupting Nick's thoughts.

"And where?" Nick quickly threw in.

"Nah, mate," the shorter of the two responded. "You'd have to talk with my dad for that kind o'stuff. I just remember the thing comin' to beg for us to undo the wall we'd built around the girl so he could have access to her again."

Nick frowned in utter confusion.

"What are you talkin' about?" Gorman exclaimed. This was making no sense to him and it clearly showed on his expression.

"You need to talk to m'dad," the young man simply said.

"So-o, can you take us to him?" Nick asked derisively.

After a short consultation with the taller young man in that other language, the shorter one said, "Come back tonight an' we'll see what we can arrange." With that, the two walked off back into the brush and were almost instantly gone from view.

Again, there was absolutely nothing to be seen and Nick wondered if he was in some bizarre alternate dimension where nothing was as it seemed.

"Well," Gorman said as he yanked open the door on the driver's side of the vehicle. "We'll head on over to Dondaraga Station for some tucker, right? Then, we'll come back by here 'fore the night's too far gone. What d'you say?"

"Dondaraga?" Nick asked.

Gorman nodded. "Best tucker a man can get out here. Not bad view, neither."

Turned out the view was a saucy red-headed Sheila named Nicola Weigert who was the current station owner's only daughter. It seemed the owner, a certain Geoff Weigert, was away with his wife on a business trip in Sydney for the week and his 28 year old only child had been left in charge of running the station while he was gone. Gorman and she apparently had a thing for each other, judging by the longing looks the two kept giving each other. Nick felt distinctly like a third wheel all throughout the meal.

The food was excellent, however. This Nicola could've been a professional chef in New York with her culinary skills and Nick told her so. She merely blushed and brushed off the compliment as she wished them a good evening and a safe journey back into town.

∞

I wish we didn't have to do this without him knowing.

Mikhail threw a sad half-smile toward Sarah, gently squeezing her fingers. *I understand, sweetheart*, he silently replied, *but Nera said anything more might cause a ripple effect that could possibly cause a change that would alter things all together.*

Sarah nodded acceptance, but inside she said, *I just don't understand why Nera couldn't go ahead and tell us the rest of it. I mean, why wouldn't she answer any of my questions? It just doesn't make sense. And I'll tell you another thing. I don't trust her. I wish she'd just go off and leave Thomas alone.*

Mikhail lifted her hand in his and kissed the backs of her fingers, silently chuckling and saying, *I know, my heart. I know.*

Sarah didn't know what he found so funny about all of this. She didn't find any of it in the least bit amusing. This Nera, whoever, or *what*ever, she was did not strike Sarah as one without a plan and Sarah wanted to know what it was. If it involved her son, she darned well wanted to know about it.

I have this, for now, Mikhail informed her, his voice floating across the pool of her consciousness like the flitting of a dragonfly across the surface of a still pond. *Why not go and see to your blog thing.*

Sarah gave him a quick glance. She *did* want to start her blog up again. After the things Lisa had told her about how she and other humans had been tracking Sarah's vision blog after Sarah had disappeared so they could discover where she'd gone, Sarah had decided it might be worth a shot to start the blog up again to see if she might be able to locate the mates for the remaining four Seraphim.

Three, Mikhail's voice reminded her quietly in her mind.

She looked over toward him, a streak of sadness piercing her heart. Israfil's plight weighed heavily on both their minds, but Sarah was bound and determined to do what she could for *everyone* involved here.

After all, these were her family members now and she would do anything she could to help each one of them find his or her one true soulmate so they might find the same type of happiness she and Mikhail now shared, even Israfil. Plus, according to what little Nera had let slip, they *all* needed to find their soulmates, and quickly, before some major calamity occurred, though she hadn't specified what type of calamity it was or when it was supposed to happen. To Sarah, that meant there was still the possibility of Israfil finding happiness, too.

Additionally, Sarah had another reason for needing to begin her blog again. She'd been toying with the idea of contacting her remaining family members within the human realm through the internet to feel them out as far as which ones would be willing to accept life within the Angelic realm and which ones would choose to remain within the human realm. She'd have to be sneaky about things, to be certain, in order to keep those tracking her at bay, but she believed she should be able to figure out a way to accomplish both tasks through her blog.

Sarah paused a moment before accepting Mikhail's offer. She could suddenly feel him trying to erect a buffer around himself again and she quickly slid her own into place without even thinking about it. He clearly had something on his mind and he didn't want her nosing around in his thoughts. After only a moment's hesitation, Sarah gave him a quick nod and stood. Normally, when she threw up her own buffer, she remained linked with Mikhail without him knowing it. He truly seemed to want his privacy today, however, so Sarah went ahead and blocked off all links with him.

"Go take care of the blog, my heart" Mikhail softly said. Sarah threw a small smile at him and then slipped out of the room to head toward the little room off the bedroom where a computer awaited her. If she could reach any of the potential mates out there for her new siblings, and if she could contact her own human siblings, this would all be worth a shot.

She sat down at the computer Mikhail had had installed for her. Sarah felt strange. First of all, she didn't like being away from Mikhail without being linked with him on some level, at least. Secondly, she still hadn't figured out how her human siblings could be brought over into the Angelic realm without causing a big stir among the Angels living there. That one was going to take a lot more thought and Sarah still didn't feel truly comfortable discussing it with Mikhail because of everything he'd already done for her family and her.

Lastly, Lisa had informed Sarah there were people in the human dimension who were tracking her blog and that they were dissecting it to see if they could find hidden clues within it to tell them where she'd gone and how they could get there themselves. She'd never done anything like that, at least not intentionally. She didn't even know how she could do something like that.

She decided it would be safest just to start writing and see what resulted.

She began typing, stiltedly at first, but then the words seemed to come more freely, and before she knew it, she had a full entry complete and ready to be posted. It read as follows:

Hello to the human race. This is Sarah Baker blogging again.

I know I promised that the last blog entry I made was to be the last of the Vision Blog, and, technically speaking, that was the truth. This is my new blog. I can't really call it a vision blog because I don't plan on writing about any of my visions here. I guess I should entitle it The Ultimate Guide, since what I'm hoping to accomplish with it is for those of you out there who belong here with me to be able to locate me through it.

Does that sound confusing?

Well, it shouldn't. I have been informed that there is now a price on my head and that there are many out there who are unhappy with the things I wrote before. For those of you who are part of this group, I have only pity for you, for you have a very long way to go before you will be ready for what is to come next. Neither I, nor my family members, wish you any harm and I would like you to know that I am actually rooting for you. I know you will come to see the error of your ways some day, whether it be in this lifetime or another.

I have also been informed there are those among you who have been searching for me, despite the madness currently gripping your world. One of your number has already managed to find me, though I believe she had a little help from someone from this place. This is good, however, for she belongs here and, as it turned out, her presence was required for an important task. But there are still more of you who belong here, as well. More are required.

That is why I have started this new blog. I am hoping those among you who actually belong where I am will feel the pull toward this place and will be able to figure out the origins of this transmission. That should lead you close enough that you'll be detectable by those of us within this place. Of course, we're not experienced, by any means, at discovering new ones belonging here with us, so you'll have to excuse us our tardiness if we're not immediately there to greet you.

There is hope, however. I will tell you that you cannot even imagine the wonders that await you, should you find your way to this place. Those around you cannot stop you, if you are truly meant to be with us. If what I have written here tugs at your heartstrings, pulls at your consciousness, and makes you feel like getting up and doing something, then there may just be a place here for you, after all.

Why not take the chance? Why not see if you can figure it out? Trust me, you would not mind being in this place, even if you don't really belong here and you're just good at figuring out things. I never could have imagined the wonders I've seen and experienced since coming to live here. I can guarantee you that your life will be infinitely improved should you make it this far.

As for the rest of you, especially my fellow Americans, I cannot think what I can say that has not already been said to try to sway you from your madness. You have grown too dependent upon others to do for you. Either that, or you have now bowed your head, and done as you've been told for so long that you've forgotten how to stand up straight and show some backbone!

If you are able to change a bad situation, then you have the responsibility to change it. If you are not able to change a bad situation, perhaps one you see or one you're living in, then you should find a way to get out of it, even if it requires you to give up everything you own and move. If you're not working and you are able to work, go find a job, even if that means taking one you are far over-qualified for and which pays far less than that which you were making before!

I recall my great grandfather telling me stories of how he, during the great depression, would work in someone else's fields to get just enough vegetables to feed his wife and himself and to earn enough for one room at an old lady's house, and that his wife would help out other, wealthy women around town, working as a maid to them, just to earn enough for whatever they needed that they couldn't get from the fields.

When I was last among you, I recall seeing "Now Hiring" signs all over the place. Sure, they were for jobs no one wanted, like at fast food joints and janitorial positions. So what? Money is money! If your family is starving and you're able to work and you're not doing it simply because it's easier to sit at home and collect a check from the government, you're not being true to yourself or to your family, if you've got one.

Countless soldiers have died over the past couple of centuries so that you would be able to live in a free society, yet you sit there and collect government entitlement checks. Countless soldiers are still putting their lives on the line so that you and your children will have the chance to go out and get jobs. Are you being fair to them by not doing that? Are you being fair to yourself?

It's hard right now, I know. I remember looking for a job while I went to school. I took whatever I could get, whenever I could get it. This included things like working in a discount retail store as a sales clerk and at a mall as a security guard. Do you think I didn't find those things distasteful? Think again.

I was raised by what equated to a Southern Belle. Just thinking about some of the things I've done over the past few years to keep my kid fed and clothed and in the right schools makes me shudder. However, it was what I had to do to get by, and, if I hadn't been found by those from this place, I would still be doing whatever I could to make sure I earned enough for my small family.

Yes, I got help from my family. That's what families are for, don't you know? We humans are not alone, ever. We have families for a reason. We look after each other. Friends do the same. We look after our friends. The world I left, however, seemed as if it was turning into some sort of totalitarian state, where only the small percentage of those with all the money were the ones who actually got to choose anything, while all the rest did only that which they were told when they were told and nothing else.

What kind of life is that? You don't have to go there. Cling tightly to your family and friends. Help them all. Believe in helping others and that human spirit of kindness will be returned to you, in kind. Your life will become so much richer and so much less stressful once you decide to live that way. Of course, you actually have to open your heart and mind to others in order to accomplish this, and that, for many of you, will be beyond your ability, I'm afraid.

That is all I can say to those of you who do not truly belong where I am. To those of you who do feel the pull, I think I've given you enough in this one blog entry to allow you to find me, if you look hard enough. I'll try to get another entry out to you soon. In the meantime, I and everyone else in this place where I am will be on the lookout for anyone who figures it out.

Good luck, and I look forward to meeting those who pick up this challenge and are successful.

Yours,
Sarah Baker

Sarah looked it over for typos and anything else she might need to change, hoping the clues she'd thought of wouldn't be too obvious, or too difficult to notice. Everything seemed just about right, though, and so she saved it on the desktop and then logged onto the internet.

Finding a free website service, she entered a made up name and address and built a simple website where she could run the blog. Once that was done, Sarah pulled up the blog entry she'd saved, copied it, pasted it onto the new website she'd built, and then exited the site. She then went out to a free email address service and created an account under a different name.

Writing under this email address, she sent messages to her human family members still residing within the human dimension. She was careful what she put in the subject lines and worded things in such a manner as to make sure her family members would open the emails without believing them to be spam. Within the body of the emails, again she was very careful how she worded things. But she was able to let them know Thomas, her parents, and she were all okay and that they would be hearing from her again soon. Once everyone had been sent an email, Sarah exited the whole system and turned off the computer.

She didn't know if this was going to work, or not. She wasn't sure if things from this dimension actually showed up on the internet in the human dimension. Things posted in the human realm made it through to the Angelic dimension, though, so why wouldn't it work in reverse?

She hoped it did.

She stood and put a hand to her aching back, arching back a little to ease her tired muscles. Sarah could almost hear Sheely yawning and, after only a second of thinking about the big comfortable bed just in the next room, she headed for the door. The last few days, and weeks, had been a bit eventful and she admitted she hadn't been getting enough sleep for Sheely or for herself. It had been a long time since she'd been pregnant and she'd forgotten how much it could take out of a woman.

She silently made her way to their bedroom and, climbing up onto the big bed, she crawled beneath the covers without even undressing. She sent out her psychic net, linking again with the one Nera wanted her to monitor. Everything was still fine there. She could feel Mikhail's energies still surrounding the area, though she didn't bother him, and she knew things would be okay if she got a few hours of shut-eye. She believed she would still be able to maintain her monitoring while she slept.

After yawning again for the third time in as many minutes, Sarah turned onto her side and adjusted the pillow beneath her head to a more comfortable position. She didn't like being in the bed without Mikhail's warm figure hugging her, but Sheely and she were both tired. Her last thoughts were that she hoped the blog worked so that her new siblings could come to know the same joyful and loving relationship she and Mikhail now shared and that her old human siblings would choose to come to live within the Angelic realm where they would be safe from others and from whatever catastrophe was coming.

Just before she closed her eyes, a flash of a vision, just a flash, mind you, blinked before her mind's eye. She didn't catch anything of any significance, however, and so she closed her eyes and a peaceful slumber gently claimed her mind, allowing her to sleep soundly for perhaps the first time since she and her mate had come to live in the Badlands.

Chapter 23

"How long have the two of you been seeing each other?" Nick asked as the police vehicle headed away from the station. It was long dark by now and there were a million stars out. Nick marveled at the sight up in the heavens and he wondered how anyone out in this godforsaken part of the world could ever find the heart to sleep at night knowing they'd miss seeing such a wondrous show all night.

"Me an' Nicola?" Gorman asked. At Nick's nod, the giant man blushed a little in the dim light from the dashboard and gruffed, "Ahem, ah, well, we haven't, ah, well, I mean, we're not officially, um, strictly speakin', that is…"

"Look," Nick interrupted. "Be her man or don't. Stop all this mamby-pamby bullshit and man-up."

Gorman blinked a few times in astonishment. Who the hell did this yank think he was, anyway?

Nick shrugged after a moment and said, "Whatever, man. I just don't think it's fair to the girl to keep stringin' her along like that simply because you don't have the balls to stand up in front of everybody and tell them she's your woman. If you're not willin' to at least do that, you need to let her go so she can go find a real man."

"Bloody hell!" Gorman growled, slamming on the brakes. Neither one of them was wearing a seatbelt and so they both had to push against the dashboard in order to keep from flying through the windshield. Gorman turned to face Nick as soon as the vehicle stopped. "Listen, Mister high-an'-mighty-New York

320

journalist," he barked furiously. "I don't know how things work back in America. But, here in the outback, we keep our business to ourselves and we keep ourselves to our own bloomin' business! So, you just stay the hell out o' mine, you understand?"

Nick pursed his lips and silently regarded the much larger older man for a moment before nodding and saying, "Sure, I'll stay out of it. I just thought I'd lend a little helping advice, seein' as how you seem to be having so much difficulty putting your relationship out there for everyone to see."

Gorman merely grunted and resumed driving into the pitch black desert.

"And, just so you know, in America men don't give a shit who knows who we're seeing. We just see what we want and we go and get it. There's none of this sneakin' around crap."

Gorman remained silent.

A couple of minutes later, Nick said, "I think that's one of the main attractions of America for most foreigners. We don't bow our heads and ask if we can please have the things we want. When we find something we want, we go out and get it. If we can't get it, we work to find a way to get it. There is simply nothing we consider out of our reach or unobtainable."

He became silent for a moment, but then continued, explaining, "At least, that's how it used to be. Now, I think there's a whole new breed of Americans being raised that will be much more like the rest of the world. They depend far too much on the government and far too little on themselves. Hell, most of the kids in America today can best be described as being part of the entitlement generation, depending entirely on their parents or the government, or both, for everything. They have no clue how to think for themselves or how to do for themselves."

He shook his head. "So, I guess I really have no right to offer advice to anyone since my own people can't even manage to get their shit straight." He looked over at Gorman and said, "Sorry."

Gorman slammed on the brakes again, nodding and saying, "No worries."

Nick nodded back and then frowned, wondering why the other man was just sitting there staring back at him. Then, from the corner of his eye, Nick caught movement in the dim headlights and turned just in time to see the two young Aborigine men who'd met with them earlier in the day. The two were approaching the vehicle with what had to be a walking piece of black leather close behind them.

Nick blinked and looked closer. It turned out the walking leather was actually a very old man caked in several different shades of dirt, or mud, or clay of some sort. Intricate designs had been drawn all over the old man's leathery skin with the stuff and the closer he got, the older he appeared to be. Nick wondered if the man was over a hundred as he took in various wrinkles and gray sprinkles in the old man's hair.

Gorman cleared his throat and opened the driver's side door. Nick quickly followed suit.

The four younger men nodded to one another as the group assembled in front of the truck in its headlight beams. The decrepit old man said nothing as he joined them.

Nick looked around for a second, wondering if there was some sort of special protocol one had to follow when talking with a tribal elder. Then, the strangest thing happened. The old geezer silently approached Nick and started poking him all over. He would softly jab him here with his index finger or poke him there with the stick he carried. He didn't say anything, but just kept circling Nick and poking at him.

After another round of this, Nick was getting quite annoyed and was wondering if he'd be breaking some tribal law if he poked back at the old man, when suddenly, the poking stopped and the old man hurled a litany of commands at the two young natives. Then, without a glance even in Nick's direction, the leathery old man turned and walked off, disappearing instantly into the pitch black surroundings.

"W-Wait!" Nick shouted after him. The old man was already gone, however. He'd already been swallowed whole by the night and Nick turned confused eyes on the two young natives still standing before the truck's headlights.

Oddly, the two were looking at him as if they didn't quite know what to make of him.

"What did he say?" Nick asked. "Can he tell us where the girl was taken or who took her?"

"Nah," the shorter of the two said. "He didn't mention the girl." Silence followed.

"Well, what did he say, then?" Gorman asked in frustration.

"He said this one need to come see the ceremony tomorrow night so he can find his way home," the shorter man said, indicating Nick.

"What the bloody hell does that mean?" Gorman demanded.

The shorter man shrugged and said, "Guess he best go to the ceremony t'find out."

Gorman threw a look of utter helplessness over at Nick.

"Well," Nick sighed, "when and where is this ceremony?" He had no idea what the younger man meant when he said Nick needed to attend in order to be able to find his way home, but after the information regarding the hair strand they'd found at the missing girl's flat, Nick was more certain than ever that this case was directly related to the Baker case. He had nothing more to go on at this point and, since he refused to do a half-assed job with anything, he was determined to discover whatever he could about the two disappearances, however he had to. If that meant he had to do what some crazy old witch doctor told him to do, then that's what he would do.

"Meet back here at sunset," the young man said. "It's a long way, but we should be able to make it in time from here."

Nick threw a questioning look to Gorman to see if that would work for him. Gorman merely nodded. "We'll be here at sunset, then," Nick said to the younger man. All he got in response was a nod and a slight wave as the two dark men turned and, yet again, disappeared almost immediately into the light brush surrounding the area.

Nick and Gorman were quiet all the way back to town, each one wrapped in his own private thoughts. Gorman was wrapped up in thoughts of guilt. This yank came in here and "bam", just set him straight about what he needed to do, as a man. Gorman knew he was right, but he didn't have to admit it to the guy.

The sooner this American was gone, the better Gorman would feel. This case had not been his favorite from the get-go, but to have to put up with someone who saw and understood as much as this Nick Shvedov did, well, it was too much for Gorman's tastes.

As for Nick, he believed whatever he was going to discover at the ceremony tonight would either be the thing to put this whole story over the edge or it would turn out to be some spiritual mumbo-jumbo that led to nothing and he would be no closer to understanding what was going on than he'd been before. Either way, he felt a sense of relief simply because he knew he would be going home tomorrow.

∞

Azra'il had one last stop to make before he could finally be on his way. He had just the barest minimum of Angels accompanying him on his journey and those were his closest, most trusted advisors he'd worked with for millennia. They were all already awaiting him near the outskirts of town.

Their team was to travel by vimanas to a point just east of the area where Azra'il could still detect two human threads and then the team would walk the rest of the way, keeping hidden from anyone's notice as best they could.

The last stop he had to make was to be for the benefit of his office assistants, so they would be able to keep things running smoothly during his absence. Just because he had decided to go out to this encampment where Mikhail and his brothers had settled with the humans, the Great Sanhedrin would not cease its operations. There were still all the day-to-day operations to consider for the city, along with the new task of monitoring the human digital transmissions for any signs of the Designers' return to their realm, and Azra'il could not neglect his duties just because he had been called away on other business.

Additionally, it was necessary to ensure everything continue on as if he was still actively working within the city walls so that Seraphim City's citizens would not be alerted to anything troubling going on. His goal here was to keep the peace throughout his entire absence. If word got out that he was no longer even within the bounds of the city's walls, mass hysteria would be sure to follow.

This last stop was the part he'd been dreading most, however. There were so many things he normally handled himself that he did not even know where to begin. He sat at his desk and flipped through the virtual calendar he kept, looking through past entries to ensure he would not miss any regularly recurring tasks he normally handled each month, writing and assigning tasks as he went. His list kept getting longer and longer.

The aides who had come to assist him with his preparations became increasingly nervous as the list he was writing kept growing and growing. They were not happy about the fact that the one remaining Seraph in Seraphim City was about to go out into the wilds of the Badlands, himself, in search of the very same Seraphim he and the Great Sanhedrin had banished from within the city walls. There was no telling if their leader would return or not, judging by the grisly manner in which the last squadron of elite Sanhedrin Guardsmen had been defeated and murdered, and the aides were all nervous.

What would become of the Angels if Lord Azra'il did not return? How would those in the Angelic realm survive? Their world was becoming mired in such turmoil, all because of humans, and the Angels within the city limits had had just about enough. And now, in the midst of all that was going on in the Angelic world, there was information coming in to indicate that the human realm was also in turmoil and that there were entire groups of humans who had found out about the Angelic realm and who were desperately seeking entry into it.

Certain factions of Angels within the city walls were so worried about this that they were now gathering in secret to discuss plans should there be a human invasion into the Angelic dimension. Even within the hallowed halls of the council building itself, one could lately turn any corner and find groups of council members gathered together, whispering about such things.

The whole business with the Seraphim almost seemed to be taking a back seat even to the idea of a human invasion into the Angelic realm. And now, Lord Azra'il had decided he would go on a journey to the Badlands himself, to discover more about the humans who had already caused such upheaval within the Angelic dimension that several civilian Angels and a multitude of elite Sanhedrin Guardsmen were dead.

Lord Azra'il thought to use his own brand of stealth to discover the information the elite Sanhedrin Guardsmen had been unable to discover. However, there were several members of both Sanhedrin houses who privately doubted his ability to discover anything of any value related to this cause. There was even one very outspoken member who could nightly be found on the streets of the city talking with its citizenry about the possibility of there being a war between the realms for the first time in history, should there be a human invasion into the Angelic realm.

The aides each had formed his, or her, own opinions regarding humans, but they were nearly all the same. No one wanted them here. No one wanted to even think of humans crossing the barrier into the Angelic dimension. They all just wanted the humans to leave those in this realm alone.

All knew of the humans' penchant for self-destruction, along with the destruction of everything surrounding them, and the Angels within the Angelic realm had had enough. The majority of the Angels of Seraphim City had voted just yesterday, in overwhelming numbers and having become angered to such a degree, that the blessed Great Designers' edict in which it had been declared the Angels' official duty to watch over and protect humans from themselves was to be no longer in effect.

Most of the Angels living within the walls of Seraphim City today could not care less about the survival of the human race. For the past few hundred years, the Angelic race had witnessed every sick and twisted atrocity one could even conceive of within the human realm, and some an Angel could *not* even conceive of they'd witnessed.

Humans, it seemed, had lost all sense of humility, all sense of spirituality, all sense of community, love, and faith. They displayed no morals, no respect for life, and simply no sign that they were actual sentient beings anymore.

When the blessed Great Designers had declared it the duty of all Angel-kind to watch over and nurture and protect the human race, that race had actually shown signs that it could eventually develop into a great society with the potential to become useful members in a worldwide society. Now, all Angel-kind watched and waited with bated breath as this drama unfolded.

The Angels were at the point that they were going to have to completely abandon humankind. Would the blessed Great Designers return in time to save humans from themselves? The Angels simply did not know the answer to that question. But as far as the Angels were concerned, humans were no longer under the Angelic realm's jurisdiction.

Azra'il finally finished making his list and issued this assignment to one Angel and another assignment to another Angel. By the time he was finished issuing assignments and wrapping up his business with the aides, the sun was already setting. He and his group of travelers would have to fly by night, it seemed. And still he was not ready to leave, even as the plethora of aides finally left his office.

Azra'il was tired. He stopped what he was doing for a moment, laying down his pen and bowing his head to massage his temples. He'd not gotten a single night's rest since Djibril had brought that damned human into the Angelic realm, not really, and it didn't appear he would be getting one anytime soon, either.

He sighed and reached for his pen once more as the door to his office opened without any knock. Annoyed, he looked up and then stopped, his face draining of color. Garnabiel, the Angel who was called to watch over the bodies of the holiest of the dead, stood just inside the door to the office, silently closing the door behind him.

Azra'il sat stunned, but finally found his voice and asked, "Wh-Why have you come?" It was all he could manage, for he feared the answer to his question.

The Angel hesitated, and then quietly said, "Obbieuth, Garnabieuth, and I have been called."

"For whom?" Azra'il demanded, his pulse suddenly racing. Garnabiel merely stared at him in silence. After just a moment, the Angel lowered his eyes and looked away out of respect for his leader. Azra'il slumped back in his chair, dazed at the realization that one of his siblings was...

∞

The screaming was awful, unlike any they'd ever heard, and the Angels rushed to their queen's bedchamber to help her. When they entered, they found her sitting up in bed, screaming and kicking and punching at an invisible foe as whatever demon she faced within her dream continued to torment her.

The closest assistant to the Queen rushed to her lady's side and grabbed her by the shoulders, taking a punch or two in the process. She shook her queen with all her might, calling to her, desperately trying to wake the lady. The others crowded in close as soon as it appeared the queen was indeed waking from the horrible nightmare.

She seemed dazed and confused by the crowd of people surrounding her, but her tears and sobs continued, as loud as when she'd been enthralled by the dream.

"My Queen," the assistant sitting with her on the bed implored, "please tell us what is wrong?"

Suriyah stared in shock for a moment at the young Angel and then started wildly shaking her head back and forth, again and again, tears still streaming down her face, sobs still wracking her body. There was nothing anyone could do, not now, not ever!

"My lady," the assistant shouted, "please!"

Suriyah suddenly pushed at the Angel, shouting, "Go! All of you! Just go!" She rose as she shouted, physically shoving the crowd of Angels out of her room with her shields as much as her arms. As soon as they were gone and the door was tightly secured behind them, Suriyah re-sheathed her shields and crawled back onto her bed, pulling out the crystal pendant hanging on the chain she always wore around her neck.

If ever there would be a time when the crystal might show her some vision, she prayed to all that was good and holy that this would be such a time. She closed her eyes and concentrated, calming her nerves and her pulse until, suddenly she felt a familiar floating sensation overcome her senses. Her body was reduced to weightlessness and she could almost feel herself floating in a warm pool of swirling colors.

Slowly, almost without conscious thought, Suriyah opened her eyes and gazed into the crystal pendant. It was glowing a bright shade of green and Suriyah lost track of the idea that her physical self even existed any longer as she became enraptured by the images playing out just inside the little pendant. They were sharply defined in their clarity and there was no mistaking the message.

Suriyah's form began trembling again as the vision played out once more within the tiny crystal and then it was over. The green light emitting from within the crystal disappeared and the thing turned clear once more. Suriyah could not believe what she had just witnessed, but she knew the crystal did not lie.

A violent sob tore from deep within her as the understanding of the images she'd been shown came crashing down around her. There was nothing she could do, no one she could contact. This thing, this thing was happening now, and when it was done, all Hell would break loose on both realms!

∞

Israfil made his way across the barrier without feeling much at all. He was moving so fast that even the slight sting he usually felt when crossing between dimensions was absent all together. Everything was dark below him and what few lights there were along the black landscape almost appeared as streaks.

Time was of the essence, here. There was no time for noticing how things looked or even where he was going. He simply had to get to his destination without any delay or else. He wished he'd had time to consult with Thomas about this, but there'd been no time. Unfortunately, everyone was almost completely out of time.

Israfil tightened his six shields around himself and poured as much of his energy as he dared into moving just a little bit faster until he felt as if he would lose consciousness. Fortunately, his target location suddenly became visible to him just up ahead and he sighed a little in relief. Landing upon the ugly, multi-leveled concrete structure, he quickly made his way across the top level and down into the bowels of the building. He never once dropped his shields as he raced down the shaft of the deserted stairway.

At the very bottom level, he swiftly pulled to a halt as he detected others about. This was where everything was to happen, he was certain of it. He had seen this very part of the stairwell in the vision he'd had back in his temporary room as he'd lain listening for any signs of disturbance within the forces surrounding those he considered his responsibility. The moment he'd detected this new threat, he'd donned his shields and left without a word to anyone. Now, he held his breath even as he waited for what he believed was to come next.

∞

Baphomet looked around their spacious living room, wondering what it was that suddenly seemed out of place.

What's wrong? Lisa's voice asked silently in his mind.

Baphomet merely shook his head. He didn't know what the problem was, he just felt like something was not quite right.

He let go of her hand for a moment and stood, looking around the room to see what could possibly have caught his attention so. Everything looked fine and undisturbed.

He bowed his head, tilting it a little, as he checked his link with Mikhail. Everything seemed okay on that front. After a moment more of wracking his brain to discover what was amiss, he shook his head and shrugged, returning to his seat beside Lisa, taking her hand back with his.

Something still bothered him, though. Something just was not right and he could not figure out what the problem was. Then it occurred to him that Israfil should have poked his head in by now to see what was wrong. After all, he'd been monitoring Lisa and Baphomet since they'd been put together at the complex. Each and every time there had been something to bother either one of them even the slightest bit, Israfil showed up, almost immediately, to see what was wrong and how he could help.

Surely he is not still upset about the other day? thought Baphomet as he let go of Lisa's hand and rose again to go in search of his brother. Try as he might, however, Baphomet was unable to locate Israfil. That had him worried. Israfil had been no more than twenty feet away from Baphomet since he'd returned to the complex the last time and Baphomet was worried that something had happened. Why else would he be feeling this way?

As he turned back into the room, Lisa stood, placing her hands at the small of her back and arching back for a moment to ease the muscles there. Then, she reached out a hand for him and said, "I'm sure he's fine. He's probably just over at the main house for something."

"Maybe," was all Baphomet said.

"Come on," Lisa said as she passed him up. "Let's go over and see if we can find him." She grabbed a sweater one of the Angels had sent over for her. "I could use the walk, anyway."

∞

Mikhail sat listening, wondering what on earth his brother was doing. He'd tried to do what Baphomet had always been able to do, which was to go into another's thoughts and see more than just the context associated with that one moment in time, but he couldn't. He watched his sibling with his mind's eye as the Seraph moved.

Just then, a flash of bright white shot across his mental vision in such a blindingly fast blink, Mikhail was temporarily stunned. He hadn't caught any details, though, and he couldn't recall anything from the flash. There was something about it, however, that felt different to him. It seemed to carry more importance, whatever the message or meaning was.

Mikhail turned his concentration from his sibling to the bright flash, wondering if there was some way he could pull it back up. He thought he'd caught a glimpse of just the slightest bit of...

All of a sudden, Mikhail bolted from his chair and took off running for the door to the next room where Sarah soundly slept. He had heard her when she'd gone in there to rest earlier, but he needed her... now!

Epilogue

Djibril paused as he crept down the back stairway to the sub-basement to the building. This area was located beneath the financial district, just beneath the Underground that serviced this most prestigious building within the district.

He felt again that strange energy fluctuation he'd felt at several of the other locales. It wasn't like the others', those of the terrorists, nor was it anything similar to Iblis' or Satariel's energies. This one carried a unique frequency signature to it, but he had definitely detected it before.

Djibril searched for something more, something that would help him identify the signature, but there was no more information detectable. The signature moved off in a different direction suddenly and he paused for a moment, wondering if he should concentrate on following it or if he should continue on down to the location where he believed the terrorists were about to carry out their heinous deed.

It only took him a second to realize how foolish that question was. He had to follow the terrorists, of course. With all the morning commuters already arriving at their posts in the building above, if the plot was allowed to been seen through to fruition, several thousand innocent humans would surely die.

He crept silently down the remaining stairs, keeping to the shadows as much as possible. At the bottom, there was one door leading out into a darkened area. The door had a small rectangular area cut into it where a glass allowed Djibril to look out onto the other side. He saw movement there, along with hearing a couple of masculine voices speaking a mix of Arabic and Farzi, though it was dark in the room beyond.

Just then, Djibril heard a noise directly behind him.

It was funny, when he thought about it. Throughout the past one million years, Djibril had never suffered much. He'd never wanted for anything or felt anything but physical need. Somehow, when he and his siblings had come into being on this planet, they'd managed to survive childhood, then puberty, so that when they became adults, they experienced no difficulty living within their own realm.

The thing that always pulled at Djibril's consciousness, however, was the fact that he and his siblings seemed to feel an irresistible pull toward the human realm. Even before the blessed Great Designers had come along and informed them of the Seraphim's purpose on this planet as the guardians of all humans, Djibril and his siblings had felt a desire to observe and protect them anyway.

Over the past few millennia, however, Djibril and his four brothers who'd lived with him within the walls of Seraphim City had become almost reluctant to have anything to do with those in the human realm. Why?

Djibril could think of no one particular reason why they should have come to feel this way. The only thing he could imagine it could be, for him at least, was the fact that, after caring for a race of beings for so long, it was very difficult to watch as they tore themselves apart.

It was widely known that the Shaitans and the Jinn frequented the human realm, causing all manner of chaos and destruction. The Great Sanhedrin had taken it upon itself to become the overseer of all things within the human realm. They were the ones who directed the Seraphim as to when one of them should go into the human realm to fix a problem and which Seraph should go.

Djibril had been sent many times, as had Mikhail, although Mikhail was normally sent when there was some sort of battle to be fought and won. Djibril had mainly been sent during the past few millennia as a teacher, a guide. Israfil had been sent as a healer, although Mikhail, too, had healing abilities and it was common knowledge among the humans that the Arch Angel Michael could heal sick loved ones.

When Djibril thought about the humans and how the amount of time the Seraphim of Seraphim City had spent out in the human realm had become less and less over the years, he realized it must have been the same for his siblings. They had all worked for so long to help the humans to survive and thrive, yet all seemed to have been for naught.

Humans no longer believed in the lessons Djibril and his brothers had taught them. They had forgotten the skills their earlier cultures had learned. They had lost the sense of morality that used to strengthen the blood running through their veins. There was no good left in the hearts of mankind and it angered Djibril to realize this.

He wanted to remind them of all of these things. He wanted to pound that humility and morality back into their hearts. He wanted to remind them that they were all connected and that it was their duty to take care of all human children and the planet on which they all lived.

Instead, he was here, in the dark, at the bottom of a stairwell, trying yet again to save the silly human population from itself. A tremendous sense of anger built inside him and seemed to explode through his mind. Just then, he turned to discover the origin of a sound he'd heard behind him.

∞

The sword that flashed in the dim light was actually a Katana, several hundred years old. It had been hand-crafted in

336

the early 1400's and passed down by an ancient, but very prestigious Japanese family line until its current owner had purchased it a little over two years ago. The hilt was made of the richest jade and it was perfect, still, except for a line of notches its latest owner had studiously and carefully cut into it after each mission.

Now, as the blade swung soundlessly through the air, the black-clad figure standing in its path had no time to move or to defend itself as the metal sliced smoothly, first through the skin, then through muscle and meat, bisecting the esophagus, and then on back to the spinal cord, where it became lodged within one of the hard vertebral bones of the spinal column there. The spinal column's owner silently crumpled to the dirty floor beneath his feet, taking the Katana with him.

The black-clad figure reached for the jade hilt. The metal would not budge and the blade's owner placed a foot onto the prone figure on the floor and tugged harder. Two more hard pulls and the blade came free of the bone. Within a minute, all nine of the men on the other side of the doorway were lying on the dirty floor of that room with their bodies all decapitated, as well. The black-clad figure surveyed the damage. One more dead than had been counted on, but that was just a bonus. The black-clad figure smiled a wicked smile beneath the mask. One more dead Muslim male just meant the world was a safer place today and that this mission had very much been worth the risk taken.

Whose head was lost? Who is this black-clad owner of the dread Katana? If you enjoyed *Infinite G*, and you'd like to know the answers to these questions and more, be sure to read *The Assassin*, book three of the **Seraphim Calls** series.

Take a sneak peek at this intriguing new addition to the series on the next page.

Seraphim Calls... can you hear them?

The Assassin

Thomas woke from the dream he'd been having only to discover that it seemed he was still immersed within the dream. His mind seemed very sluggish and he had difficulty pulling himself upright, and then getting up from the bed. Something was calling to him, though, and he knew he had to move.

He stumbled out into the hallway, weaving and bumping into the walls of the hallway as he made his way toward the master suite. He had to get there. He *had* to. There were no Angels in attendance as he opened the main door to the suite and stumbled into the receiving room. He passed over to the bedroom his mother and Mikhail shared, not even bothering to knock as he turned the handle and practically fell inside.

There, he stopped dead in his tracks, his eyes nearly bugging out of their sockets at the scene confronting him. Mikhail and his mother were both lying on the floor of the room, just at the foot of the bed, writhing and twisting in agony as they gasped desperately for breath. Their mouths were agape and they clawed frantically at their own throats with their hands, digging deep into the soft flesh there. Thomas stared in mute horror as blood gushed from the claw marks each made.

Realization finally dawned and Thomas ran to his mother's side, grabbing her hands and pulling them back from her throat. She fought him, though her eyes were rolled up into the back of her head. Still, she gasped and gagged, as if she couldn't breathe. Her mouth was wide open, but no air was getting through!

"Mom!" Thomas screamed. "Mom! Mikhail!" Over and over he screamed as he fought for control of her stiff and bloodied hands. Mikhail still clawed at his own throat, the blood still flowing freely all over and around his writhing form. His eyes were also rolled back into his head as he gasped and gagged.

They each made gurgling sounds, as if liquid was running down their throats and into their lungs and Thomas finally decided it must be blood from where they'd gored themselves in the neck. He yelled their names a couple more times, but had no luck obtaining any kind of a response from them. Then, a thought occurred to him and he changed his call, yelling instead for the one person who might actually be able to help him.

"Nera!" he screamed, as loud as he could. "Help me, Nera! Help!" There was no response. Tears were now flowing freely down his cheeks, but Thomas did not care. His mother was no longer struggling with him and Mikhail's fingers suddenly stilled their clawing and dropped off to his sides. Both of them closed their eyes and then they both stopped moving.

That's when Thomas felt it.

Something was approaching.

He'd never felt anything like it before. He could almost hear it as it approached. It sounded almost like a heartbeat, but heavy and low. It made the very air around him vibrate with each beat as it grew closer and closer to the room.

Was it Nera? Thomas swallowed and prayed that it would be Nera and that she would come and help them.

He tensed as the door to the room slowly swung open.